超級英語閱讀訓練

FUN學美國英語課本精選 二版

Michael A. Putlack &
e-Creative Contents_著
Cosmos Language Workshop_譯

2

SUPER READING TRAINING BOOK 2

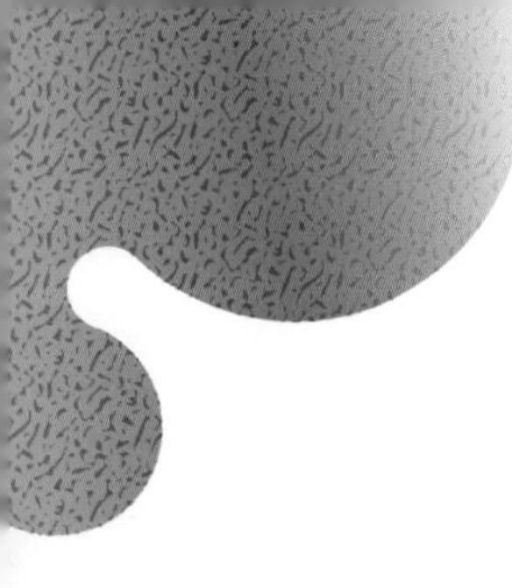

Preface 前言

用美國教科書來學習英語，是目前甚受歡迎的英語學習風潮，就像美國兒童學習母語一樣，透過教科書中各科的知識來奠定英語基礎。本書的所有內容都是美國教科書最基本的課程，對於非英語系國家的我們來說，是非常有用的英語學習書。

美國的教育過程著重統合教育，將各個科目彼此連結，本書並配上生動的照片圖解，幫助學生提高學習效率。透過這種精心編寫的內容與編輯方式來學習英語，除了能幫助學習正確的英語，也能夠在各個科目的教育過程中，自然而然地熟悉與運用英語。讓你不用出國，也能體驗美國課程，全面提升英語能力！

1 本套書完整收錄美國一年級到六年級的各學科核心內容，並依文章長度與難易度，共分為兩冊。

- 超級英語閱讀訓練 1：FUN 學美國英語課本精選
- 超級英語閱讀訓練 2：FUN 學美國英語課本精選

2 每一冊皆精選 90 篇文章，分析美國最多人使用的四大教科書內容，文章範疇遍及各個學科與領域。

3 依據美國教科書的英文單字和閱讀文章，並穿插上百張的照片資料，精心編寫與設計，幫助學生以最輕鬆的方式，達到最大的學習效果。

4 讀完課文之後，隨即有題目練習，測驗讀者是否能抓出文章的「主旨」（main idea）和細節（details），並有字彙能力（vocabulary）測驗。這些題型是各種英文考試最常見的出題型式，透過這些簡單的練習，除了能幫助理解文章，也能幫助培養日後參加各種英語檢定考試的能力。

本套書旨在幫助讀者打好紮實的英語基礎，朝向高等的英語能力邁進。書中羅列各種範疇的主題，幫助讀者熟悉各種學科和領域的背景知識和用語，培養能進一步閱讀《時代》、《紐約時報》的能力。無論是求學、參加英文檢定或是在職場工作，亦或是想參加多益、托福等各種英文考試，或者想到國外留學、在國際企業或跨國公司工作，本書都可以幫助您一圓美夢！

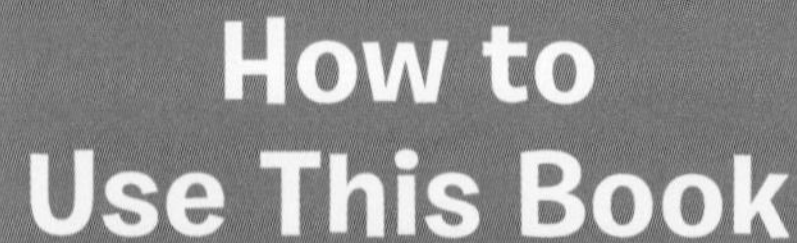

本書的使用步驟

本書設計有「課本」(Main Book)和「訓練書」(Training Book)兩大部分：

課　本　精選各學科範疇的菁華，全書以全英文呈現。

訓練書　針對字彙、閱讀和聽力做設計，並特別標示出英語的句子結構，幫助理解句意與文法結構。

STEP 1 閱讀課文

首先，先閱讀搭配了各式照片和圖片的課文。在這過程中，如果出現不認識的詞彙或片語，先不要看翻譯，也不要查字典，而是藉由在閱讀的過程中，培養由上下文掌握內容的能力。在這階段，要參考文章所穿插的照片或圖片，這些圖片具有「圖像字典」的功能，能幫助理解文章內容。如果有無法推知的詞彙或片語，就把它們圈出來，在回答文章下方的題目之後，再查看「訓練書」。

STEP 2 做文章下方的題目

讀完課文之後，隨即有題目練習，測驗你是否能抓出文章的「主旨」(main idea)和細節(details)，並有字彙能力(vocabulary)測驗。這些題型是各種英文考試最常見的出題型式，透過這些簡單的練習，除了能幫助理解文章，也有助於培養日後參加各種英語檢定考試的能力。

STEP 3 查看訓練書

訓練書除了附有答案和翻譯以外，還標示了文章的句子結構，根據文法和片語詞組來斷句，以幫助理解句意與文法結構。透過這種斷句的練習，除了能提升英文的理解力，也能加強詞彙和句型的掌握能力。

STEP 4 對照課本與訓練書

接下來，要一面看訓練書，一面確認課文中不認識的詞彙或片語的意思，並完全了解課文內容。首先，先把〈Words to Know〉的詞彙掃視一遍，然後一邊讀英文課文，一邊對照中文翻譯。

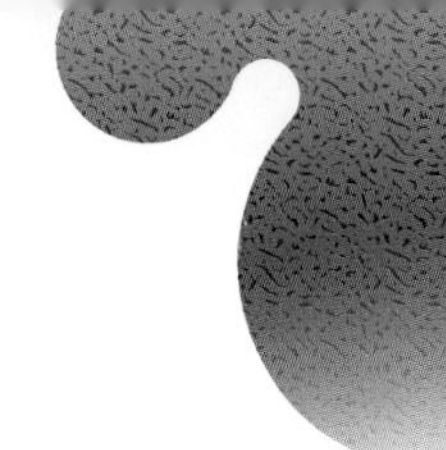

STEP 5 自己練習翻譯與斷句

接下來，不要看翻譯，試著自己翻譯英文課文。這時，你可以練習斷句，這會對文章理解有很大的幫助。如果有無法掌握的，就再一次確認英文詞彙、片語的中文意思，直到充分理解。

STEP 6 邊聽音檔邊閱讀

熟悉英文的發音，比用眼睛看英文，來得更為重要。本書的課文皆由專業的母語人士所讀誦，每一篇文章最少反覆聽兩遍，以熟悉正確的發音和音調。在聽課文的誦讀時，可以參考訓練書的斷句處，並注意聽母語人士的發音、音調和連音等。你也可以在訓練書上標示出音調和連音的地方。然後再聽兩遍，並大聲地跟著唸。這時，要盡量去模仿母語人士的唸誦與發音。在本書中，西方歷史的地名和人名很常出現，這些發音要特別留意，並盡可能熟悉。

STEP 7 不聽錄音，自己大聲唸出課文

再接下來，暫時不要再聽音檔，自己練習把課文大聲讀誦出來，並且盡量模仿母語人士的發音與語調。發音或語調不順暢的地方，要再多聽音檔來練習，直到熟練為止。

STEP 8 重新再閱讀英文課文

現在再次回到課本，仔細閱讀英文課文，並再做一次題目。這一次要要求自己能夠充分理解文章內容與句法結構，要能完全掌握文章與題目。

The Introduction of Training Book

訓練書特色說明

透過「斷句」掌握「即讀即解」的竅門

為了能更快、更正確地閱讀英文，就需要能夠掌握英文的句子結構。而要培養英文句子結構的敏銳度，最好的方法就是以各「意義單元組」來理解句子，也就是將英文句子的「意義單元組」（具一個完整意義的片語或詞組），用斷句（chunk）的方式分開，然後再來理解句子。只要能理解各個「意義單元組」，那麼再長的句子，都能被拆解與理解。

聽力也是一樣，要區分「意義單元組」，這樣能幫助很快聽懂英文。例如下面這個句子可以拆解成兩個部分：

I am angry at you.

I am angry / at you
我生氣　對你

我們會發現，這個句子由兩個「意義單元組」所組成。不管句子多長多複雜，都是由最簡單的基本句型（主詞＋動詞）發展而成，然後再在這個主要句子上，依照需求，添加上許多片語，以表現各式各樣的句意。

在面對英文時，腦子裡能立刻自動快速分離基本句型和片語，就能迅速讀懂或聽懂英文。在讀誦英文時，從一個人的斷句，大致就能看出個人的英文能力。現在再來看稍微長一點的句子。經過斷句以後，整個句子變得更清楚易懂，閱讀理解就沒問題了：

Leonardo da Vinci painted / the most famous portrait / in the world: / the Mona Lisa.
里奧納多達文西畫了　最有名的肖像畫　全世界　（就是）蒙娜麗莎

一個句子有幾個斷句？

一個句子有幾個斷句？有幾個「意義單元組」？這是依句子的情況和個人的英語能力，而有不同的。一般來説，以下這些地方通常就是斷句的地方：

★ 在「主詞＋動詞」之後
★ 在 and、but、or 等連接詞之前
★ 在 that、who 等關係詞之前
★ 在副詞、不定詞 to 等的前後

另外，主詞很長時，時常為了要區分出主詞，在主詞後也會斷句。例如：

Your neighbors / are the people / who live near you.
你的鄰居　是人們　住在你附近

In our community, / people help each other / and care about one another.
在我們社區　人們互相幫助　並彼此關心

對初學者來說，一個句子裡可能會有很多斷句的斜線，而當閱讀能力越來越強之後，你需要斷句的地方就會越來越少，到後來甚至能一眼就看懂句子，不需要用斷句的方式來幫助理解。

本訓練書因為考慮到初學者，所以盡可能細分可斷句處，只要是能分為一個「意義單元組」的地方，訓練書上就標示出斷句。等你的英文實力逐漸提升，到了覺得斷句變成是一種累贅，能夠不用再做任何標記就能讀懂課文時，就是你的英文能力更進一階的時候了。透過斷句的練習，熟悉英語的排列順序和結構，你會驚訝地發現到，自己的閱讀能力突飛猛進！

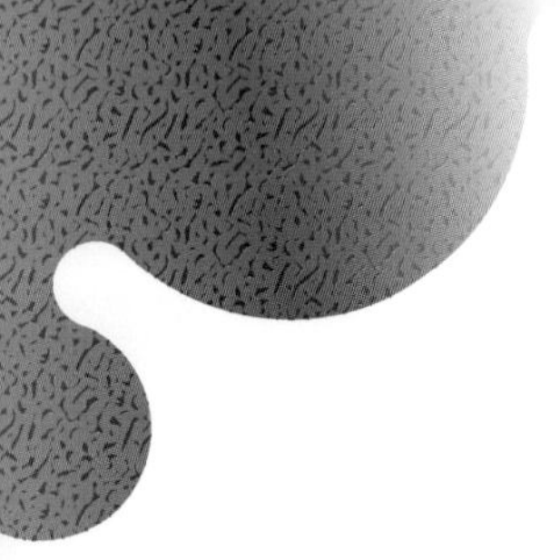

The Structure of Main Book

課本架構

11 National Parks

The United States has many national parks. These are protected areas. So people cannot develop or damage them.

The first national park was Yellowstone National Park. It is an area with stunning scenery and many wild animals. The Grand Canyon is also a national park. It is one of the largest canyons in the world.

Every year, millions of people visit these parks. They tour the parks and go hiking. Some even camp in the parks. They learn about the land and how to preserve it, too.

課文
藉由閱讀課文，培養掌握上下文的能力

Some National Parks in the U.S.

▲ Yellowstone National Park

▲ Grand Canyon National Park

▲ Yosemite National Park

❶ **What is special about the Grand Canyon?**

a. Many wild animals live there.
b. It was the first national park.
c. It is a very large canyon.

❷ **Answer the questions.**

a. What was the first national park? ______
b. What is one of the world's largest canyons? ______
c. What do people do at national parks? ______

文意理解測驗
透過主旨 (main idea) 和細節 (details)，測驗是否讀懂課文內容

❸ **Write the correct word and the meaning in Chinese.**

canyon	damage	stunning	go hiking	preserve

a. ______: a deep valley with steep rock sides and often a stream or river flowing through it
b. ______: to go for long walks in the countryside
c. ______: to save; to conserve

字彙能力測驗
確認是否理解英文詞彙片語的真正意義

32

The Structure of Training Book

訓練書架構

Good Neighbors 好鄰居

Your neighbors / are the people / who live near you. In our **community**, / people help **each other** / and **care about one another**. If you want / to have a good neighbor, / you **have to** / be a good neighbor / first. There are / many ways / to do this.

First, / you can be nice / to your neighbors. Always **greet** them / and say, "Hello." **Get to know** them. **Become friends / with them**. Also, don't be noisy / at your home. And **respect** / your neighbors' **privacy**. If they have / any **problems**, / **help** them **out**. They will help you / too / **in the future**. If you do / all of these things, / you can be / a good neighbor.

單字提示
- 藉由文中重點單字畫記，理解字彙如何運用

課文斷句
- 透過分離基本句型，迅速讀懂英文
- 反覆聽音檔，練習把課文大聲唸出來

你的鄰居 neighbor 就是住在你家附近的人。在我們的社區 community 裡，人們會互相幫忙 help each other、彼此關心 care about one another。若是想要有個好鄰居，你必須先成為一個好鄰居 be a good neighbor。要做到這點有很多方法 many ways。

首先 first，你可以對鄰居表示友好 be nice。要經常和他們打招呼 greet，並且說「你好」。去認識他們 get to know them，和他們成為朋友 become friends。還有，不要在家裡製造噪音 don't be noisy，並且要尊重鄰居的隱私 respect privacy。他們若是遇到問題 problems，你可以幫助他們 help them out，將來 in the future 他們也會幫助你的。如果這些你都做到了，你就是個好鄰居 good neighbor。

中文翻譯與重要字彙片語中英對照

- **community** 社區 · **each other** 互相（兩者之間） · **care about** 關懷
- **one another** 互相（三者以上） · **have to** 必須 · **greet** 打招呼
- **get to know** 認識 · **become friends with sb.** 與某人做朋友
- **respect** 尊重 · **privacy** 隱私 · **problem** 問題 · **help out** 幫助擺脫困難
- **in the future** 日後；未來

單字學習

6

Table of Contents

Chapter 1

Social Studies

Culture

Culture & Economics

The American Government System

Geography

Geography Skills

American Geography

History

American History

World History

Science

Life Science

A World of Living Things

Ecosystems

Exploring the Human Body

Earth Science

Weather and Space

Mathematics

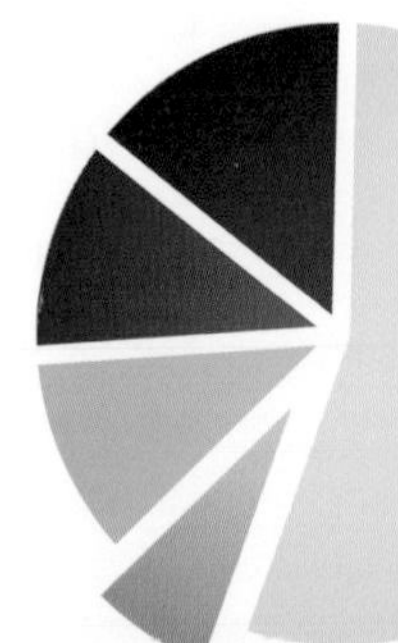

Language • Visual Arts • Music

Language and Literature

Visual Arts

Music

Social Studies

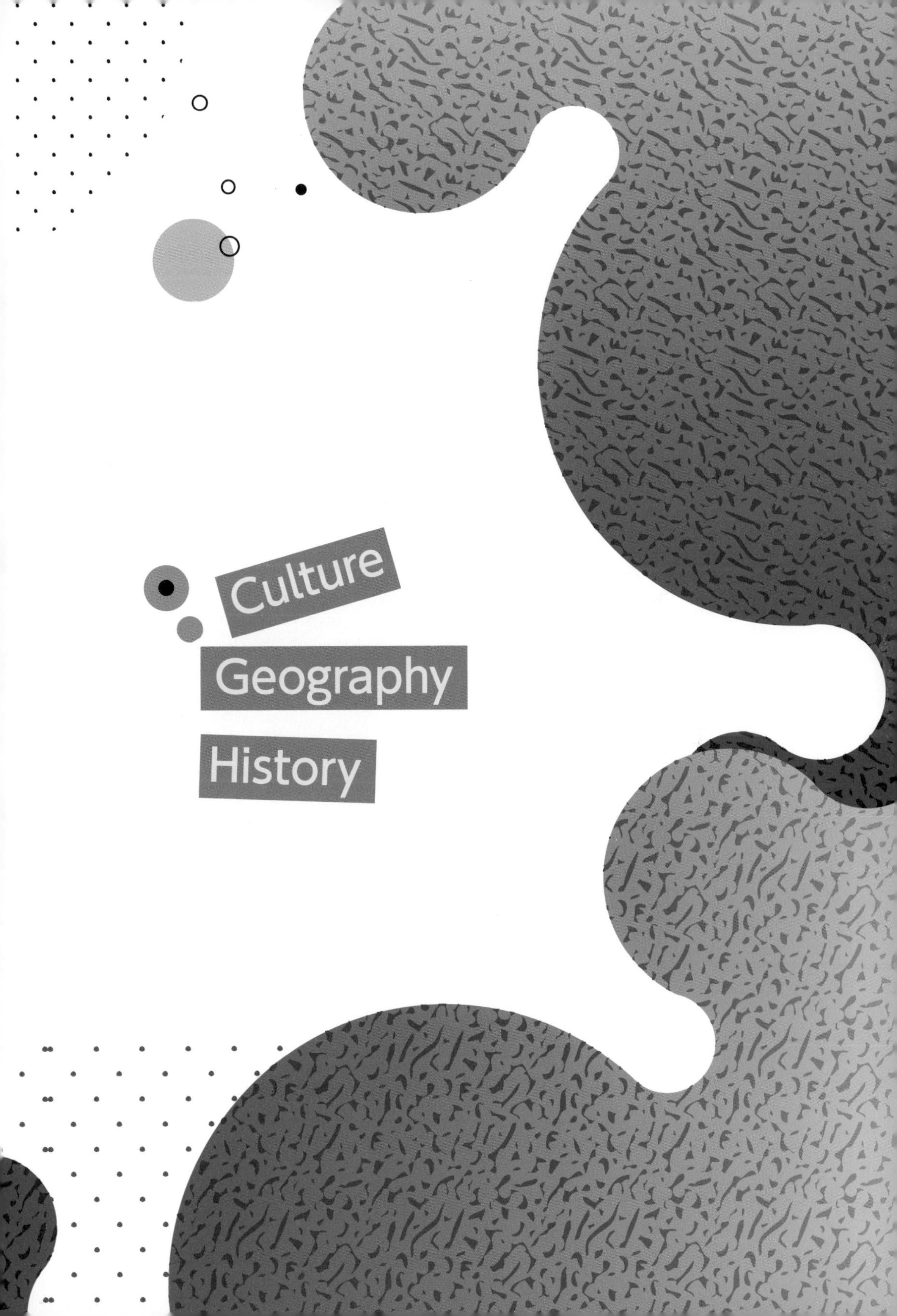
Culture
Geography
History

Culture

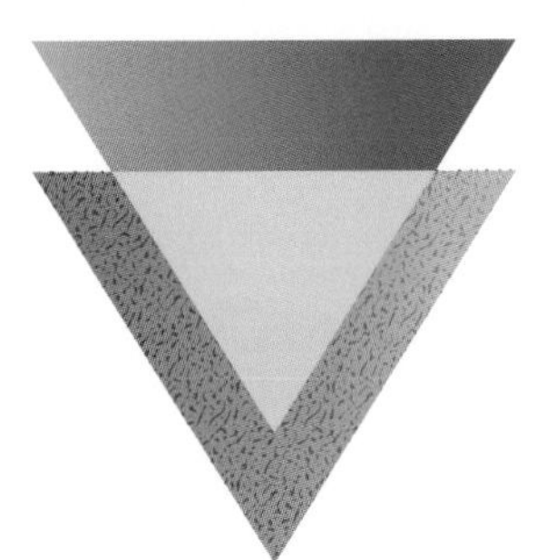

Culture & Economics

The American Government System

01 Kinds of Communities

People live in many different places. Some like big cities. Others like living in the countryside. And others like neither place. They prefer small cities or towns.

Big cities are urban communities. Some cities have millions of people. People in big cities live closely together. They often live in apartments. They might use the bus or subway very often.

Rural communities are in the countryside. They have small populations. Farmers live in rural areas. People live in houses and often drive cars.

Suburban communities are small cities near big ones. Many families live there. But they might work in a big city. They might drive or take buses and subways.

Good Citizens

▲ respect each other

▲ care for their neighbors

▲ treat others with kindness

1 What is the main idea of the passage?

a. People prefer small cities or towns.
b. There are three kinds of communities.
c. Rural communities have small populations.

2 Fill in the blanks.

a. Big cities might have ______________ of people.
b. ___________ communities are in the countryside.
c. _______________ communities are near big cities.

3 Write the correct word and the meaning in Chinese.

rural	urban	take	population	prefer

a. ___________________: the number of people who live in a particular area
b. ___________________: to like one thing more than another
c. ___________________: relating to or located in a city

Different Customs and Cultures

Every country has its own customs and traditions. A custom is a special way of doing something. A tradition is a custom that is passed down over time. These customs and traditions make different cultures in different countries. We should know about other people's customs and cultures. And we should always respect them.

For example, in America, people wear their shoes in their homes. But in some Asian countries like Japan and Korea, people take off their shoes before going inside their homes. In many Asian countries, people use chopsticks while Americans and Europeans eat with forks and knives. But in India and some other countries, people often eat with their hands. There are many other differences. But all of these cultures are special. We should try to know and learn about them.

Different Eating Cultures

▲ Many Asians use chopsticks.

▲ Westerners eat with forks and knives.

▲ Indians often eat with their hands.

1 What is the main idea of the passage?

a. People in Japan and Korea take off their shoes in their homes.
b. Americans and Indians have different eating styles.
c. We need to know about foreign customs and cultures.

2 Fill in the blanks.

a. Different customs and traditions make different ______________.
b. Americans wear their ____________ in their homes.
c. People in ____________ often eat with their hands.

3 Write the correct word and the meaning in Chinese.

pass down	custom	respect	chopsticks	take off

a. ____________________: two thin sticks used in East Asian cultures for eating food
b. ____________________: a special way of doing something; a tradition
c. ____________________: to give something to younger people

03 The Story of Israel

03

▲ Abraham

In the past in the Middle East, there were many different religions. People often prayed to many gods. There were mountain gods. There were gods of rivers, lakes, and seas. There were all kinds of gods. However, one religion began that worshipped only one god.

There was a man named Abram. He was said to be a descendant of both Noah and Adam. He lived in a land called Canaan. There, the god Yahweh made a covenant with Abram. Yahweh promised Abram many descendants and said that the land he was living on would forever be theirs. In return, Abram had to worship only Yahweh. Abram agreed. His name changed to Abraham, which means "father of many nations."

▲ The building of Noah's Ark

Abraham's descendants through his son Isaac became the Israelites. Isaac and his wife Rebecca later had twins: Jacob and Esau. Jacob's descendants founded the twelve tribes of the Israelites. They made the city Jerusalem the center of their political power. For a time, they were powerful. Later, they were made slaves and taken to Egypt. And then many years later, Moses freed the Israelites and returned them to their land.

▲ Moses striking the rock

1 What does "Abraham" mean?

a. father of many nations
b. a descendant of Noah and Adam
c. founder of Israel

2 What is NOT true?

a. Most people in the Middle East worshipped only one god.
b. Abram only worshipped Yahweh.
c. Isaac was the son of Abraham.

3 Write the correct word and the meaning in Chinese.

religion	worship	covenant	Israelite	descendant

a. ____________________: a formal agreement or promise
b. ____________________: a person born or living in the ancient kingdom of Israel
c. ____________________: a child; an offspring

04 Money Management

When people work, they get paid. This money is called earnings. With their earnings, they can do two things: spend or save their money. Most people do a combination of these two.

First, they have to spend their money on many things. They have to pay for their home. They have to pay for food and clothes. And they have to pay for insurance, transportation, and even entertainment costs. Usually, there is some money left over. People often save this money. They might put it in the bank. Or they might invest in the stock market.

Unfortunately, some people spend too much money. They spend more than they earn. So they go into debt. Debt is a big problem for many people.

People can plan to buy something if they budget their income, spending, and savings. A budget helps people to manage money and to save it.

Budget Items

▲ rent

▲ food

▲ insurance

▲ education

▲ transportation

▲ entertainment

▲ clothing

1 How do people go into debt?

a. By paying for food and clothes.
b. By investing in the stock market.
c. By spending more money than they earn.

2 What is NOT true?

a. The money people make from working is their savings.
b. Some people put their savings in the bank.
c. Budgets help people manage their money.

3 Write the correct word and the meaning in Chinese.

stock market	earnings	budget	debt	invest in

a. ________________: the business or activity of buying and selling stocks
b. ________________: to use money for something in order to earn more money
c. ________________: to plan and control how much one will spend; a plan on how to spend money

05 Basic Economics

05

In free-market economies, companies decide what and how much of a product they will produce. However, they are interested in making profits. So they do not want to produce too much or too little of a product. They want to produce exactly the right amount necessary. So they often pay attention to the law of supply and demand.

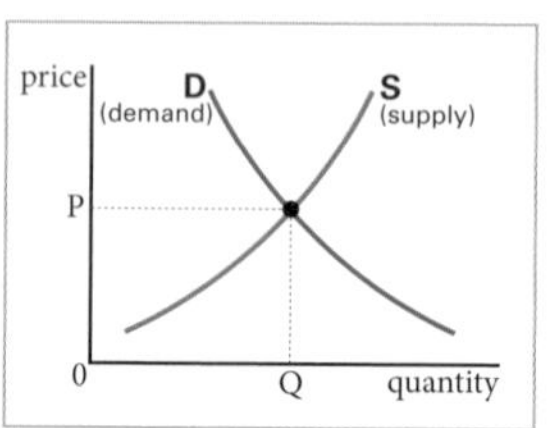

▲ the law of supply and demand

This law states that when the supply of a product is low yet demand is high, then the price will be high. However, if the supply of a product is high yet demand is low, then the price will be low. Companies want to find a median. They want just the right amount of supply and just the right amount of demand.

But, there are often other factors that companies must consider. Once they make something, they must deliver it to the market. This way, people can purchase the product. This is called distribution. Distribution is often done by trucks, trains, ships, and airplanes. Without an effective distribution system, even in-demand products will not sell well.

Once products are at the market, they must be consumed. This means that people purchase them. The amount of consumption depends on many things. It depends on the supply and demand, of course. And the price is also another important factor.

▲ production

▲ consumption

1 **What is the passage mainly about?**

a. The law of supply and demand.
b. Distribution and consumption.
c. Some important economic factors.

2 **What is true? Write T (true) or F (false).**

a. Companies are interested in earning profits. ____
b. The law of supply and demand is important in economics. ____
c. A low demand and a high supply usually result in a high price. ____

3 **Write the correct word and the meaning in Chinese.**

distribution	make a profit	consume	pay attention to	demand

a. ____________________: the amount of desire for a product or service
b. ____________________: to buy
c. ____________________: the process of giving something to a group of people

The Three Branches of Government

The government is made up of three branches. They are the executive, legislative, and judicial branches. These three branches of the government make and enforce laws. All three of them have their own duties and responsibilities.

The legislative branch is Congress. Congress proposes bills and discusses them. Then Congress votes on the bills. If the bills pass and the president signs them, then they become laws.

After a law has been passed, it must be carried out, or enforced. The executive branch enforces laws. The executive branch is the president and everyone who works for him.

The judicial branch is the court system. The judicial branch determines if laws have been broken. When people break the law, the judicial branch takes care of their cases.

The Government in the USA

▲ the White House

▲ the Capitol Building

▲ the Supreme Court

1 When does a bill become a law?

a. After Congress passes it.
b. After the president signs it.
c. After Congress discusses it.

2 Fill in the blanks.

a. The three branches of the government make and enforce __________.
b. Congress is the ______________ branch.
c. The ___________ system is the judicial branch.

3 Write the correct word and the meaning in Chinese.

vote on	enforce	Congress	judicial branch	propose

a. ____________________: to make sure that a law or rule is obeyed by people
b. ____________________: the legislature of the United States government
c. ____________________: the branch of government that decides if laws have been broken; the court system

The American Presidential Election System

In the United States, there are many political parties. But two are very powerful. They are the Republican Party and the Democratic Party. About two years before the presidential election, members of both parties start running for president. They want to be their party's presidential nominee. They raise money and travel around the country giving speeches.

Every four years, the U.S. elects a president. In an election year, every state has either a primary or a caucus. This is where they elect delegates. The candidates want to get as many delegates as possible. New Hampshire has the first primary in the country. Iowa has the first caucus. As the states hold their primaries and caucuses, unpopular politicians drop out of the race. When one candidate has enough delegates, he or she becomes the party's nominee. In July or August, both parties have conventions. They officially nominate their presidential and vice presidential candidates there. Then, the race for president really begins. The candidates for both parties visit many states. They give speeches. They try to win voters. On the first Tuesday in November, the American voters decide who the next president will be.

Famous Primaries and Caucuses

◂ The New Hampshire Primary is the first primary in the country.

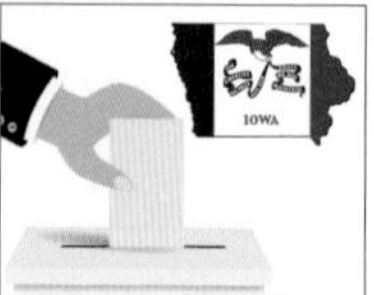

◂ The Iowa Caucus is the first caucus in the country.

◂ Many states hold their primaries and caucuses on Super Tuesday.

1 How does a candidate become a party's presidential nominee?

a. By winning the Iowa Caucus.
b. By winning on Election Day.
c. By winning enough delegates.

2 Fill in the blanks.

a. The ____________ Party and the Democratic Party are the most powerful parties in the U.S.
b. The U.S. elects a new president every _________ years.
c. New Hampshire has the first ____________ in the country.

3 Write the correct word and the meaning in Chinese.

political party	primary	caucus	delegate	nominee

a. ________________: an election in which people in a particular state in the U.S. choose their candidate for president
b. ________________: a person who has been selected to run in an election
c. ________________: a person who is chosen or elected to vote or act for others

08 A Nation of Immigration

In 1789, the United States became a country. It was a huge land. And the country expanded and got bigger. But, at that time, few people lived in the U.S. The country needed immigrants. So, during the nineteenth century, millions of people moved to the U.S.

The first Europeans to come to America were English, Dutch, Spanish, and French. Then, between 1870 and 1924, they also came from Ireland, Germany, Italy, Russia, and other countries. Millions of them came to America. These immigrants worked hard. But they often made little money. Yet they slowly improved their lives. And they helped the U.S. become a great and powerful country.

▲ Immigrants arriving at New York City, 1887

▲ Polish immigrants working on the farm, 1909

▲ the Statue of Liberty, a symbol of freedom to immigrants

1 In the 19th century, where did most immigrants to America come from?

a. Europe. b. Asia. c. Africa.

2 Fill in the blanks.

a. The United States became a country in __________.

b. Many immigrants came to the U.S. in the ______________ century.

c. Immigrants often made __________ money at first.

3 Write the correct word and the meaning in Chinese.

make money	expand	immigrant	improve	Statue of Liberty

a. _______________: a large monumental statue symbolizing liberty on Liberty Island in New York Bay

b. _______________: to become larger

c. _______________: a person who moves from one country to another to live

Geography

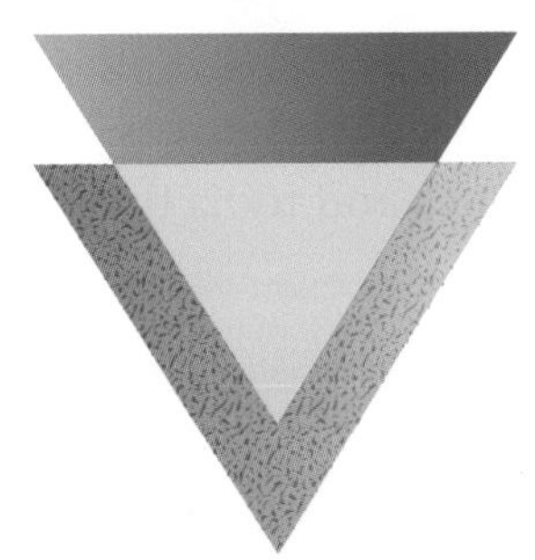

09 Kinds of Resources

There are many kinds of resources on the earth. Four of them are very important. They are renewable, nonrenewable, human, and capital resources.

Renewable resources can be used again and again. They can be replaced within a short time. Some energy resources are renewable. The energy from the sun, tides, water, and wind is renewable. Also, trees and animals are renewable. But humans still need to take good care of them. We should not waste them at all.

Nonrenewable resources are limited in supply. Once we use them, they disappear forever. They can't be replaced. Many energy resources are like this. Coal, gas, and oil are all nonrenewable.

Human resources are people and the skills they have. This also includes the knowledge and information that humans have.

People make products using renewable and nonrenewable resources. Machines are often used to produce goods. The machines and tools that are used to produce goods are called capital resources.

Renewable Resources **Nonrenewable Resources**

▲ solar energy ▲ wind power ▲ water power ▲ coal ▲ oil ▲ gas

1 What is NOT true?

a. Renewable resources can be replaced within a short time.
b. Nonrenewable resources cannot be used again.
c. Coal, gas, and oil are all renewable.

2 Answer the questions.

a. What are the four important kinds of resources? ______________________
b. What are some renewable energy resources? ______________________
c. What are capital resources? ______________________

3 Write the correct word and the meaning in Chinese.

human resources	renewable	capital resources	replace

a. ______________: people and the skills they have
b. ______________: able to be used again
c. ______________: machines and tools used to produce goods

10 Extreme Weather Conditions

Many people live in areas with four seasons. It's hot in summer and cold in winter. The weather in spring and fall is either warm or cool. These are very normal weather conditions. But sometimes there are extreme weather conditions. These can cause many problems for people.

Sometimes, it might not rain somewhere for a long time. Lakes, rivers, and streams have less water in them. Trees and grasses die. People and animals become very thirsty. This is called a drought.

Other times, it rains constantly for many days. Water levels become much higher than normal. Water often goes on the ground and even onto city streets. These are called floods.

In many warm places near the water, there are tropical storms. These storms drop heavy rains and have very strong winds. Tropical storms can drop several inches of rain in a few hours. Some places might get two or three tropical storms every year.

▲ drought

▲ flood

▲ tropical storm

1 What is the main idea of the passage?

a. Extreme weather can cause problems.
b. Floods often cause many problems.
c. Tropical storms drop large amounts of rain.

2 Answer the questions.

a. What happens during a drought? ______________________
b. What is it called when the water level becomes too high? ______________
c. What do tropical storms do? ______________________

3 Write the correct word and the meaning in Chinese.

normal	thirsty	extreme	flood	drought

a. ______________: a large amount of water covering an area that is usually dry
b. ______________: a period in which no or very little rain falls
c. ______________: feeling a need or desire to drink

Understanding Hemispheres

11

Earth is a big planet. But we can make it smaller by dividing it into sections. We call these sections hemispheres. One hemisphere is half of the earth.

There is an imaginary line that runs from east to west all around the earth. It is in the center of the earth. We call it the equator. The equator divides the Northern Hemisphere from the Southern Hemisphere. The Northern Hemisphere includes Asia and Europe. North America is also in it. Below the equator is the Southern Hemisphere. Australia and Antarctica are in it. So are most of South America and Africa.

We can also divide the earth into the Eastern and Western hemispheres. The line that does this is the prime meridian. It runs from north to south. It goes directly through Greenwich, England. The Eastern Hemisphere includes Europe, Africa, and Asia. The Western Hemisphere includes North and South America.

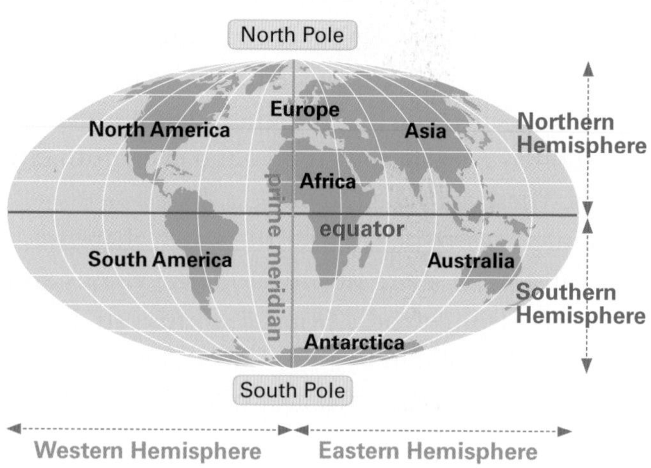

1 What goes through Greenwich, England?

a. The equator. b. The prime meridian. c. The Southern Hemisphere.

2 What is NOT true?

a. The equator runs from east to west.
b. Australia is in the Northern Hemisphere.
c. Earth has the Eastern Hemisphere and the Western Hemisphere.

3 Write the correct word and the meaning in Chinese.

hemisphere	prime meridian	imaginary	equator	divide

a. ____________________: to separate into parts or groups
b. ____________________: the imaginary line from the North Pole to the South Pole that passes through Greenwich in England
c. ____________________: one half of the earth

The Earth's Climate Zones

There are three main climate zones on the earth. They are the tropical, temperate, and polar climate zones.

The tropical zones are found near the equator. Basically, they are found between the Tropic of Cancer and the Tropic of Capricorn. In general, the tropical zone has hot weather most of the year. Many areas in the tropical zone have very wet weather, but this is not always the case.

The temperate zones are the largest of the three main climate zones. One temperate zone lies between the Tropic of Cancer and the Arctic Circle. The other temperate zone lies between the Tropic of Capricorn and the Antarctic Circle. Most of the world's population lives in temperate zones. Temperate zones are neither too hot nor too cold. They experience changing seasons all year long. For the most part, the weather is not too extreme in these places.

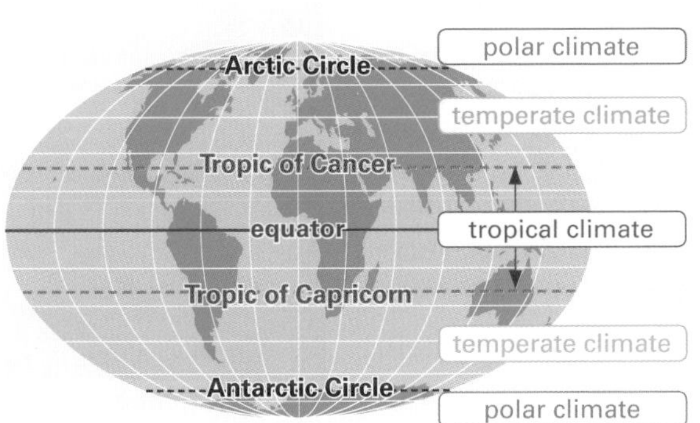

The polar zones are found north of the Arctic Circle and south of the Antarctic Circle. The weather in these places is constantly cold. Few people live in these places. Few animals live in them as well.

1 In which zone do most of the world's people live?

a. The tropical zone. b. The temperate zone. c. The polar zone.

2 Fill in the blanks.

a. The three main climate zones are the tropical, temperate, and __________ climate zones.

b. Tropical zones often have hot, __________ weather.

c. One of the temperate zones is between the Tropic of Capricorn and the __________ __________.

3 Write the correct word and the meaning in Chinese.

tropical zone	Tropic of Cancer	temperate zone	Antarctic Circle

a. ____________________: an area in which there are four distinct seasons

b. ____________________: a line of latitude about 23 degrees north of the equator

c. ____________________: a line of latitude about 66 degrees south of the equator

13 Climbing Mount Everest

Mount Everest is in the Himalaya Mountains. It is located near the border of Nepal, Tibet, and China. At 8,848 meters high, it is the highest mountain in the world. People call it "The Top of the World."

For years, people wanted to be the first to climb the mountain. But no one could get to the top. Many people tried, but none of them succeeded. Some of them even died.

But, in 1953, at last two men were successful. They were Sir Edmund Hillary and Tenzing Norgay. Hillary was from New Zealand. Norgay was a Sherpa. Sherpas are expert mountain climbers from Tibet and Nepal. They are often employed as guides for mountaineering expeditions in the Himalayas, particularly Mt. Everest. There were nine people on the team. They also had hundreds of porters and twenty Sherpas. It took them several days to get near the top. Some men came very close. But they couldn't get there. Finally, on May 29, 1953, Hillary and Norgay got to the top of the mountain. They were the first people to stand on top of the world!

Earth's Highest Mountains

▲ Mount Everest (8,848 m)

▲ K2 (8,611 m)

▲ Kanchenjunga (8,586 m)

▲ Lhotse (8,516 m)

1 Who was Tenzing Norgay?

a. A Sherpa who climbed Mount Everest.
b. One of Sir Edmund Hillary's porters.
c. One of Sir Edmund Hillary's relatives.

2 What is true? Write T (true) or F (false).

a. Sir Edmund Hillary climbed Mount Everest in 1953. ______
b. Sherpas come from New Zealand. ______
c. Sir Edmund Hillary climbed Mount Everest all by himself. ______

3 Write the correct word and the meaning in Chinese.

border	mountaineering	Sherpa	expedition	porter

a. ____________________: the activity of climbing mountains
b. ____________________: a journey for a specific purpose; the people engaged in such an activity
c. ____________________: the official line separating two countries or states

14 The Midwest Region of the United States

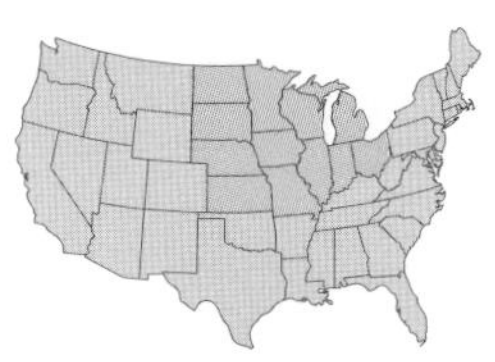

The American Midwest covers an enormous amount of land. It starts with Ohio, Michigan, and Indiana. It goes as far west as North and South Dakota, Nebraska, and Kansas. There are a total of twelve states in the Midwest.

Actually, the Midwest is in the east and central part of the country. But, a long time ago, the United States was much smaller. The only states in the country were beside the Atlantic Ocean. So people called the lands west of them the Midwest.

The land in the Midwest is almost completely identical. It is full of plains and prairies. The Midwest is very flat land. There are no mountains in it. Most hills only rise a few hundred feet high. However, the Great Lakes are in the Midwest. These are five huge lakes located between the U.S. and Canada.

Nowadays, people in the Midwest often work in industry or agriculture. In Detroit and other cities, making automobiles is a huge business. However, there are also many farmers. They grow corn, wheat, and other grains. And they also raise pigs and cows.

Some Geographical Features

▲ the Great Lakes

▲ the Great Plains

▲ the Badlands

1 What city in the Midwest makes automobiles?

a. Chicago. b. Cincinnati. c. Detroit.

2 Answer the questions.

a. How many states are in the Midwest? __________

b. Where were all of the American states located a long time ago?

____

c. What are the Great Lakes? __________

3 Write the correct word and the meaning in Chinese.

enormous	prairie	identical	raise	agriculture

a. __________: a large area of flat, grassy land in North America

b. __________: to keep and take care of animals

c. __________: farming; the act of growing crops

15 Yellowstone National Park

15

One of the most beautiful places in the U.S. is Yellowstone National Park. It is located mostly in Wyoming. But parts of it are in Montana and Idaho, too.

For many years, people had heard about a beautiful land in the west. But few ever saw it. Then more people began visiting the area in the 1800s. Also, the artist Thomas Moran visited Yellowstone. He made many beautiful landscapes of the region. This helped Yellowstone to become the first national park in 1872.

Many different animals live in Yellowstone. Bison, wolves, elk, eagles, and lots of other animals live there. Much of the land is forest. But there are also plains. And there are even geysers there. Geysers shoot hot water into the air. The most famous geyser is called Old Faithful. It has this name because it erupts on a regular schedule all the time.

▲ Grand Prismatic Spring

▲ Old Faithful

▲ bison

1 What is the main idea of the passage?

a. Yellowstone National Park is a beautiful place.
b. Old Faithful is located in Yellowstone National Park.
c. Thomas Moran visited Yellowstone in the 1800s.

2 What is true? Write T (true) or F (false).

a. Thomas Moran was a photographer. ____
b. Yellowstone became the first national park in the U.S. ____
c. Old Faithful is the name of a geyser in Yellowstone. ____

3 Write the correct word and the meaning in Chinese.

geyser	landscape	regular	erupt	bison

a. ______________: a large wild animal like a cow with long hair and a big head
b. ______________: an underground pool of water that often sends great bursts of hot water into the air
c. ______________: occurring at fixed intervals

16 The West Region of the United States

California is one of the richest states in America. It has a large amount of land. And it also has more people than any other state. It has plenty of natural resources, too. But everything is not perfect there. California has two major problems: earthquakes and forest fires.

The San Andreas Fault runs through California. Because of it, the state gets many earthquakes. Some of them are very powerful. For example, there was a strong earthquake in San Francisco in 1906. It destroyed many buildings. And it started numerous fires. Over 3,000 people died after it. There have also been many other strong earthquakes. Some people fear that the "big one" will hit someday. They think an earthquake will cause a huge amount of damage.

During summer and fall, much of California is dry. So forest fires, or wildfires, often start. These fires can spread rapidly. They burn many forests. But they also can burn people's homes and buildings. They often kill people before firefighters can put them out.

Some Geographical Features

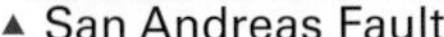
▲ San Andreas Fault

▲ Sierra-Nevada Mountains

▲ Death Valley

1 What is the "big one"?

a. a forest fire b. an earthquake c. a volcano

2 Fill in the blanks.

a. There was a strong ________________ in San Francisco in 1906.
b. California is often dry in the ______________ and fall.
c. ____________ __________ can burn forests, homes, and buildings.

3 Write the correct word and the meaning in Chinese.

earthquake	hit	rapidly	numerous	wildfire

a. __________________: a sudden shaking of the ground
b. __________________: a fire that starts in a rural area and spreads rapidly
c. __________________: occur in and cause damage to an area suddenly

The Lady's Husband
pointed teeth, quivering nostrils . . . Jean Lenoir pacing up and
down to hide his fear, talking about the guinguette à deux sous.
'There are others who deserve this and I wish they were
going down with me!'
But the next day, at the crack of dawn, he was alone. No one
from the guinguette was there with him.
Despite the heat, Maigret felt a sudden chill. And he looked
at this dapper haberdasher with his gold-tipped cigarette with
fresh eyes. Then he turned to where the Bassos' boat was being
moored at the bank, half-naked people leaping ashore to greet

History

American History

World History

17 The *Mayflower*

17

In Britain, there was a group of people called Pilgrims. They were different from most people there. They had certain religious beliefs that others did not share. So they wanted to leave Britain and go to the New World. They hired a ship called the *Mayflower* to take them to America.

▲ the Pilgrims departing on the *Mayflower*

They left in 1620 and landed in America after two months of sailing. They were supposed to go to the Hudson River area. But they landed at a place called Plymouth Rock. It was in modern-day Massachusetts on Cape Cod. Still, the Pilgrims decided to settle there.

▲ the first Thanksgiving at Plymouth

The first winter was hard. Many Pilgrims died. But the Native Americans there made peace with them. Their leader was Samoset. He brought Squanto to stay with the Pilgrims. Squanto and other Native Americans taught the Pilgrims how to farm the land properly. That year, the Pilgrims harvested many crops. They had a big three-day festival with the Native Americans. That was the first Thanksgiving.

Every year, the Pilgrim colony became stronger and stronger. More colonists came from Britain. So the colony became very successful.

1 What did the Native Americans do for the Pilgrims?

a. They showed the Pilgrims how to have a big festival.
b. They showed the Pilgrims how to settle in Plymouth Rock.
c. They showed the Pilgrims how to farm the land.

2 What is NOT true?

a. The Pilgrims sailed to America on the *Mayflower*.
b. Squanto was the leader of the Native Americans.
c. The first Thanksgiving was held in 1621.

3 Write the correct word and the meaning in Chinese.

Pilgrim	harvest	festival	be supposed to	Thanksgiving

a. ______________________: one of the English colonists settling at Plymouth in 1620
b. ______________________: an event that is held to celebrate a particular thing
c. ______________________: to gather crops from the fields; the gathering of crops

18 The Colonies Become Free

18

After the first English settlers arrived in Jamestown, more and more people moved from Europe to America. They lived in places called colonies. As the years passed, there were 13 colonies.

These colonies were ruled by the king of England. But many colonies did not want to be ruled by England. They wanted to be free. On July 4, 1776, many leaders in the colonies signed the Declaration of Independence. In the declaration, they wrote that Americans wanted to be free and start their own country. The colonies fought a war with England. The war lasted for many years. George Washington commanded the American soldiers and led them to victory.

After the war, the colonies became a country. The country was called the United States of America. Today, Americans celebrate Independence Day on July 4.

▲ The American soldiers fought the English in the Revolutionary War.

▲ George Washington was the commander of the American soldiers.

▲ Americans celebrate Independence Day on July 4.

1 What happened on July 4, 1776?

a. The 13 American colonies became a country.
b. The Declaration of Independence was signed.
c. War began between England and America.

2 What is true? Write T (true) or F (false).

a. There were 13 English colonies in America. ____
b. George Washington was the English leader. ____
c. American Independence Day is July 4. ____

3 Write the correct word and the meaning in Chinese.

victory	independence	Revolutionary War	command

a. ____________: freedom
b. ____________: the fact of winning a competition or battle
c. ____________: to lead; to order

19 The French and Indian War Leads to Revolution

19

▲ The Boston Tea Party was an act by colonists against the Tea Act.

▲ British troops killed five American civilians in the Boston Massacre.

In the eighteenth century, countries in Europe often fought wars against each other. They usually fought in Europe. But sometimes they fought in other places. One of these other places was in America.

In the 1750s and 1760s, the British and French fought a war in North America. Some people called it the French and Indian War. Others called it the Seven Years' War. Basically, the British and American colonists were on one side. The French and Native Americans were on the other side.

The British won the war. So the French left most of North America. They had to give many of their colonies to the British. But the war was very expensive for the British. So King George III of Britain wanted to raise taxes in the colonies. He said the British had protected the colonies. So they should pay higher taxes.

The British passed many taxes. These included the Stamp Act and the Tea Act. There were many others, though. The Americans hated the taxes and thought they were unfair. They called them the Intolerable Acts. Eventually, Britain's actions led to war in the colonies. The Americans revolted. And then they gained their freedom from Britain. That happened because of the American Revolution.

1 What eventually caused the American Revolution?

a. The Seven Years' War. b. King George III. c. The Native Americans.

2 Answer the questions.

a. What was the other name of the French and Indian War? ____________

b. Who won the French and Indian War? ____________

c. What did the Americans call the Stamp Act and the Tea Act? ____________

3 Write the correct word and the meaning in Chinese.

Stamp Act	tax	intolerable	unfair	revolt

a. ____________: a law passed by the British Parliament in 1765 to raise revenue in the American colonies

b. ____________: not treating people in an equal way; not morally right

c. ____________: to rebel; to fight back against one's leaders

The Bill of Rights

▲ the Bill of Rights

In 1787, the states' leaders started to write the Constitution. The Constitution is the supreme law of the land. But many Americans were not happy. They were worried about the strength of the national government. They knew a strong government could take away their rights. So they wanted to add some amendments to the Constitution. These would give specific rights to the people and the states. So they wrote 10 amendments to the Constitution. Together, they were called the Bill of Rights. The Bill of Rights was ratified in 1791 and then became law.

▲ Freedom of speech is granted in the First Amendment.

The First Amendment is about freedom. People have freedom of speech, religion, and the press and the right to assemble peacefully. The Second Amendment gives people the right to have guns. The Third Amendment says the government cannot put soldiers in people's houses. The Fourth Amendment protects people from illegal searches and arrests. The Fifth Amendment says a person cannot be tried twice for the same crime. The Sixth Amendment gives people the right to a speedy trial. The Seventh Amendment gives people the right to a jury trial. The Eighth Amendment protects people from high bail. The Ninth and Tenth amendments protect the people and states by giving them all rights not mentioned in the Constitution.

1 What is the passage mainly about?

a. The Bill of Rights and its amendments.
b. The process involved in writing the Bill of Rights.
c. The number of amendments in the Bill of Rights.

2 What is true? Write T (true) or F (false).

a. The American people wanted a strong national government. ____
b. The Bill of Rights became law in 1787. ____
c. The first 10 amendments are the Bill of Rights. ____

3 Write the correct word and the meaning in Chinese.

Constitution	assemble	amendment	speedy trial	ratify

a. ____________________: to approve; to accept as legal
b. ____________________: a criminal trial held after minimal delay
c. ____________________: to come together in a single place

21 The American Civil War

21

The Civil War was the bloodiest war in American history. It was fought for many reasons. One big reason was slavery. The South had slaves. The North did not.

The Civil War began after Abraham Lincoln became president. It started in 1861. The North had more men. It also had more railroads and more industries. But the South had better generals than the North. There were many battles during the war. At first, the South seemed to be winning the war. But, in 1863, General Robert E. Lee lost at Gettysburg. The next day, the South lost the Battle of Vicksburg. The North began winning after that.

Two Union generals were very important. General William T. Sherman cut through the South. His March to the Sea from Atlanta to the port of Savannah destroyed much of the South's will to fight. General Ulysses S. Grant led the Union forces. He finally defeated the South, so General Lee surrendered to him. Five days later, John Wilkes Booth assassinated President Lincoln.

▲ Robert E. Lee

▲ William T. Sherman

▲ Ulysses S. Grant

▲ The Battle of Gettysburg

▲ Surrender of General Lee to General Grant.

1 Who was the leader of the Union forces during the Civil War?

a. General Robert E. Lee. b. General William T. Sherman.
c. General Ulysses S. Grant.

2 Fill in the blanks.

a. Abraham Lincoln was president when the __________ __________ started.
b. General Sherman went on the __________ to the Sea.
c. John Wilkes Booth killed President __________ after the war ended.

3 Write the correct word and the meaning in Chinese.

general	assassinate	bloody	will	surrender

a. __________________: extremely violent and involving a lot of injuries
b. __________________: to kill an important person usually for political reasons
c. __________________: to give in; to stop fighting or resisting

The Roaring Twenties and the Great Depression

In the 1920s, the American economy was very strong, and life was good. World War I had just ended. So people were interested in peace, not war. They had jobs and were making a lot of money. There were new technologies being created, and people could afford to buy them. They began moving to the suburbs and living in houses. People had leisure time, so they could go out and enjoy themselves.

Then, on October 24, 1929, the stock market crashed. Suddenly, life changed for millions of people. Instantly, people lost billions of dollars in stock. Companies went bankrupt. As they went out of business, millions of people lost their jobs. The unemployment rate climbed. The president at the time, Herbert Hoover, was blamed for the economic problems.

In 1932, Franklin Roosevelt was elected the new president of the United States. Roosevelt had a plan to end the Great Depression. His plan was called the New Deal. He increased the influence of the government on the economy. He tried to have the government give people jobs. During the 1930s, life in the U.S. was very difficult. It was only when World War II began in 1941 that the Great Depression ended. Then, the U.S. economy began to recover.

Famous Events in American History

▲ the transcontinental railroad

▲ the Roaring Twenties

▲ the Great Depression

1 What is the main idea of the passage?

a. The New Deal caused the Great Depression to become worse.
b. The Great Depression ended good economic times in the U.S.
c. The American economy in the 1920s was very strong.

2 What is NOT true?

a. The American economy was good in the 1920s.
b. The stock market crashed in 1929.
c. Franklin Roosevelt was president when the stock market crashed.

3 Write the correct word and the meaning in Chinese.

Great Depression	leisure time	afford	recover	go bankrupt

a. ____________________: time available for ease and relaxation
b. ____________________: to lose all of one's money
c. ____________________: to begin to get stronger and return to its earlier state

23 What Do Historians Do

Historians study the past. They are concerned about past events and people who lived in the past. But historians do not just learn names, dates, and places. Instead, they try to interpret past events. They want to know why an event happened. They want to know why a person acted in a certain way. And they want to know how one event caused another to occur.

To do this, historians must study many sources. First, they use primary sources. These are sources that were recorded at the same time an event occurred. They could be journals. They could be books. They could be newspaper articles or photographs. In modern times, they could even be videotaped recordings. Historians use primary sources to get the opinions of eyewitnesses to important events. They also use secondary sources. These are works written by people who did not witness an event. Good historians use both primary and secondary sources in their work.

There are many kinds of history. Some historians like political history. Others study military history. Some focus on economics. And others prefer social or cultural history. All of them are important. And all of them help us understand the past better.

▲ Important people in history are historical figures.

▲ Historic sites are where important events occurred.

▲ Historical events are events that made an impact on history.

1 What is the passage mainly about?

a. What primary and secondary sources are.
b. How historians learn about the past.
c. Why historians like to study the past.

2 What is NOT true?

a. Historians want to know about the past.
b. Historians often use primary sources.
c. Good historians only use primary sources.

3 Write the correct word and the meaning in Chinese.

interpret	primary source	eyewitness	journal	military

a. ____________________: a source that was recorded when a certain event occurred
b. ____________________: a magazine dealing with a specialized subject
c. ____________________: relating to or belonging to the armed forces

Rome: From Republic to Empire

24

According to legend, the brothers Romulus and Remus founded Rome in 753 B.C. Rome grew larger until around 620 B.C., when a group of people called the Etruscans conquered it. The Etruscans ruled Rome for 111 years. In 509 B.C., the Roman people overthrew King Tarquin the Proud. They were free again.

The Romans made a new kind of government. It was called a republic. Under the republic, they elected a small number of people to be their leaders. These leaders were called patricians. Up to 300 of them could be elected to the Senate. For the next 500 years, Rome remained a republic.

▲ Carthaginian general Hannibal leading his army in the Punic Wars

Rome began to grow more powerful. It soon controlled all of the Italian peninsula. From 264 B.C. to 146 B.C., it fought the Punic Wars against Carthage. The Romans won and became the masters of the Mediterranean Sea. Soon, the republic was enormous. But it became corrupt. A general—Julius Caesar—challenged the rule of the Senate and became a dictator. Yet he was murdered in 44 B.C., and the republic was ruled by three leaders.

Eventually, those three men fought each other. Octavian won and became the first Roman emperor. The republic was gone. Now it was the Roman Empire.

▲ Octavian, the first Roman emperor

1 What happened in Rome in 44 B.C.?

a. The Punic Wars ended.
b. Julius Caesar was murdered.
c. Rome became an empire.

2 What is true? Write T (true) or F (false).

a. Rome was conquered by the Etruscans in 753 B.C. ____
b. There were 300 members of the Roman Senate. ____
c. Rome fought the Punic Wars against Carthage. ____

3 Write the correct word and the meaning in Chinese.

patrician	republic	corrupt	dictator	overthrow

a. ______________: to remove a leader or government from power by force
b. ______________: a government in which the leaders are voted into office
c. ______________: doing dishonest things in order to gain money or power

25 The Middle Ages

The Roman Empire fell in 476. It was conquered by Germanic invaders. In the east, there was still the Byzantine Empire. It was the eastern part of the Roman Empire. It lasted for almost 1,000 more years. It was finally defeated in 1453.

But in Western Europe, after the fall of the Western Roman Empire, the Dark Ages began. This term is sometimes applied to the first 300 years after the fall of Rome and sometimes to the whole Middle Ages. During this time, only a few people could read and write. The people had hard lives. They often just struggled to survive. Most people farmed the land. Their lives were very simple then.

Throughout the Middle Ages, there were very slow improvements in people's lives. Some kings ruled their lands fairly. Others were very harsh. They treated their people like slaves. And they taxed them very much. Many people died of starvation. Others died because of diseases. The Black Death killed almost half of the people in Europe in the fourteenth century. The Middle Ages were a very difficult time for most people.

Famous Events in the Middle Ages

▲ the Crusades

▲ Black Death

▲ Hundred Years' War

1 What is NOT true?

a. The Roman Empire was conquered by Germanic invaders.
b. The Byzantine Empire was in Western Europe.
c. The Dark Ages happened after the fall of the Roman Empire.

2 When did the Byzantine Empire fall?

a. In 300. b. In 476. c. In 1453.

3 Write the correct word and the meaning in Chinese.

harsh	the Middle Ages	invader	struggle	starvation

a. ________________: someone who uses force to enter another country
b. ________________: hunger; extreme suffering or death caused by a lack of food
c. ________________: strict, unkind, and often unfair

Marco Polo and the Silk Road

China and Europe are very far from each other. Today, people can fly between the two in a few hours. But in the past, it took months or years to go from one place to the other. When people traveled from China to Europe, they went on the Silk Road.

The Silk Road was not a real road. It was a large group of trade routes. But, by following it, people could get from the Mediterranean Sea to the Pacific Ocean. It was called the Silk Road because the Chinese transported silk to the west on it.

The Silk Road became very famous because of Marco Polo. He was an Italian adventurer. With his father and uncle, he left Italy and returned twenty-five years later in 1295. He had taken the Silk Road to China. He had many adventures. He even became an advisor to the emperor. When he came back, he wrote a book, *The Travels of Marco Polo*, about his travels and became very famous.

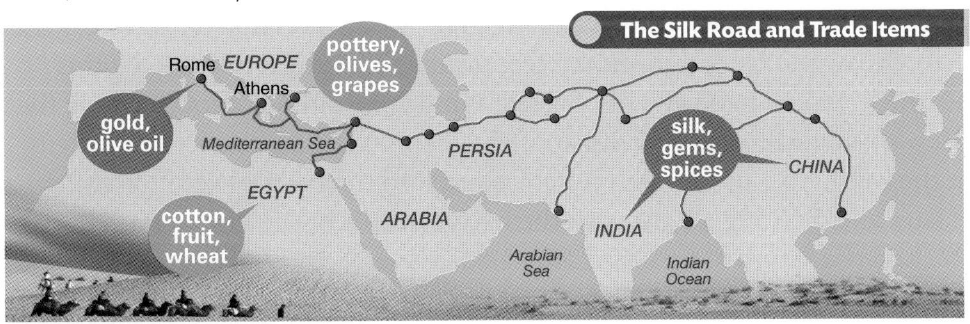

1 **What was the Silk Road?**

a. It was a real road.
b. It was a large group of trade routes.
c. It was Marco Polo's road.

2 **Answer the questions.**

a. How did people go from China to Europe in the past? ______________________

b. Who transported silk on the Silk Road? ______________________

c. What did Marco Polo do after he went back to Italy? ______________________

3 **Write the correct word and the meaning in Chinese.**

transport	adventurer	trade route	emperor	advisor

a. ______________: someone who seeks dangerous or exciting experiences
b. ______________: someone who gives advice in a particular field
c. ______________: a route that is used by traders

The Age of Exploration

27

In 1453, the Ottoman Turks defeated the Byzantine Empire. They captured its capital city Constantinople. Suddenly, the land route from Europe to Asia became more dangerous. At that time, many Europeans purchased spices from China and other Asian countries. But now they could not get them from land. So they tried to get their spices by sea. This began the Age of Exploration.

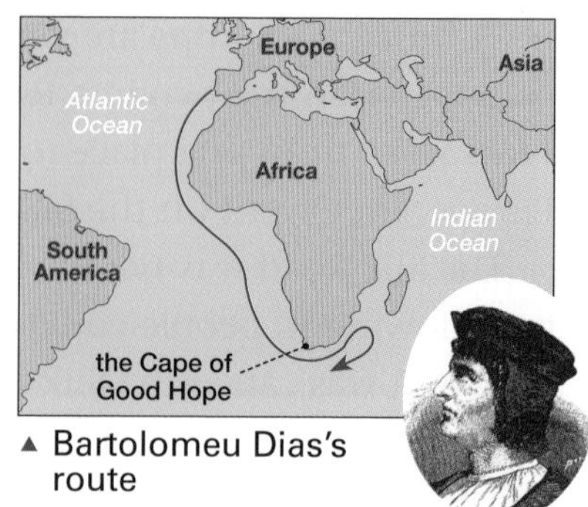

▲ Bartolomeu Dias's route

Many Europeans began sailing south around Africa. At first, the Portuguese and Spanish started sailing south. But then other Europeans started to follow them. In 1488, Bartolomeu Dias became the first European to sail to the Cape of Good Hope in Africa. This was the southernmost point of Africa. He had discovered the way to India by water. In 1498, Vasco da Gama sailed across the Indian Ocean and landed in India. He returned to Portugal in 1499. By this time, the Americas had been discovered. But people did not know how big the earth was. Finally, in 1519, Ferdinand Magellan set sail from Spain. He sailed past the southern part of South America and into the Pacific Ocean. Magellan was later killed during a fight with the native people of the Philippines. But, in 1522, his crew returned to Spain. They had sailed around the world!

Early Portuguese Explorers

▲ Gil Eanes ▲ Vasco da Gama ▲ Ferdinand Magellan

1 What did Vasco da Gama do?

a. He sailed to the Cape of Good Hope.
b. He sailed around the world.
c. He sailed all the way to India.

2 What is NOT true?

a. The Europeans defeated the Byzantine Empire in 1453.
b. Bartolomeu Dias sailed around the southern part of Africa.
c. Magellan's crew was the first to sail around the world.

3 Write the correct word and the meaning in Chinese.

capture	route	spice	crew	southernmost

a. ____________________: a seasoning; something that gives food an extra taste
b. ____________________: a group of people who work on and operate a ship
c. ____________________: a particular way or direction between places

28 The Spread of Islam

In 632, Muhammad died. He was the founder of Islam. At his death, there were few Muslims. And they had very little land. But after Muhammad's death, Islam began to spread rapidly.

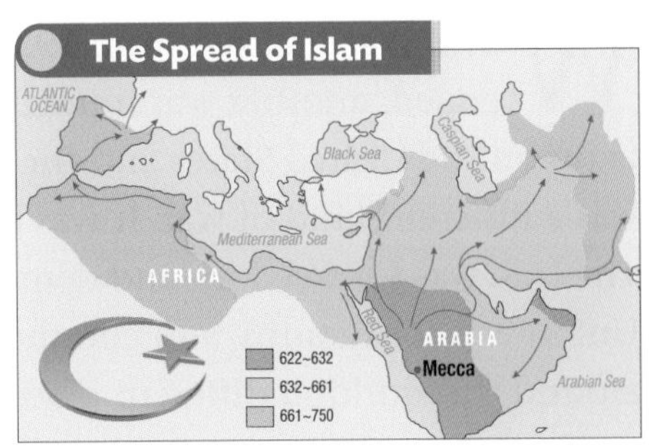

Soon after Muhammad's death, Muslim leaders selected caliphs to govern the Muslim community. During the reigns of the first four caliphs (from 632 to 661), Islam spread throughout the Arabian Peninsula. By 661, Islam conquered land from Persia in the Near East to Egypt in Africa. From 661 to 750, the Umayyad dynasty ruled the Islamic world. They spread Islam throughout northern Africa. In 711, an Islamic army crossed the Mediterranean Sea and entered Spain. In a few years, they had captured Spain. The Muslims went north and entered France. But, in 732, Charles Martel defeated an Islamic army near Tours. The Muslim advance to the north was stopped.

Meanwhile, the Muslims could not defeat the Byzantine Empire in the east. They advanced on Constantinople several times. But they always lost. Later, however, the Ottoman Empire arose in the east. It challenged the Byzantines. By the fifteenth century, the Byzantine Empire was weak. In 1453, the Ottomans conquered it. They made Constantinople their capital. From there, they would rule a vast Islamic empire until the twentieth century.

▲ Mehmed II, Sultan of the Ottoman Empire, entered Constantinople and conquered it.

1 What is the passage mainly about?

a. How Muhammad founded Islam.
b. How Islam advanced throughout the world.
c. How the Ottoman Empire defeated the Byzantine Empire.

2 Fill in the blanks.

a. The founder of Islam was ________________.
b. The first four ____________ ruled from 632 to 661.
c. The ______________ Empire defeated the Byzantine Empire in 1453.

3 Write the correct word and the meaning in Chinese.

founder	caliph	Muslim	dynasty	Islam

a. ________________: a Muslim ruler
b. ________________: a period when a country is ruled by a family of rulers
c. ________________: a follower of Islam

29 The Cold War

29

World War II lasted from 1939 to 1945. When it ended, another war immediately began. It was between the United States and the Soviet Union. But this was a different kind of war. It was called the Cold War. The U.S. was for freedom and democracy. The Soviet Union was for tyranny and communism. So they battled around the world in different places.

There were many events in the Cold War, but few involved actual fighting. The Berlin Blockade of 1948 and 1949 was one incident. So was the construction of the Berlin Wall in 1961. Of course, there were some wars. Both the Korean War and the Vietnam War were a part of the Cold War since the U.S. and the Soviet Union supported opposite sides. Even the Space Race in the 1950s and 1960s was a part of the Cold War. And so was the nuclear race. Both countries had thousands of nuclear weapons, but they never used them.

Eventually, the Cold War ended in the 1980s. Thanks to U.S. President Ronald Reagan, the Soviet Union began to collapse. In 1989, the Berlin Wall came down. The countries of Eastern Europe started becoming free. And, in 1991, the Soviet Union ended. The Cold War was over.

Important Cold War Events

▲ Berlin Airlift

▲ Korean War

▲ Vietnam War

▲ Berlin Wall

1 Which event was a part of the Cold War?

a. World War II. b. The Space Race. c. The election of Ronald Reagan.

2 Fill in the blanks.

a. The United States supported freedom and ________________.

b. The __________ Blockade was in 1948 and 1949.

c. Both the Korean War and the Vietnam War were a part of the ________ ________.

3 Write the correct word and the meaning in Chinese.

communism	Cold War	collapse	tyranny	nuclear weapon

a. ____________________: to suddenly fail or stop existing

b. ____________________: a system in which goods are owned in common

c. ____________________: a government ruled by a cruel ruler who has total power; a dictatorship

30 Globalization

In the years after World War II, the world greatly changed. Much of this was due to new technology. For instance, the jet was developed. This increased the speed that people could travel. There were also advances in telecommunications. Computers and the Internet were invented. It became much easier for people to communicate with others all around the world. This has led to the spread of globalization.

Basically, the world is becoming a smaller place. In the past, what happened in one country rarely affected other countries. Or it took a long time for any effects to occur. But the world is different today. Because of globalization, what happens in one part of the world can affect places all around it.

Thanks to globalization, people can now do business more easily with those in other countries. When you go to the supermarket, you can see various foods from all of the different countries. This happens because of globalization. Also, people are learning more about other countries these days. This leads to more understanding about other countries. In the age of globalization, there has not been a single world war. And the world is becoming richer. Globalization has surely been good for the world.

▲ Thanks to technology, we live in a globalized world.

1 What is the passage mainly about?

a. The various effects of globalization.
b. The modern way of doing business.
c. The speed that people can communicate nowadays.

2 Fill in the blanks.

a. There was much new technology developed after ________ ________ ____.
b. Because of globalization, the ________ is becoming smaller.
c. It is ________ to do business with people in other countries these days.

3 Write the correct word and the meaning in Chinese.

due to	telecommunications	advance	affect	globalization

a. ________________: communications involving technological developments
b. ________________: to change or influence something
c. ________________: progress in science, technology, etc.

Science

Life Science
Earth Science
Physical Science

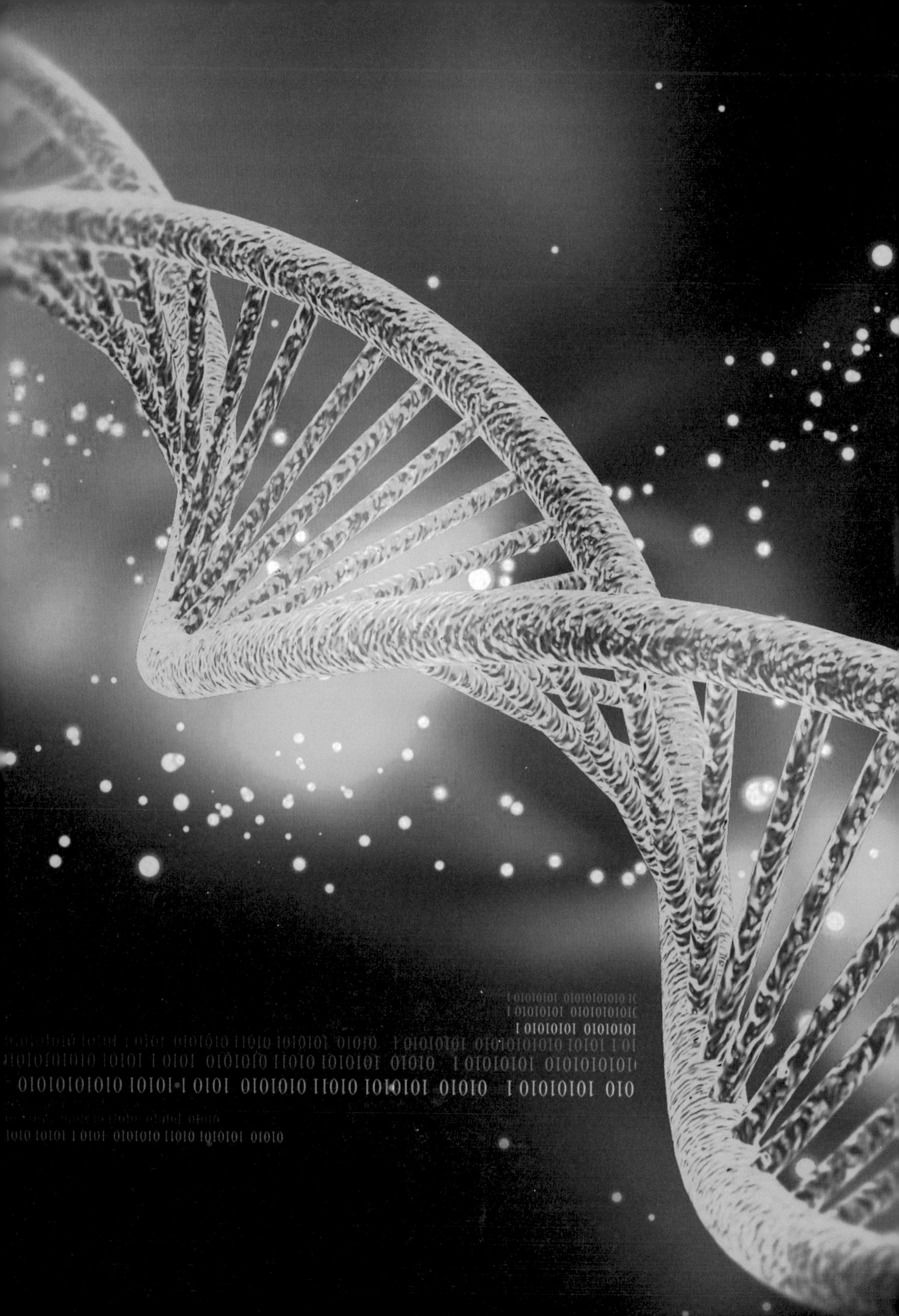

Life Science

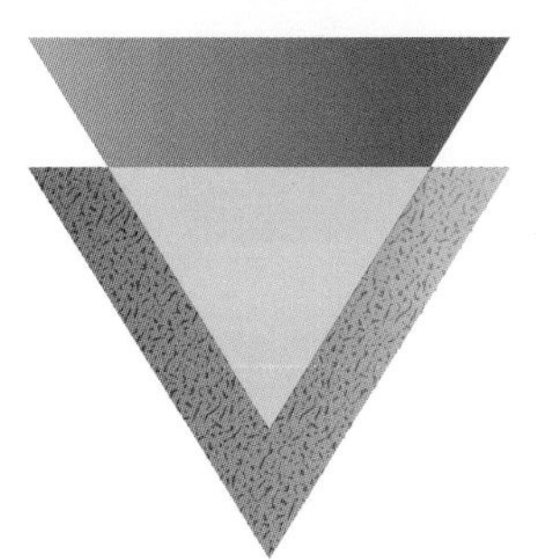

A World of Living Things

Ecosystems

Exploring the Human Body

31 Organisms

There are millions of types of organisms on the earth. An organism is any creature that is alive. These include animals, plants, fungi, and microorganisms. All organisms are made of cells. Some have just one cell. Others have billions and billions of them.

Microorganisms are very, very small. In fact, you can't even see them without a microscope. Bacteria and protists are microorganisms. These are often one-celled organisms. So everything they need to survive is in a single cell. How do they reproduce? They simply divide themselves in half. This is called asexual reproduction.

But most organisms are multi-celled. So they may have a few cells. Or they could have trillions of them. Multi-celled organisms have specialized cells. These cells often do one specific thing. They could be used to defend the organism from disease. They could be used for reproduction. They could be used for digestion. Or they could be used for many other purposes.

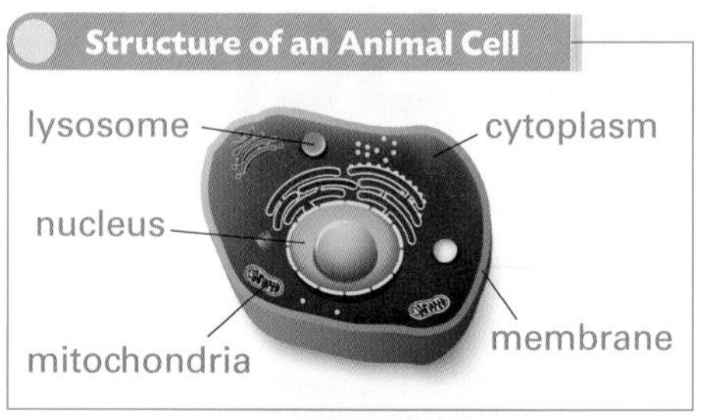

Structure of an Animal Cell

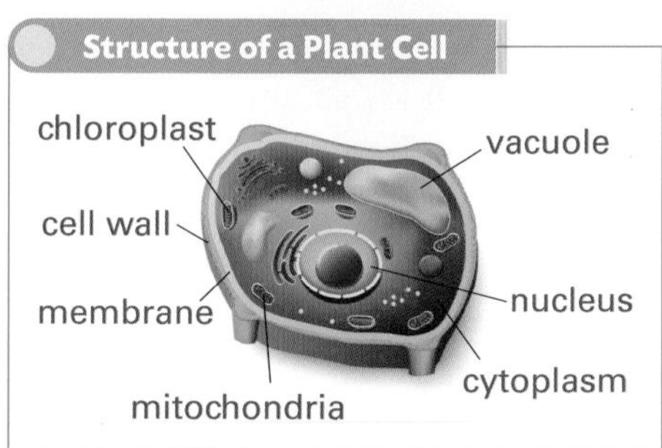

Structure of a Plant Cell

▲ Amoebas are one-celled organisms.

1 What is asexual reproduction?

a. Reproduction involving male and female cells
b. The dividing of a cell in half
c. The creating of a multi-celled organism

2 What is true? Write T (true) or F (false).

a. You need a microscope to see a microorganism. ____
b. Multi-celled organisms have one cell. ____
c. Cells have many different uses. ____

3 Write the correct word and the meaning in Chinese.

fungi	reproduce	microorganism	protist	asexual

a. ________________: lacking sex or functional sex organs
b. ________________: to produce young animals or plants
c. ________________: an organism that has only one cell

32 Kingdoms

There are many organic creatures on Earth. Some are very different from others. But many have some similarities. So scientists have divided organisms into five separate kingdoms. These kingdoms are animals, plants, protists, fungi, and bacteria. All of the creatures in each kingdom are similar in some way.

The animal kingdom is the biggest. It has over 800,000 species. Most animals are either vertebrates or invertebrates. Animals include mammals, reptiles, birds, amphibians, and insects.

The second largest kingdom is the plant kingdom. Plants include trees, bushes, flowers, vines, and grasses.

The third kingdom is the protists. They are animals that have only one cell. They include protozoans, algae, and diatoms.

The fourth kingdom is the fungi. Most fungi are mushrooms. But there are also certain molds, yeasts, and lichen, too.

The final kingdom is the bacteria. These are some kinds of bacteria and various pathogens, such as viruses.

▲ animal kingdom

▲ plant kingdom

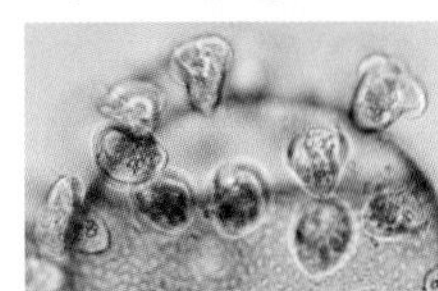
▲ protist kingdom

▲ fungi kingdom

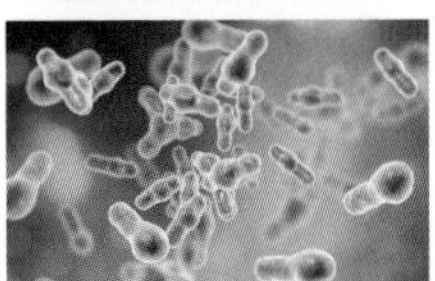
▲ bacteria kingdom

1 What is the passage mainly about?

a. The five kingdoms of organisms.
b. The number of species in each kingdom.
c. The similarities of the organisms in the five kingdoms.

2 What is true? Write T (true) or F (false).

a. The biggest kingdom is the plant kingdom. _____
b. Insects and algae belong to the protist kingdom. _____
c. Mushrooms and yeasts are fungi. _____

3 Write the correct word and the meaning in Chinese.

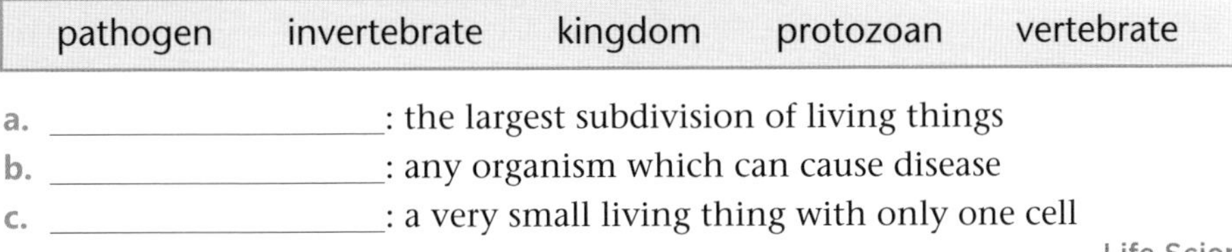

pathogen	invertebrate	kingdom	protozoan	vertebrate

a. ____________________: the largest subdivision of living things
b. ____________________: any organism which can cause disease
c. ____________________: a very small living thing with only one cell

33 Heredity

33

People often look very similar to their parents. They might have the same face. Or they have the same color hair or eyes. They might be tall or short like their parents. Why do they look this way? The answer is heredity.

Heredity is the passing of traits from a parent to his or her offspring. This happens because of genes. Genes contain DNA. DNA is the basic building block of life. Both parents pass on their genes to their offspring. So the offspring may resemble the mother, father, or both.

There are dominant and recessive genes. Dominant genes affect the body more than recessive genes. Recessive genes exist in a body. But they do not affect it. Dominant genes, however, affect the organism. Genes do not just determine an organism's physical characteristics. They also determine the organism's mental characteristics. This can include intelligence. And it may even affect personality, too.

▲ Genes are transferred from parents to their offspring.

▲ Learned behavior is taught to an animal.

▲ Instinctive behavior comes naturally to an animal.

1 What is the main idea of the passage?

a. There are both dominant and recessive genes.
b. DNA is the basic building block of life.
c. People pass their genes on to their offspring.

2 Answer the questions.

a. Why do children often look like their parents? ____________________
b. What do genes have? ____________________
c. What kinds of genes are there? ____________________

3 Write the correct word and the meaning in Chinese.

heredity	trait	offspring	recessive gene	intelligence

a. ____________________: a distinguishing quality or characteristic
b. ____________________: the passing of traits from parents to offspring
c. ____________________: a gene that exists in the body but is overshadowed by a dominant gene

34 Sexual and Asexual Reproduction

All plants need to reproduce in order to create new plants. There are two ways they can reproduce. The first is sexual reproduction. The second is asexual reproduction.

Sexual reproduction involves a male and female of the same species. Plants that reproduce this way have flowers. Flowers are where their reproductive organs and seeds are. The male reproductive organ is the stamen. It has pollen that needs to be carried to the female part of the plant. The female part is the pistil. When the pollen gets transferred, the plant has been pollinated. This causes seeds to grow in the flower. Soon, the seeds germinate, which means they are growing into young plants.

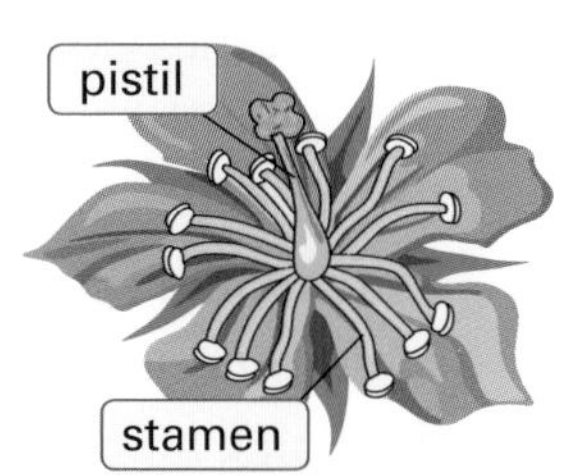

The second method is asexual reproduction. In this method, there is only one parent plant. Asexual reproduction can happen in many ways. For example, a new plant may simply start growing from an old plant. Other plants reproduce from bulbs. Onions and potatoes are both bulbs. Parts of these plants can simply begin growing roots, and thus they become new plants. In the case of asexual reproduction, there is no pollen, and there are no male and female plants. New plants simply grow from old ones.

▲ sexual reproduction

▲ asexual reproduction

1 What is the main idea of the passage?

a. The reproductive organs of plants are in their flowers.
b. Onions and potatoes can reproduce asexually.
c. Plants can reproduce sexually or asexually.

2 What is NOT true?

a. Plants can reproduce in two different ways.
b. When seeds germinate, they can grow into new plants.
c. Asexual reproduction requires male and female parts.

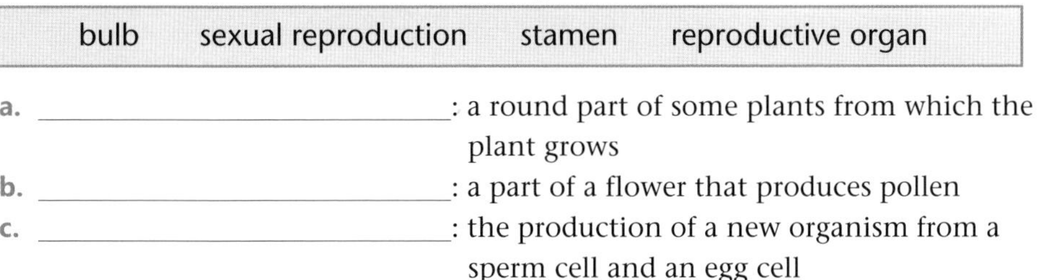

3 Write the correct word and the meaning in Chinese.

bulb	sexual reproduction	stamen	reproductive organ

a. ______________________: a round part of some plants from which the plant grows
b. ______________________: a part of a flower that produces pollen
c. ______________________: the production of a new organism from a sperm cell and an egg cell

35 Pollination and Fertilization

35

Plants that reproduce sexually have both male and female parts. A plant must be pollinated in order to reproduce. Pollen from the stamen—the male part—must reach the pistil—the female part. There are two major ways this happens. The first is the wind. Sometimes, the wind carries pollen from one plant to another. However, this is not a very effective method. Fortunately, many animals help pollinate plants. Usually, the animals are insects, such as bees and butterflies. Plants' flowers often produce nectar, which insects like. As the insects collect a plant's nectar, they pick up pollen. As the insects go from plant to plant, the pollen on them rubs off on the pistils of other plants. This pollinates the plants.

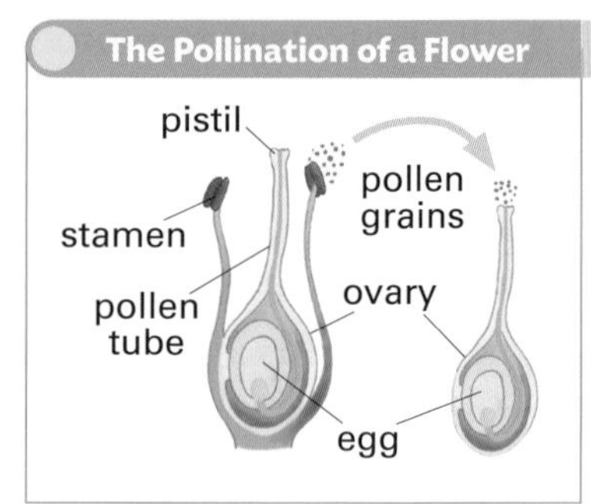

Now that the pollen has been transferred, the plant must be fertilized. The stigma of a plant has a pollen tube. At least one grain of pollen must go down that tube. This is not easy because the tube is so small, so plants often need many grains of pollen to ensure that one will go down the tube. Once that happens, then the male and female cells can unite. This results in the fertilization of the plant. And it can now reproduce.

▲ Bees help pollination.

1 Which animal often pollinates flowers?

a. Bees. b. Bears. c. Birds.

2 Answer the questions.

a. What is the male part of the plant? ______________________

b. What is the female part of the plant? ______________________

c. Where in the stigma must the pollen go to fertilize a plant?

____

3 Write the correct word and the meaning in Chinese.

pollinate	pollen	nectar	grain	fertilization

a. ______________: a sweet substance produced by flowers

b. ______________: a very small individual piece of a substance

c. ______________: to place pollen from one flower on another flower

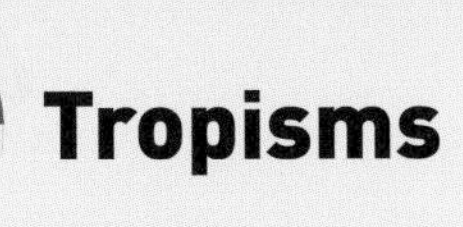

36 Tropisms

People know that animals often adapt to their environment. This is called evolution. It can take place over a very long time. And it can change animals very much. Plants can also adapt. Their adaptations are called tropisms.

A tropism is the response of a plant to an external stimulus. An external stimulus can be light, moisture, or gravity. Tropisms are involuntary, but they help plants survive in their environment.

Plants need light in order to live. Without light, they cannot undergo photosynthesis. So plants will always grow toward light. If they are in shadows or dark places, they will bend toward the light that they need to survive.

The same is true of moisture. Without water, plants will die. Plants' roots will grow toward the parts of the ground that have moisture. Plants' leaves will adapt so that they can trap as much moisture as possible.

Gravity is another force which causes tropisms. Stems will always move against gravity. This means that they will move in an upward direction. However, roots move with gravity. This means that they move downward.

▲ The response of plants to light is called phototropism.

▲ The response of plants to water is called hydrotropism .

▲ The response of plants to gravity is called gravitropism.

1. **What is the adaptation of a plant called?**
   a. Evolution. b. Tropism. c. Stimulus.

2. **What is NOT true?**
   a. Evolution is a change in plants.
   b. Plants may react to light or gravity.
   c. Plants will try to bend toward light.

3. **Write the correct word and the meaning in Chinese.**

evolution	stimulus	tropism	involuntary	gravity

a. ________________: the fact of living things turning towards or away from something
b. ________________: the process by which organisms adapt to their environments
c. ________________: the force that attracts objects towards one another, especially the force that makes things fall to the ground

37 The Five Kingdoms of Life

37

There is an amazing variety of life on the earth. Scientists have classified all forms of life into five different kingdoms. Each kingdom has its own characteristics.

The first is the Monera Kingdom. There are about 10,000 species in it. Members of this kingdom are prokaryotes that are unicellular. Its members include various kinds of bacteria and some algae.

The second is the Protista Kingdom. There are around 250,000 species in it. Members of this kingdom include protozoans and some kinds of algae.

The third is the Fungi Kingdom. There are around 100,000 species in it. Members of this kingdom are similar to plants. But they do not use photosynthesis to create nutrients. Mushrooms are members of this kingdom.

Biological Classification

kingdom
▼
phylum | division
▼ ▼
class
▼
order
▼
family
▼
genus
▼
species

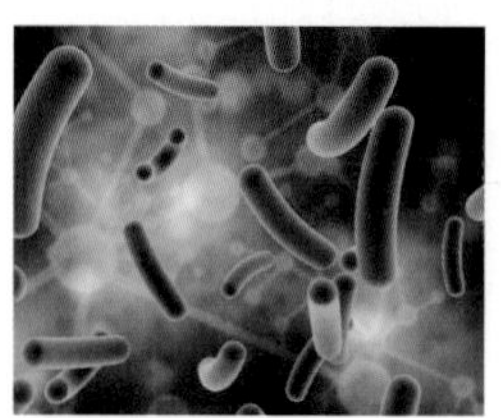

▲ Monera Kingdom

The fourth is the Plantae Kingdom. There are around 250,000 species in it. Plants, trees, flowers, and bushes all belong to this kingdom.

The fifth is the Animalia Kingdom. It is the biggest with over 1,000,000 species in it. It is formed by multicellular animals.

1 Which organisms belong to the Protista Kingdom?

a. Protozoans. b. Mushrooms. c. Prokaryotes.

2 What is true? Write T (true) or F (false).

a. There are around 250,000 species in the Monera Kingdom. ____

b. Mushrooms belong to the Fungi Kingdom. ____

c. The Plantae Kingdom has the greatest number of species. ____

3 Write the correct word and the meaning in Chinese.

Monera Kingdom	prokaryote	photosynthesis	unicellular

a. ________________: an organism lacking a true nucleus

b. ________________: the process by which a plant uses the energy from the light of the sun to produce its own food

c. ________________: having or consisting of a single cell; one-celled

38 Gregor Mendel

These days, scientists can do amazing things with genetics. They can modify the genetic structure of plants. This can let them produce more fruit or grain. Some are even resistant to diseases. But the field of genetics is very young. It is barely over 100 years old. And it was all started by a monk called Gregor Mendel.

Gregor Mendel enjoyed gardening. He especially liked to grow peas in his garden. While doing that, he noticed that some pea plants had different characteristics. He saw that some were tall while others were short. The colors of their flowers were different. And there were other differences, too. He wanted to know why. So he started experimenting with them.

Mendel started crossbreeding plants with one another. He learned about dominant and recessive genes this way. He created hybrids, which are plants that carry the genes of different plants. He grew many generations of peas and learned a lot about them. What Mendel learned became the basis for modern genetics.

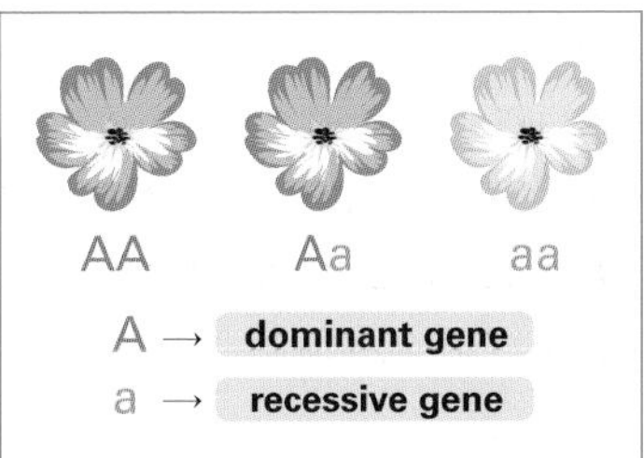

Mendel did most of his work with peas in the 1850s and 1860s. But, at first, people ignored his work. It was not until the early twentieth century that people began to study his research. Then they realized how much he had really accomplished.

▲ hybrid

1. **Why did Gregor Mendel conduct experiments with peas?**
   a. He was curious why some plants were different from others.
   b. He was interested in learning how to crossbreed plants.
   c. He wanted to invent the science of genetics.

2. **Fill in the blanks.**
   a. Gregor Mendel is the father of ______________.
   b. Gregor Mendel conducted experiments on __________ plants.
   c. Gregor Mendel learned about ________________ and recessive genes.

3. **Write the correct word and the meaning in Chinese.**

genetics	resistant	crossbreed	hybrid	recessive gene

a. ____________________: to interbreed; to produce a hybrid
b. ____________________: an animal or plant that is produced from two different kinds of animals or plants
c. ____________________: not harmed or affected by something

39 Pollination and Germination

39

All plants reproduce somehow. This allows them to produce offspring that will grow into mature plants. There are two important steps in plant reproduction. The first is pollination. The second is germination.

Most plants have both male and female reproductive organs. However, they must come into contact with each other in order for the plant to reproduce. This happens through pollination. Pollen from the male part of a plant must reach the female part of the plant. This can happen in many ways. The wind may sometimes blow the pollen from one part to the other. But this is very ineffective. Many times, animals such as bees, butterflies, and other insects pollinate plants. As they go from plant to plant, pollen gets stuck to their bodies. When they land on a new plant, some of it rubs off. Many times, this pollinates the plant. Once the pollen goes from the anther (the male part) to the stigma (the female part), the plant has been pollinated and can start to reproduce.

▲ self-pollination

▲ cross-pollination

The other important step is germination. Germination happens after a plant's seeds have been formed. At first, the plant's seeds are dormant. However, when they germinate, they come to life and begin to grow. If the conditions are good, then the seed will become a seedling. Eventually, it will mature and become a plant.

seedling

▲ germination

1. **What is the passage mainly about?**
   a. Why germination happens.
   b. Where plants' reproductive organs are.
   c. How plants reproduce.

2. **What is NOT true?**
   a. Pollination happens before germination.
   b. Insects frequently pollinate plants.
   c. Germination is what forms a plant's seeds.

3. **Write the correct word and the meaning in Chinese.**

seedling	pollination	germination	anther	dormant

a. ____________________: inactive; asleep

b. ____________________: a young plant that has grown from a seed

c. ____________________: the top part of a stamen of a flower that contains pollen

What Is a Food Web

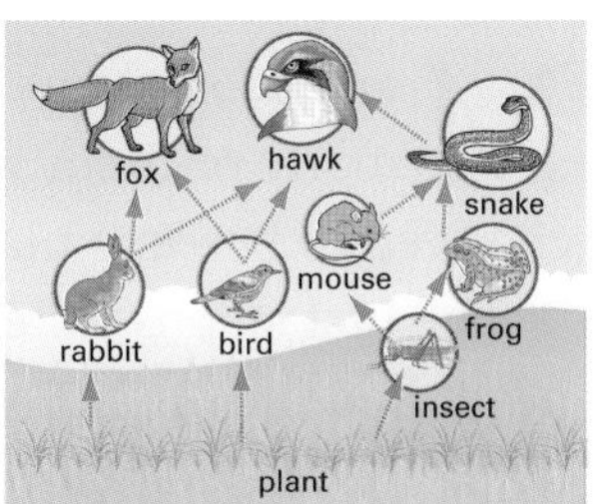

▲ food web

A food chain shows the feeding relationship in an ecosystem. However, most feeding relationships are not simple because most organisms eat or are eaten by many different things. So we often use a "food web" to show the relationship between all of the species in an ecosystem. A food web is a map of overlapping food chains. Each food web contains several food chains.

All food webs begin with producers. They are plants that use the sun's energy to make their own food. These plants are eaten by animals, called consumers. Consumers are organisms that eat other organisms. Consumers can be classified into three groups according to the type of food they eat.

Herbivores are plant eaters. They only eat plants. Cows and horses are herbivores. So are rabbits. Huge animals can be herbivores, too. Both elephants and rhinoceroses only eat plants. Carnivores are meat eaters. They are often hunters. They are predators and must find prey to catch and eat. The members of the cat family, dogs, wolves, foxes, and other sharp-toothed animals are all carnivores. Sharks are also meat eaters. Some animals eat both plants and animals. They are called omnivores. Humans are omnivores. So are pigs, bears, and even chickens.

▲ herbivore

Every food chain and food web ends with decomposers such as bacteria. They break down dead organisms into substances that can be used by producers.

▲ omnivore

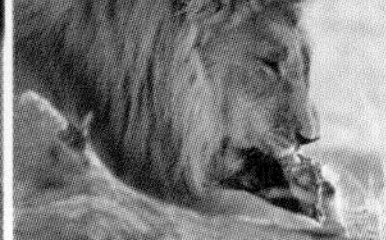
▲ carnivore

1 What is the passage mainly about?

a. The feeding relationships in an ecosystem
b. The three groups of animals
c. The various animals that are omnivores

2 Answer the questions.

a. How many groups of consumers are there? ______________________
b. What do herbivores eat? ______________________
c. What do omnivores eat? ______________________

3 Write the correct word and the meaning in Chinese.

ecosystem	herbivore	carnivore	omnivore	decomposer

a. ________________: an animal that only eats other animals
b. ________________: all the living things in an area and the way they affect each other and the environment
c. ________________: an organism that makes dead plants and animals decay

41 How Ecosystems Change

41

Many ecosystems are thriving communities that are full of life. However, many of them were once empty and were barren lands. But they changed to become places with many kinds of organisms.

The first step is called primary succession. This happens in a place that has never had life on it. Soil must be made first. Then pioneer species come to the land. These are low-level organisms like lichens and mosses. Over time, the soil starts to be able to support more complicated organisms. These are various grasses. Once there is some minor vegetation, animals like insects and birds move in. Eventually, bushes and trees start to grow. Finally, even larger animals move into the land.

Eventually, the ecosystem will grow enough that a climax community will be formed. This means that the ecosystem is fairly stable. The ecosystem will not change anymore unless something from outside affects it. It could be an invasive species. Or it could be a natural disaster. But unless something affects the ecosystem, it will never change.

Stages of Succession

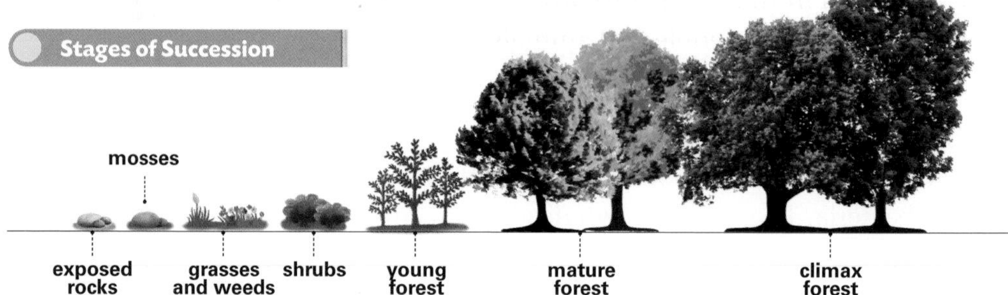

1 **What is a pioneer species?**

a. Organisms that invade an ecosystem.
b. Various kinds of grasses.
c. The first organisms that live on a land.

2 **What is NOT true?**

a. Primary succession is the first step in the changing of an ecosystem.
b. Lichens are some of the first plants to live in a barren area.
c. Climax communities form quickly on barren lands.

3 **Write the correct word and the meaning in Chinese.**

barren	primary succession	thriving	invasive species

a. ____________________: having or showing vigorous vegetal or animal life
b. ____________________: any species that is not native to an environment
c. ____________________: empty; abandoned; lifeless

The Carbon and Nitrogen Cycles

Carbon is one of the most important elements. All living things are made from carbon. But it is constantly changing forms. This is called the carbon cycle. In the atmosphere, carbon is often present in the form of carbon dioxide. This is a compound that has one carbon atom and two oxygen atoms. Plants breathe in the carbon dioxide and use it to produce nutrients. The carbon then becomes part of the plants. These plants die and then often get buried. Over time, these plants may turn into fossil fuels like coal or petroleum. People later burn these fossil fuels, which releases carbon dioxide into the atmosphere.

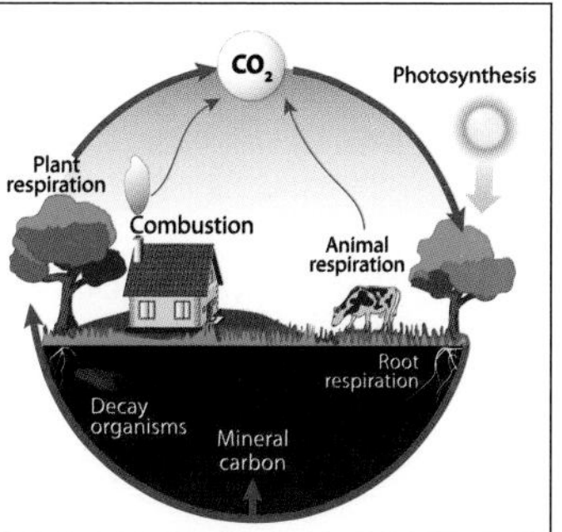

▲ carbon cycle

Another important element is nitrogen. There is also a nitrogen cycle. Nitrogen is actually the most common element in the atmosphere. Around 80% of the air we breathe is nitrogen. We don't need nitrogen like we need oxygen. But nitrogen is still important. There is often nitrogen in the soil. Plants absorb the nitrogen from the soil. When people and animals eat the plants, they release the nitrogen into their bodies. Bacteria in people's and animals' bodies can fix the nitrogen so that the bodies can use it. Later, when the people and animals die and decompose, the nitrogen returns to the soil or the atmosphere. Then it can be reused again.

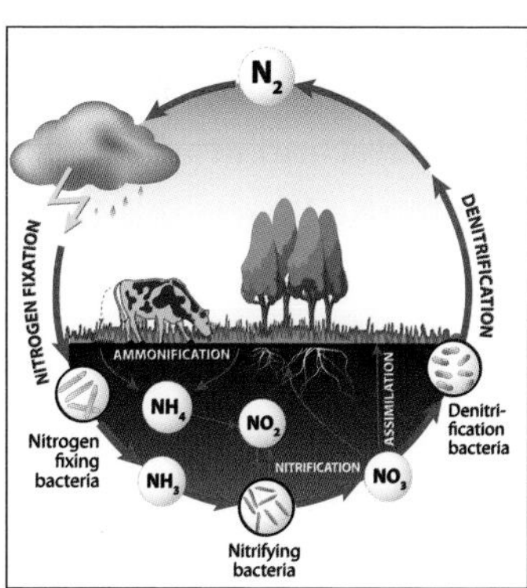

▲ nitrogen cycle

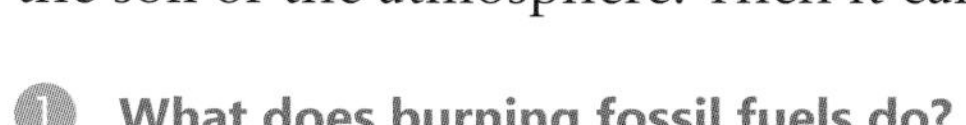

1 What does burning fossil fuels do?

a. It helps plants and animals decompose.
b. It releases carbon dioxide into the air.
c. It helps create nitrogen for the atmosphere.

2 Answer the questions.

a. What is all life made from? ______________________
b. What may some plants turn into after they die? ______________________
c. How much of the atmosphere is nitrogen? ______________________

3 Write the correct word and the meaning in Chinese.

present	fossil fuel	compound	absorb	decompose

a. ______________: to take something in
b. ______________: a chemical that combines two or more elements
c. ______________: a fuel such as oil, coal, or gas formed from the decay of organisms

The Circulatory System

43

Human Heart

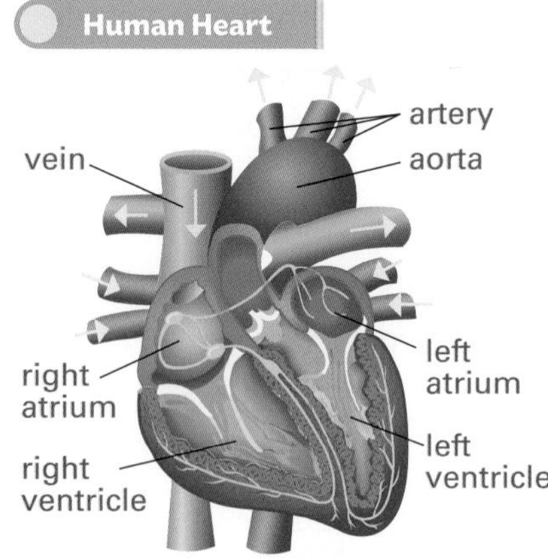

The circulatory system is the part of the body that controls the flow of blood. It has many parts. The most important is the heart. However, there are also arteries and veins that send blood throughout the body.

The heart has four chambers. They are the left and right atria and the left and right ventricles. First, blood flows into the right atrium. Then it goes to the right ventricle and into the lungs. In the lungs, oxygen is added to the blood. Then the blood returns to the heart. It goes into the left atrium and then into the left ventricle. From there, it leaves the heart by going to the aorta.

The aorta is the body's main artery. It feeds blood to the rest of the body. The body has both arteries and veins. Together, they are called blood vessels. These blood vessels take oxygen-rich blood and transport it everywhere in the body. The body then uses the blood, which loses its oxygen. Then, other veins and arteries take the oxygen-depleted blood back to the heart, and the cycle begins again.

▲ circulatory system

1 What is the passage mainly about?

a. How blood moves through the body.
b. How the aorta sends blood throughout the body.
c. Where the arteries and veins are.

2 What is NOT true?

a. The circulatory system controls the flow of blood.
b. The heart has four ventricles.
c. The main artery in the body is the aorta.

3 Write the correct word and the meaning in Chinese.

circulatory system	atrium	artery	aorta	depleted

a. ____________________: the main artery in the body
b. ____________________: reduced; no longer sufficient
c. ____________________: the upper chamber of each half of the heart

44 The Immune System

Every day, the body is attacked by bacteria, viruses, and other invaders. It is the body's immune system that fights these invaders. It helps keep the person healthy. The immune system is made up of various cells, tissues, and organs.

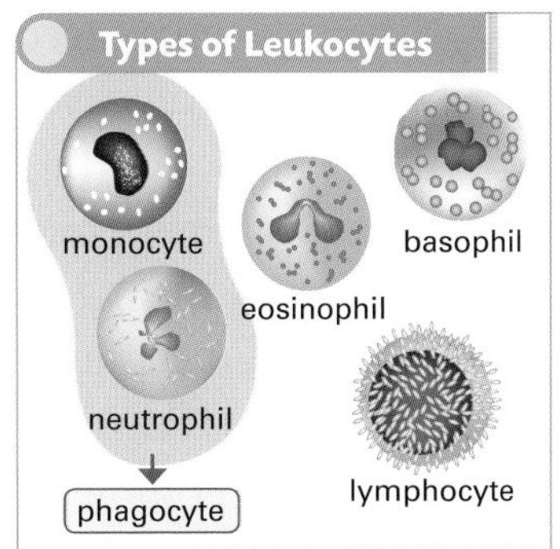

White blood cells are very important. They are also called leukocytes. They move through the body in lymphatic vessels. There are two types of leukocytes. The first try to destroy invading organisms. These are phagocytes. The second are lymphocytes. They help the body remember various invaders. This way, it can destroy them in the future.

Antigens often invade the body. The body then produces antibodies. They fight the antigens. If the antibodies succeed, they will always remain in the body. This lets the body fight the disease again in the future. This is very effective against viruses.

People are often born immune to certain diseases. This is called innate immunity. But there is adaptive immunity, too. This happens when the body recognizes threats to it. It then learns how to defeat them. Also, thanks to vaccinations, people can become immune to many diseases. Vaccinations help improve the strength of the immune system.

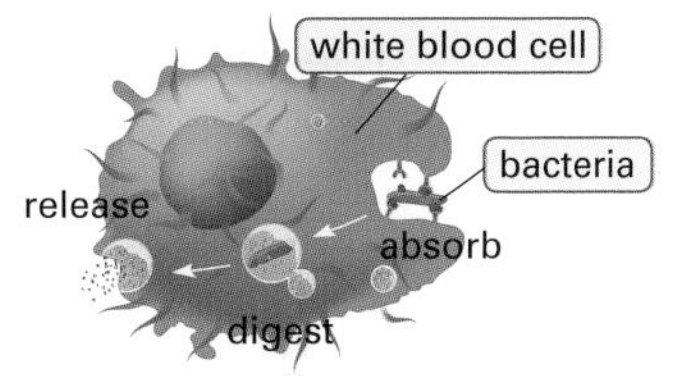

▲ phagocytosis

antibody
antigen
lymphocyte

▲ antigens and antibodies

1. **What does a vaccination do?**
   - a. It makes a person immune to a certain disease.
   - b. It creates leukocytes in the body.
   - c. It increases the number of antigens in a body.

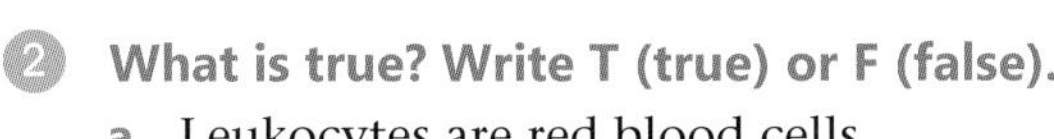

2. **What is true? Write T (true) or F (false).**
   - a. Leukocytes are red blood cells. ____
   - b. The body sometimes produces antibodies. ____
   - c. People are often born with innate immunity. ____

3. **Write the correct word and the meaning in Chinese.**

phagocyte	immune system	leukocyte	antibody	antigen

a. ______________: a cell that engulfs and digests invading microorganisms

b. ______________: a substance in the body that fights antigens

c. ______________: a substance that causes your body to produce antibodies

45 The Development of a Baby

When a woman becomes pregnant, a baby starts to grow in her body. For the next nine months, she will have another life inside her. Until the baby is born, the baby is called a fetus. The fetus goes through several stages of development over nine months.

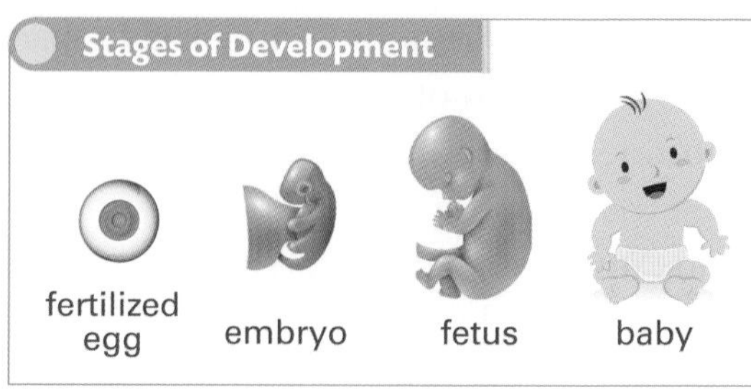

At first, the new life is just an embryo. It starts growing cells and becoming larger. After three weeks, the body's organs begin to develop, and it takes a human shape. After two months, most of the organs are completely developed. Only the brain and spinal cord are not.

In the ninth week, the embryo is now said to be a fetus. The fetus starts to develop more quickly now. By week fourteen, doctors can determine if it is a male or a female. And after about four or five months of pregnancy, the mother can feel her baby moving around inside her. By the sixth month, the fetus is able to survive outside the womb. The fetus still needs about three more months to develop inside the mother. Finally, during the ninth month, most babies are born.

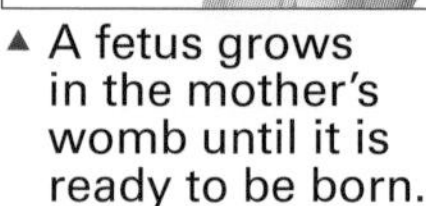

▲ A fetus grows in the mother's womb until it is ready to be born.

1 When can a mother feel her baby inside her?

a. After two months of pregnancy.
b. After four or five months of pregnancy.
c. After six months of pregnancy.

2 Fill in the blanks.

a. An unborn baby inside the mother is called a __________.
b. Most of the fetus's organs are completely developed in two __________.
c. A fetus can survive outside the __________ by the sixth month.

3 Write the correct word and the meaning in Chinese.

pregnant	fetus	embryo	spinal cord	womb

a. ______________: the part of a woman's body in which a baby develops; a uterus
b. ______________: a developing baby before it is born
c. ______________: the inner part of your spine that contains nerves

Earth Science

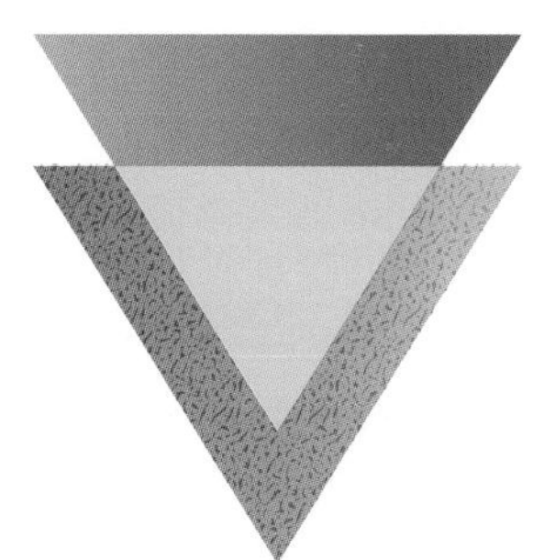

Weather and Space

Earth's Surface

The Universe

46 Weather Equipment

46

Meteorologists are people who study the weather. They tell us if it will be hot or cold. They tell us if it will be sunny or rainy. They have lots of equipment to help them.

The most common piece of equipment is the thermometer. A thermometer measures the temperature of the air. By looking at it, people can tell exactly how hot or cold it is. Another common instrument is the barometer. This measures the air pressure. So people can know if it is going to rain or not. Usually, when the air pressure drops, bad weather is coming. And when it goes up, good weather is coming. There is other equipment, too. A rain gauge measures the amount of rain that has fallen in a place. And an anemometer is used to measure how fast the wind is blowing. It's really useful on windy days! And some people even have weather vanes on their homes. They show which direction the wind is blowing.

Celsius

Fahrenheit

Weather Equipment

▲ weather vane

▲ barometer

▲ rain gauge

▲ thermometer

1 What does dropping air pressure indicate?

a. There is bad weather coming.　　b. There is good weather coming.
c. There will be sunny skies.

2 Answer the questions.

a. What equipment measures the temperature? ____________________
b. What does a barometer do? ____________________
c. What equipment measures the wind speed? ____________________

3 Write the correct word and the meaning in Chinese.

equipment	meteorologist	weather vane	barometer	rain gauge

a. ____________________: someone who study the weather
b. ____________________: an instrument that shows the direction of the wind
c. ____________________: an instrument that measures air pressure

The Water Cycle

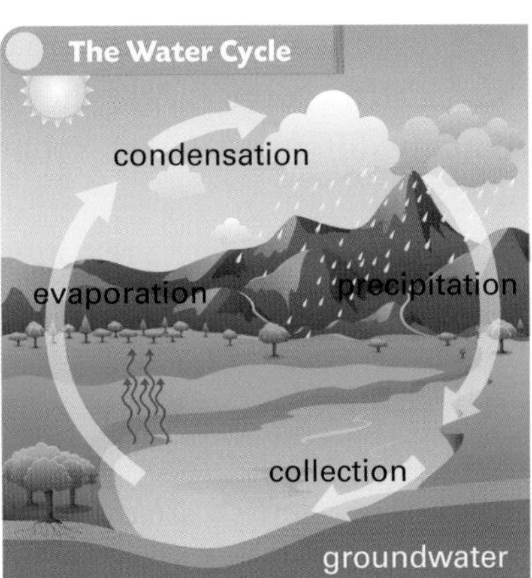

There is a limited amount of water on the earth. In fact, for billions of years, the amount of water has not changed. However, water can often appear in many different forms. These all make up the water cycle.

The first stage is evaporation. This happens when the sun's heat on rivers, lakes, seas, and oceans causes water to turn into water vapor. The water vapor then rises into the air.

The second stage is condensation. As water vapor rises, the air gets colder. This causes the water vapor to turn into tiny water droplets. These droplets come together to form clouds.

The third stage is precipitation. The water droplets fall to the ground in some form. The most common kind of precipitation is rain. But, in cold weather, snow, sleet, or ice may fall instead.

The final stage is collection. When water falls to the ground, it may flow into rivers, lakes, seas, or oceans. Or it may go down into the ground. There, it becomes groundwater. But the water cycle goes on and on.

rain
snow
sleet

1 What is condensation?

a. The turning of water vapor into water droplets.
b. The falling of water to the ground as rain.
c. The changing of water into water vapor.

2 What is true? Write T (true) or F (false).

a. The amount of water on the earth is always changing. ____
b. Evaporation is the first stage of the water cycle. ____
c. Rain, sleet, and snow are all kinds of precipitation. ____

3 Write the correct word and the meaning in Chinese.

water cycle	evaporation	condensation	precipitation	sleet

a. ____________________: the falling of water to the ground
b. ____________________: a mixture of snow and rain
c. ____________________: the process in which a gas changes into a liquid

48 Ocean Resources and Conservation

48

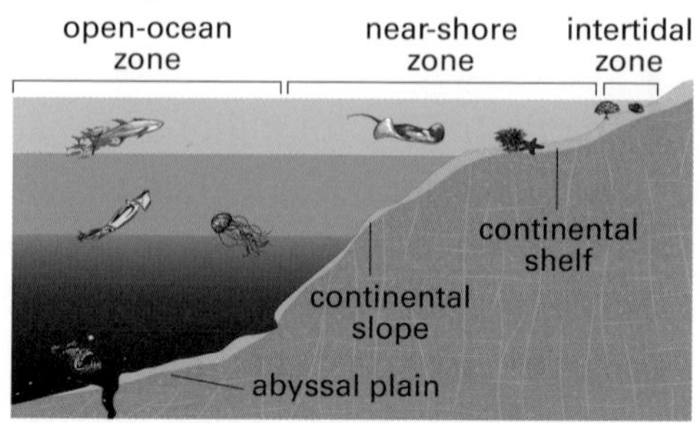

Oceans cover around 71% of the earth's surface. And they are full of many different resources that can benefit humanity.

For one, the oceans are a great source of fish and seafood. Fishermen from numerous countries sail the oceans to catch fish for people to eat. However, humans are catching too many fish. Fish stocks are starting to become smaller. So humans need to be careful. They should not overfish areas. Instead, they should catch smaller numbers of fish. Then, more fish can grow and repopulate the oceans.

The oceans also have many valuable resources beneath their floors. For instance, oil and natural gas are pumped from beneath the seafloor in many places. But, again, humans need to be careful. Sometimes, oil spills release large amounts of oil into the water. This can kill many fish, birds, and other sea creatures.

There are even large amounts of certain ores beneath the ocean. Gold, silver, and other valuable metals could be mined in the future. And people can even use the oceans for energy. Tidal energy could provide cheap and abundant energy in the future. But we need to take good care of our oceans. They have many resources, but we need to conserve them, too.

▲ ocean life

1 What is the main idea of the passage?

a. There are fewer resources in the oceans nowadays.
b. It is possible to create energy from the world's oceans.
c. Oceans have many resources that must be used wisely.

2 Answer the questions.

a. How much of the earth's surface do the oceans cover? ____________________
b. What happens when there is an oil spill in the ocean? ____________________
c. What might tidal energy be able to do? ____________________

3 Write the correct word and the meaning in Chinese.

humanity	repopulate	oil spill	mine	abundant

a. ____________________: to dig coal or another substance out of the ground
b. ____________________: available in large quantities
c. ____________________: to increase the number of species after a decline

The Formation of the Earth

Billions of years ago, the sun formed. There was a huge disk of rocks and gases in the solar system. Eventually, these rocks and gases began to form planets. This was about 4.5 billion years ago. The earth was the third planet from the sun. At first, the earth was extremely hot. But, over millions of years, it began to cool down. As the earth cooled, water vapor started forming in the atmosphere. This caused the creation of clouds all over the planet. Soon, the clouds began dropping huge amounts of water all over the planet. This caused the creation of the earth's oceans, seas, rivers, and lakes.

But the earth 4.5 billion years ago looked different from the earth of today. Today, there are seven continents. In the past, this was not true. There have been different numbers of continents. Once, there was just one continent on the whole planet. Why? One clue is the theory of plate tectonics. There are many plates that make up the earth's crust. These plates are huge pieces of land. And they are constantly moving. As the earth ages, the plates slowly move around. Today, there are seven continents. In the future, perhaps there will be more or less.

Continental Drift

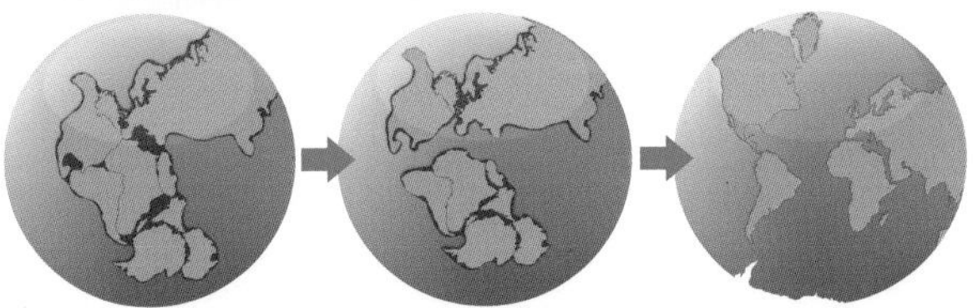

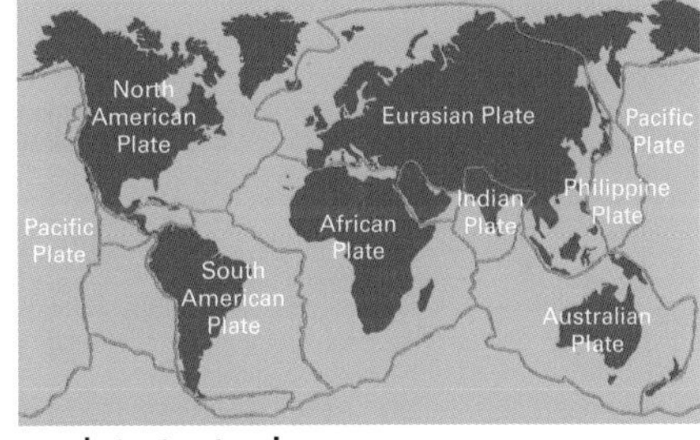

▲ plate tectonics

1 How long did it take for the earth to cool down?

a. Several thousand years. b. Several million years. c. 4.5 billion years.

2 Fill in the blanks.

a. The earth started to form about ________ ____________ years ago.

b. There are seven ________________ on the earth today.

c. According to the theory of ______ __________, the plates are constantly moving.

3 Write the correct word and the meaning in Chinese.

plate tectonics	continent	atmosphere	crust	creation

a. ________________: one of the great divisions of land of the earth

b. ________________: the thick outer surface of the earth

c. ________________: the theory that the earth's crust is divided into plates that are always moving

50 Earthquakes

Sometimes, the ground suddenly begins to shake. Buildings and bridges move back and forth. They might even fall down. Places in the ground begin to crack. This is an earthquake. Earthquakes happen all the time all around the earth. Most of the time, they are so small that we cannot even feel them. But sometimes there are very large earthquakes. These can cause great damage, kill many people, and even change the way the earth looks.

The earth's crust is its top part. The crust is formed of many plates. These are called tectonic plates. There are seven large plates and around twelve smaller ones. These plates are enormous. But they also move really slowly. Sometimes they move back and forth against each other. This causes earthquakes.

The Richter scale measures the power of earthquakes. A level 2 quake is ten times as powerful as a level 1 quake. For each whole number increase, the power of the earthquake increases by ten. Levels 1 to 4 are weak earthquakes. Level 5 earthquakes can cause some damage. Levels 6 and 7 can be dangerous. Levels 8 and 9 can cause huge amounts of death and destruction.

The Richter Scale

Description	micro	minor		light	moderate	strong	major	great	
Magnitude	1.0–1.9	2.0–2.9	3.0–3.9	4.0–4.9	5.0–5.9	6.0–6.9	7.0–7.9	8.0–8.9	9.0 and greater

1. **What forms the crust?**
   a. Earthquakes. b. The Richter scale. c. Tectonic plates.

2. **Answer the questions.**
   a. How many large tectonic plates are there on the earth? ______________
   b. What measures an earthquake's power? ______________
   c. What do weak earthquakes measure? ______________

3. **Write the correct word and the meaning in Chinese.**

crack	tectonic plate	Richter scale	quake	destruction

   a. ______________: a plate that makes up part of the earth's crust
   b. ______________: an earthquake
   c. ______________: to break or split without complete separation of parts

51 Volcanic Eruptions

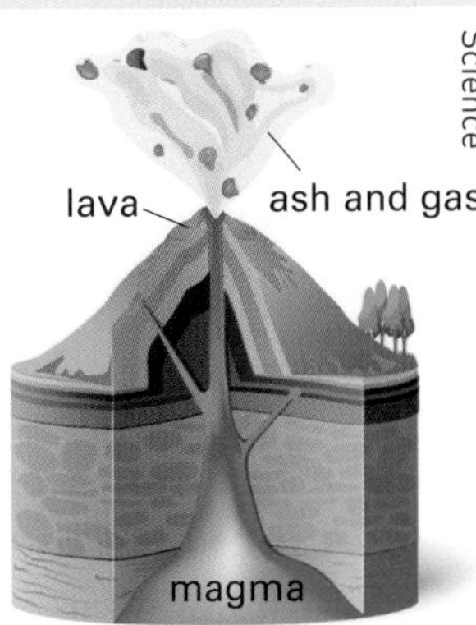

Sometimes, volcanoes suddenly erupt. They spew tons of ash, gas, and lava. They might even kill large numbers of people. What is it that makes a volcano erupt?

Deep in the earth, there is usually a lot of pressure. Also, the temperature deep underground can be very high. In fact, it is often high enough to melt rocks. Melted rock that is beneath the ground is called magma. The magma is constantly trying to move up toward the surface. Under the earth, there are large pools of magma that have gathered together. These are called magma chambers. These magma chambers often exist beneath volcanoes. Eventually, the pressure beneath the earth becomes too great. The magma forces its way to the surface. This causes a volcano to erupt. When a volcano erupts, it often expels ash and gas. It can also expel magma. Magma that is on the surface is called lava. The lava often creeps down the sides of the volcano until it eventually cools and hardens.

The size of the eruption depends on the amount of pressure that is released. Some volcanoes release a steady amount of lava. These have a low amount of pressure. Other volcanoes erupt explosively. They can shoot ash miles into the air. They can expel lava and gas very far in the area. These are the most dangerous eruptions. Mt. Vesuvius, Krakatoa, and Mt. St. Helens all had explosive eruptions that killed many people.

▲ Krakatoa

▲ Mt. St. Helens

1 What is the passage mainly about?

a. The eruptions of some famous volcanoes.
b. What causes a volcano to erupt.
c. The difference between magma and lava.

2 Fill in the blanks.

a. Melted rock that is underground is called ______________.
b. Magma gathers in pools called ______________ ______________.
c. Volcanoes can expel lots of __________, gas, and lava when they erupt.

3 Write the correct word and the meaning in Chinese.

magma	spew	lava	explosive	eruption

a. ____________________: to explode; to erupt
b. ____________________: very loud and sudden, like an explosion
c. ____________________: hot liquid rock below the surface of the earth

52 Mass Extinctions

52

Every once in a while, a mass extinction occurs on the earth. When this happens, large numbers of species all go extinct at once. Scientists have identified at least five mass extinctions during the earth's history. During these mass extinctions, up to 95% of all life on the planet was killed. The last mass extinction happened about 65 million years ago. Scientists refer to it as the K-T Extinction.

▲ Dinosaurs lived in the Cretaceous Period.

▲ An asteroid struck the earth and caused a tremendous change.

65 million years ago, the earth looked very different. There were no humans. Instead, dinosaurs ruled the land and the seas. This was a time called the Cretaceous Period. Then, suddenly, there was a mass extinction. Scientists are not exactly sure what happened. But most of them believe that an asteroid or comet struck the earth. This caused a tremendous change in the planet. Large amounts of dust were thrown into the atmosphere. This blocked the sun. No sunlight could reach the earth, so many plants died. The animals that ate the plants then died. And the animals that ate those animals died, too.

The K-T Extinction killed all of the dinosaurs. And about half of the other species on the planet died, too. Of course, all life did not die. In fact, some life flourished. After the K-T Extinction, mammals began to increase in number. Eventually, humans evolved. So, without the K-T Extinction, humans might not ever have existed.

1 **How much life on the earth can a mass extinction kill?**

a. 5% b. 65% c. 95%

2 **What is NOT true?**

a. There have been at least five mass extinctions on the earth.
b. All of the dinosaurs died during the K-T Extinction.
c. Most mammals were killed during the K-T Extinction.

3 **Write the correct word and the meaning in Chinese.**

Cretaceous Period	mass extinction	asteroid	flourish

a. ______________________: a rocky object that orbits the sun in outer space; a minor planet

b. ______________________: the period from about 144 to 65 million years ago

c. ______________________: to grow well

The Inner and Outer Planets

The solar system has eight planets in it. These planets are divided into two groups. We call them the inner and outer planets. These two groups have their own characteristics.

The inner planets are Mercury, Venus, Earth, and Mars. They are all fairly close to the sun. Also, these planets are all small and made up of solid, rocklike materials. The earth is the largest of the inner planets. And the inner planets all have zero, one, or two moons.

The outer planets are very different from the inner planets. The outer planets are much colder than the inner planets. They are farther from the sun. The outer planets are Jupiter, Saturn, Uranus, and Neptune. They are all very large. Jupiter is the largest planet in the solar system. The outer planets are mostly made up of gas. Also, the outer planets have many moons. Jupiter has at least 63 moons. The others also have many moons.

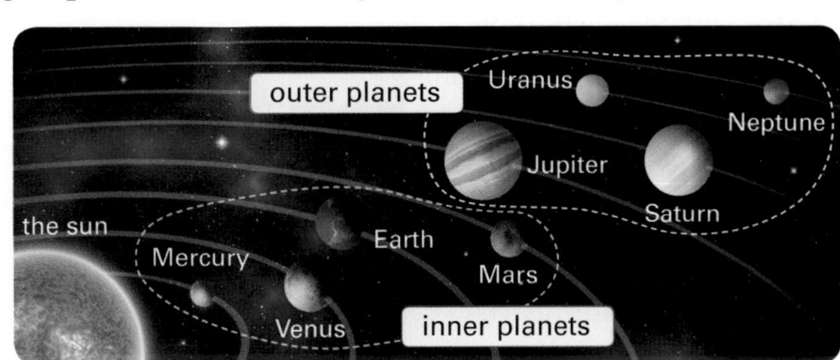

1 What is the main idea of the passage?

a. The solar system has eight planets in it.
b. The inner and outer planets have many differences.
c. The outer planets are much colder than the inner planets.

2 What is true? Write T (true) or F (false).

a. The inner planets are made up of gas. ____
b. Saturn is one of the outer planets. ____
c. Jupiter has at least 63 moons. ____

3 Write the correct word and the meaning in Chinese.

characteristic	solid	moon	inner planets	outer planets

a. ____________________: an object similar to a planet that goes around another planet
b. ____________________: the four planets farthest away from the sun
c. ____________________: hard or firm, keeping a clear shape

54 Are We Alone

54

▲ An extraterrestrial is an alien.

For thousands of years, men have looked at the stars and asked, "Are we alone?" Men are fascinated by the stars and the possibility of there being life on other planets. Myths in many cultures tell stories about aliens coming to the earth. But no one knows if there really are aliens or not.

Nowadays, scientists are searching for life on other planets. Some believe there could be life on Mars. Others think the moons Europa or Io could have life. And others are looking at other star systems. They are trying to find Earth-like planets.

What does life need to survive on other planets? Life on the earth is all carbon based. That kind of life needs a star to provide heat and light. It needs an atmosphere with oxygen. It needs water. Of course, other forms of life could be based on different elements. We don't know what they would need to survive. But we do know one thing: Men will continue looking for extraterrestrial life until we find it.

▲ Scientists are searching for life on Mars.

1 **What is the passage mainly about?**

a. The search for Earth-like planets in the solar system.
b. The requirements for life on other planets.
c. The possibility of life in places other than on the earth.

2 **Fill in the blanks.**

a. There are many myths about ____________ coming to the earth.
b. Some scientists are searching for __________ on other planets.
c. Some people believe the planet ___________ could have aliens on it.

3 **Write the correct word and the meaning in Chinese.**

be fascinated by	star system	element	extraterrestrial

a. ___________________: originating or existing outside the earth
b. ___________________: a large number of stars with a perceptible structure
c. ___________________: an important basic part of something

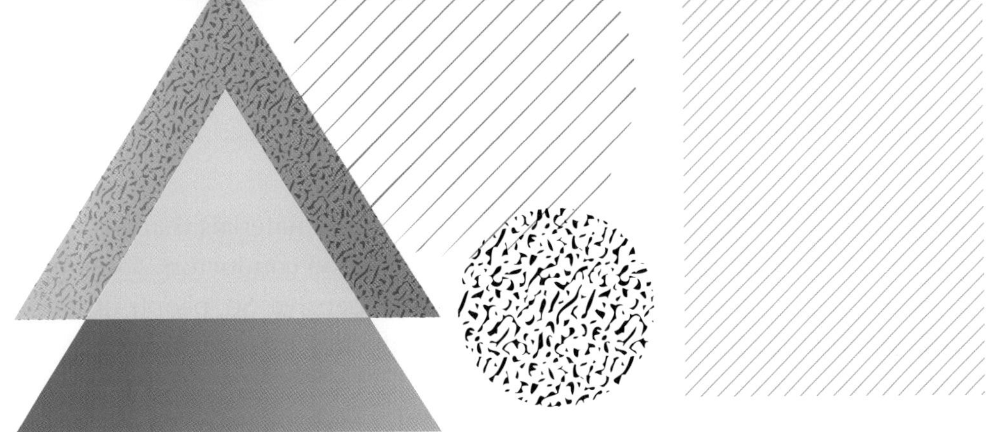

Physical Science

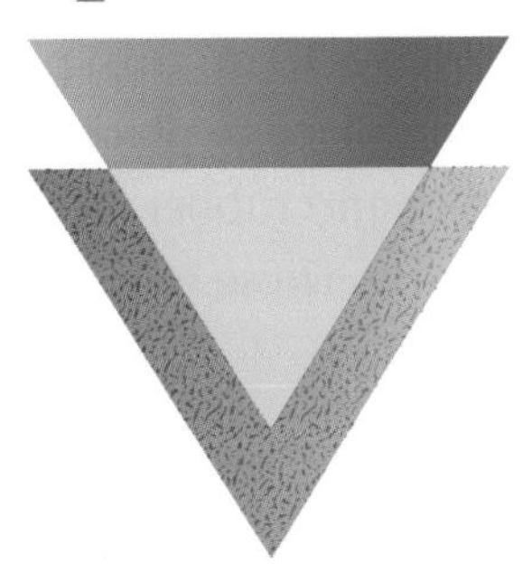

Matter and Energy

55 Conductors and Insulators

55

Electricity can move thanks to conductors. These are materials that let electricity move freely. Gold and silver are very good conductors. Some people make wires out of them. But they are both expensive. So, people often use other conductors to make wires. Most electrical wires are made from a conducting metal, such as copper.

What are some other conductors? Lots of metals are conductors. So is graphite. Water is an excellent conductor. That's why it's a bad idea to go swimming in thunderstorms. Lightning can strike the water and hurt or even kill a person. The human body is also a conductor. That's why people need to be careful around electricity.

Of course, people may want to stop the flow of electricity. To do this, people use insulators. They prevent electricity from moving from place to place. What are some of them? Plastics are very good insulators. Paper and rubber are also insulators. And glass and porcelain are two more insulators. These materials are all useful for stopping the flow of electricity.

▲ copper ▲ gold ▲ silver ▲ glass ▲ rubber ▲ paper

1 **Why is electricity dangerous to humans?**

a. Because humans are good insulators.
b. Because the human body stops the flow of electricity.
c. Because the human body is a conductor.

2 **Answer the questions.**

a. What does a conductor do? ______________________
b. What does an insulator do? ______________________
c. What are some insulators? ______________________

3 **Write the correct word and the meaning in Chinese.**

conductor	thunderstorm	insulator	wire	porcelain

a. ______________: a long thin piece of metal like a thread
b. ______________: something through which electricity can flow
c. ______________: a hard white substance that is made by baking clay

56 Sir Isaac Newton

Sir Isaac Newton lived in the seventeenth and eighteenth centuries. He was one of the greatest scientists who ever lived. He worked with light. He invented calculus. And he also discovered gravity and the three laws of motion.

Supposedly, Newton was sitting under an apple tree one day. An apple fell and hit him on the head. So he started thinking about gravity. He realized that it was gravity that caused objects to fall to the ground.

Newton's three laws of motion are incredibly important to physics. The first law says that the state of motion of an object does not change until a force is applied to it. It is often called the *law of inertia*. The second law of motion is called the *law of acceleration*. It is often written as $F = ma$. That means "force equals mass times acceleration." This is the most important of the three laws. The third law says that for every action, there is an equal and opposite reaction. The third law means that all forces are *interactions*.

Newton's Laws of Motion

▲ the law of inertia

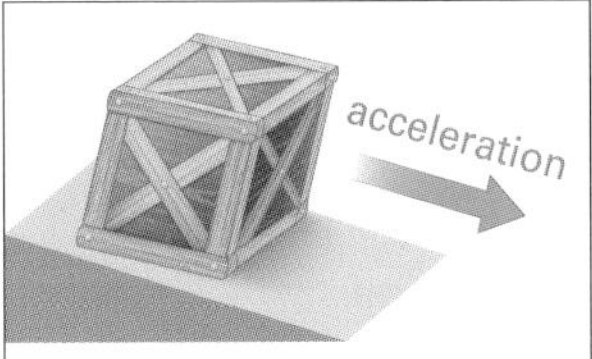

▲ the law of acceleration

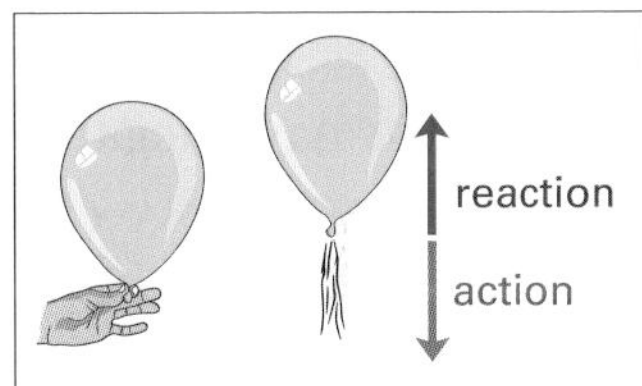

▲ the law of action and reaction

1 What is the *law of inertia*?

a. All objects will fall to the ground because of the force of gravity.
b. An object in motion does not change its state until an outside force affects it.
c. For every action, there is an equal and opposite reaction.

2 What is true? Write T (true) or F (false).

a. Sir Isaac Newton lived in the twentieth century. _____
b. Newton discovered gravity. _____
c. Newton came up with three laws of motion. _____

3 Write the correct word and the meaning in Chinese.

calculus	acceleration	gravity	force	inertia

a. ________________: the physical force that keeps something in the same position or moving in the same direction
b. ________________: a branch of mathematics that deals with changing values
c. ________________: the rate at which the speed of an object increases

57 Elements

The entire universe is made of matter. And matter is made of elements or compounds. Compounds are chemical combinations of two or more elements. What is an element? It is a substance that is made up of only one kind of atom, such as helium or gold. Atom is the smallest unit of an element.

There are more than 110 elements. Most are natural. So they appear in nature. But scientists have made a few elements. They only appear in labs.

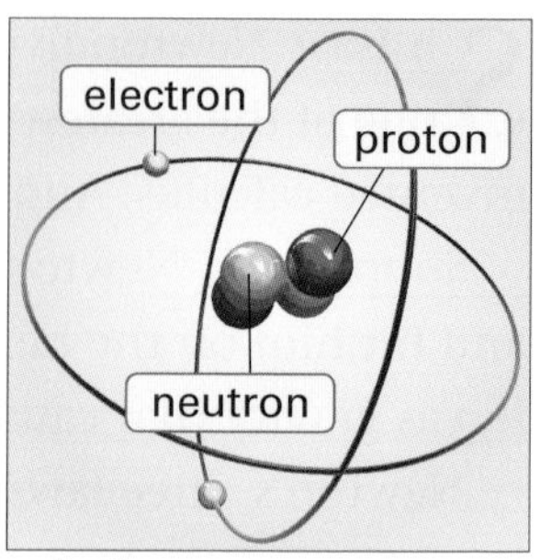

▲ helium atom
(2 protons and 2 neutrons)

All elements have a similar structure. They have a nucleus. This is the element's core, the center of an atom. Inside the nucleus are protons and neutrons. Elements have different numbers of them. For example, hydrogen has 1 proton and 0 neutrons. Helium has 2 protons and 2 neutrons. Oxygen has 8 protons and 8 neutrons. Gold has 79 protons and 118 neutrons. Outside the nucleus are electrons. They orbit the nucleus.

Electrons have negative charges. But protons have positive charges. Also, an element usually has the same number of protons and electrons. But they can sometimes be different.

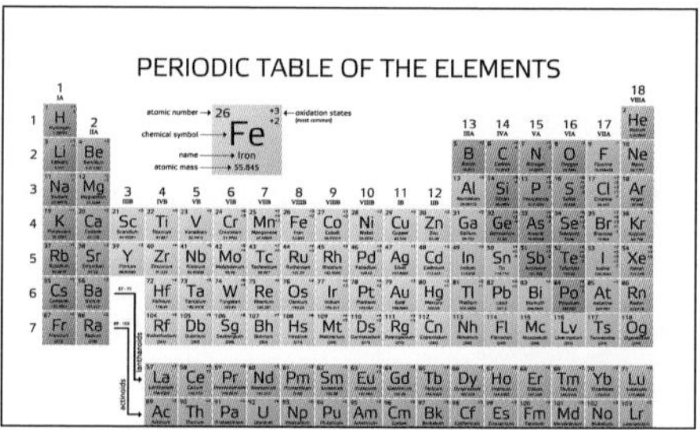

▲ periodic table of the elements

1. How many protons does gold have?
   a. 8　　b. 79　　c. 118

2. What is true? Write T (true) or F (false).
   a. There are more than 110 elements. ______
   b. Most elements are man-made. ______
   c. Protons and neutrons are in the nucleus. ______

3. Write the correct word and the meaning in Chinese.

matter	element	atom	nucleus	proton

   a. ______________: the part of the nucleus of an atom that has a positive electrical charge
   b. ______________: the smallest unit of an element
   c. ______________: physical substance in the universe

58 Atoms and Their Atomic Numbers

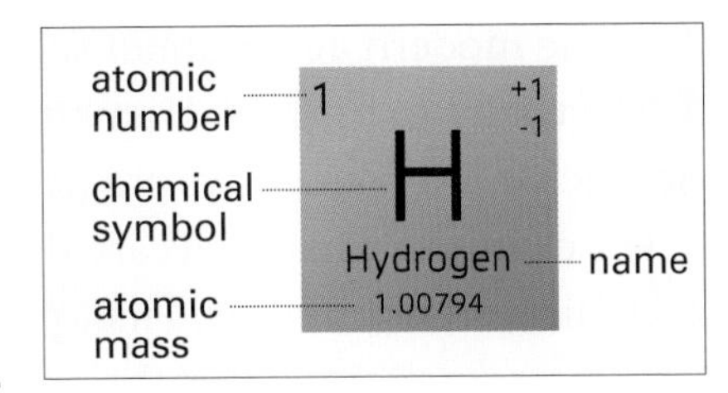

All atoms have different numbers of protons, neutrons, and electrons. The protons are positively charged and are in the nucleus. Neutrons are also in the nucleus. But they have no charge. And electrons orbit the nucleus. They have negative charges. The number of protons and neutrons in an atom is often—but not always—the same.

Every element has a different number of protons. This helps make it different from other elements. An element's atomic number is the same as its number of protons. For example, hydrogen has only 1 proton. So this means that it has an atomic number of 1. It is the first element on the periodic table of elements. Helium is the second element. It has an atomic number of 2. This means that it has 2 protons in its nucleus.

There are more than 110 different elements. Scientists often recognize them according to their atomic numbers. Carbon is the basis for all life on Earth. Its atomic number is 6. Oxygen is an important element. Its atomic number is 8. Iron is another important element. 26 is its atomic number. Gold has an atomic number of 79. And uranium's atomic number is 92.

1 Which element has an atomic number of 2?

a. Helium. b. Carbon. c. Hydrogen.

2 What is true? Write T (true) or F (false).

a. Neutrons have no charge. ____
b. An element's atomic number is the number of electrons it has. ____
c. Hydrogen has an atomic number of 2. ____

3 Write the correct word and the meaning in Chinese.

orbit	charge	atomic number	hydrogen	periodic table

a. ______________: the number of protons in an atom
b. ______________: to travel around something in a curved path
c. ______________: the first element on the periodic table of elements

Energy and Environmental Risks

In the modern age, human society runs on energy. Most machines need electricity to operate. Humans have many different ways to create electricity. But some ways are harmful to the environment.

For example, fossil fuels are the most common kind of energy. They include coal, oil, and natural gas. First, people have to mine them from the ground. This can sometimes harm the environment. However, scientists are creating cleaner and more efficient ways to do that these days. So the environment is not damaged as much. But when people burn these fossil fuels, they can release gases that might harm the environment.

Tidal energy is another way to make electricity. This uses the ocean tides to make electricity. But some kinds of tidal energy can kill many fish and other sea creatures. Also, dams can create lots of clean hydroelectric energy. But dams create lakes and change the courses of rivers. So they can change the environment very much.

Nuclear energy is a very powerful form of energy. It is cheap. It is also very clean. But many people are afraid of it because it uses radioactive materials. Also, there have been some accidents at nuclear power plants in the past. But the technology is much better these days. So many countries are starting to build more nuclear power plants now.

▲ fossil fuel

▲ a tidal power plant

1 What is the main idea of the passage?

a. Fossil fuels are the most common kind of energy.
b. Technology is creating lots of clean energy.
c. Making and using energy can harm the environment.

2 Fill in the blanks.

a. Mining fossil fuels from the ground can sometimes harm the ______________.
b. Tidal energy uses the ocean ___________ to make electricity.
c. ____________ energy is cheap and clean but uses radioactive materials.

3 Write the correct word and the meaning in Chinese.

fossil fuel	tidal energy	nuclear energy	hydroelectric

a. ____________________: a fuel such as coal or oil
b. ____________________: using water power to produce electricity
c. ____________________: energy developed from the tides

60 The Scientific Method of Inquiry

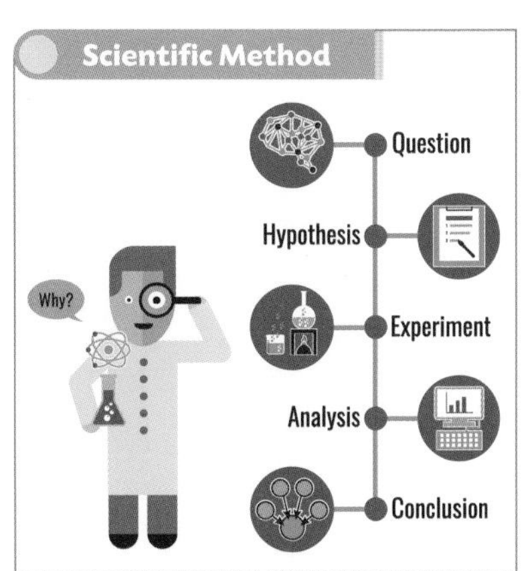

Scientists have a method they use when they are trying to learn something new. It is called the scientific method of inquiry.

The first step is to ask a question. It could be "Why do birds fly south for the winter?" Or it could be "How much heat does it take for gold to melt?" It could be about anything.

Then, the scientist must do research. He or she should learn as much about the topic as possible. Next, the scientist makes a hypothesis. This is an educated guess. It could be "Birds fly south for the winter because they are cold." Or it could be "Gold melts at 200 degrees Fahrenheit." Now, the scientist has a hypothesis, so it must be tested. Scientists do this by conducting experiments. Some do experiments in labs, and others do them outdoors.

After the experiments are complete, the scientist must analyze the data. Then he should compare it with the hypothesis. Was the hypothesis right or wrong? Even with a wrong hypothesis, scientists can still learn a lot. Finally, they should write about their results. That way, other people can learn, too.

1 How can a scientist test a hypothesis?

a. By asking a question.
b. By doing research.
c. By doing an experiment.

2 Fill in the blanks.

a. Scientists use the scientific ______________ of inquiry to learn.
b. A ________________ is an educated guess.
c. Scientists conduct experiments in __________ or outdoors.

3 Write the correct word and the meaning in Chinese.

inquiry	hypothesis	an educated guess	conduct	Fahrenheit

a. ____________________: a guess that is likely to be right because it is based on knowledge of the situation
b. ____________________: to do something in an organized way
c. ____________________: a scientific explanation that one thinks may be true and that can be tested

Mathematics

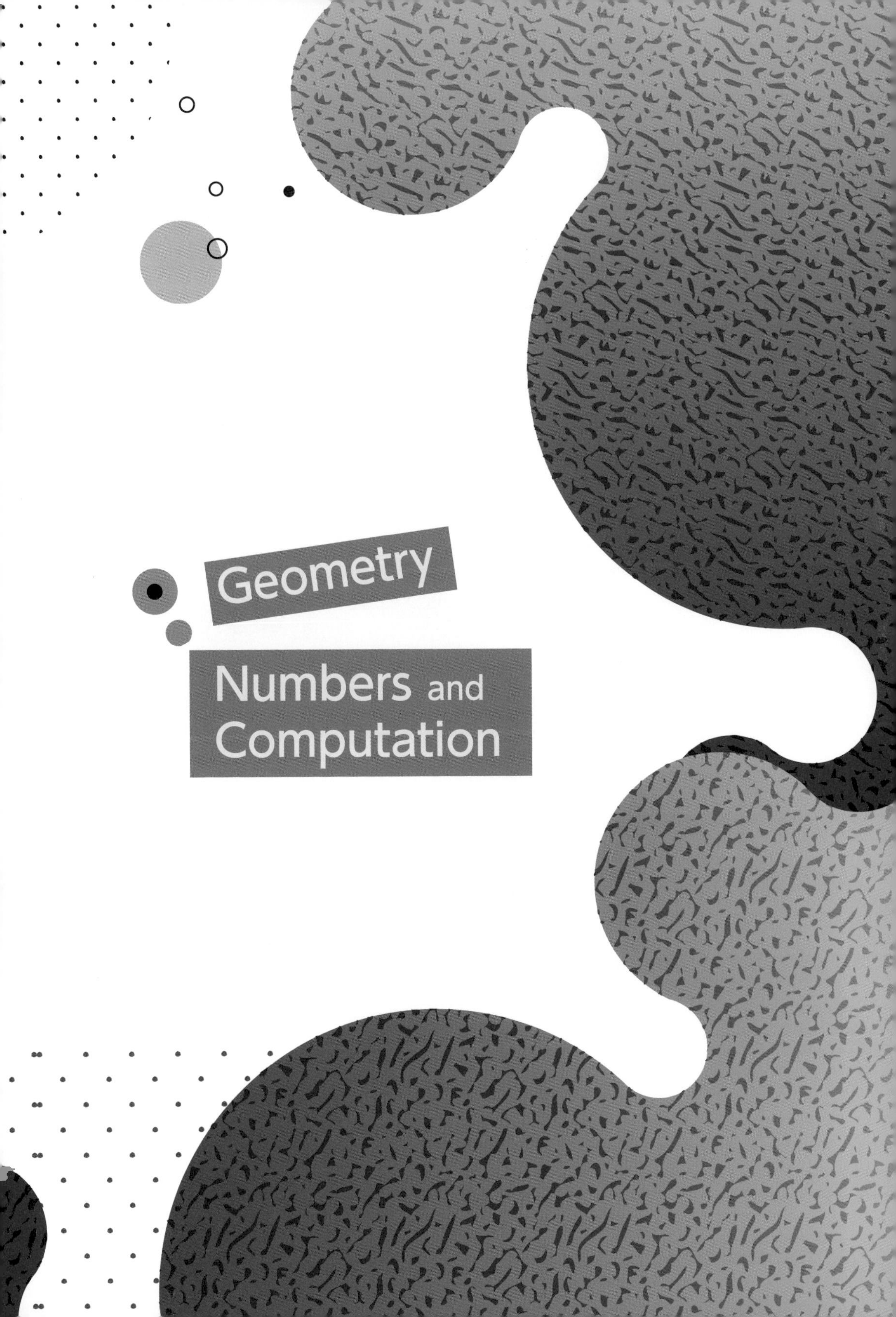
Geometry
Numbers and Computation

Geometry

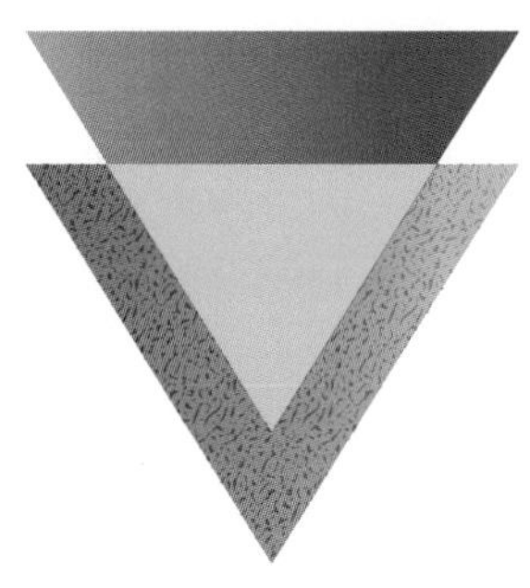

61 Angles

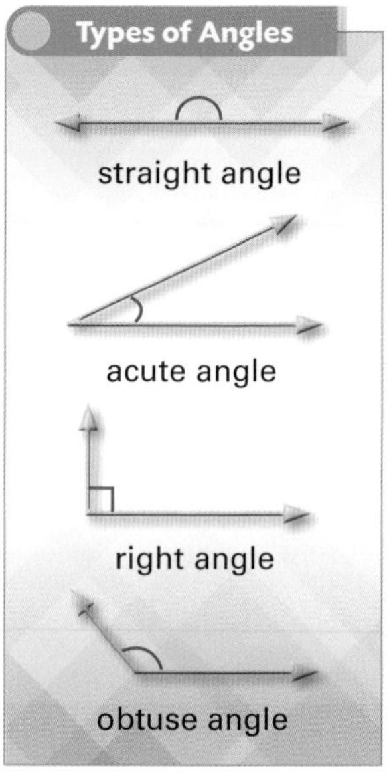

When two line segments meet at the same endpoint, they form an angle. The size of an angle is measured in degrees. An angle can measure anywhere from 0 to 180 degrees. There are four different kinds of angles. What type they are depends on how many degrees they have.

A straight angle measures 180°. A straight angle forms a line.

The next kind of angle is an acute angle. This angle measures more than 0° but less than 90°. All triangles have at least one acute angle, and many have three of them.

A right angle occurs when two perpendicular lines intersect. These two lines form a ninety-degree angle. This is called a right angle. All of the angles in a square or rectangle are right angles. Some triangles have one right angle, so they are called right triangles.

The last kind of angle is an obtuse angle. An obtuse angle is more than 90° but less than 180°. Some triangles have obtuse angles, but a triangle can never have more than one obtuse angle.

▲ protractor

1 What is the measurement of a straight angle?

a. 0°   b. 90°   c. 180°

2 What is NOT true?

a. An acute angle is between 0° and 90°.
b. A right angle is greater than an obtuse angle.
c. An obtuse angle is greater than an acute angle.

3 Write the correct word and the meaning in Chinese.

straight angle	acute angle	right angle	obtuse angle

a. ____________________: an angle that measures between 90 and 180 degrees
b. ____________________: an angle that measures 180 degrees
c. ____________________: an angle that measures more than 0 degrees but less than 90 degrees

62 Triangles

Triangles are geometrical figures that have three sides. There are several kinds of triangles. They depend on the type of angles in the triangles and the lengths of the sides of the triangles.

The first three types of triangles are acute, right, and obtuse triangles. An acute triangle is one where all three angles in the triangle are acute. So each angle is less than 90°. A right triangle has one angle that is 90°. And the other two angles are acute. Finally, an obtuse triangle has one angle that is more than 90° but less than 180°. The other two angles in it are acute.

Next, there are three types of triangles that are characterized by the length of the triangles' sides. They are equilateral, isosceles, and scalene triangles. Equilateral triangles have three sides that are the same length. All three angles are always 60°, so they are also acute triangles. Isosceles triangles have two sides with equal length. And all three sides in a scalene triangle are of different lengths.

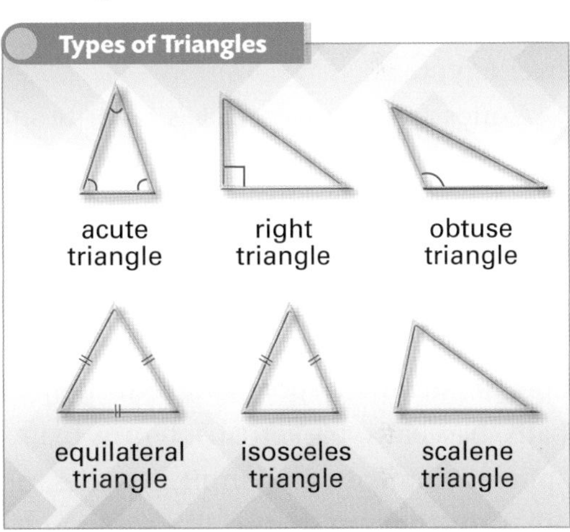

1 What is a triangle that has two sides that are the same length?

a. A scalene triangle.
b. An equilateral triangle.
c. An isosceles triangle.

2 Fill in the blanks.

a. Every angle in an __________ triangle is less than 90°.
b. A __________ triangle has one angle that is 90°.
c. The sides of an equilateral triangle are all the __________ length.

3 Write the correct word and the meaning in Chinese.

equilateral triangle	obtuse triangle	isosceles triangle	geometrical

a. ____________________: a triangle that has three sides that are the same length
b. ____________________: a triangle that has two sides with equal length
c. ____________________: consisting of points, lines, curves, or surfaces

Solid Figures in Real Life

Solid figures include cubes, prisms, pyramids, cylinders, cones, and spheres. Everywhere you look, you can see solid figures.

Many buildings are rectangular prisms. A door is one, too. So are the bulletin board in your classroom and this book you are reading right now.

Pyramids are not very common. But some of them are really famous. Think about Egypt for a minute. What comes to mind? The pyramids, right? There are huge pyramids all over Egypt.

Cones are among people's favorite solid figures. Why is that? The reason is that ice cream cones are solid figures. There are often many cones in areas where there is road construction, too. Construction workers put traffic cones on the street to show people where they can and cannot drive.

Of course, spheres are everywhere. People would not be able to play most sports without them. They need soccer balls, baseballs, basketballs, tennis balls, and many other spheres. Oranges, grapefruit, peaches, plums, and cherries are fruits that are shaped like spheres, too.

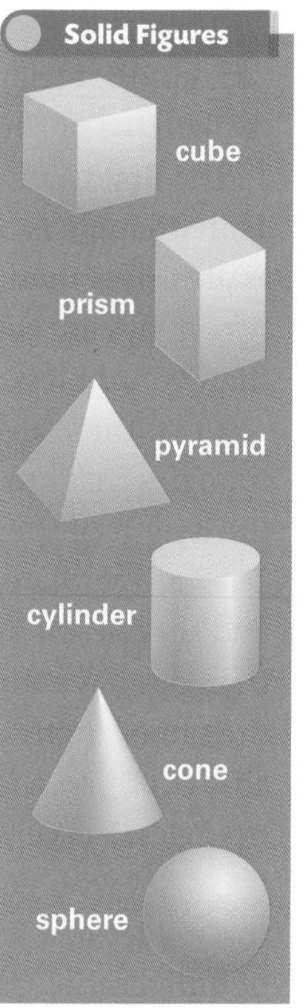

1 What is the passage mainly about?

a. Solid figures that exist in reality.
b. What solid figures look like.
c. How common some solid figures are.

2 Answer the questions.

a. What kind of solid figures are doors? ____________________
b. What kind of solid figures are the famous buildings in Egypt? ____________
c. What kind of solid figures are traffic cones? ____________________

3 Write the correct word and the meaning in Chinese.

cone	rectangular prism	solid figure	cylinder	sphere

a. ____________________: a solid or hollow tube with long straight sides and two circular ends the same size
b. ____________________: a three-dimensional shape
c. ____________________: a solid figure in the shape of a rectangle

64 Dimensions

The physical world we live in has three dimensions. These three dimensions can all be measured and charted on a graph. They are length, width, and depth.

Length is the first dimension. It is represented by a simple line. On a three-dimensional graph, it is represented by the x-axis, which runs horizontally.

The second dimension is width. When an object exists in two dimensions, it can take the shape of a plane figure, such as a square, rectangle, triangle, or circle. In other words, it can be represented in both length and width. On a three-dimensional graph, width is represented by the y-axis, which also runs horizontally.

The third dimension is depth. It is also called height. When an object exists in three dimensions, it can take the shape of a solid figure, such as a cube, pyramid, sphere, or prism. On a three-dimensional graph, depth is represented by the z-axis, which runs vertically.

The fourth dimension is time. Scientists have a name for a cube that exists in four dimensions. They call it a tesseract.

So how many dimensions are there? Scientists are not sure. Some believe that there may be eleven dimensions. Others claim that there are even more. Right now, scientists are searching for extra dimensions. They have not found any yet, but they believe they exist.

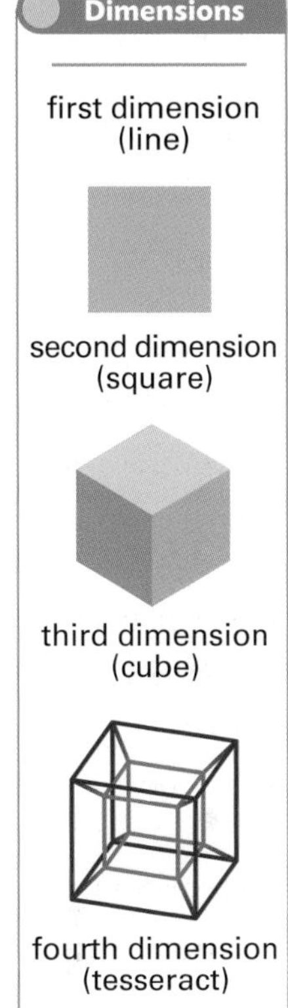

1 What is a tesseract?

a. A three-dimensional figure. b. A graph with three dimensions.
c. A cube with four dimensions.

2 Answer the questions.

a. How many dimensions are in the physical world? ______________________
b. What are these dimensions? ______________________
c. What is the fourth dimension? ______________________

3 Write the correct word and the meaning in Chinese.

second dimension	third dimension	horizontally	tesseract

a. ______________: positioned from side to side rather than up and down
b. ______________: a cube inside another cube
c. ______________: depth or height; a solid

$3,800.00
8%
8%
13%
21%
Site
Decorations
Publicity
Miscellaneous
$800.00
$700.00
$600.00
$500.00
$400.00
$300.00
$200.00
$100.00
$0.00
Site
Decorations
Publicity
,800.00
13%
8%
8%
21%
13%
16%
21%

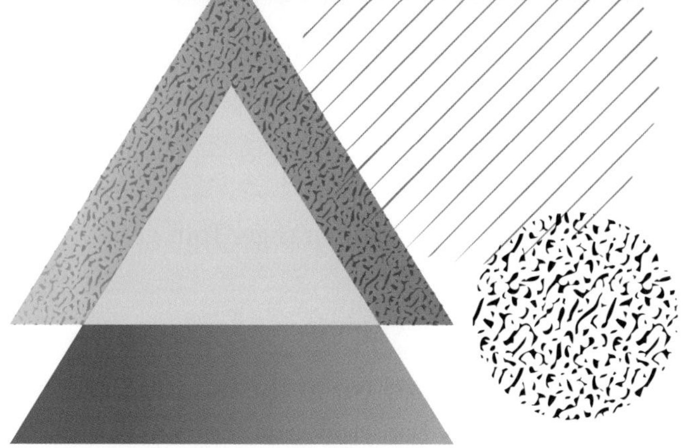

Numbers and Computation

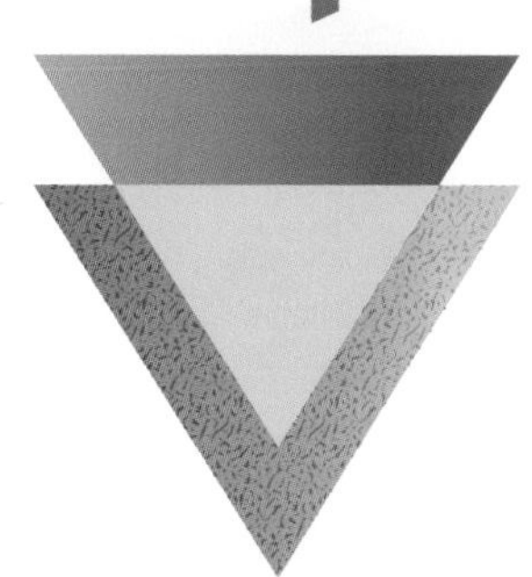

Solve the Problems

65

1 Two oranges are the same size. Amy gets $\frac{1}{2}$ of one orange. Tom gets $\frac{1}{5}$ of the other. Who gets more of the orange?

→ $\frac{1}{2}$ is greater than $\frac{1}{5}$. So, Amy gets the larger piece.

2 Eric has one candy bar. He eats $\frac{1}{3}$ of the candy bar in the morning. Later in the day, he eats another $\frac{1}{3}$ of the candy bar. How much of the candy bar is left over?

→ He ate $\frac{2}{3}$ of the candy bar. So there is $\frac{1}{3}$ left over.

3 Mary makes a pie. She cuts it into 8 pieces. Steve takes $\frac{1}{4}$ of the pie. Then Chris takes $\frac{1}{2}$ of the pie. How much pie remains?

→ $\frac{1}{4}=\frac{2}{8}$. And $\frac{1}{2}=\frac{4}{8}$. $\frac{2}{8}+\frac{4}{8}=\frac{6}{8}$. So $\frac{6}{8}$ of the pie is gone. Now there are $\frac{2}{8}$ (or $\frac{1}{4}$) of the pie remaining.

4 Daniel goes shopping. He has $5\frac{1}{2}$ dollars. His brother goes shopping with him. His brother has $5\frac{2}{3}$ dollars. Who has more money?

→ $\frac{2}{3}$ is greater than $\frac{1}{2}$. So Daniel's brother has more money.

How to Read Fractions

	$\frac{1}{2}$ one half
	$\frac{3}{6}$ three sixths
	$1\frac{1}{2}$ one and one half
	$3\frac{1}{4}$ three and one fourth
	$2\frac{2}{3}$ two and two thirds

1 **What is the passage mainly about?**
- a. How to solve word problems for fractions.
- b. The most difficult word problems.
- c. Using addition in mathematics.

2 **What is NOT true?**
- a. Amy has more of the orange than Tom.
- b. Eric eats $\frac{1}{3}$ of the candy bar in the morning.
- c. Steve takes more of the pie than Chris.

3 **Complete the sentences with the words below.**

greater than	left over	remains	three sixths

a. How much is __________ __________ if you subtract four from nine?

b. Mary cut the pie into six pieces. Joe took three of them. There were __________ __________ left.

c. When you take away three from seven, four __________.

Collecting and Organizing Data

People often conduct research. They may research a topic and find as much information as they can about it. Perhaps they want to know the daily temperature in a region for an entire year. Or maybe they want to know how many books students read during a semester. First, they decide what information they want. Then they collect the data.

But the raw data they collect could be useless by itself. So they need to organize it. One common way to organize data is to use charts and diagrams. This lets people see the visual results of their data. For example, perhaps the researchers have some data on how many books each student reads. They can put that data onto a bar graph. This will let them analyze it more easily. Or, maybe they know the average temperature for each day of the year. They can organize it into a circle graph. This will show them the percentage of hot, warm, cool, and cold days the area gets. By using these visual aids, they can interpret their data much more easily.

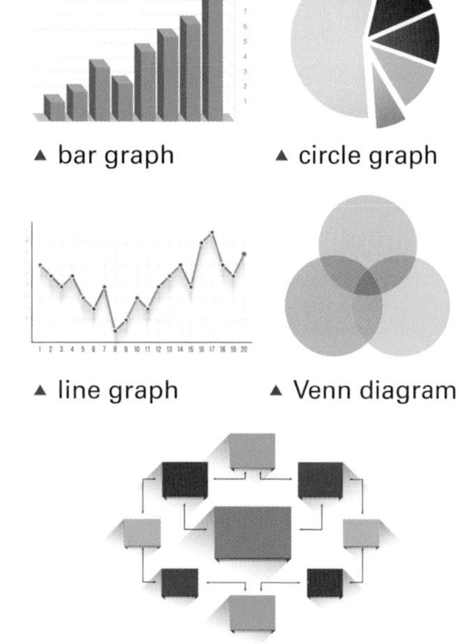

▲ bar graph ▲ circle graph

▲ line graph ▲ Venn diagram

▲ flow diagram

1. **What is the main idea of the passage?**
   - a. There are several ways to organize data.
   - b. Graphs help people organize data.
   - c. A researcher needs to collect some data.

2. **What is NOT true?**
   - a. People use charts to organize their information.
   - b. Bar graphs use circles to show the data.
   - c. Diagrams are visual aids.

3. **Write the correct word and the meaning in Chinese.**

semester	analyze	raw data	average	interpret

a. ____________________: data that has not been analyzed

b. ____________________: to explain the meaning of something

c. ____________________: to study or examine something in detail

67 Roman Numerals

67

We count with numbers today. The decimal system we use is very easy. But not every culture has counted the same way. Many systems are different. In ancient Rome, the Romans used Roman numerals. But these were not actually numerals. Instead, they were letters.

The Romans used the letters I, V, X, L, C, D, and M to stand for certain quantities. For example, I was 1, V was 5, X was 10, L was 50, C was 100, D was 500, and M was 1,000. To make larger numbers, they just added more letters. So 2 was II, and 3 was III. 6 was VI, and 7 was VII. However, the number 4 was not IIII. Instead, it was IV. Why did they do that? When a letter was going to change to one with a greater value, the Romans put the smaller letter in front of the bigger letter. That meant they should subtract that amount, not add to it. So 9 was IX. 40 was XL. 90 was XC. And 900 was CM.

Doing that was not difficult. But Romans could not count very high since it was hard to write large numbers. For example, what was 3,867? In Roman numerals, it was MMMDCCCLXVII. How about doing addition, subtraction, multiplication, or division? Can you imagine dividing MMCCXII by CCLXIV?

Roman Numerals

I = 1	IV = 4	VII = 7	X = 10	D = 500
II = 2	V = 5	VIII = 8	L = 50	M = 1000
III = 3	VI = 6	IX = 9	C = 100	

1 How do you write the number 4 in Roman numerals?

a. III b. VI c. IV

2 What is true? Write T (true) or F (false).

a. The Romans used letters for numbers. ____
b. V meant 10 to the Romans. ____
c. XL was 90 to the Romans. ____

3 Write the correct word and the meaning in Chinese.

Roman numeral	decimal system	instead	quantity	stand for

a. ____________: a number system that uses a base of 10
b. ____________: a letter that represents a number
c. ____________: the amount of something

The Order of Operations

In math, some problems are easy to solve. For example, this problem: 2+3=5. That is a simple problem. But sometimes there are more complicated problems. For example, how about this problem: 2+3×4? How do you solve this? Do you do the addition or the multiplication first? Is the answer 14 or 20?

In math, there is something called the order of operations. These tell the order in which you should solve a math problem. There are three simple rules:

1) Do the calculations inside parentheses first.
2) Moving from left to right, solve all multiplication and division problems first.
3) Moving from left to right, solve all addition and subtraction problems next.

Let's look at the problem above one more time: 2+3×4. How do we solve it? First, we must multiply 3×4. That's 12. Then we add 2+12. That's 14. So the correct answer is 14.

How about a more complicated problem? Look at this problem: 3×(3+4)−1. First, we must solve the problem in parentheses. So 3+4 is 7. Next, we do the multiplication problem. So 3×7 is 21. Last, we do the subtraction problem. So 21−1 is 20. The answer is 20.

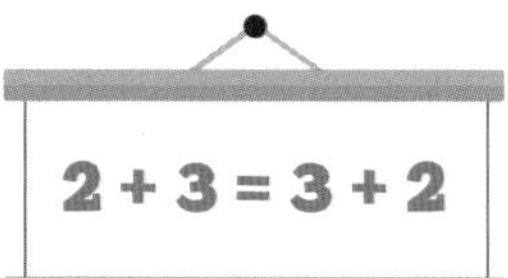

▲ **Commutative property of addition:** Numbers can be added in any order, and the sum will be the same.

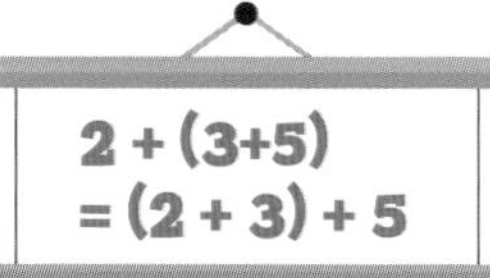

▲ **Associative property of addition:** Numbers can be grouped in any way, and the sum will be the same.

1 What is the order of operations?

a. The order in which a math problem should be solved.
b. Addition, subtraction, multiplication, and division.
c. Doing the calculations inside parentheses first.

2 Fill in the blanks.

a. You should solve problems in ______________ first.
b. Solve multiplication and ______________ problems before you solve addition and subtraction problems.
c. You should always move from ________ to right when solving a math problem.

3 Write the correct word and the meaning in Chinese.

calculation	solve	operation	multiply	parenthesis

a. ____________________: to add a number to itself a particular number of times
b. ____________________: the process of calculating something
c. ____________________: a mathematical process

Percentages, Ratios, and Probabilities

The weatherman may say, "There is a 70% chance of rain." He is telling you the probability of rain. At 70%, this means that, in the current weather conditions, it will rain 70 times out of 100. Weather forecasts often use percentages. So do sports. An announcer may say, "The basketball player shoots 52%." This means that for every 100 shots he takes, he makes 52.

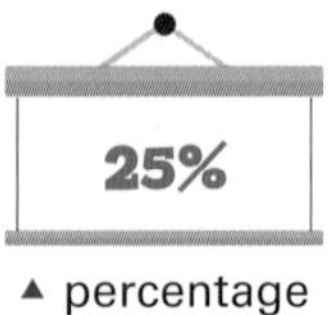

▲ percentage

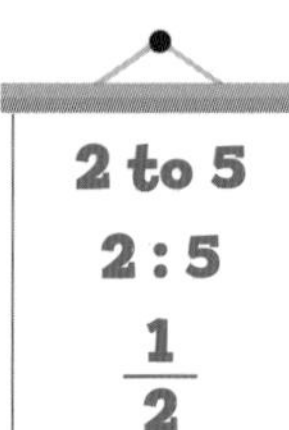

▲ ratio

Ratios are a way to compare two things to one another. For example, a classroom has 20 children. There are 12 boys and 8 girls. You can say, "The ratio of boys to girls is 12 to 8." Or you can write the ratio as 12:8. Perhaps there are 5 cats and 8 dogs. You can say the ratio of cats to dogs is 5 to 8 or 5:8.

Probability expresses the odds, or chances, of something happening. If you flip a coin, there is a 1 in 2 chance of a certain side showing because a coin has two sides. If you roll a die, there is a 1 in 6 chance of the number 4 appearing. Perhaps there are 10 cookies. Three are oatmeal cookies. If you grab one cookie at random, there is a 3 in 10 chance you will get an oatmeal cookie.

1 What do "odds" express?

a. the percentage of a number
b. the chances of something happening
c. how often something has happened

2 What is NOT true?

a. Weather forecasts often use ratios.
b. Probability is the chance that something will happen.
c. There is a 1 in 6 chance of the number 4 appearing when you roll a die.

3 Write the correct word and the meaning in Chinese.

odds	percentage	weather forecast	at random	ratio

a. ____________________: the chance of something happening
b. ____________________: a type of comparison between two things
c. ____________________: by chance; without being chosen intentionally

70 Square Roots

5 x 5 = 25
squaring

exponent/power
$5^2 = 25$
base perfect square

divisor
25 ÷ 5 = 5
square root

You have probably multiplied a number by itself before. For example, two times two is four. (2×2=4) Four times four is sixteen. (4×4=16) Five times five is twenty-five. (5×5=25) And ten times ten is one hundred. (10×10=100) When you multiply a number by itself, you are squaring it.

However, what happens when you do an inverse operation? An inverse operation of squaring is finding the square root of a number. When the divisor of a number and the result are the same, then that is the square root of the number.

For instance, the square root of 4 is two. (=2) Why is that? The reason is that four divided by two is two. (4÷2=2) The divisor and the result are the same. Also, the square root of 49 is seven. Forty-nine divided by seven is seven. And the square root of 100 is ten. One hundred divided by ten is ten.

However, not all square roots are whole numbers. In fact, they are usually irrational numbers. For example, what is the square root of three? It is not a whole number. Instead, it is 1.73205. It actually goes on to infinity because it can never be solved. And how about the square root of six? It is 2.44948. It too goes on to infinity and cannot be solved. Actually, the majority of numbers have square roots that are irrational numbers.

1. **What is the inverse operation of squaring a number?**
   a. Finding its root. b. Finding its square root. c. Finding its cube root.

2. **What is true? Write T (true) or F (false).**
   a. The square root of five is twenty-five. ____
   b. When you multiply a number by itself, you get the square root. ____
   c. The square root of three is an irrational number. ____

3. **Write the correct word and the meaning in Chinese.**

square root	inverse operations	whole number	to infinity

a. ____________: a number, such as 1, 4, or 15, that has no digits after the decimal point
b. ____________: a number that, when multiplied by itself, equals a certain number
c. ____________: without limit or end

Probability and Statistics

71

The probability of something is the chance that it will happen. This is often expressed as a percentage. For example, if you flip a coin, the probability of it being heads is fifty percent. If you roll a die, the probability of it being the number one is 16.67%, or $\frac{1}{6}$. You can determine the probability by taking the number of ways something can happen and dividing it by the total number of outcomes.

Statistics, on the other hand, is the field of math that collects, organizes, and interprets data. Once data has been collected, one of the easiest ways to analyze it is with graphs. For data that involves probability, circle graphs—or pie charts—are the best to use. These can be divided into 100 percentage points. Perhaps there is a fifty percent chance of something happening, a twenty-five percent chance of something else happening, and a twenty-five percent chance of something different happening. This can easily be shown on a circle graph.

On the other hand, other statistics are best recorded on a bar graph. These are simple charts with an x-axis and a y-axis. For example, perhaps the person is recording some students' best subjects. The classes are English, math, science, and history. These classes go on the x-axis, which is horizontal. The number of students that do well in each class goes on the y-axis, which is vertical. This makes the data easy to see and to interpret.

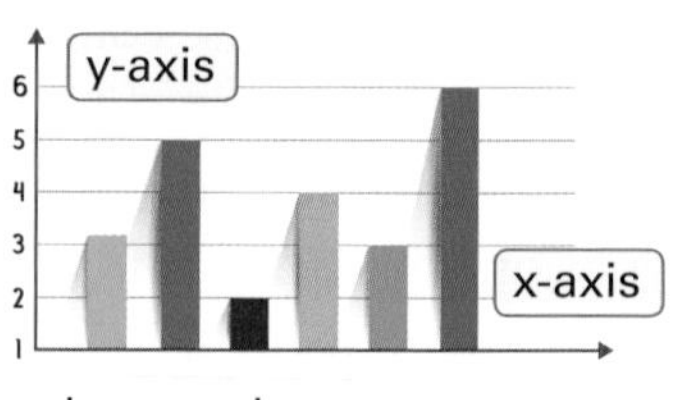

▲ bar graph

1 What is the y-axis on a chart?

a. A horizontal line. b. A diagonal line. c. A vertical line.

2 Fill in the blanks.

a. The chance of something happening is its ______________.

b. Statistics is the field of math that collects, organizes, and interprets ________.

c. A __________ __________ is also called a pie chart.

3 Write the correct word and the meaning in Chinese.

pie chart	outcome	statistics	x-axis	y-axis

a. ______________: a circular chart divided into triangular areas

b. ______________: the science of collecting, organizing, and interpreting data

c. ______________: a vertical line on a chart

72 The Metric System

The metric system is a system of measurement that uses the base-10 system. It measures length, volume, weight, pressure, energy, and temperature. There are several units in the metric system. But, since it uses the base-10 system, converting them is quite easy.

The meter is the unit used to measure length in the metric system. But there are also millimeters, centimeters, decimeters, decameters, hectometers, and kilometers. So, in 1 meter, there are 10 decimeters, 100 centimeters, and 1,000 millimeters. Also, in 1 kilometer, there are 10 hectometers, 100 decameters, and 1,000 meters. The most common units of length are the millimeter, centimeter, meter, and kilometer.

The liter is the unit used to measure volume in the metric system. However, there are also milliliters, centiliters, deciliters, decaliters, hectoliters, and kiloliters. The method to convert them is the same as for meters.

The gram is the unit used to measure weight in the metric system. The most common units of weight are the gram and the kilogram. There are other units, but they are not commonly used.

Finally, the metric system uses Celsius to measure temperature. 0 degrees Celsius is the temperature at which water freezes. 100 degrees Celsius is the temperature at which water boils.

Prefixes Used in the Metric System

Kilo- means thousand
1 kilometer (km) = 1,000 m

Hecto- means hundred
1 hectometer (hm) = 100 m

Deka- means ten
1 decameter (dam) = 10 m

Deci- means tenth
1 decimeter (dm) = 0.1 m

Centi- means hundredth
1 centimeter (cm) = 0.01 m

Milli- means thousandth
1 millimeter (mm) = 0.001 m

1. **How many hectometers are in one kilometer?**
   a. 10 b. 100 c. 1,000

2. **What is NOT true?**
   a. The meter measures length in the metric system.
   b. A decameter is bigger than a centimeter.
   c. The liter is used to measure weight in the metric system.

3. **Write the correct word and the meaning in Chinese.**

metric system	base-10 system	volume	convert	Celsius

a. ______________: the amount of space in a container
b. ______________: to change from one system to another
c. ______________: a system of measurement based on the meter

Language • Visual Arts • Music

Language and
Literature
Visual Arts
Music

Language and Literature

73 The Norse Gods

73

Norse mythology comes from Northern Europe. The Norse were Vikings. They lived in the area that is Norway, Sweden, and Finland today. The Vikings loved to fight and make war. So their stories often are very violent.

There were many Norse gods. Odin was their leader. He was very wise. Odin always had two ravens. They were thought and memory. They told him everything that happened in the land. Thor was the god of thunder. He was the most powerful of all the gods. He carried a great hammer that he often used to kill giants. Loki was the god of mischief and fire and was a half giant. He was also a trickster, so he caused many problems for the gods, especially Thor. Frigg was Odin's wife and was also the goddess of marriage. And Freya was the goddess of love. There were also many other Norse gods and goddesses.

The gods lived at Asgard. They often had to fight their enemies, like frost giants and trolls. There are many stories about their deeds that people still enjoy reading.

Norse Gods

▲ Odin

▲ Thor

▲ Loki

▲ Frigg

▲ Freya

▲ Hel

1 **Which Norse god had two ravens that spoke to him?**

a. Odin. b. Loki. c. Thor.

2 **Fill in the blanks.**

a. Norse mythology comes from countries in ______________ ____________.

b. The leader of the Norse gods was ___________.

c. The Norse gods all lived at ____________.

3 **Write the correct word and the meaning in Chinese.**

Viking	raven	mischief	deed	troll

a. __________________: one of the Scandinavian people who attacked the coasts of Europe in the Middle Ages

b. __________________: a dwarf or giant in Scandinavian folklore inhabiting caves or hills

c. __________________: trouble; a trick

74 The *Iliad* and the *Odyssey*

74

Two of the greatest works of literature are also very old. They are the epic poems the *Iliad* and the *Odyssey*. Both were told by Homer and tell stories about the ancient Greeks.

The *Iliad* is about the Trojan War. Paris abducted Helen and took her to Troy. Helen was the most beautiful woman in the world. So all of the Greeks joined together to fight the Trojans. There were many great Greek warriors. There were Agamemnon, Menelaus, Odysseus, and Ajax. But Achilles was the greatest warrior of all. The war lasted for ten years. Many people died. Finally, thanks to Odysseus, the Greeks used the Trojan Horse to win. The Greeks pretended to leave. They left behind a giant horse. The Trojans took the horse into their city. But many Greek warriors were hiding inside it. At night, the Greeks came out of the horse. Inside the city, they managed to capture and defeat Troy.

▲ Achilles

The *Odyssey* tells the tale of Odysseus's return home after the war. It took him ten years to get home. He had many strange adventures. He had to fight a fearsome Cyclops. He met magical women like Circe and Calypso. And all of his men died. Finally, though, with help from the gods, Odysseus arrived home.

▲ Cyclops

1 What is the main idea of the passage?

a. The *Iliad* is about the Trojan War.
b. Odysseus took ten years to get home after the Trojan War.
c. The *Iliad* and the *Odyssey* tell stories from ancient Greece.

2 What is true? Write T (true) or F (false).

a. The *Iliad* was about the adventures of Odysseus. _____
b. The Trojans hid in the Trojan Horse. _____
c. Odysseus and all of his men arrived home after ten years. _____

3 Write the correct word and the meaning in Chinese.

epic poem	Trojan War	abduct	adventure	pretend to

a. ____________________: an exciting, unusual, and sometimes dangerous experience
b. ____________________: a long poem that features heroes, gods, and magic
c. ____________________: to seize and take away a person by force

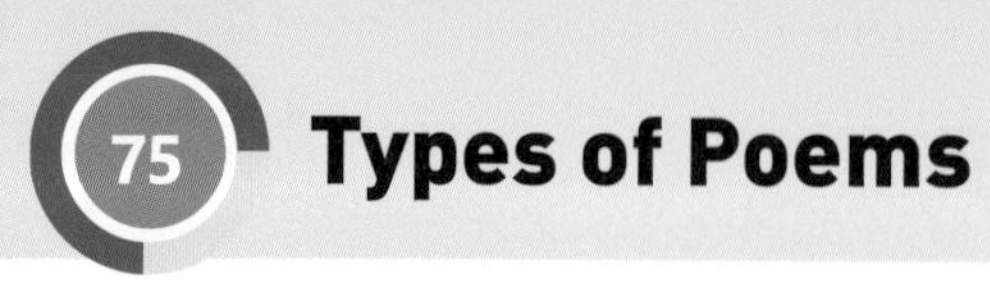

75 Types of Poems

Poets have many different types of poems to choose from when they write. They can write very long or very short poems. They can write about many different subjects. And they can write with different rhyme schemes and in different meters.

One of the oldest types of poems is the epic. This is a very long poem. It can often be thousands of lines long. An epic poem is typically about a hero and his adventures. There have been many famous epic poems in history. The *Iliad, Odyssey, Aeneid, Beowulf,* and *Gilgamesh* are just a few of the many epic poems.

▲ Beowulf

On the other hand, many poems are very short. Sonnets are one type of short poem. They are poems with fourteen lines. Usually, the last two lines in a sonnet rhyme. Sonnets can be about many different topics. William Shakespeare wrote many famous sonnets. Couplets can be long or short poems. Each stanza in a couplet has two lines. The last word in each line rhymes. Quatrains are very short poems. They only have four lines. And cinquains have five lines. Limericks are also poems with five lines. And haikus are poems with only three lines. The first and third lines have five syllables. And the second line has seven syllables. They are some of the shortest of poems.

1 What type of poem has only three lines?

a. A couplet. b. A haiku. c. A cinquain.

2 What is true? Write T (true) or F (false).

a. Epic poems are short poems. ____

b. A sonnet has fourteen lines. ____

c. Quatrains and limericks both have four lines. ____

3 Write the correct word and the meaning in Chinese.

poet	stanza	rhyme scheme	sonnet	couplet

a. ________________: a type of poem with fourteen lines

b. ________________: the pattern of rhymes in the lines of a poem

c. ________________: a section of a poem consisting of a group of lines that form a unit

Understanding Sentences

All sentences must have a subject and a verb. Some sentences can be very short. For example, "I ate," is a complete sentence. Why? It has a subject and a verb. Other sentences can be very, very long.

People often make mistakes when making English sentences. One common mistake is the run-on sentence. Look at this sentence:

I went to the park I saw my friend.

It's a run-on sentence. A run-on sentence is a combination of two sentences that either needs punctuation or a conjunction. Here's a complete sentence:

I went to the park, and I saw my friend.

All sentences need to have subject-verb agreement. It means that if the subject is singular, the verb must be singular. And if the subject is plural, the verb must be plural. Look at this sentence:

Jason like to play computer games.

It's a wrong sentence. Why? It doesn't have subject-verb agreement.
Here is the correct complete sentence:

Jason likes to play computer games.

So watch out for run-on sentences, and always make sure your subjects and verbs agree. Then you'll be making lots of complete sentences.

1 **What does a run-on sentence need?**

a. A subject. b. Punctuation. c. Subject-verb agreement.

2 **What is NOT true?**

a. All sentences must have a subject and a verb.
b. If the subject is singular, the verb must be plural.
c. Subject-verb agreement is important in English.

3 **Write the correct word and the meaning in Chinese.**

run-on sentence	punctuation	agree	complete sentence

a. ____________________: to be the same or suggest the same thing
b. ____________________: symbols such as commas, periods, and question marks
c. ____________________: a sentence with an improper combination of two or more complete sentences

77 Common Proverbs

77

Proverbs are short expressions that people sometimes use. They typically pass on some type of wisdom. The English language has a very large number of proverbs.

One proverb is "Absence makes the heart grow fonder." It means that people usually have good memories of events or people from the past. Of course, at the time, they might not have thought much of them. However, over time, the "absence" changed their memories, so they remember the events or people fondly.

"All that glitters is not gold" is another important proverb. Gold is very valuable, and it glitters brightly. But many other things glitter, too. However, they may not be valuable. In fact, they may even be harmful. So this proverb is a warning. People should be careful because not every shiny, good-looking thing is like gold.

"He who hesitates is lost" is a popular expression. This proverb tells people not to hesitate. They should make a decision and go with it. If they hesitate or wait too long, they might lose an important opportunity.

Finally, "It's no use crying over spilt milk" is another common proverb. Sometimes bad things might happen to a person. But that person should not cry about it. Instead, the person should accept what has happened and move on. That is the meaning of that proverb.

1 What is the main idea of the passage?

a. People use many proverbs in everyday life.
b. A lot of proverbs are about valuable things like gold.
c. Proverbs contain wisdom in a short passage.

2 What is NOT true?

a. Proverbs rarely teach some kind of wisdom to people.
b. "All that glitters is not gold" is a proverb that warns people.
c. "It's no use crying over spilt milk" tells people to move on from the past.

3 Write the correct word and the meaning in Chinese.

proverb	absence	fond	glitter	move on

a. ____________________: cherished with great affection
b. ____________________: a wise saying
c. ____________________: to accept that a situation has changed and be ready to deal with new experiences

78 Figures of Speech

Writers can be creative. To do this, they can use figures of speech. There are many of these. Four are similes, metaphors, hyperbole, and personification.

Similes and metaphors are both comparisons. But they are not the same. Similes use "as" or "like" to compare two things. For example, "strong as an ox" and "dark like night" are similes. Metaphors are comparisons between two unlike things that seem to have nothing in common. "The stars are diamonds in the sky" and "There is a sea of sand" are metaphors.

Hyperbole is also a figure of speech. It is a form of exaggeration. People often exaggerate when they speak or write. For instance, "There were a million people in the store" is hyperbole. "I worked all day and all night" is, too.

Finally, people often give objects and animals human characteristics. This is personification. "The wind is whispering" is one example. So is "My dog is speaking to me." The wind and the dog are not humans. But in both cases, they have human characteristics. So they are examples of personification.

▲ simile

▲ metaphor

▲ hyperbole

▲ personification

1 Which comparison uses "like" or "as"?

a. Hyperbole. b. A simile. c. A metaphor.

2 Fill in the blanks.

a. Similes and metaphors are two kinds of ____________ of speech.
b. ______________ is a form of exaggeration.
c. ____________________ gives animals or objects human characteristics.

3 Write the correct word and the meaning in Chinese.

simile	metaphor	comparison	hyperbole	personification

a. ____________________: a word or phrase that ordinarily designates one thing is used to designate another
b. ____________________: an expression comparing one thing with another, always including the words "as" or "like"
c. ____________________: language that describes something as better or worse than it really is

Greek and Latin Roots

79

English has more words than any other language. Why is this? One reason is that English borrows words from many other languages. Then it turns these words into new English words. Many of these words come from Greek and Latin. These are called roots. By studying roots, a person can learn the meanings of many different words in English.

For instance, the root *hydro* comes from Greek. It means "water." From that root, we get the words hydrate, dehydrate, hydrant, hydrogen, and many others. The root *aster* comes from Greek. It means "star." From *aster*, we get the words asteroid, asterisk, astronomy, astronaut, and many others. *Geo* also comes from Greek. It means "earth." The words geology, geometry, and geography all come from it.

Of course, there are many roots from Latin, too. For instance, the root *vid* means to "see." From that root, we get video, visual, visualize, and many others. The root *script* means to "write." From it, we get transcript, inscription, and others. And *port* means to "carry." From that root, we get transport, portable, export, and import, among others.

Without borrowing from other languages, English would have very few words. But, thanks to Latin and Greek—and other languages, too—English has many, many words.

The Root *Aster*

asteroid

astronaut

asterisk

astronomy

1 What is the main idea of the passage?

a. Many English words come from Latin and Greek.
b. English has fewer words than both Latin and Greek.
c. Many people study Latin and Greek roots.

2 Fill in the blanks.

a. Studying ___________ helps a person learn the meanings of many different words in English.
b. *Geo* is a root word that comes from ___________.
c. The root *vid* means to "_________."

3 Write the correct word and the meaning in Chinese.

root	hydrate	asterisk	geology	visualize

a. ___________________: the symbol *
b. ___________________: the base form of a word
c. ___________________: the scientific study of the history and structure of the earth

Visual Arts

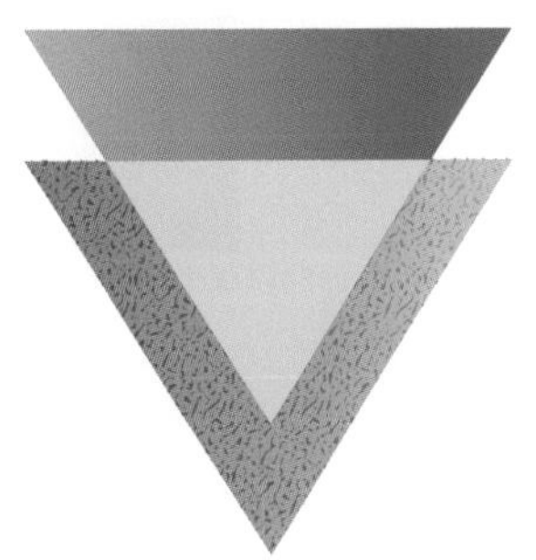

80 Gothic Cathedrals

80

In the Middle Ages, religion was a very important part of people's lives. Almost everyone went to church on Sunday. So building churches was important. Some towns and cities built huge churches. They were called cathedrals. There were many different styles. One important style was Gothic. The Gothic Age lasted from around the twelfth to sixteenth centuries.

Gothic cathedrals were enormous. Their builders made them to impress many people. So they look like they are reaching up into the sky. The reason that they are so high is that they have buttresses. These are supports that help the cathedrals stay up. The cathedrals also had many stained-glass windows. These showed scenes from the *Bible*. Also, they allowed a lot of light to enter the cathedrals. Inside the cathedrals, the ceilings were very high. This made them look even more impressive. The outsides of cathedrals often had many sculptures. These were called gargoyles. The gargoyles looked like monsters. They were used to ward off evil spirits.

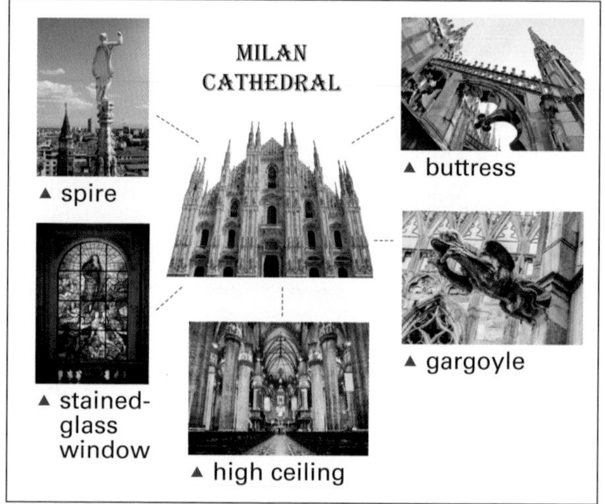

1 **What is a cathedral?**
- a. A Gothic building.
- b. A building with stained-glass windows.
- c. A very large church.

2 **Answer the questions.**
- a. What helped support cathedrals? ______________________
- b. What did stained-glass windows show? ______________________
- c. What are gargoyles? ______________________

3 **Write the correct word and the meaning in Chinese.**

Gothic	enormous	buttress	stained-glass	gargoyle

- a. ______________: a structure for supporting or giving stability to a building
- b. ______________: a stone statue of an ugly creature
- c. ______________: relating to colored glass that often shows pictures of various scenes

81 Islamic Architecture

Islam began in the seventh century. Since then, there have been many styles of buildings designed by Muslims. They all combine to make up Islamic architecture.

In Islam, art is restricted. There should be no images of Allah – the god of Islam. Also, there should be no pictures of people either. So many of Islam's most creative people became architects.

One of the main features of Islamic architecture is the minaret. These are tall towers. They are found in every mosque. There are usually four minarets at every mosque. There is one at each corner of the building. They can be very high towers. Domes are also very popular features. Domes are rounded roofs of buildings. Many mosques have impressive domes.

As for famous buildings, there are many. The Dome of the Rock is in Jerusalem. It is one of the earliest examples of Islamic architecture. The Sultan Ahmed Mosque is in Istanbul, Turkey. It is another well-known building. And the Taj Mahal is located in India. Some say it is the most beautiful building in the entire world.

▲ Dome of the Rock

1. **In what way is there a restriction in Islamic art?**
   a. There should be tall towers at each corner of a building.
   b. There should be no images of people.
   c. Buildings should have domes.

2. **What is true? Write T (true) or F (false).**
   a. Islamic art allows images of Allah. ____
   b. Minarets are tall towers. ____
   c. Many mosques have domes. ____

3. **Write the correct word and the meaning in Chinese.**

architecture	minaret	mosque	dome	Muslim

   a. ________________: a tall tower outside an Islamic mosque
   b. ________________: a roof shaped like the top half of a ball
   c. ________________: a place where Muslims go to worship

82 Renaissance Artists

82

During the Renaissance, there were many brilliant artists. These included Raphael, Botticelli, Giotto, and Donatello. But two are considered greater than the others. One is Leonardo da Vinci. The other is Michelangelo Buonarroti.

Leonardo da Vinci was a true Renaissance man. He could do many things well. He was an engineer and scientist. He was an inventor, architect, and artist. He was one of the greatest men in history. As an artist, he painted one of the world's most famous pictures: the *Mona Lisa*. Another famous painting is *The Last Supper*. It shows Jesus and his apostles together. Leonardo made many other famous works. But those two are the most well known.

Michelangelo was an incredible sculptor. He created two of the most famous statues of all time. The first was *David*. The second was *Pietà*. *Pietà* is a sculpture of Mary holding the body of Jesus after he died. Michelangelo was also a great painter. He painted the frescoes on the ceiling of the Sistine Chapel. The most famous of these frescoes is the *Creation of Adam*. It shows God and Adam reaching out to one another.

Famous Renaissance Works

▲ *Pietà*

▲ *Mona Lisa*

▲ *The Birth of Venus*

▲ *David*

▲ *The Last Supper*

▲ *The Creation of Adam*

1 What kind of work is the *Creation of Adam*?

a. A fresco. b. A sculpture. c. A statue.

2 Answer the questions.

a. When did Raphael and Botticelli paint? ________________

b. What kind of a person was Leonardo da Vinci? ________________

c. What were two of Michelangelo's most famous statues? ________________

3 Write the correct word and the meaning in Chinese.

brilliant	Renaissance man	apostle	incredible	fresco

a. ________________: a picture that is painted onto wet plaster on a wall

b. ________________: a person who has wide interests and is expert in several areas

c. ________________: a follower

83 Classical Art

The ancient Greeks loved art. They made all kinds of works of art. This included pottery, paintings, sculptures, and murals. The Greeks even considered their buildings to be works of art. So they made beautifully designed buildings as well.

Many examples of pottery have survived from ancient Greece. Pottery in ancient Greece had two functions. People used it to eat or drink from. And they used it for decorations. Many Greek ceramics have beautiful pictures painted on them. These pictures often show stories from Greek mythology.

Sculpture was highly prized in ancient Greece. The Greeks made sculptures from either stone or bronze. Many stone sculptures have survived to today. But few bronze sculptures have. The Greeks depicted the people in sculptures exactly as they looked in real life.

As for architecture, many Greek buildings still exist today. One important feature of these buildings is their columns. The Greeks made three types of columns: Doric, Ionic, and Corinthian. Doric columns were the simplest. They had very plain designs. Ionic columns had flutes, or lines, carved into them from the top to the bottom. They were also more decorative than Doric columns. Corinthian columns were the most decorative ones of all. Their tops—called capitals—often had flowers or other designs on them. And they also had flutes.

1 What is the passage mainly about?

a. The types of artwork created in ancient Greece.
b. The forms of columns that the ancient Greeks made.
c. The pottery and sculptures made by the ancient Greeks.

2 Answer the questions.

a. What kinds of works of art did the ancient Greeks make? ______________
b. What did the Greeks make sculptures from? ______________
c. What were the three types of columns the Greeks made? ______________

3 Write the correct word and the meaning in Chinese.

mural	decoration	ceramics	flute	column

a. ______________ : the objects produced by shaping and baking clay
b. ______________ : a painting on a wall
c. ______________ : a long, vertical, rounded groove in the shaft of a column

From Baroque to Realism

84

From around the late sixteenth century to the early eighteenth century, there was a new type of art in Europe. It was called Baroque. There were Baroque artists in every European country. So they all had slightly different styles. But there were many similarities that Baroque artists shared.

For one, there were often contrasts between light and dark in Baroque paintings. The artists also focused on movement. And they stressed facial expressions in the figures they painted. This was one way they tried to show emotions in their paintings. The works of Baroque artists also had symbolic or moralizing meanings. Many Baroque artists painted religious topics, too.

One very important characteristic was that Baroque artists were realists. So they painted their subjects as realistically as possible. They knew about perspective. So they could show things such as size and distance. They were also able to use the space in their paintings very well. This ability made many Baroque artists quite famous. Today, people still admire the works of artists such as El Greco, Rembrandt, and Caravaggio.

▲ *The Calling of Saint Matthew* by Caravaggio

▲ *The Night Watch* by Rembrandt

▲ *The Opening of the Fifth Seal* by El Greco

1 **Where were most Baroque painters?**

a. In America. b. In Asia. c. In Europe.

2 **What is NOT true?**

a. The Baroque Period ended during the seventeenth century.
b. Baroque paintings have contrasts between light and dark.
c. Many Baroque paintings showed people's emotions.
d. El Greco and Rembrandt were two Baroque artists.

3 **Write the correct word and the meaning in Chinese.**

stress	contrast	symbolic	perspective	admire

a. ____________________: representing something else
b. ____________________: an obvious difference between two or more things
c. ____________________: a way of drawing objects in a picture so as to give the appearance of distance or depth

85 Nineteenth Century American Landscapes

85

In the nineteenth century, much of America was not settled. So there were few cities. Not many people lived in the countryside. So there were many beautiful places for artists to paint landscapes.

One group of landscape artists was called the Hudson River School. The Hudson River flows through New York. These artists painted the land in this area. Much of it was forest. But there were also farms, fields, and many mountains. Thomas Cole was the first Hudson River School artist. Frederic Edwin Church and Asher Durand were two others. The Hudson River School artists were Romantics. So they idealized the landscapes they painted. They painted the scenes the way they wanted the land to look, not the way that it actually looked.

▲ *Distant View of Niagara Falls* by Thomas Cole

▲ *Fallen Monarchs* by William Bliss Baker

Around the same time, there was another school of artists. They were called Naturalists, or Realists. They painted nature as it appeared. William Bliss Baker was one of these artists. He also painted in the Hudson River area. But his paintings look very different from the Hudson River School artists' paintings. Baker's works are realistic. His painting *Fallen Monarchs* is one of the most beautiful of the Naturalist paintings.

1. **What kinds of artists were the Hudson River School artists?**
   a. Naturalists. b. Romantics. c. Realists.

2. **What is true? Write T (true) or F (false).**
   a. The Hudson River School artists painted in New York City. ____
   b. Thomas Cole idealized his landscapes. ____
   c. William Bliss Baker was a Naturalist. ____

3. **Write the correct word and the meaning in Chinese.**

school	idealize	scene	Romantic	Naturalist

a. ______________: to make ideal; to represent something in an ideal form
b. ______________: a writer, musician, or artist whose work stresses emotion and imagination
c. ______________: a group of writers, artists, etc. whose work or ideas are similar

Music

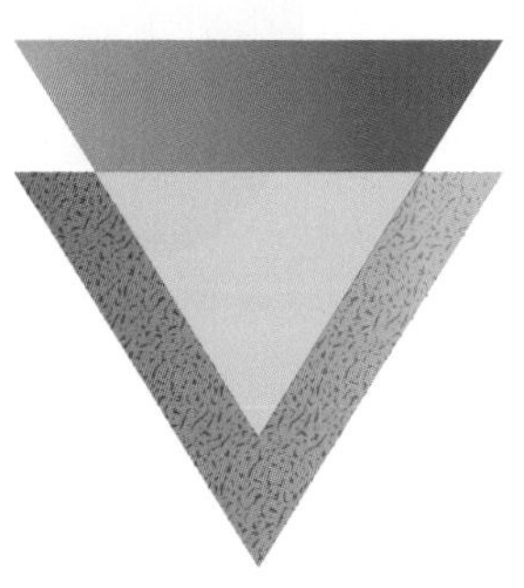

Composers and Their Music

There have been many great classical music composers. Three of the greatest were Johann Sebastian Bach, Wolfgang Amadeus Mozart, and Ludwig van Beethoven.

▲ Bach

▲ Mozart

Bach came first. He composed music during the Baroque Period. Much of his music was for the church. He wrote tunes for orchestras, choirs, and solo instruments. *The Brandenburg Concertos* are some of his most famous works.

Mozart was one of the most brilliant musicians of all time. He was a child genius. He started writing music at a very young age. He wrote all kinds of music. His opera *The Marriage of Figaro* is still famous. So is his *Great Mass in C Minor*.

▲ Beethoven

Beethoven was a great pianist and composer. His *Moonlight Sonata* was very famous. He went deaf later in his life. But he still conducted orchestras. His *9th Symphony* is one of the greatest of all pieces of classical music.

▲ young Mozart

1 **Who wrote *The Brandenburg Concertos*?**

a. Wolfgang Amadeus Mozart.

b. Ludwig van Beethoven.

c. Johann Sebastian Bach.

2 **What is true? Write T (true) or F (false).**

a. Bach lived during the Baroque Period. ____

b. Mozart went deaf later in life. ____

c. Beethoven composed *Moonlight Sonata*. ____

3 **Write the correct word and the meaning in Chinese.**

composer	conduct	choir	genius	go deaf

a. ____________________: to direct the performance of musicians or a piece of music

b. ____________________: a person who writes music

c. ____________________: someone who is much more intelligent or skillful than other people

87 Musical Dynamics

When musicians play their instruments, they must do more than just read the notes and then play them. They must know the speed that they should play the music. And they must also know the dynamics. This means they must know if they should play softly or loudly. How do they know that? They can look for certain letters on their sheet music.

On the sheet music, they will see the letters *p*, *pp*, *mp*, *f*, *ff*, or *mf*. These letters are all related to musical dynamics. They indicate the softness or the loudness that the musician should play.

p stands for piano. It means the music should be played softly. There are also *pp* and *mp*. *pp* means pianissimo, which stands for "very soft." And *mp* means mezzo piano. This means "moderately soft."

Of course, some music should be played loudly. When a musician sees *f*, it means forte. That stands for "loud." Just like with soft music, there are two more degrees of loudness. The first is *ff*. That's fortissimo, which means "very loud." And there is *mf*. That's mezzo forte, which means "moderately loud."

Musical Notation

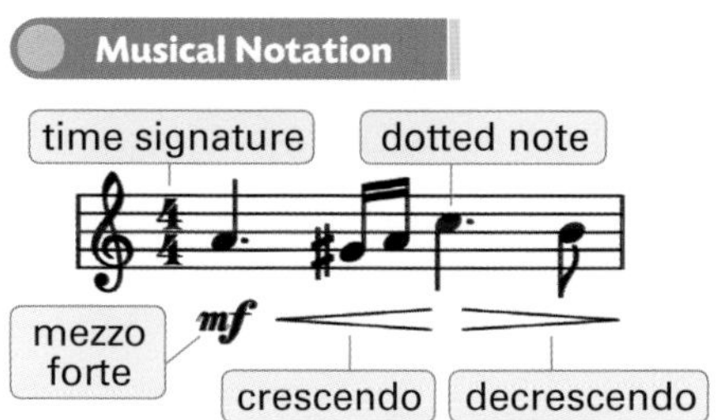

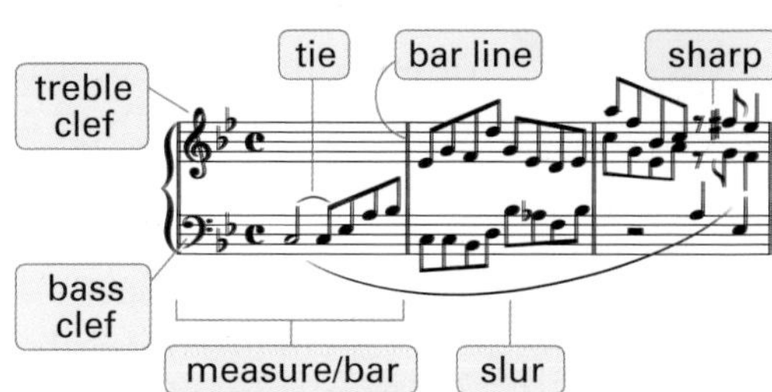

1 Which symbol means fortissimo?

a. *f*. b. *mf*. c. *ff*.

2 Fill in the blanks.

a. Letters like *p*, *pp*, and *mp* appear on __________ music.
b. *pp* stands for ______________.
c. Forte stands for "__________."

3 Write the correct word and the meaning in Chinese.

sheet music	dynamics	be related to	moderately	indicate

a. ______________: to some degree but not to a great degree
b. ______________: the variation and gradation in the volume of musical sounds
c. ______________: music in its printed or written form, especially single sheets of paper not formed into a book

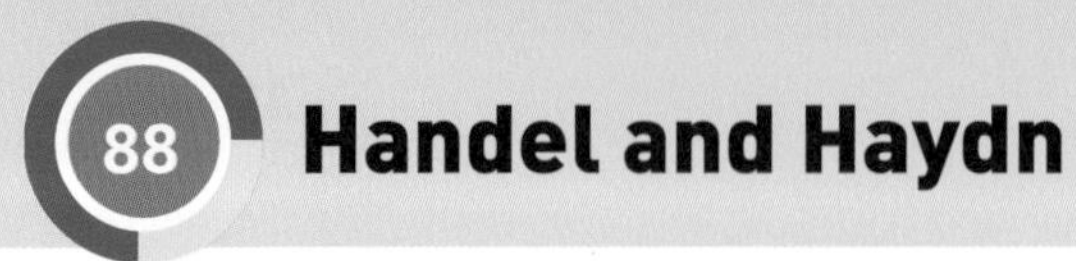

88 Handel and Haydn

▲ Handel

Two of the greatest of all classical music composers were George Friedrich Handel and Joseph Haydn.

Handel lived during the Baroque Period in the eighteenth century. He was German. But he lived in England for a long time. Some of his music is very popular and well-known all around the world. He wrote *Water Music* and *Music for the Royal Fireworks*. These are two easily recognizable pieces of music. But his most famous music by far is his *Messiah*. It is an oratorio that tells the life of Jesus Christ. From the *Messiah*, the most famous piece is the *Hallelujah* chorus. Today, when orchestras play the *Hallelujah* chorus, the audience always stands up. Why? When King George II of Great Britain first heard it, he stood up during that part.

▲ Haydn

Joseph Haydn was one of the best composers of the Classical Period. He composed hundreds of sonatas, symphonies, and string quartets. He also influenced many other composers. Beethoven was the greatest of all his students. Two of his best works are the *Surprise Symphony* and *The Creation*, an oratorio.

1 What is the passage mainly about?

a. The lives and works of two classical composers.
b. The best works of Handel and Haydn.
c. The religious pieces of music that Handel wrote.

2 What is NOT true?

a. Handel lived during the eighteenth century.
b. *Water Music* is a famous piece of music by Handel.
c. Haydn wrote the *Messiah*.

3 Write the correct word and the meaning in Chinese.

well-known	oratorio	audience	sonata	string quartet

a. ____________________: a group of four musicians who all play stringed instruments
b. ____________________: a long piece of classical music for singers and an orchestra, usually based on a religious story
c. ____________________: a piece of classical music for one instrument

89 Spirituals

Music is often associated with religion. In Christianity, there are many kinds of songs people sing. There are hymns, carols, chants, and others. Another type of music is the spiritual.

Spirituals were first written in the eighteenth century in the United States. They were written because there was a revival of interest in religion in the U.S. then. Spirituals were often very inspiring songs. They were about stories and themes from the *Bible*. In style, they were a kind of folk music or folk hymn. Spirituals were often sung by black Americans. Yet there were also many white spirituals, too. Many of the blacks who made these spirituals were slaves from Africa. So spirituals had a strong African influence. They later combined with European and American influences. The result was spirituals.

Nowadays, spiritual music is called gospel music. It is a form of music that is very religious. All kinds of people sing and listen to gospel music. It inspires people and gives them comfort as well.

▲ people singing Christmas carols

▲ Spirituals were originally sung by African-Americans.

▲ Spirituals often inspire the people who hear them.

1. **What style of music were the first spirituals similar to?**
   a. Folk music. b. Chants. c. Gospel music.

2. **Fill in the blanks.**
   a. Hymns, carols, and chants are kinds of music associated with ____________.
   b. The first spirituals appeared in the U.S. in the ______________ century.
   c. People call spirituals ___________ music today.

3. **Write the correct word and the meaning in Chinese.**

spiritual	comfort	folk music	inspiring	carol

a. _________________: traditional music from a particular country or region
b. _________________: a traditional song sung at Christmas
c. _________________: a religious folk song that was sung originally by African-Americans

The Classical Period of Music

90

▲ Schubert

The years between 1750 and 1820 saw some of the greatest music ever created. This time is now called the Classical Period of music. Among the composers who wrote during this period were Mozart, Beethoven, Haydn, and Schubert.

By 1750, people were getting tired of the Baroque Period. So they worked on new forms of music. Thus arose the Classical Period. It has several important characteristics. For one, the mood of the music often changed. In a single piece of music, there was not just one mood anymore. Instead, the mood could suddenly change anytime during a piece. The same was true of the rhythm of the music. Music from this period followed several different rhythmic patterns. There were often sudden pauses. Or the music would suddenly go from being very slow to very fast or from very soft to very loud.

Also, music from the Classical Period has beautiful melodies. The works the composers created are typically easy to remember. Of course, they are still sophisticated works. But the ease with which people can remember them has helped increase their popularity. Even today, the works of composers from this period are among the most popular of all classical music.

1 **What was a characteristic of music in the Classical Period?**

a. The works were very complicated.
b. The music had several moods.
c. The music was difficult to play.

2 **Fill in the blanks.**

a. The Classical Period of music lasted from ___________ to 1820.
b. The ______________ Period came right before the Classical Period.
c. The mood of the music during the Classical Period could often __________ suddenly.

3 **Write the correct word and the meaning in Chinese.**

get tired of	mood	typically	popularity	sophisticated

a. __________________: a quality that something such as a piece of music has that makes you have a particular feeling
b. __________________: having refined or cultured tastes; advanced
c. __________________: the state of being liked or accepted by many people

MOZART
MDCCLVI · MDCCXCI

SUPER READING TRAINING BOOK 2

Table of Contents

Social Studies

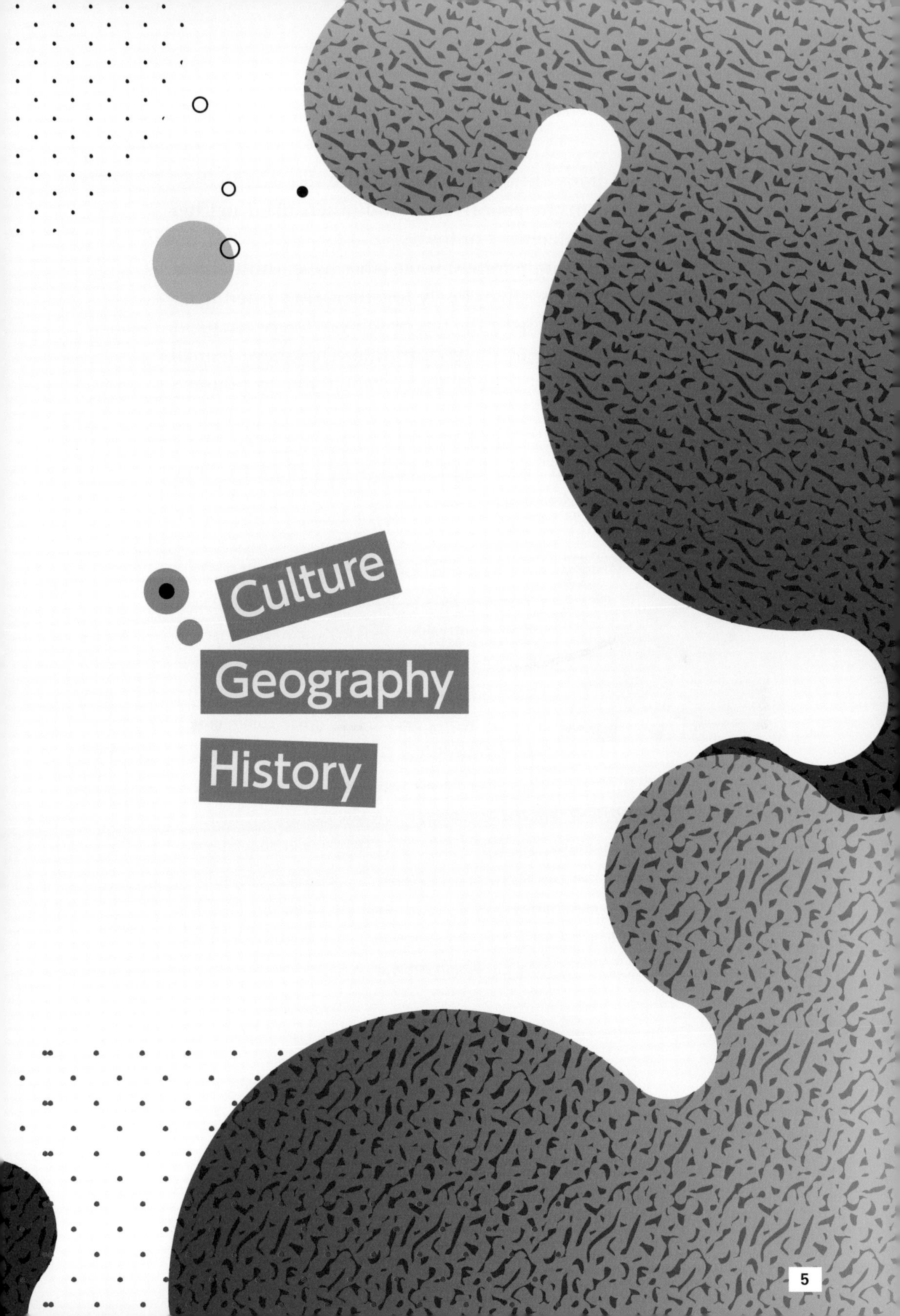
Culture
Geography
History

01 Kinds of Communities 社區的種類

People live / in many different places. **Some** like / big cities. **Others** like / living / in the countryside. And others like / **neither** place. They **prefer** / small cities / or towns.

Big cities / are **urban** communities. Some cities have / **millions of** people. People in big cities / live closely together. They often live / in apartments. They **might** use / the bus or subway / very often.

Rural communities / are in the countryside. They have / small **populations**. Farmers live / in rural areas. People live in houses / and often drive cars.

Suburban communities / are small cities / near big ones. Many families live / there. But they might work / in a big city. They might drive / or take buses and subways.

單字提示
- 藉由文中重點單字畫記，理解字彙如何運用

課文斷句
- 透過分離基本句型，迅速讀懂英文
- 反覆聽音檔，練習把課文大聲唸出來

人們住在許多不同的地方 **different places**。有些人喜歡大城市 **big city**，有些人喜歡住在鄉間 **countryside**，還有些人這兩個地方都不喜歡，他們偏好 **prefer** 小城市 **small city** 或市鎮 **town** 居住。

大城市就是都市社區 **urban community**，有些城市的市民高達數百萬 **millions of people**。生活在大城市的市民居住空間擁擠 **live closely together**，他們通常住在公寓 **apartment**，經常搭乘公車或地鐵 **bus or subway**。

鄉村社區 **rural community** 位於鄉間，那裡的人口較少 **small populations**。農夫們都住在鄉村 **rural area**。當地人住在平房 **house** 裡，通常都是自己開車。

近郊社區 **suburban community** 是鄰近大城市 **near big cities** 的小型城市。有很多家庭 **many families** 住在郊區，但是卻在大城市工作。居民也許是自己開車 **drive**，或是搭乘公車和地鐵 **take buses and subways**。

中文翻譯與重要字彙片語中英對照

Words to Know

- **some . . ., others . . .** 有些人……，有些人則……
- **neither** 兩者皆非
- **prefer** 偏好
- **urban** 城市的
- **millions of . . .** 數百萬的……
- **might** 可能
- **rural** 鄉下的
- **population** 人口
- **suburban** 郊區的

單字學習

02 Different Customs and Cultures 不同的風俗與文化

Every country has / **its own** customs and traditions. A custom is / a special way / of doing something. A **tradition** is / a custom / that **is passed down** / **over time**. These customs and traditions / make different cultures / in different countries. We should know / about other people's customs and cultures. And we should always respect / them.

For example, / in America, / people wear their shoes / in their homes. But / in some Asian countries / like Japan and Korea, / people **take off** their shoes / before going inside their homes. In many Asian countries, / people use **chopsticks** / **while** Americans and Europeans / eat / with forks and **knives**. But / in India and some other countries, / people often eat / with their hands. There are / many other **differences**. But all of these cultures / are special. We should try / to know and learn / about them.

每個國家都有自己的習俗 **customs** 和傳統 **traditions**。習俗是一種特定的行事方法 **a special way of doing something**，傳統則是隨著時間傳遞下來的 **be passed down over time** 習俗。這些習俗和傳統在不同的國家中形成了不同的文化 **make different cultures**。我們應該認識其他人的習俗和文化，並且應該永遠尊重它們 **should always respect them**。

舉例來說 **for example**，在美國 **in America**，人們在家會穿鞋子 **wear their shoes in homes**，但在日本和韓國等亞洲國家 **in some Asian countries**，人們進入住家前會先脫鞋 **take off their shoes**。還有，在許多亞洲國家 **in many Asian countries**，人們使用筷子 **use chopsticks** 吃東西，美國人和歐洲人 **Americans and Europeans** 用餐時則使用刀叉 **with forks and knives**，但在印度和一些其他國家，人們用手 **with their hands** 進食。還有許多其他差異 **many other differences**，然而所有的文化都是獨特的，我們應該試著去了解和學習 **know and learn**。

Words to Know

- **custom** 風俗習慣
- **culture** 文化
- **one's own** 自己的
- **tradition** 傳統
- **be passed down** 被傳遞下來
- **over time** 隨著時間
- **for example** 舉例來說
- **take off** 脫掉（衣物）
- **chopsticks** 筷子
- **while** 而（對照語氣）
- **knife** 刀子
- **difference** 差異性

03 The Story of Israel 以色列的故事

In the past / in the Middle East, / there were / many different **religions**. People often prayed / to many gods. There were / mountain gods. There were / gods of rivers, lakes, /and seas. There were / all kinds of gods. However, / one religion began / that **worshipped** only one god.

There was a man / named Abram. He **was said to** be / a **descendant** / of both Noah and Adam. He lived in a land / called Canaan. There, / the god **Yahweh / made a covenant** / with Abram. Yahweh **promised** Abram / many descendants / and said / that the land he was living on / would forever be theirs. **In return**, / Abram had to worship / only Yahweh. Abram agreed. His name changed to Abraham, / which means / "father of many nations."

Abraham's descendants / through his son Isaac / became **the Israelites**. Isaac and his wife Rebecca / later had twins: / Jacob and Esau. Jacob's descendants founded / the twelve **tribes** of the Israelites. They made the city Jerusalem / the center of their **political power**. **For a time**, / they were **powerful**. Later, / they were made slaves / and taken to Egypt. And then / many years later, / Moses freed the Israelites / and returned them / to their land.

中東 **in the Middle East** 以前有許多不同的宗教 **many different religions**，人們常向許多神祇祈求，有山神、河神、湖神與海神，各種神 **all kinds of gods** 都有。然而，有一個宗教開始只崇拜單一神祇 **only one god**。

有一位叫做亞伯蘭 **Abram** 的男子，據說他是諾亞與亞當 **Noah and Adam** 的後裔 **descendant**。他住在一處稱做迦南的地方 **land called Canaan**，神明耶和華 **the god Yahweh** 在那裡和亞伯蘭立下約定 **make a covenant**。耶和華承諾給他很多後代子孫，並表示要將他現居之處永遠贈與他們，代價就是亞伯蘭只能崇拜 **worship** 耶和華。亞伯蘭答應了，並將名字改成了亞伯拉罕 **changed to Abraham**，意思就是「諸國之父」**father of many nations**。

亞伯拉罕的後裔，從他的兒子以撒開始 **through his son Isaac** 都成了以色列人 **the Israelites**。以撒與他的妻子利百加 **Rebecca** 不久後生下一對雙胞胎 **twins**，取名為雅各與以掃 **Jacob and Esau**。雅各的子孫創立了以色列的 12 支派 **twelve tribes**，將城市耶路撒冷 **the city Jerusalem** 變成政治權力的中心。他們強盛了一段時期，後來成為奴隸 **slaves** 被帶往埃及 **be taken to Egypt**。在很多年之後，摩西 **Moses** 解放了以色列人 **free the Israelites**，並讓他們重回他們的土地。

Words to Know

- **religion** 宗教
- **worship** 信奉；崇拜
- **be said to** 據說；傳說
- **descendant** 後代子孫
- **Yahweh** 耶和華
- **make a covenant** 訂立契約
- **promise** 承諾；應允
- **in return** 回報
- **the Israelites** 以色列人
- **tribe** 部落；種族
- **political power** 政治權力
- **for a time** 一度；暫時
- **powerful** 強大的

04 Money Management 金錢管理

When people work, / they **get paid**. This money is called / **earnings**. With their earnings, / they can do two things: / spend / or save their money. Most people do / a **combination** of these two.

First, / they have to / spend their money / on many things. They have to pay / for their home. They have to pay / for food and clothes. And they have to pay / for **insurance**, / **transportation**, / and even **entertainment costs**. Usually, / there is some money / left over. People often save / this money. They might put it / in the bank. Or they might **invest** / in the **stock market**.

Unfortunately, / some people spend / too much money. They spend more / than they earn. So they **go into debt**. Debt is a big problem / for many people.

People can plan / to buy something / if they **budget** / their **income**, **spending**, and savings. A budget helps people / to **manage** money / and to save it.

人們工作 work 所得到的報酬 get paid 稱為收入 earnings。有了收入，人們就可以進行消費和儲蓄 spend or save 這兩件事。大部分的人會將兩者互相搭配。

首先，他們必須將錢花費 spend money 在許多事情上，像是房子 pay for home、食物 food、衣服 clothes、保險、交通費甚至是娛樂開銷等方面。通常在這些花費外，還會有一些錢剩下來 some money left over。人們通常會把這些錢存在銀行 put it in the bank 或是投資股票市場 invest in the stock market。

遺憾的是，有些人開銷太大 spend too much money，他們入不敷出，因而開始欠債 go into debt。債務對許多人來說是個很大的問題。

其實，人們可以透過計畫性的購物來妥善安排他們的收入 income、開銷 spending 以及儲蓄 savings。預算 budget 幫助人們管理金錢 manage money 並進行儲蓄。

Words to Know

- **get paid** 得到報酬
- **earnings** 收入；工資
- **combination** 結合；聯合
- **insurance** 保險
- **transportation** 交通運輸
- **entertainment** 娛樂
- **cost** 花費
- **invest** 投資
- **stock market** 股票市場
- **go into debt** 負債
- **budget** 編列預算；按照預算來計畫
- **income** 收入
- **spending** 花費；費用
- **manage** 管理；控制

05 Basic Economics 基礎經濟學

In **free-market economies**, / companies decide / what and how much of a **product** / they will produce. However, / they **are interested in** / **making profits**. So they do not want to produce / too much or too little / of a product. They want to produce exactly / the right **amount necessary**. So they often **pay attention to** / the law of **supply** and **demand**.

This law states / that when the supply of a product / is low / yet demand is high, / then the price will be high. However, / if the supply of a product / is high / yet demand is low, / then the price will be low. Companies want to find / a **median**. They want / just the right amount of supply / and just the right amount of demand.

But, / there are often / other **factors** / that companies must **consider**. Once / they make something, / they must deliver it / to the market. This way, / people can **purchase** / the product. This is called / **distribution**. Distribution is often done / by trucks, trains, ships, and airplanes. Without an **effective** distribution system, / even in-demand products / will not sell well.

Once / products are / at the market, / they must **be consumed**. This means / that people purchase them. The amount of **consumption** / depends on many things. It **depends on** / the supply and demand, / of course. And the price is / also another important factor.

在自由市場經濟 **free-market economy** 中，由公司來決定生產的產品與數量，然而，他們在乎的是獲利 **make profits**，便不願生產過多或過少，只想生產剛好需要的數量 **produce exactly the right amount necessary**。因此，他們通常會留意供需法則 **the law of supply and demand**。

該法則說明了當產品供不應求時，價格則會上漲。若是供過於求的話，價格則會下跌。公司多想取中間值 **find a median**，他們希望供給量剛好 **the right amount of supply**，需求量也剛好 **the right amount of demand**。

不過公司需要考慮進去的還有其他因素 **other factors**。一旦產品生產，他們就要送到市場上 **deliver to the market**，民眾才能購買產品，這就稱為物流 **distribution**，多以貨車、火車、船隻與飛機 **by trucks, trains, ships, and airplanes** 來運輸。若無有效的物流系統，即使是受歡迎的產品 **in-demand product** 都會銷售不佳。

產品一旦上市，就必須被消費 **consumed**，也就是讓民眾買走。購買的數量取決於許多事，如供給與需求 **the supply and demand**，價格 **price** 也是另一個重要的因素。

Words to Know

- **free-market economy** 自由市場經濟體制 • **product** 產品 • **be interested in** 對……感興趣
- **make a profit** 創造利潤 • **amount** 數量 • **necessary** 必要的；必需的
- **pay attention to** 注意；留意 • **supply** 供應 • **demand** 需求 • **median** 中間值
- **factor** 因素 • **consider** 考量 • **purchase** 購買 • **distribution** 分發；分配
- **effective** 有效率的 • **be consumed** 被消耗；被消費 • **consumption** 消費
- **depend on** 視情況而定

06 The Three Branches of Government 政府的三大部門

The government / is made up of / three branches. They are / the **executive, legislative**, and **judicial** branches. These three branches of the government / make and **enforce** laws. All three of them / have their own **duties** / and **responsibilities.**

The legislative branch / is Congress. Congress **proposes** bills / and **discusses** them. Then Congress votes / on the bills. If the bills pass / and the president signs them, / then they become laws.

After a law has been passed, / it must **be carried out**, / or enforced. The executive branch / enforces laws. The executive branch / is the president / and everyone / who works for him.

The judicial branch / is the **court system**. The judicial branch **determines** / if laws have been broken. When people break the law, / the judicial branch takes care of / their cases.

政府分為三個部門 **three branches**：行政部門 **executive branch**、立法部門 **legislative branch** 以及司法部門 **judicial branch**。這三個部門負責法律的制訂及執行 **make and enforce laws**，它們有各自的權責 **duty and responsibility**。

立法部門為國會，負責提議 **propose**、討論 **discuss** 並表決法案 **vote on the bills**，法案一旦通過並經總統簽署，就正式成為法律 **become laws**。

法律通過後會被執行，行政部門負責執行法律 **enforce laws**，行政部門是指總統以及其屬下。

司法部門為法院系統 **court system**，負責裁決 **determine** 違法與否 **if laws have been broken**，當人們違反法律，司法部門就會處理他們的案件。

Words to Know

- **branch** 部門
- **executive** 行政的
- **legislative** 立法的
- **judicial** 司法的
- **enforce** 實施；執行
- **duty** 職務；職責
- **responsibility** 責任
- **propose** 建議；提出
- **discuss** 討論
- **be carried out** 被執行
- **court system** 法院系統
- **determine** 判決；裁定

The American Presidential Election System
美國總統選舉制度

In the United States, / there are / many **political parties**. But two are very powerful. They are / the **Republican** Party / and the **Democratic** Party. About two years / before the **presidential election**, / members of both parties / start running for president. They want to be / their party's presidential **nominee**. They **raise money** / and travel around the country / giving speeches.

Every four years, / the U.S. elects a president. In an election year, / every state has / either a **primary** / or a **caucus**. This is / where they elect **delegates**. The **candidates** want to get / **as** many delegates **as possible**. New Hampshire has / the first primary / in the country. Iowa has / the first caucus. As the states hold / their primaries and caucuses, / unpopular **politicians** / **drop out** of the race. When one candidate has / enough delegates, / he or she becomes / the party's nominee. In July or August, / both parties have **conventions**. They **officially nominate** / their presidential and **vice** presidential candidates / there. Then, / the race for president / really begins. The candidates for both parties / visit many states. They give speeches. They try to win voters. On the first Tuesday / in November, / the American voters decide / who the next president will be.

美國有許多政黨 **political party**，其中勢力最大的兩黨是共和黨 **the Republican Party** 與民主黨 **the Democratic Party**。總統大選 **presidential election** 的前兩年左右，兩黨的黨員開始競選總統 **run for president**，他們想獲得黨的提名成為總統候選人 **presidential nominee**。這些人會進行募款 **raise money**，並到全國各地演講 **give speeches**。

美國每四年選一次總統。在選舉年 **election year** 的時候，各州會舉行初選或是黨代表大會 **primary or caucus**，這時他們也會選出黨代表 **elect delegates**，而候選人則希望盡量爭取黨代表的支持。新罕布夏州是全美國第一個進行初選的州，愛荷華州則是第一個召開黨代表大會的州。各州進行初選或黨代表大會期間，支持度低的從政者 **unpopular politicians** 會退選 **drop out of the race**。一旦某位候選人得到足夠的黨代表支持，就能獲得提名代表黨參選總統 **the party's nominee**。到了七月或八月，兩黨召開大會，正式提名正副總統的候選人。接著，總統選戰 **the race for president** 正式展開。兩黨的參選人造訪各州、進行演講，努力贏得選民支持 **try to win voters**。十一月的第一個星期二，美國選民會決定誰將成為下一屆的總統 **the next president**。

Words to Know

- **political party** 政黨 · **republican** 共和主義的 · **democratic** 民主主義的
- **presidential** 總統的 · **election** 選舉 · **nominee** 被提名人 · **raise money** 募款
- **primary** 初選 · **caucus** 黨代表大會 · **delegate** 會議代表 · **candidate** 候選人
- **as . . . as possible** 盡可能地…… · **politician** 政治家；政客 · **drop out** 脫離
- **convention** 大會；會議 · **officially** 正式地 · **nominate** 提名 · **vice** 副的

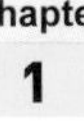

08 A Nation of Immigration 移民之國

In 1789, / the United States / became a country. It was a huge land. And the country **expanded** / and got bigger. But, / at that time, / few people lived / in the U.S. The country needed **immigrants**. So, / during the nineteenth **century**, / **millions of** people / moved to the U.S.

The first **Europeans** / to come to America / were English, **Dutch**, **Spanish**, and **French**. Then, / between 1870 and 1924, / they also came / from **Ireland**, **Germany**, Italy, **Russia**, and other countries. Millions of them / came to America. These immigrants / worked hard. But / they often made / little money. Yet / they slowly **improved** / their lives. And they helped the U.S. / become a great and powerful country.

1789 年，美利堅合眾國成為了一個國家 **become a country**。它的國土廣闊，而且國家規模擴張後變得更為龐大 **expand and get bigger**。但是在當時，很少人居住在美國。美國需要移民 **need immigrants**，因此在 19 世紀時，上百萬民眾 **millions of people** 遷徙至美國 **move to the U.S.**。

來到美國的第一批歐洲人 **the first Europeans** 有英國人 **English**、荷蘭人 **Dutch**、西班牙人 **Spanish** 和法國人 **French**。接著在 1870 年到 1924 年之間，還有來自愛爾蘭 **Ireland**、德國 **Germany**、義大利 **Italy**、俄羅斯 **Russia** 和別國 **other countries** 的人民，共有數百萬的人來到了美國。這些移民工作勤奮 **work hard**，但通常錢賺得卻很少 **make little money**。不過漸漸地，他們的生活獲得了改善 **slowly improve their lives**。而他們也幫助美國成為了一個非凡又強大的國家。

Words to Know

- **immigration** 移民
- **expand** 擴大；擴展
- **immigrant** 移民
- **century** 世紀
- **millions of** 上百萬的
- **European** 歐洲人
- **Dutch** 荷蘭人
- **Spanish** 西班牙人
- **French** 法國人
- **Ireland** 愛爾蘭
- **Germany** 德國
- **Russia** 俄羅斯
- **improve** 改善；加強

09 Kinds of Resources 資源的種類

There are / many kinds of resources / on the earth. Four of them / are very important. They are / **renewable**, nonrenewable, human, and **capital** resources.

Renewable resources / can be used / again and again. They can **be replaced** / within a short time. Some energy resources / are renewable. The energy / from the sun, **tides**, water, and wind / is renewable. Also, / trees and animals / are renewable. But humans still need to / take good care of them. We should not waste them / at all.

Nonrenewable resources / **are limited** / in supply. **Once** we use them, / they **disappear** forever. They can't be replaced. Many energy resources / are like this. **Coal**, gas, and oil / are all nonrenewable.

Human resources / are people and the skills / they have. This also **includes** / the **knowledge** and information / that humans have.

People make products / using renewable and nonrenewable resources. Machines are often used / to **produce** goods. The machines and **tools** / that are used to produce goods / are called capital resources.

地球上有許多種不同的資源 **many kinds of resources**，其中有四種非常重要，它們是可再生資源 **renewable resources**、不可再生資源 **nonrenewable resources**、人力資源 **human resources** 以及資本資源 **capital resources**。

可再生資源可以重複利用 **use again and again**，並且可以在短時間之內更新 **can be replaced**。有些能源資源 **some energy resources** 屬於可再生資源，像是太陽能、潮汐能、水力以及風力。此外，樹木與動物 **trees and animals** 也屬於可再生資源。然而，人們依舊要加以小心愛護 **take good care of them**，不可隨意浪費。

不可再生資源的供應有限 **limited in supply**，一旦使用了，它們便會永久消失。它們無法更新 **can't be replaced**。許多能源資源都屬此類，煤、天然氣以及石油 **coal, gas, and oil** 都不可再生 **nonrenewable**。

人力資源是指人以及他們所具備的技能 **people and skills they have**，這當中也包含了人所擁有的知識與資訊 **knowledge and information**。

人們使用可再生與不可再生資源來製造產品，機器亦被用來生產商品。用來生產商品的機器與工具 **machine and tools** 稱作資本資源。

Words to Know

- **resources** 資源 • **renewable** 可再生的 • **capital** 資本 • **be replaced** 被更換；被替代
- **tide** 潮汐 • **be limited** 有限的 • **once** 一旦 • **disappear** 消失 • **coal** 煤 • **include** 包括
- **knowledge** 知識 • **produce** 製造 • **tool** 工具

10 Extreme Weather Conditions 極端的天氣狀況

Many people live / in areas / with four seasons. It's hot in summer / and cold in winter. The weather / in spring and fall / is either warm / or cool. These are / very normal weather conditions. But sometimes / there are / extreme weather conditions. These can **cause** / many problems / for people.

Sometimes, / it might not rain / somewhere / for a long time. Lakes, rivers, and **streams** / have less water / in them. Trees and **grasses** / die. People and animals / become very thirsty. This is called / a **drought**.

Other times, / it rains **constantly** / for many days. **Water levels** / become much higher / than normal. Water often goes / on the ground / and even onto city streets. These are called / **floods**.

In many warm places / near the water, / there are **tropical storms**. These storms / **drop** heavy rains / and have very strong winds. Tropical storms / can drop / several inches of rain / in a few hours. Some places might get / two or three tropical storms / every year.

很多人住在有四季 **four seasons** 變化的地區，通常夏天炎熱，冬天寒冷，春天和秋天的天氣非暖即涼。這些都是非常正常的天氣狀況 **normal weather condition**，但有時候也會有極端的天氣狀況 **extreme weather condition** 發生，這通常給人們帶來許多麻煩 **cause many problems**。

有時候，某個地方可能有好長一段時間沒降雨 **not rain**，湖泊、河川以及溪流的水量減少 **have less water**，草木枯死，人們和動物感到口渴難耐 **become very thirsty**，這就是所謂的乾旱 **drought**。

有時候，雨可能會持續下 **rain constantly** 很多天，水位 **water level** 也會高出 **become much higher** 正常值。此時水常常會流至平地，甚至淹到市區街道，這就是所謂的水災 **floods**。

許多溫暖近海的地區會有熱帶風暴 **tropical storm**，這些暴風雨會挾帶豪雨 **drop heavy rains** 狂風 **have very strong winds**。熱帶風暴能在幾小時內降下數英寸高的雨量。有些地方每年 **every year** 都可能會有兩到三個的熱帶風暴。

Words to Know

- **extreme** 極端的；激烈的
- **weather condition** 天氣狀況
- **cause** 造成
- **stream** 小河；溪流
- **grass** 草地；牧地
- **drought** 旱災
- **constantly** 不斷地；持續地
- **water level** 水平面；地下水位
- **flood** 洪水；水災
- **tropical storm** 熱帶風暴
- **drop** 落下；滴下

Understanding Hemispheres 了解兩大半球

Earth is a big **planet**. But we can make it smaller / by **dividing** it / into sections. We call these sections / hemispheres. One hemisphere / is half of the earth.

There is / an **imaginary** line / that runs from **east** to **west** / all around the earth. It is / **in the center of** the earth. We call it / **the equator**. The equator divides / the **Northern** Hemisphere / from the **Southern** Hemisphere. The Northern Hemisphere / includes / Asia and Europe. North America / is also in it. **Below** the equator / is the Southern Hemisphere. Australia and Antarctica / are in it. So are / most of South America and Africa.

We can also divide Earth / into the Eastern and Western hemispheres. The line / that does this / is **the prime meridian**. It runs / from north to south. It **goes directly** / **through** Greenwich, England. The Eastern Hemisphere / includes / Europe, Africa, and Asia. The Western Hemisphere / includes / North and South America.

地球是一個大行星 **big planet**，但我們可以將它分成較小的區塊 **section**，這些區塊稱為半球 **hemisphere**。每一個半球都是地球的二分之一 **half of the earth**。

有一條假想線 **imaginary line** 貫穿地球的東西之間 **from east to west**，它位於地球的中心，我們稱之為赤道 **the equator**。赤道將地球分為北半球 **the Northern Hemisphere** 以及南半球 **the Southern Hemisphere**，北半球包含了亞洲、歐洲以及北美洲；赤道以下的區塊稱為南半球，它包含了澳洲、南極洲以及大部分的南美洲和非洲。

我們也可以將地球分為東半球 **the Eastern Hemisphere** 和西半球 **the Western Hemisphere**，區分東西兩半球的稱為本初子午線 **the prime meridian**，這條線由北向南 **from north to south** 延伸，剛好通過英國的格林威治 **go directly through Greenwich, England**。東半球包含歐洲、非洲以及亞洲；西半球包含北美洲和南美洲。

Words to Know

- **hemisphere** 半球
- **planet** 行星
- **divide** 劃分
- **imaginary** 想像的；虛擬的
- **east** 東方
- **west** 西方
- **in the center of** 在……的中心
- **the equator** 赤道
- **northern** 北方的
- **southern** 南方的
- **below** 在……下方
- **the prime meridian** 本初子午線
- **go through** 通過
- **directly** 直接地

12 The Earth's Climate Zones 地球的氣候區

There are / three main climate zones / on the earth. They are / the **tropical**, **temperate**, and **polar** climate zones.

The tropical zones / are found / near the equator. **Basically**, / they are found / between **the Tropic of Cancer** / and **the Tropic of Capricorn. In general**, / the tropical zone / has hot weather / most of the year. Many areas / in the tropical zone / have very wet weather, / but **this is not** always **the case**.

The temperate zones / are the largest / of the three main climate zones. One temperate zone / lies / between the Tropic of Cancer / and **the Arctic Circle**. The other temperate zone / lies / between the Tropic of Capricorn / and **the Antarctic Circle**. Most of the world's **population** / lives / in temperate zones. Temperate zones / are neither too hot / nor too cold. They **experience** / changing seasons / all year long. **For the most part**, / the weather is / not too extreme / in these places.

The polar zones / are found / north of the Arctic Circle / and south of the Antarctic Circle. The weather / in these places / is constantly cold. Few people live / in these places. Few animals live / in them / **as well**.

地球上總共有三大氣候區 **three main climate zones**，分別是熱帶地區 **tropical zone**、溫帶地區 **temperate zone** 與寒帶地區 **polar zone**。

熱帶氣候區位於赤道附近 **near the equator**，基本上，就在北回歸線 **the Tropic of Cancer** 與南回歸線 **the Tropic of Capricorn** 之間。熱帶氣候區大致上全年氣候炎熱 **hot weather**，熱帶氣候區中的許多地方氣候潮濕 **very wet weather**，但又不全然是如此。

溫帶氣候區則是三大氣候區中最大的 **the largest** 區域。其中一個溫帶氣候區位於北回歸線與北極圈 **the Arctic Circle** 之間，另一個則在南回歸線與南極圈 **the Antarctic Circle** 之間。全球多數人口居住於溫帶氣候區。溫帶氣候區既不過於炎熱也不過於寒冷，終年都能感受四季的變化 **changing seasons**。這些區域的天氣通常不會太過極端。

寒帶氣候區則位於北極圈與南極圈。這些地區的天氣終年酷寒，鮮少有人與動物居住 **few people live** 在此地。

Words to Know

- **climate zone** 氣候帶；氣候區
- **tropical** 熱帶的
- **temperate** 溫帶的
- **polar** 極地的
- **basically** 基本上
- **the Tropic of Cancer** 北回歸線
- **the Tropic of Capricorn** 南回歸線
- **in general** 一般地
- **this is not the case** 這不是實際情況
- **the Arctic Circle** 北極圈
- **the Antarctic Circle** 南極圈
- **population** 人口
- **experience** 經驗；體驗
- **for the most part** 大多數情況下
- **as well** 同樣地；也

13 Climbing Mount Everest 攀登聖母峰

Mount Everest / is in the Himalaya Mountains. It is located / near the **border** / of Nepal, Tibet, and China. At 8,848 meters high, / it is the highest mountain / in the world. People call it / "The Top of the World."

For years, / people wanted to be / the first / to climb the mountain. But no one could / get to the top. Many people tried, / but none of them / succeeded. Some of them / even died.

But, / in 1953, / **at last** / two men were **successful**. They were / Sir Edmund Hillary and Tenzing Norgay. Hillary was from New Zealand. Norgay was a **Sherpa**. Sherpas are / **expert** mountain climbers / from Tibet and Nepal. They **are** often **employed** / as **guides** / for **mountaineering expeditions** / in the Himalayas, / **particularly** Mt. Everest. There were nine people / on the team. They also had / hundreds of **porters** / and twenty Sherpas. It took them / several days / to get near the top. Some men / came very close. But they couldn't get there. Finally, / on May 29, 1953, / Hillary and Norgay / got to the top of the mountain. They were / the first people / to stand on top of the world!

聖母峰 **Mount Everest** 屬喜馬拉雅山脈群 **in the Himalaya Mountains**，位於尼泊爾、西藏和中國的邊界。其高 8,848 公尺，是世界上最高的山 **the highest mountain**。人們稱它為「世界之頂」**The Top of the World**。

長久以來，許多人都想成為第一個攀上此山的人，但從沒有人 **no one** 到過山頂 **get to the top**。許多人嘗試攀爬，不但無人成功，更有人喪命於此。

然而就在 1953 年，終於 **at last** 有兩個人成功了。他們是來自紐西蘭的艾德蒙・西拉瑞爵士 **Sir Edmund Hillary** 和雪巴人丹增・諾蓋 **Tenzing Norgay**。雪巴人 **Sherpa** 是來自西藏和尼泊爾的登山專家 **expert mountain climber**，他們常被雇用 **employed** 為前往喜馬拉雅山（特別是聖母峰）登山探險 **mountaineering expeditions** 的嚮導 **guides**。那一個團隊有九個人，他們雇用了數百個搬運工和二十個雪巴人。他們花了數日才接近山頂 **get near the top**。有些人離終點很近 **come very close**，卻無法抵達。最後在 1953 年 5 月 29 號，西拉瑞和諾蓋抵達了山頂。他們是第一批站在世界之頂 **stand on the top of the world** 的人。

Words to Know

- **mount** 山
- **border** 邊境
- **at last** 最後；終於
- **successful** 成功的
- **Sherpa** 雪巴人
- **expert** 熟練的；專業的
- **be employed** 受僱
- **guide** 導遊
- **mountaineering** 登山；爬山
- **expedition** 遠征；探險
- **particularly** 特別是；尤其是
- **porter** 搬運工；腳夫

14

The Midwest Region of the United States
美國的中西部

The American Midwest / covers / an **enormous amount** of land. It starts with / Ohio, Michigan, and Indiana. It goes / as far west as North and South Dakota, Nebraska, and Kansas. There are / a total of twelve states / in the Midwest.

Actually, / the Midwest / is in the east and **central** part / of the country. But, / a long time ago, / the United States was much smaller. The only states / in the country / were beside the Atlantic Ocean. So people called / the lands / west of them / the Midwest.

The land in the Midwest / is almost **completely identical**. It **is full of** / **plains** and **prairies**. The Midwest / is very flat land. There are no mountains / in it. Most hills only **rise** / a few hundred feet high. However, / **the Great Lakes** /are in the Midwest. These are / five huge lakes / located between the U.S. and Canada.

Nowadays, / people in the Midwest / often work / in industry or **agriculture**. In Detroit and other cities, / making **automobiles** / is a huge business. However, / there are also many farmers. They grow / corn, **wheat**, and other **grains**. And they also **raise** / pigs and cows.

美國中西部 **the American Midwest** 涵蓋了廣大的土地 **enormous amount of land**，它自俄亥俄州、密西根州以及印第安納州起，向西遠至南、北達科他州、內布拉斯加州以及堪薩斯州。中西部總共有十二個州 **twelve states**。

事實上 **actually**，中西部地區位於美國東部及中央地帶 **in the east and central part**。但是在很久以前，美國比現在小很多。這個國家僅有的州全部皆臨大西洋岸 **beside the Atlantic Ocean**，所以人們才稱他們的西邊的土地為中西部。

中西部的土地都大致相似 **identical**，充滿了平原和草原 **full of plains and prairies**。中西部的土地都非常平坦 **very flat land**，山地不存在於此區。大部分的山丘 **hills** 只有幾百英尺高而已。然而，五大湖 **the Great Lakes** 位於中西部，是坐落於美國和加拿大之間的五座大湖泊 **five huge lakes**。

現今，居住於中西部的居民通常從事工業或農業 **industry or agriculture**。在底特律及其他城市，汽車製造 **making automobiles** 是一個巨大的工業。然而，那裡也有許多農夫 **many farmers**，他們種植 **grow** 玉米、小麥以及其他穀物 **grains**。同時他們也飼養 **raise** 豬隻和母牛。

Words to Know

- **enormous** 龐大的 • **amount** 數量 • **actually** 實際上 • **central** 中央的
- **completely** 完全地；徹底地 • **identical** 同一的；完全相同的 • **be full of** 充滿
- **plain** 平原 • **prairie** 大草原 • **rise** 高聳；高出 • **the Great Lakes** 五大湖
- **agriculture** 農業 • **automobile** 汽車 • **wheat** 小麥 • **grain** 穀物 • **raise** 養育；飼養

15 Yellowstone National Park 黃石國家公園

One of the most beautiful places / in the U.S. / is Yellowstone National Park. It is located / **mostly** in Wyoming. But parts of it / are in Montana and Idaho, / too.

For many years, / people had heard / about a beautiful land / in the west. But few ever saw it. Then / more people began / visiting the area / in the 1800s. Also, / the **artist** Thomas Moran / visited Yellowstone. He made many beautiful **landscapes** / of the region. This helped Yellowstone / to become the first national park / in 1872.

Many different animals / live in Yellowstone. **Bison**, **wolves**, **elk**, **eagles**, and lots of other animals / live there. Much of the land / is forest. But there are also plains. And there are / even **geysers** / there. Geysers **shoot** hot water / into the air. The most famous geyser / is called Old **Faithful**. It has this name / because it **erupts** / **on a regular schedule** / all the time.

美國最漂亮的地方就是黃石國家公園 **Yellowstone National Park**。它大部分位於 **be located** 懷俄明州，也有少部分位於蒙大拿州和愛達荷州。

多年以來，人們聽聞過西部美麗的土地 **beautiful land**，卻鮮少人真正見識過。在 1800 年代，人們開始造訪此地。此外，藝術家湯瑪斯．莫蘭 **Thomas Moran** 也曾來過黃石。他創作許多此區美景的畫作 **make many beautiful landscapes**，這幫助黃石公園在 1872 年成為第一個國家公園 **the first national park**。

許多不同的動物居住在黃石公園。北美野牛、狼、駝鹿、老鷹以及許多其他動物都生活於此。這裡大部分的土地都是森林 **forest**，但也有些是平原 **plains**，甚至有間歇泉。間歇泉將熱水噴至空氣中，其中最有名的 **the most famous** 間歇泉稱做「老忠實噴泉」。它因噴發時段固定 **erupt on a regular schedule** 而享有此名。

Words to Know

- **mostly** 大多數地；大部分地 • **artist** 藝術家 • **landscape** 風景；景色 • **bison** 北美野牛
- **wolf** 狼 • **elk** 麋鹿 • **eagle** 老鷹 • **geyser** 噴泉 • **shoot** 射出；噴出 • **faithful** 忠實的
- **erupt** 爆發；噴出 • **on a regular schedule** 規律地照行程表行事

16 The West Region of the United States 美國的西部

California is / one of the richest states / in America. It has / **a large amount of** land. And it also has / more people / than any other state. It has / **plenty of** natural resources, / too. But everything is not perfect / there. California has / two **major** problems: / earthquakes and forest fires.

The San Andreas **Fault** / runs through California. Because of it, / the state gets / many earthquakes. Some of them / are very powerful. For example, / there was / a strong earthquake / in San Francisco / in 1906. It **destroyed** / many buildings. And it started / numerous fires. Over 3,000 people / died / after it. There have also been / many other strong earthquakes. Some people **fear** / that the "big one" will hit / someday. They think / an earthquake will cause / a huge amount of **damage**.

During summer and fall, / much of California / is dry. So forest fires, / or **wildfires**, / often start. These fires can **spread** / **rapidly**. They burn / many forests. But they also can burn / people's homes and buildings. They often kill people / before firefighters can / **put** them **out**.

加州 **California** 是美國最富裕的州之一 **one of the richest states**，它擁有大量的土地以及高於其他州的人口，同時蘊藏豐富的天然資源 **natural resources**。然而，並非一切都如此完美。加州有兩個主要的問題 **two major problems**：地震 **earthquake** 以及森林大火 **forest fire**。

聖安德烈斯斷層 **the San Andreas Fault** 貫穿加州 **run through California**，基於此因，加州地震頻繁 **get many earthquakes**。其中有些地震非常強大。舉例來說，1906 年舊金山發生過一次強震，它摧毀了眾多建築物 **destroy many buildings** 並引起許多火災 **start numerous fire**。超過 3,000 人命喪於此次災害。加州還有許多其他的強烈地震，有些人擔憂將來會發生一次「大地震」**the "big one"**，他們相信這會帶來偌大的損害 **cause a huge amount of damage**。

夏秋之際 **during summer and fall**，加州大部分地區都很乾燥。因此，森林大火或是野火 **forest fires, or wildfires** 時常發生。這些火勢蔓延地很快 **spread rapidly**，它們燒光了許多森林 **burn many forests**，也燒毀了人們的家園和建築物 **burn homes and buildings**，它們常在消防隊員撲滅前就帶走許多人的性命 **kill people**。

Words to Know

- **a large amount of** 很多
- **plenty of** 大量的
- **major** 主要的；重要的
- **fault** 斷層
- **destroy** 破壞
- **fear** 害怕；恐懼
- **damage** 損害
- **wildfire** 野火
- **spread** 漫延；擴散
- **rapidly** 快速地
- **put out** 撲滅（火）

17 The *Mayflower* 五月花號

In Britain, / there was / a group of people / called Pilgrims. They were different / from most people there. They had / certain **religious beliefs** / that others did not share. So they wanted to leave Britain / and go to the New World. They **hired** a ship / called the *Mayflower* / to take them to America.

They left in 1620 / and landed in America / after two months of sailing. They **were supposed to** / go to the Hudson River area. But they landed at a place / called Plymouth Rock. It was in modern-day Massachusetts / on Cape Cod. Still, / the Pilgrims decided / to settle there.

The first winter was hard. Many Pilgrims died. But the Native Americans there / **made peace** with them. Their leader was Samoset. He brought Squanto / to stay with the Pilgrims. Squanto and other Native Americans / taught the Pilgrims / how to **farm the land** / **properly**. That year, / the Pilgrims **harvested** / many crops. They had / a big three-day **festival** / with the Native Americans. That was / the first **Thanksgiving**.

Every year, / the Pilgrim colony / became stronger and stronger. More colonists / came from Britain. So the colony / became very successful.

英國 **in Britain** 有一群稱為清教徒 **Pilgrims** 的人，他們與大部分的英國人不同。這些人擁有某種宗教信仰 **have certain religious beliefs** 不被認同，因此他們想離開英國，前往新大陸 **want to go to the New World**。清教徒雇了一艘名為「五月花號」**the Mayflower** 的船，帶他們前往美洲。

清教徒於 1620 年離開，在海上航行兩個月後 **after two months of sailing** 抵達美洲 **land in America**。他們原本的目的地是哈德遜河一帶，卻在普利茅斯岩 **Plymouth Rock** 登陸，位置在現今科德角的麻薩諸塞州。儘管如此，清教徒仍決定定居於此 **settle there**。

第一個冬天相當煎熬，許多清教徒因此喪生。不過當地的印地安人 **the Native American there** 和他們和平相處 **make peace**，印地安首領薩莫塞特 **Samoset** 帶著史廣多 **Squanto** 與清教徒一起生活。史廣多和其他印地安人教導清教徒如何種田 **teach how to farm**。那一年，清教徒的作物豐收 **harvest many crops**，和印地安人舉辦了一場為期三天的盛大宴會 **have a big three-day festival**，這也是第一次的感恩節 **the first Thanksgiving**。

每一年 **every year**，清教徒殖民地 **the Pilgrim colony** 越來越壯大，更多的殖民從英國前來，此處成為非常成功 **become very successful** 的殖民地。

Words to Know

- **religious belief** 宗教信仰
- **hire** 雇用；聘請
- **be supposed to** 應該
- **make peace** 交好
- **farm the land** 耕種
- **properly** 正確地；恰當地
- **harvest** 收穫；收成
- **festival** 慶典
- **Thanksgiving** 感恩節

The Colonies Become Free 殖民地獲得自由

After the first English **settlers** / arrived in Jamestown, / more and more people / moved from Europe / to America. They lived in places / called colonies. As the years passed, / there were 13 colonies.

These colonies were ruled / by the king of England. But many colonies / did not want to / be ruled by England. They wanted to / be free. On July 4, 1776, / many leaders in the colonies / signed / **the Declaration of Independence**. In the declaration, / they wrote / that Americans wanted to / be free / and start their own country. The colonies **fought a war** / with England. The war **lasted** / for many years. George Washington **commanded** / the American soldiers / and **led them** / **to victory**.

After the war, / the colonies became a country. The country was called / the United States of America. Today, / Americans celebrate / **Independence Day** / on July 4.

在第一批英國移民抵達詹姆士鎮後，越來越多人從歐洲前往美國。這些人居住在稱為「殖民地」**colony** 的地方。隨著時間過去，出現了 13 個殖民地 **13 colonies**。

這些殖民地由英國國王統治 **ruled by the King of England**，但是大多數的殖民地不希望受到英國的治理，它們想要的是自由 **want to be free**。1776 年 7 月 4 號，殖民地許多領袖簽訂了獨立宣言 **sign the Declaration of Independence**。獨立宣言的內容表示，美國人民希望獲得自由，建立自己的國家。殖民地與英國開戰 **fight a war with England**，戰爭持續了好幾年。喬治．華盛頓 **George Washington** 指揮美國士兵，帶領他們迎向勝利 **lead them to victory**。

戰爭結束後，殖民地成為了一個國家 **become a country**，就是我們所稱的美利堅合眾國 **the United State of America**。今天美國人在 7 月 4 號 **July 4** 慶祝美國獨立紀念日 **Independence Day**。

Words to Know

- **settler** 殖民者；移居者
- **the Declaration of Independence**《獨立宣言》
- **fight a war** 發動戰爭
- **last** 持續
- **command** 命令；統領
- **lead . . . to** 引導；致使
- **victory** 勝利
- **Independence Day** 美國獨立紀念日

19 The French and Indian War Leads to Revolution

法印戰爭導致革命

In the eighteenth century, / countries in Europe / often fought wars / against each other. They usually fought / in Europe. But sometimes / they fought / in other places. One of these other places / was in America.

In the 1750s and 1760s, / the British and French / fought a war / in North America. Some people called it / the French and Indian War. Others called it / the Seven Years' War. **Basically**, / the British and American colonists / were **on one side**. The French and Native Americans / were **on the other side**.

The British won the war. So the French left / most of North America. They had to give / many of their colonies / to the British. But the war was very expensive / for the British. So King George III of Britain / wanted to **raise taxes** / in the colonies. He said / the British had protected the colonies. So they should / pay higher taxes.

The British passed / many taxes. These included / the Stamp **Act** and the Tea Act. There were many others, / though. The Americans hated the taxes / and thought / they were **unfair**. They called them / the **Intolerable** Acts. **Eventually**, / Britain's actions led to war / in the colonies. The Americans **revolted**. And then / they **gained** their freedom / from Britain. That happened / because of the American Revolution.

18 世紀歐洲各國 **countries in Europe** 之間經常發生戰爭 **often fight wars**，通常在歐洲本土打仗，然而有時候也會在其他地方發動戰爭，美洲就是其中之一。

在 1750 至 1760 年代之間，英國人與法國人 **the British and French** 在北美爆發一場戰爭，有人稱之為「法印戰爭」**the French and Indian War**，有些人則稱其為「七年戰爭」**the Seven Years' War**。基本上，英國和美國殖民地站在同一陣線 **on one side**；法國和印地安人在另一陣線 **on the other side**。

英國獲得勝利，法國因此退出大部分的北美，並讓出許多殖民地給英國。然而對英國而言，戰爭付出的代價非常昂貴 **very expensive**，因此，英國國王喬治三世 **King George III** 想要提高殖民地的賦稅 **raise taxes in the colonies**。他宣稱英國保護殖民地，所以殖民地居民要負擔更高的稅。

英國通過許多稅法，其中包含《印花稅法》**the Stamp Act** 和《茶稅法》**the Tea Act**，其他新增的稅法也不可勝數。美國人憎恨課稅，認為並不公平。他們將新增的稅法稱為「不可容忍法案」**the Intolerable Acts**。最終，英國的種種行為導致了殖民地的戰爭。美國人起義 **the Americans revolt**，並脫離英國獲得自由 **gain freedom**。這也就是美國獨立戰爭的原因。

Words to Know

- **revolution** 革命 • **basically** 在根本上 • **on one side** 在一邊
- **on the other side** 在另一邊 • **raise** 提高；增加 • **tax** 稅捐 • **Act** 法令；法案
- **unfair** 不公平的 • **intolerable** 不能忍受；無法容忍的 • **eventually** 最後；終於
- **revolt** 起義；造反 • **gain** 獲得

The Bill of Rights 權利法案

In 1787, / the states' leaders / started to write / the **Constitution**. The Constitution / is **the supreme law** / of the land. But many Americans / were not happy. They were worried about / the **strength** of the national **government**. They knew / a strong government / could take away their rights. So they wanted to / add some **amendments** / to the Constitution. These would give / **specific** rights / to the people and the states. So they wrote 10 amendments / to the Constitution. Together, / they were called / the Bill of Rights. The Bill of Rights / **was ratified** / in 1791 / and then became law.

The First Amendment / is about freedom. People have / freedom of speech, religion, and **the press** / and the right / to **assemble peacefully**. The Second Amendment / gives people / the right to have guns. The Third Amendment says / the government cannot put soldiers / in people's houses. The Fourth Amendment / protects people / from **illegal searches** and **arrests**. The Fifth Amendment says / a person cannot **be tried** twice / for the same **crime**. The Sixth Amendment / gives people / the right to a **speedy** trial. The Seventh Amendment / gives people / the right to a jury trial. The Eighth Amendment / protects people / from high **bail**. The Ninth and Tenth amendments / protect the people and states / by giving them / all rights / not mentioned in the Constitution.

1787 年，美國的領導者開始起草《美國憲法》**the Constitution**，這是國家的最高法律 **the supreme law**。然而許多美國人民並不開心，因為他們擔心國家政府的力量，他們深知這樣的強權政府會奪走 **take away** 人民的權力。於是他們希望在《美國憲法》中增加修正案 **amendments**，賦予人民和政府特定的權力。他們立下十條憲法修正案 **10 amendments**，統稱為《權利法案》**the Bill of Rights**。《權利法案》於 1791 年生效 **ratified**，正式成為法律 **become law**。

第一條修正案與自由 **freedom** 相關，人民擁有言論、宗教與新聞的自由，以及和平集會 **assemble peacefully** 的權利。第二條修正案允許人民持有武器 **have guns**。第三條修正案聲明政府不得於民房駐軍 **cannot put soldiers in people's houses**。第四條修正案保障人民不受非法搜查與拘捕 **protect from illegal searches and arrests**。第五條修正案說明，任何人不得因同一罪行而受二次審判 **cannot be tried twice for the same crime**。第六條修正案規定人民有權要求迅速審判 **speedy trial**。第七條修正案賦予人民要求陪審團審判 **jury trial** 的權利。第八條修正案禁止過高的保釋金 **protect from high bail**。第九及第十條修正案保障人民及政府行使《美國憲法》中未規定事項的權利 **all rights not mentioned in the Constitution**。

Words to Know

- **the Bill of Rights** 權利法案
- **constitution** 憲法
- **the supreme law** 最高法律
- **strength** 權力；力量
- **government** 政府
- **amendment** 修正案
- **specific** 特定的
- **be ratified** 被批准
- **the press** 報刊；新聞界
- **assemble** 集合；聚集
- **peacefully** 和平地
- **illegal** 非法的
- **search** 搜查
- **arrest** 逮捕
- **be tried** 被審判
- **crime** 罪行；犯罪
- **speedy** 迅速的
- **bail** 保釋金

21 The American Civil War 美國南北戰爭

The Civil War / was the **bloodiest** war / in American history. It was fought / for many reasons. One big reason / was slavery. The South had slaves. The North did not.

The Civil War began / after Abraham Lincoln became president. It started in 1861. The North had / more men. It also had / more **railroads** / and more industries. But the South had / better **generals** / than the North. There were many battles / during the war. At first, / the South seemed to / be winning the war. But, / in 1863, / General Robert E. Lee / lost at Gettysburg. The next day, / the South lost / the Battle of Vicksburg. The North began winning / after that.

Two **Union** generals / were very important. General William T. Sherman / **cut through** the South. His **March** to the Sea / from Atlanta / to the **port** of Savannah / destroyed much of the South's **will** / to fight. General Ulysses S. Grant / led the Union **forces**. He finally defeated the South, / so General Lee **surrendered** to him. Five days later, / John Wilkes Booth / **assassinated** President Lincoln.

南北戰爭 **the Civil War** 是美國史上死傷最慘的戰爭 **the bloodiest war**。戰爭發生的原因有很多，主要原因 **one big reason** 是奴隸 **slavery** 問題。南方 **the South** 有奴隸；北方 **the North** 則沒有。

南北戰爭發生於亞伯拉罕・林肯成為總統後的 1861 年 **start in 1861**。當時北方人力較充足 **more men**，也擁有較多的鐵路 **more railroads** 和工業 **more industries**。但是南方的將領則比北方的出色 **better generals**。這場戰爭有過許多戰役 **many battles**。戰爭之初 **at first**，南軍看似佔有優勢 **seem to be winning**。但是在 1863 年，羅伯特・E・李將軍在蓋茲堡之役中大敗 **lose**。隔天，南軍又敗於維克斯堡之役。在這之後，北軍開始勢如破竹 **the North begins winning after that**。

聯邦軍的兩個將軍 **two Union generals** 非常重要。威廉・T・謝爾曼將軍 **General Sherman** 切斷了南軍 **cut through the South**。他的向海岸行軍計畫 **March to the Sea** 由亞特蘭大向沙凡那港市進軍，摧毀了許多南軍反抗的意志 **will to fight**。尤利賽斯・S・格蘭特將軍 **General Grant** 帶領聯邦的軍隊打敗了南軍。李將軍最後向他投降 **surrender**。五天之後 **five days later**，約翰・威爾克斯・布斯刺殺了林肯總統 **assassinate President Lincoln**。

Words to Know

- **bloody** 血淋淋的；殺戮的 • **railroad** 鐵路 • **general** 將軍 • **Union** 聯盟
- **cut through** 切斷 • **march** 行軍 • **port** 港口 • **will** 意願；決心 • **force** 軍隊
- **surrender** 投降 • **assassinate** 暗殺

The Roaring Twenties and the Great Depression

咆哮的二〇年代和經濟大蕭條

In the 1920s, / the American **economy** / was very strong, / and life was good. World War I / had just ended. So people were interested in / peace, not war. They had jobs / and were making a lot of money. There were / new technologies being created, / and people could afford to / buy them. They began / moving to the suburbs / and living in houses. People had **leisure time**, / so they could go out / and enjoy themselves.

Then, / on October 24, 1929, / the **stock market crashed**. Suddenly, / life changed / for millions of people. Instantly, / people lost / **billions of** dollars / in stock. Companies **went bankrupt**. As they **went out of business**, / millions of people / lost their jobs. The **unemployment rate** / climbed. The president at the time, / Herbert Hoover, / **was blamed for** / the economic problems.

In 1932, / Franklin Roosevelt was elected / the new president / of the United States. Roosevelt had a plan / to end the Great Depression. His plan was called / the New Deal. He **increased** / the **influence** of the government / on the economy. He tried to / have the government / give people jobs. During the 1930s, / life in the U.S. / was very difficult. It was / only when World War II began in 1941 / that the Great Depression ended. Then, / the U.S. economy / began to **recover**.

1920 年代 **in the 1920s** 的美國經濟強盛、生活富足 **life is good**。由於第一次世界大戰才剛結束，人民嚮往和平不要戰爭。他們有工作，能賺大錢，也買得起許多新創的科技產品 **new technologies being created**。人們搬到郊區，住進房子，有了閒暇時間 **have leisure time** 能夠走出戶外享受愜意的生活。

然而 1929 年 10 月 24 日當天股市狂洩 **the stock market crashed**，數百萬人的生活瞬間變調。人們一下子就從股票中損失了數十億 **lose billions of dollars**，企業紛紛破產 **go bankrupt**。公司一倒閉，數百萬人民也頓失工作 **lose jobs**，失業率 **unemployment rate** 隨之攀升。當時的總統赫伯特・胡佛被指責為造成經濟問題的罪魁禍首。

1932 年富蘭克林・羅斯福 **Franklin Roosevelt** 被選為新一屆的美國總統。羅斯福提出一個終止經濟大蕭條 **end the Great Depression** 的政策，稱為「新政」**the New Deal**。他提高了政府在經濟中的影響力，並試圖由政府提供人們就業機會。在 1930 年代期間 **during the 1930s**，美國的生活非常艱苦，這樣的日子直至 1941 年的第二次世界大戰 **World War II** 才終止。不久，美國的經濟開始復甦。

Words to Know

- **roaring** 咆哮的
- **the Great Depression**（美國）經濟大蕭條
- **economy** 經濟
- **leisure time** 休閒時間
- **stock market** 股市
- **crash** 暴跌
- **billions of** 數十億的
- **go bankrupt** 破產
- **go out of business** 停業
- **unemployment rate** 失業率
- **be blamed for** 為……被責備
- **increase** 增加
- **influence** 影響力
- **recover** 恢復

23 What Do Historians Do 歷史學家做些什麼？

Historians study / **the past**. They **are concerned about** / past **events** / and people / who lived in the past. But historians do not just learn / names, dates, and places. Instead, / they try to **interpret** / past events. They want to know / why an event happened. They want to know / why a person acted / in a certain way. And they want to know / how one event caused another to **occur**.

To do this, / historians must study / many **sources**. First, / they use **primary** sources. These are sources / that **were recorded** at the same time / an event occurred. They could be / **journals**. They could be / books. They could be / newspaper **articles** or **photographs**. In modern times, / they could even be / videotaped recordings. Historians use primary sources / to get the opinions / of **eyewitnesses** / to important events. They also use / **secondary** sources. These are works / written by people / who did not witness an event. Good historians use / both primary and secondary sources / in their work.

There are / many kinds of history. Some historians like / **political** history. Others study / **military** history. Some **focus on** economics. And others prefer / social or cultural history. All of them / are important. And all of them help us / understand the past better.

歷史學家 **historian** 研究過去 **study the past**，他們關切過去的事件以及生活在昔日的人們。歷史學家不只是單純得知人名、日期和地點，而是試著詮釋過去的事件 **interpret past events**，了解事情發生的原因以及人的某種行為 **in a certain way** 動機。他們也想知道事件彼此之間的因果關係。

因此，歷史學家必須研究許多資料 **study many sources**。首先，他們必須運用事件發生時所記錄下來的第一手資料 **primary source**，可能是期刊 **journal**、書籍 **book**、報章 **newspaper article** 或照片 **photograph**，現在也有可能是錄影紀錄 **videotaped recording**。歷史學家從原始資料中得知重要事件目擊者 **eyewitnesses** 的觀點。此外，他們也會採用非事件目擊者所記錄的第二手資料 **secondary source**。優秀的歷史學家會在研究過程中同時採用這兩種資料。

歷史分為許多種類 **many kinds of history**，有的歷史學家喜歡政治史 **political history**，有的研究軍事史 **military history**，有人著重於經濟史 **economics**，也有人偏好社會史 **social history** 或文化史 **cultural history**。這些歷史都很重要，它們能幫助我們更加了解過去。

Words to Know

- **historian** 歷史學家 • **the past** 過去 • **be concerned about** 關心 • **event** 事件
- **interpret** 解釋；說明 • **occur** 發生 • **sources** 來源；出處 • **primary** 原始的
- **be recorded** 被記錄 • **journal** 期刊 • **article** 文章 • **photograph** 照片
- **eyewitness** 見證人；目擊者 • **secondary** 次要的；第二的 • **political** 政治的
- **military** 軍事的 • **focus on** 集中於

24 Rome: From Republic to Empire 羅馬：從共和到帝制

According to legend, / the brothers Romulus and Remus / founded Rome / in 753 B.C. Rome grew larger / until around 620 B.C., / when a group of people / called **the Etruscans** / conquered it. The Etruscans ruled Rome / for 111 years. In 509 B.C., / the Roman people **overthrew** / King Tarquin the Proud. They were free / again.

The Romans made / a new kind of government. It was called / a republic. Under the republic, / they elected / a small number of people / to be their leaders. These leaders were called / **patricians. Up to** 300 of them / could be elected / to **the Senate**. For the next 500 years, / Rome remained a republic.

Rome began to / grow more powerful. It soon controlled / all of the Italian **peninsula**. From 264 B.C. to 146 B.C., / it fought **the Punic Wars** / against **Carthage**. The Romans won / and became the masters / of **the Mediterranean** Sea. Soon, / the republic was enormous. But it became **corrupt**. A general—Julius Caesar— / **challenged** the rule of the Senate / and became a **dictator**. Yet he **was murdered** / in 44 B.C., / and the republic was ruled / by three leaders.

Eventually, / those three men / fought each other. Octavian won / and became the first Roman emperor. The republic was gone. Now it was the Roman Empire.

根據傳說，羅繆勒斯與雷摩斯 **Romulus and Remus** 兄弟倆於西元前 753 年建立了羅馬 **found Rome**。羅馬逐漸強盛壯大，直到西元前 620 年伊特拉斯坎人 **the Etruscans** 攻取此國 **conquer Rome**。伊特魯里亞人統治羅馬有 111 年之久。在西元前 509 年時，羅馬人推翻國王驕傲者塔克文 **overthrow King Tarquin**，重獲自由 **free again**。

羅馬人建立一種稱為共和國 **republic** 的新政府。在此種體制之下，他們選出一小群人作為領袖，稱為羅馬貴族 **patrician**，多達 300 人可受選進入元老院 **the Senate**。羅馬共和國體制持續有 500 年之久。

羅馬開始越來越強盛 **grow more powerful**，很快就控制了整個義大利半島。它與迦太基 **against Carthage** 的布匿戰爭從西元前 264 年打到了西元前 146 年，羅馬贏得了勝利 **the Romans win**，成為整個地中海的霸主 **the master of the Mediterranean Sea**。羅馬共和國很快地龐大起來，但也變得腐敗 **corrupt**。一名叫做尤利烏斯・凱薩的將軍挑戰元老院的權威，並成為了一位獨裁者 **become a dictator**，然而他卻在西元前 44 年遭到謀殺 **be murdered**，而共和國則是由三位領袖統治 **be ruled by three leaders**。

最終他們互相鬥爭，屋大維 **Octavian** 贏得勝利，成為首位羅馬皇帝 **become the first Roman emperor**。共和國已不復存在，成為了羅馬帝國 **the Roman Empire**。

Words to Know

- **Republic** 共和政體 • **the Etruscans** 伊特拉斯坎人 • **overthrow** 推翻
- **patrician**（古羅馬）貴族 • **up to** 高達…… • **the Senate**（古羅馬）元老院
- **peninsula** 半島 • **the Punic Wars** 布匿戰爭（羅馬與迦太基間的三次戰爭）
- **Carthage** 迦太基 • **the Mediterranean Sea** 地中海 • **corrupt** 腐敗的；貪污的
- **challenge** 挑戰；質疑 • **dictator** 獨裁者 • **be murdered** 被謀殺

25 The Middle Ages 中世紀

The Roman Empire fell / in 476. It **was conquered** / by **Germanic** invaders. In the east, / there was still / the Byzantine Empire. It was / the eastern part / of the Roman Empire. It **lasted** / for almost 1,000 more years. It was finally defeated / in 1453.

But in Western Europe, / after the fall of the Western Roman Empire, / **the Dark Ages** began. This **term is** / sometimes / **applied to** the first 300 years / after the fall of Rome / and sometimes / to the whole Middle Ages. During this time, / only a few people could / read and write. The people had / hard lives. They often just **struggled** / to **survive**. Most people / farmed the land. Their lives were / very simple / then.

Throughout the Middle Ages, / there were / very slow **improvements** / in people's lives. Some kings / ruled their lands / fairly. Others were very **harsh**. They treated their people / like slaves. And they taxed them / very much. Many people / died of **starvation**. Others died / because of diseases. **The Black Death** killed / almost half of the people / in Europe / in the fourteenth century. The Middle Ages were / a very difficult time / for most people.

羅馬帝國於 476 年 **in 476** 瓦解，它被日耳曼人 **by Germanic invaders** 征服。在東方，拜占庭帝國 **the Byzantine Empire** 仍存在，它就是東羅馬帝國。直至一千多年後，東羅馬帝國才於 1453 年被擊敗 **be defeated**。

然而在西歐，西羅馬帝國瓦解後 **after the fall of the Western Roman Empire**，黑暗時代 **the Dark Ages** 來臨。黑暗時代一詞適用於羅馬帝國瓦解後的前三百年間或是整個中世紀。這段期間，只有少數人 **only a few people** 能夠閱讀和寫字 **read and write**。人們的生活非常艱苦 **have hard lives**，生活僅能糊口 **struggle to survive**。大部分的人以農為業，生活過得非常簡單。

在中世紀期間，人們的生活沒有很大的改善 **very slow improvements**。有些國王公平地對待他的臣民；但有些國王則非常殘酷。這些國王把他們的人民當成奴隸對待，並嚴加課稅。許多人死於飢餓 **die of starvation** 或是疾病 **disease**，黑死病 **the Black Death** 在十四世紀奪走了幾乎歐洲半數人的性命。對大部分的人來說，中世紀是一場苦難 **very difficult time**。

Words to Know

- **the Middle Ages** 中古時期
- **be conquered** 被……征服
- **Germanic** 日耳曼民族的
- **last** 持續
- **the Dark Ages** 黑暗時代
- **term** 名詞
- **be applied to** 指的是
- **struggle** 掙扎
- **survive** 求生
- **throughout** 貫穿；徹底
- **improvement** 改善
- **harsh** 嚴苛
- **starvation** 飢餓
- **the Black Death** 黑死病

Marco Polo and the Silk Road 馬可波羅與絲路

China and Europe / are very far / from each other. Today, / people can fly / between the two / in a few hours. But in the past, / it took months or years / to go / from one place to the other. When people traveled / from China to Europe, / they went / on the Silk Road.

The Silk Road was / not a real road. It was / a large group of **trade routes**. But, / by **following** it, / people could get / from the Mediterranean Sea / to the Pacific Ocean. It was called / the Silk Road / because the Chinese **transported silk** / to the west / on it.

The Silk Road became very famous / because of Marco Polo. He was / an Italian **adventurer**. With his father and uncle, / he left Italy / and returned twenty-five years later / in 1295. He had taken the Silk Road / to China. He had many adventures. He even became an **advisor** / to the emperor. When he came back, / he wrote a book, *The Travels of Marco Polo*, / about his travels / and became very famous.

中國和歐洲相距遙遠。今日，人們只要花幾個小時 **in a few hours** 便可飛抵兩地。然而在過去，兩地往返 **from one place to the other** 需要幾個月或是幾年的時間。當人們由中國前往歐洲 **from China to Europe**，他們會經過絲路 **the Silk Road**。

絲路並非一條真的路 **not a real road**，而是許多貿易路線 **a large group of trade routes** 所組合起來的。經由此道，人們可以由地中海 **from the Mediterranean Sea** 前往太平洋 **to the Pacific Ocean**。這條商道之所以稱做絲路，是因中國人經由此處將絲綢運送 **transport silk** 至西方。

絲路因馬可波羅 **Marco Polo** 而變得非常有名。他是一位義大利的探險家 **Italian adventurer**，和父親及舅舅一起離開義大利，至 25 年後，也就是 1295 年，才返回家鄉。他經由絲路抵達中國 **take the Silk Road to China**，途中經過許多冒險 **have many adventures**，甚至成為皇帝的顧問 **advisor**。當他返回義大利，他寫了一本《馬可波羅遊記》***The Travels of Marco Polo***，這本書是關於他的遊歷，而且此書大受歡迎。

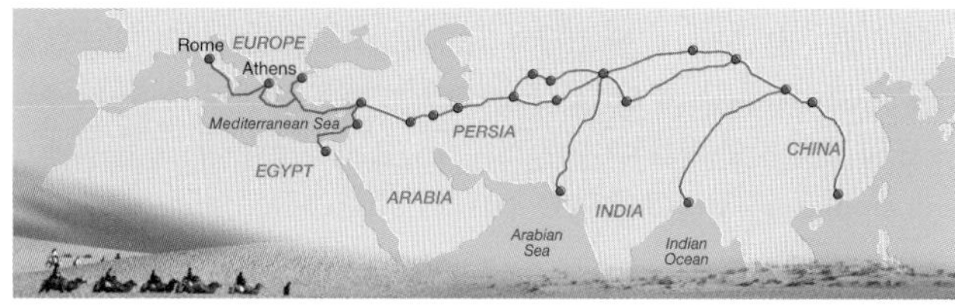

Words to Know

- **the Silk Road** 絲路
- **trade route** 貿易路線
- **follow** 跟隨
- **transport** 運送
- **silk** 絲綢
- **adventurer** 探險家
- **advisor** 顧問；指導者

27 The Age of Exploration 地理大發現

In 1453, / the Ottoman Turks defeated / the Byzantine Empire. They **captured** / its **capital city** Constantinople. Suddenly, / the **land route** / from Europe to Asia / became more dangerous. At that time, / many Europeans **purchased spices** / from China and other Asian countries. But now / they could not get them / from land. So they tried to get / their spices / by sea. This began / the Age of Exploration.

Many Europeans began / sailing south / around Africa. At first, / the Portuguese and Spanish / started sailing south. But then / other Europeans started / to follow them. In 1488, / Bartolomeu Dias became / the first European / to sail to the Cape of Good Hope / in Africa. This was / the **southernmost** point / of Africa. He had **discovered** / the way to India / by water. In 1498, / Vasco da Gama sailed / across the Indian Ocean / and landed in India. He returned to Portugal / in 1499. **By this time**, / the Americas had been discovered. But people did not know / how big the earth was. Finally, in 1519, / Ferdinand Magellan **set sail** / from Spain. He sailed / past the southern part of South America / and into the Pacific Ocean. Magellan was / later / killed / during a fight / with the native people of the Philippines. But, in 1522, / his **crew** returned to Spain. They had sailed / around the world!

1453 年，鄂圖曼土耳其人 **the Ottoman Turks** 擊敗 **defeat** 拜占庭帝國，並攻佔了首都君士坦丁堡。突然間，歐洲通往亞洲的陸路 **land route** 變得更加危險。當時，許多歐洲人會向中國和其他亞洲國家購買香料 **spices**，此時他們無法透過陸路購買，於是開始嘗試走海路 **to get spices by sea**。地理大發現 **the Age of Exploration** 於是展開。

許多歐洲人開始向南繞行非洲 **sail south around Africa**。最初只有葡萄牙和西班牙向南航行，接著其他歐洲人也開始跟隨他們的腳步。在 1488 年，巴爾托洛梅烏 · 迪亞士 **Bartolomeu Dias** 成為第一個航行至非洲最南端好望角 **sail to the Cape of Good Hope** 的歐洲人，他同時也發現了前往印度的水路。1498 年，瓦斯科 · 達伽馬 **Vasco da Gama** 航越印度洋 **sail across the Indian Ocean**，在印度登陸 **land in India**，並於 1499 年返回葡萄牙。此時，美洲已經被發現了。不過人們依舊不了解地球有多大。最後，在 1519 年，斐迪南 · 麥哲倫 **Ferdinand Magellan** 自西班牙啟航，途經南美洲的南端 **past the southern part of South America** 並深入太平洋 **into the Pacific Ocean**，而後他死於與菲律賓原住民的衝突中。然而在 1522 年，他的船員返回西班牙，完成了航行環繞世界 **sail around the world** 的創舉！

Words to Know

- **exploration** 發現；探索
- **capture** 佔領
- **capital city** 首都
- **land route** 陸路
- **purchase** 購買
- **spice** 香料
- **southernmost** 最南端
- **discover** 發現
- **by this time** 在這時
- **set sail** 啟航
- **crew**（飛機，船）機組員

28 The Spread of Islam 伊斯蘭教的傳播

In 632, / **Muhammad** died. He was / the **founder** of Islam. At his death, / there were few **Muslims**. And they had / very little land. But after Muhammad's death, / Islam began to spread / rapidly.

Soon after Muhammad's death, / Muslim leaders selected **caliphs** / to **govern** the Muslim community. During **the reigns / of the first four caliphs** (from 632 to 661), / Islam spread / throughout the Arabian Peninsula. By 661, / Islam conquered land / from Persia in the Near East / to Egypt in Africa. From 661 to 750, / the Umayyad **dynasty** ruled / the Islamic world. They spread Islam / throughout northern Africa. In 711, / an Islamic army / crossed the Mediterranean Sea / and entered Spain. In a few years, / they had captured Spain. The Muslims went north / and entered France. But, in 732, / Charles Martel defeated an Islamic army / near Tours. The Muslim **advance** / to the north / was stopped.

Meanwhile, / the Muslims could not defeat / the Byzantine Empire / in the east. They advanced on Constantinople / several times. But they always lost. Later, / however, / the Ottoman Empire **arose** / in the east. It **challenged** the Byzantines. By the fifteenth century, / the Byzantine Empire was weak. In 1453, / the Ottomans conquered it. They made Constantinople / their capital. From there, / they would rule / a **vast** Islamic empire / until the twentieth century.

伊斯蘭教的創立者 **the founder of Islam** 穆罕默德 **Muhammad** 於 632 年辭世。他去世時，穆斯林 **Muslims** 還很少，也沒有什麼土地。穆罕默德去世後 **after Muhammad's death**，伊斯蘭教開始快速傳播 **Islam spreads rapidly**。

穆罕默德辭世不久後，穆斯林領袖們選出哈里發 **caliph** 來治理伊斯蘭教社會 **govern the Muslim community**。在最初的四位哈里發的統治下（從 632 年到 661 年），伊斯蘭教的傳播普及整個阿拉伯半島 **spread throughout the Arabian Peninsula**。伊斯蘭教在 661 年攻下近東的波斯與非洲的埃及。伍邁葉王朝 **dynasty** 從 661 年 750 年統治整個伊斯蘭世界，將伊斯蘭教傳播至整個北非。一個伊斯蘭教的軍隊在 711 年時越過地中海，進入了西班牙，並在短短幾年內就佔領了西班牙。穆斯林向北走進入了法國，不過鐵鎚查理在 732 年時，於圖爾附近擊潰了伊斯蘭教的軍隊，停止了穆斯林的北征。

此時，穆斯林無法攻下東邊的拜占庭帝國，多次前往君士坦丁堡也總是敗下陣來。然而後來鄂圖曼帝國 **the Ottoman Empire** 從東方崛起，威脅到了拜占庭帝國。到了 15 世紀，拜占庭帝國衰弱不堪，鄂圖曼人於 1453 年征服了他們。他們將君士坦丁堡定為首都 **make Constantinople their capital**，他們在那裡統治著一個龐大的伊斯蘭教帝國 **rule a vast Islamic empire** 到 20 世紀。

Words to Know

- **spread** 普及；傳播 • **Islam** 伊斯蘭教 • **Muhammad** 穆罕默德 • **founder** 創立者
- **Muslim** 伊斯蘭教徒；穆斯林 • **caliph** 哈里發（伊斯蘭教中穆罕默德的繼承者） • **govern** 統治
- **the reigns of the first four caliphs** 前四位哈里發統治期間 • **dynasty** 王朝 • **advance** 前進
- **meanwhile** 同時 • **arise** 崛起 • **challenge** 挑戰 • **vast** 龐大的

29 The Cold War 冷戰

World War II lasted / from 1939 to 1945. When it ended, / another war immediately began. It was / between the United States and the Soviet Union. But this was / a different kind of war. It was called / the Cold War. The U.S. was / for freedom and democracy. The Soviet Union was / for **tyranny** and **communism**. So they battled around the world / in different places.

There were many events / in the Cold War, / but few **involved** / actual fighting. The Berlin **Blockade** of 1948 and 1949 / was one **incident**. So was / the **construction** of the Berlin Wall / in 1961. Of course, / there were some wars. Both the Korean War and the Vietnam War / were a part of the Cold War / since the U.S. and the Soviet Union / **supported opposite sides**. Even the Space Race / in the 1950s and 1960s / was a part of the Cold War. And so was / the **nuclear** race. Both countries had / thousands of nuclear weapons, / but they never used them.

Eventually, / the Cold War ended / in the 1980s. **Thanks to** U.S. President Ronald Reagan, / the Soviet Union began to **collapse**. In 1989, / the Berlin Wall **came down**. The countries of Eastern Europe / started becoming free. And, in 1991, / the Soviet Union ended. The Cold War was over.

第二次世界大戰由 1939 年持續 **last** 到 1945 年，戰爭一結束，另一場戰爭旋即爆發，這是美國與蘇聯之間的另一種型態的戰爭，稱為「冷戰」**the Cold War**。美國 **the U.S.** 擁護自由與民主 **freedom and democracy**，蘇聯 **the Soviet Union** 卻支持暴政與共產主義 **tyranny and communism**，所以他們在世界各地不同的地方較量 **battle**。

冷戰期間發生許多事件，多非涉及真正的戰爭。發生於 1948 年和 1949 年的「柏林封鎖」**the Berlin Blockade** 是其中一個事件，1961 年柏林圍牆 **the Berlin Wall** 的建造也是其一。當然，期間也發生過一些戰爭，像韓戰 **the Korean War** 與越戰 **the Vietnam War** 也屬於冷戰的一部分，因為美蘇兩方各支持一方。甚至連 1950 年代和 1960 年代的太空競賽 **the Space Race** 也屬於冷戰之一，核子競賽 **the nuclear race** 亦是，美蘇雙方皆擁有大量核武 **nuclear weapon**，不過他們從未真正使用。

冷戰最終於 1980 年代結束 **end in the 1980s**，這要歸功於美國總統隆納．雷根，蘇聯開始瓦解 **collapse**。1989 年柏林圍牆倒塌 **come down**，東歐國家開始走向自由 **become free**。接著在 1991 年，蘇聯正式垮臺 **end**，冷戰也隨之告終 **be over**。

Words to Know

- **the Cold War** 冷戰
- **tyranny** 專制
- **communism** 共產主義
- **involve** 牽扯；牽涉
- **blockade** 封鎖
- **incident** 事件
- **construction** 建造
- **support** 支持
- **opposite side** 相反的一方
- **nuclear** 核子
- **thanks to** 幸虧；由於
- **collapse** 瓦解
- **come down** 倒塌

30 Globalization 全球化

In the years / after World War II, / the world greatly changed. Much of this / was **due to** new technology. **For instance**, / the **jet was developed**. This **increased** / the speed / that people could travel. There were also advances / in **telecommunications**. Computers and the Internet / were invented. It became much easier / for people / to **communicate with** others / all around the world. This has **led to** / the **spread** of globalization.

Basically, / the world is becoming / a smaller place. In the past, / what happened in one country / rarely **affected** other countries. Or it took a long time / for any **effects** / to **occur**. But the world is different / today. Because of globalization, / what happens / in one part of the world / can affect places / all around it.

Thanks to globalization, / people can now do business / more easily / with those in other countries. When you go to the supermarket, / you can see various foods / from all of the different countries. This happens / because of globalization. Also, / people are learning more / about other countries / these days. This leads to / more understanding / about other countries. In the age of globalization, / there has not been / a single world war. And the world is becoming richer. Globalization has surely been good / for the world.

第二次世界大戰後，世界大幅地轉變，而此多歸因於新的科技 **new technology**。像是噴射機的研發，增進人民旅行的速度。電信通訊也有所進步 **advance in telecommunications**，電腦與網路的發明，使人與人的聯繫 **to communicate with others** 變得更加簡單，這也促成了全球化的展開 **the spread of globalization**。

基本上，世界越來越小 **become a smaller place**。在過去，一個國家所發生的事很少會影響到 **rarely affected** 其他國家，或是需要很久的時間之後影響才會發酵。不過現在的世界已經不一樣了，拜全球化之賜，一個地方所發生之事能影響它周遭的地區 **affect places around it**。

多虧有全球化 **thanks to globalization**，人們現在能更便利地與其他國家的人做生意 **do business more easily**。當你來到超市，能見到不同國家的各種食品 **see various foods**。這些都是因為全球化，近來人們也得知越來越多有關其他國家的資訊，這讓人們對其他國家有更深入的了解 **learn more about other countries**。在全球化的時代，還沒有發生任何一次世界大戰 **not a single world war**，世界變得更加豐富 **become richer**。全球化對世界當然是有益的 **good for the world**。

Words to Know

- **due to** 起因於 • **for instance** 舉例來說 • **jet** 噴射機 • **be developed** 被開發
- **increase** 增加 • **telecommunications** 電信 • **communicate with** 與……溝通；交談
- **lead to** 導致 • **spread** 普及 • **affect** 對……發生作用 • **effect** 影響 • **occur** 發生

Science

Life Science
Earth Science
Physical Science

31 Organisms 有機體

There are / millions of types of organisms / on the earth. An organism is any creature / that is alive. These include / animals, plants, **fungi**, and **microorganisms**. All organisms / are made of **cells**. Some have / just one cell. Others have / billions and **billions of** them.

Microorganisms / are very, very small. In fact, / you can't even see them / without a **microscope**. **Bacteria** and **protists** / are microorganisms. These are often / one-celled organisms. So everything they need to survive / is in a single cell. How do they **reproduce**? They simply divide themselves / in half. This is called / asexual reproduction.

But most organisms / are **multi-celled**. So they may have / a few cells. Or they could have / **trillions of** them. Multi-celled organisms have / **specialized** cells. These cells often do / one **specific** thing. They could be used / to defend the organism / from disease. They could be used / for reproduction. They could be used / for **digestion**. Or they could be used / for many other purposes.

地球上有數百萬種的有機體 **millions of types of organisms**。有機體是任何活著的生物。他們包含了動物、植物、真菌以及微生物。所有的有機體 **all organisms** 都由細胞組成 **made of cells**。有些有機體只有一個細胞。有些則擁有數不盡的細胞。

微生物 **microorganisms** 非常非常小 **very, very small**。事實上，沒有顯微鏡是無法看到它們的。細菌和原生生物 **bacteria and protists** 都是微生物，通常是單細胞生物 **one-celled organisms**。所以它們要維持的就只是個單一細胞生命。那麼它們要如何繁殖 **reproduce** 呢？它們將自己一分為二 **divide themselves in half**，這稱作無性生殖 **asexual reproduction**。

然而大多數的有機體 **most organisms** 屬於多細胞 **multi-celled** 生物，所以它們可能僅有一些細胞或是擁有無數個細胞。多細胞生物 **multi-celled organisms** 擁有特定的細胞 **have specialized cells**，這些細胞通常會進行專門的工作 **specific thing**，它們可以用來抵禦疾病 **to defend from disease**、繁殖 **for reproduction**、消化 **for digestion** 或是許多其他的用途 **for many other purposes**。

Words to Know

- **fungus** 真菌
- **microorganism** 微生物
- **cell** 細胞
- **billions of** 數十億的
- **microscope** 顯微鏡
- **bacteria** 細菌
- **protist** 單細胞生物；原生生物
- **reproduce** 繁殖
- **multi-celled** 多細胞的
- **trillions of** 無數
- **specialized** 特殊的
- **specific** 特定的
- **digestion** 消化

32 Kingdoms 界

There are / many **organic creatures** / on Earth. Some are / very different from others. But many have / some similarities. So scientists have divided organisms / into five separate kingdoms. These kingdoms are / animals, plants, protists, fungi, and bacteria. All of the creatures / in each kingdom / are similar / in some way.

The animal kingdom / is the biggest. It has / over 800,000 **species**. Most animals are / either **vertebrates** or **invertebrates**. Animals include / mammals, reptiles, birds, amphibians, and insects.

The second largest kingdom / is the plant kingdom. Plants include / trees, **bushes**, flowers, **vines**, and grasses.

The third kingdom / is the protists. They are animals / that have only one cell. They include / **protozoans**, **algae**, and **diatoms**.

The fourth kingdom / is the fungi. Most fungi are **mushrooms**. But there are also / certain **molds**, **yeasts**, and **lichen**, / too.

The final kingdom / is the bacteria. These are / some kinds of bacteria / and various **pathogens**, / such as **viruses**.

地球上有許多有機生物 organic creature，有的彼此之間大不相同，也有許多擁有某些相似性 similarity。因此科學家將有機體分成五個獨立的界 five separate kingdoms，分別為動物界、植物界、原生生物界、真菌界以及細菌界，每個界 each kingdom 的生物都有一定的 in some way 相似性。

最大的是動物界 the animal kingdom，包含了超過八十萬種物種 over 800,000 species，大多數可分為脊椎與無脊椎動物 vertebrates or invertebrates。動物包括哺乳動物、爬行動物、鳥類、兩棲動物以及昆蟲。

第二大的是植物界 the plant kingdom，有喬木、灌木、花卉、藤類以及青草。

第三大的是單細胞 only one cell 的原生生物界 the protists，包含原生動物、水藻和矽藻。

第四大的為真菌界 the fungi，大部分的真菌是菇類 mushrooms，也有一些是黴菌 mold、酵母菌 yeast 和地衣 lichen。

最後是細菌界 the bacteria，包含某些種類的細菌以及病毒 viruses 等各種 various 病原體 pathogens。

Words to Know

- **kingdom** 界 • **organic creature** 有機生物 • **species** 物種 • **vertebrate** 脊椎動物
- **invertebrate** 無脊椎動物 • **bush** 灌木 • **vine** 藤本植物 • **protozoan** 原生動物
- **algae** 水藻 • **diatom** 矽藻 • **mushroom** 菇類 • **mold** 黴菌 • **yeast** 酵母
- **lichen** 地衣 • **pathogen** 病原體 • **virus** 病毒

33 Heredity 遺傳

People often / look very similar / to their parents. They might have / the same face. Or they have / the same color hair or eyes. They might be / tall or short / like their parents. Why do they look / this way? The answer is heredity.

Heredity is / the passing of **traits** / from a parent / to his or her **offspring**. This happens / because of **genes**. Genes contain DNA. DNA is / the basic **building block** of life. Both parents pass on / their genes / to their offspring. So the offspring / may **resemble** / the mother, father, or both.

There are / **dominant** and **recessive** genes. Dominant genes / affect the body / more than recessive genes. Recessive genes **exist** / in a body. But they do not affect it. Dominant genes, / however, / affect the organism. Genes do not just **determine** / an organism's **physical** characteristics. They also determine / the organism's **mental** characteristics. This can include / **intelligence**. And it may even / affect **personality**, / too.

人們通常會與父母長得很像 **look similar to their parents**。他們也許會有相同的面孔、相同的髮色或是眼睛。他們也許會和父母一樣高或一樣矮。為什麼他們會長得如此相似呢？其答案在於遺傳 **heredity**。

遺傳是指由親代傳給後代 **from a parent to offspring** 的特徵 **the passing of traits**，這發生的原因來自於基因，基因內有去氧核糖核酸 **contain DNA**。去氧核糖核酸是生命的基本架構 **the basic building block of life**，父母親雙方傳遞基因給後代，所以後代才會長得像父母親其中一人，或是與父母都很相似。

基因可分為顯性和隱性的，顯性基因 **dominant gene** 帶給身體的影響 **affect the body** 比隱性基因 **recessive gene** 來得大，隱性基因存在於體內 **exist in a body**，卻不會對身體有影響 **do not affect it**。然而顯性基因則會影響生物體。基因不僅僅決定有機體的身體特徵，同時也決定了有機體的心理特徵 **mental characteristic**。這其中也包含了智力 **intelligence**、甚至是性格 **personality**。

Words to Know

- **heredity** 遺傳 • **trait** 特徵 • **offspring** 後代 • **gene** 基因 • **building block** 構成要素
- **resemble** 相像 • **dominant** 顯性的 • **recessive** 隱性的 • **exist** 存在 • **determine** 決定
- **physical** 身體的；生理的 • **mental** 心智上的 • **intelligence** 智力 • **personality** 性格

34 Sexual and Asexual Reproduction 有性生殖與無性生殖

All plants need to reproduce / in order to create / new plants. There are two ways / they can reproduce. The first / is sexual reproduction. The second / is asexual reproduction.

Sexual reproduction involves / a male and female / of the same species. Plants / that reproduce this way / have flowers. Flowers are / where their **reproductive organs** and seeds are. The male reproductive organ / is the **stamen**. It has **pollen** / that needs to be carried / to the female part of the plant. The female part / is the **pistil**. When the pollen **gets transferred**, / the plant has **been pollinated**. This causes seeds / to grow in the flower. Soon, / the seeds **germinate**, / which means / they are growing into young plants.

The second method / is asexual reproduction. In this method, / there is only one parent plant. Asexual reproduction can happen / in many ways. For example, / a new plant may / simply start growing / from an old plant. Other plants reproduce / from **bulbs**. Onions and potatoes / are both bulbs. Parts of these plants / can simply begin / growing roots, / and thus / they become new plants. In the case of asexual reproduction, / there is no pollen, / and there are / no male and female plants. New plants simply grow / from old ones.

所有的植物都需要繁殖來產生新的植物 **create new plants**，它們有兩種繁殖的方式，第一種是有性生殖 **sexual reproduction**，第二種是無性生殖 **asexual reproduction**。

有性生殖需要同種的雄株與雌株 **involve a male and a female**，以這種方式繁殖的植物會開花 **have flowers**，花朵是它們保存生殖器官和種子的地方。雄性生殖器官為雄蕊 **stamen**，上面有需要傳到雌株的花粉。雌性生殖器官為雌蕊 **pistil**，一旦花粉傳送至此 **pollen gets transferred**，植物就完成了授粉 **pollinated**，花朵裡的種子 **seeds** 開始成長。不久後種子會發芽 **germinate**，代表它們即將長成幼小植物 **grow into young plants**。

第二種生殖方式為無性生殖，這種方式只需要一株親代 **one parent plant** 便可完成。無性生殖可分為多種方式，例如，新生植物可以直接從原植物長出 **grow from an old plant**，也有植物靠鱗莖來繁殖 **reproduce from bulbs**，洋蔥和馬鈴薯就屬於鱗莖。這種植物的部分結構可直接生根，變成新植物。無性生殖不需要花粉 **no pollen**，也沒有雄株與雌株之分 **no male and female plants**，新植物直接從原植物中生長。

Words to Know

- **sexual** 有性的
- **asexual** 無性的
- **reproductive organ** 生殖器官
- **stamen** 雄蕊
- **pollen** 花粉
- **pistil** 雌蕊
- **get transferred** 傳送
- **be pollinated** 被授粉
- **germinate** 發芽
- **bulb** 鱗莖

35 Pollination and Fertilization 授粉與受精

Plants / that reproduce sexually / have both male and female parts. A plant must be pollinated / in order to reproduce. Pollen from the stamen / —the male part— / must reach the pistil / —the female part. There are / two major ways / this happens. The first is the wind. Sometimes, / the wind carries pollen / from one plant to another. However, / this is not / a very effective method. **Fortunately**, / many animals help / pollinate plants. Usually, / the animals are insects, / such as bees and butterflies. Plants' flowers often produce / **nectar**, / which insects like. As the insects collect a plant's nectar, / they pick up pollen. As the insects go / from plant to plant, / the pollen on them / **rubs off** / **on** the pistils of other plants. This pollinates the plants.

Now that the pollen has been transferred, / the plant must **be fertilized**. The **stigma** of a plant / has a **pollen tube**. **At least** / one **grain** of pollen / must go down that tube. This is not easy / because the tube is so small, / so plants often need / many grains of pollen / to ensure / that one will go down the tube. **Once** that happens, / then the male and female cells / can **unite**. This **results in** / the fertilization of the plant. And it can now reproduce.

有性生殖的植物具有雄性 **the male part** 和雌性 **the female part** 的構造，一株植物必須授粉 **must be pollinated** 才能繁殖 **in order to reproduce**，來自雄蕊（雄性構造）的花粉必須要抵達雌蕊 **pollen must reach to the pistil**（雌性構造）。這個過程主要依靠兩個方式 **two major ways**：一為風 **wind**，有時候風會將花粉攜帶至另一株植物上，然而，這並不是非常有效率的方法。所幸許多動物都能幫忙授粉，通常以昆蟲 **insects** 為主，如蜜蜂和蝴蝶。植物的花朵常會產生昆蟲喜愛的花蜜，昆蟲採集花蜜 **collect a plant's nectar** 的同時也會沾上花粉 **pick up pollen**，所以當昆蟲穿梭於植物之間，身上的花粉就會沾在其他植物的雌蕊上 **the pollen rubs off on the pistils pf other plants**，完成了授粉。

既然花粉已經傳遞完成，植物必須準備受精 **must be fertilized**。植物的柱頭有一根花粉管，至少要有一粒花粉 **one grain of pollen** 順著管子滑下 **go down the pollen tube**。然而這並不容易，因為花粉管很小，所以植物需要許多粒的花粉，才能確保有一個會滑下管中。一旦成功，雄細胞與雌細胞才能結合 **the male and female cells unite**。結果導致受精作用 **fertilization**，植物得以繁殖。

Words to Know

- **pollination** 授粉
- **fertilization** 受精
- **fortunately** 幸運地
- **nectar** 花蜜
- **rub off on** 因摩擦而沾在……上
- **now that** 既然
- **be fertilized** 授精
- **stigma** 柱頭
- **pollen tube** 花粉管
- **at least** 至少
- **grain** 顆粒
- **once** 一旦
- **unite** 混合
- **result in** 導致

36 Tropisms 向性

People know / that animals often **adapt** / **to** their **environment**. This is called / **evolution**. It can take place / over a very long time. And it can change animals / very much. Plants can also adapt. Their adaptations are called / tropisms.

A tropism is / the **response** of a plant / to an external **stimulus**. An external stimulus / can be light, **moisture**, or **gravity**. Tropisms are **involuntary**, / but they help plants / survive in their environment.

Plants need light / in order to live. Without light, / they cannot undergo / photosynthesis. So plants will always grow / toward light. If they are in **shadows** / or dark places, / they will **bend** / toward the light / that they need to survive.

The same is true of moisture. Without water, / plants will die. Plants' roots will grow / toward the parts of the ground / that have moisture. Plants' leaves will adapt / **so that** they can **trap** / as much moisture as possible.

Gravity is another force / which causes tropisms. Stems will always move / against gravity. This means / that they will move / in an **upward direction**. However, / roots move with gravity. This means / that they move downward.

我們知道動物會適應環境 **adapt to their environment**，稱為演化 **evolution**，演化的過程可能需要很長的時間，動物也會產生很大的改變。其實植物 **plants** 也會適應環境，稱為向性 **tropism**。

向性是指植物對外在刺激 **to an external stimulus** 的反應 **response**，這些刺激可能是光、水分或是地心引力 **light, moisture, or gravity**。向性是非自主的 **involuntary** 行為，卻有助於植物生存。

植物需要光 **light** 來維生，沒有光就無法行使光合作用，因此植物會一直往光源的方向生長 **grow toward light**。假如它們被陰影遮蔽或處於暗處，就會向有光的地方彎曲 **bend toward the light**，如此才能生存。

水分 **moisture** 對植物也一樣，沒有水分，植物就會死亡。植物的根 **plants' roots** 會朝著有水分的土壤生長 **grow toward the ground**，葉子也會適應環境，才能盡可能地鎖住水分。

另一種會造成向性的力量是地心引力 **gravity**，莖總是往地心引力的反方向生長 **stems move against gravity**，也就是向上生長。然而根卻是順著地心引力的方向生長 **roots move with gravity**，所以它們會往下 **downward** 紮根。

Words to Know

- **tropism** 向性
- **adapt to** 適應
- **environment** 環境
- **evolution** 進化
- **response** 回應
- **stimulus** 刺激
- **moisture** 水分
- **gravity** 地心引力
- **involuntary** 非自願性的
- **shadow** 陰影
- **bend** 彎曲
- **so that** 以便於
- **trap** 捕捉；陷入
- **upward** 向上的
- **direction** 方向

The Five Kingdoms of Life 生命五界

There is / **an amazing variety of** life / on the earth. Scientists have **classified** / all forms of life / into five different kingdoms. Each kingdom has / its own characteristics.

The first / is the **Monera** Kingdom. There are / about 10,000 species / in it. Members of this kingdom / are **prokaryotes** / that are **unicellular**. Its members include / various kinds of bacteria and some algae.

The second / is the **Protista** Kingdom. There are / around 250,000 species / in it. Members of this kingdom / include **protozoans** and some kinds of algae.

The third / is the **Fungi** Kingdom. There are / around 100,000 species / in it. Members of this kingdom / are similar to plants. But they do not use photosynthesis / to create nutrients. Mushrooms are / members of this kingdom.

The fourth / is the **Plantae** Kingdom. There are / around 250,000 species / in it. Plants, trees, flowers, and bushes / all belong to this kingdom.

The fifth / is the **Animalia** Kingdom. It is the biggest / with over 1,000,000 species / in it. It is formed / by multicellular animals.

地球上有驚人的生物種類，科學家將所有型態的生物分成五界 **five different kingdoms**，每一界都有各自的特色。

第一界是原核生物界 **the Monera Kingdom**，當中約有一萬種物種。此界的生物是單細胞的 **unicellular** 原核生物 **prokaryotes**，包含了各類的細菌與某些藻類。

第二界是原生生物界 **the Protista Kingdom**，當中約有 25 萬種物種。此界的生物包含了原生動物 **protozoans** 與某些種類的海藻 **some kinds of algae**。

第三界則是真菌界 **the Fungi Kingdom**，當中約有十萬種物種。此界中的生物類似植物，但它們不藉光合作用來製造養分。蘑菇 **mushrooms** 為此界的物種。

第四界是植物界 **the Plantae Kingdom**，當中約有 25 萬種物種。植物、樹木、花朵與灌木叢 **plants, trees, flowers, and bushes** 都屬於此界中的物種。

第五界是動物界 **the Animalia Kingdom**，擁有逾一百萬種物種，是最大的界。它是由多細胞的動物 **multicellular animals** 所組成的。

Words to Know

- **amazing** 驚人的 • **a variety of** 很多的 • **classify** 分類 • **Monera** 原核界
- **prokaryote** 原核生物 • **unicellular** 單細胞的 • **Protista** 原生生物界 • **protozoan** 原生動物
- **Fungi** 真菌界 • **Plantae** 植物界 • **Animalia** 動物界

38 Gregor Mendel 格萊高爾・孟德爾

These days, / scientists can do / amazing things / with **genetics**. They can **modify** / the **genetic structure** / of plants. This can let them produce / more fruit or **grain**. Some are even / **resistant to** diseases. But the field of genetics / is very young. It is barely / over 100 years old. And it was all started / by a **monk** / called Gregor Mendel.

Gregor Mendel enjoyed **gardening**. He especially liked / to grow peas / in his garden. While doing that, / he noticed / that some pea plants had / different characteristics. He saw / that some were tall / while others were short. The colors of their flowers / were different. And there were other differences, / too. He wanted to know / why. So he started / **experimenting** with them.

Mendel started / **crossbreeding** plants / with one another. He learned about / dominant and recessive genes / this way. He created **hybrids**, / which are plants / that carry the genes of different plants. He grew / many **generations** of peas / and learned a lot about them. What Mendel learned / became the basis / for modern genetics.

Mendel did / most of his work / with peas / in the 1850s and 1860s. But, at first, / people **ignored** his work. It was not until / the early twentieth century / that people began to study / his research. Then they **realized** / how much he had really **accomplished**.

近期的科學家能活用遺傳學 **genetics**，他們能改變植物的基因結構 **modify the genetic structure**，讓它們生產更多的水果或稻穀，有些甚至還可以抵抗疾病。但遺傳學屬於新領域，僅有逾一百年的歷史。而它是由一位名叫格萊高爾・孟德爾 **Mendel** 的修道士所開始的。

格萊高爾・孟德爾對園藝很有興趣 **enjoy gardening**，尤其喜歡在花園中種植豌豆 **grow peas**。在此過程中，他注意到有些豌豆叢有不同的特徵。有些高有些矮，花朵的顏色也不同。還有其他不同之處，想知道原因的他便開始用豌豆做起了實驗 **experiment with them**。

孟德爾開始為植物進行雜交 **crossbreed plants**，由此了解了顯性基因 **dominant gene** 與隱性基因 **recessive gene**。他創造出擁有不同植物基因的混種 **create hybrids**。他種植許多代的豌豆並從中學到很多。孟德爾所習得的便是現代遺傳學的基礎 **the basis for modern genetics**。

孟德爾大部分的研究在 1850 年到 1860 年間進行。人們起初忽略他的成果 **ignore his work**，一直到 20 世紀初人們才開始深入探討他的研究 **study his research**。那時他們才明白他的成果有多麼偉大。

Words to Know

- **genetics** 遺傳學 • **modify** 更改 • **genetic** 基因的 • **structure** 結構 • **grain** 穀物
- **resistant to** 抵抗 • **monk** 傳道士；和尚 • **gardening** 園藝 • **experiment** 實驗
- **crossbreed** 雜種 • **hybrid** 混種 • **generation** 代 • **ignore** 忽略 • **realize** 發覺；了解
- **accomplish** 完成

39 Pollination and Germination 授粉與發芽

All plants reproduce / somehow. This allows them / to produce offspring / that will grow into **mature** plants. There are / two important steps / in plant **reproduction**. The first is pollination. The second is germination.

Most plants have / both male and female **reproductive organs**. However, / they must come into contact / with each other / in order for the plant to reproduce. This happens / through pollination. Pollen / from the male part of a plant / must reach / the female part of the plant. This can happen / in many ways. The wind may sometimes / blow the pollen / from one part to the other. But this is / very **ineffective**. Many times, / animals such as bees, butterflies, and other insects / pollinate plants. As they go / from plant to plant, / pollen **gets stuck to** their bodies. When they land on a new plant, / some of it / **rubs off**. Many times, / this pollinates the plant. Once the pollen goes / from the **anther** (the male part) / to the stigma (the female part), / the plant has been pollinated / and can start to reproduce.

The other important step / is germination. Germination happens / after a plant's seeds / have been formed. At first, / the plant's seeds are **dormant**. However, / when they germinate, / they **come to life** / and begin to grow. If the **conditions** are good, / then the seed will become a seedling. Eventually, / it will mature / and become a plant.

所有植物必然會繁殖 **reproduce**，這讓它們能繁衍後代 **offspring** 以長成成熟的植物。植物的繁殖 **in plant reproduction** 有兩項重要步驟 **two important steps**，首先是授粉 **pollination**，第二個則是發芽 **germination**。

大多植物兼具雄性與雌性生殖器官 **reproductive organ**，然而它們需要彼此接觸，也就是藉由授粉來繁殖。植物雄性器官的花粉 **pollen** 必須傳遞到雌性器官，可藉由多種方式來完成。有時風會將花粉吹至另一處，不過成效不彰，多為像蜜蜂、蝴蝶與其他昆蟲類的動物來替植物授粉 **pollinate plants**。當牠們穿梭於植物間，花粉會沾到身上 **pollen gets stuck to their bodies**，所以當牠們停駐在新植物上時，會有些花粉掉落，植物大多是如此授粉。當花粉從花藥（雄性器官）傳到柱頭（雌性器官）**from the anther to the stigma**，植物便已授粉並能夠開始繁殖。

另一個重要的步驟為發芽 **germination**。植物種子成型後便會發芽。植物種子 **plant's seeds** 剛開始是休眠 **dormant** 狀態的，當它們發芽 **germinate** 時便回復生氣 **come to life** 並開始生長 **begin to grow**。若情況良好，種子會長成幼苗 **become a seedling**，成熟 **mature**，最後成為一株植物 **become a plant**。

Words to Know

- **mature** 成熟
- **reproduction** 繁衍
- **reproductive organ** 生殖器官
- **ineffective** 無效率的
- **get stuck to** 黏到
- **rub off** 擦掉
- **anther** 花藥
- **dormant** 休眠的
- **come to life** 甦醒
- **condition** 情況

40 What Is a Food Web 何謂食物網

A food chain shows / the feeding relationship / in an ecosystem. However, / most feeding relationships / are not simple / because most **organisms** / eat or are eaten by / many different things. So we often use / a "food web" / to show the relationship / between all of the species / in an ecosystem. A food web is / a map / of **overlapping** food chains. Each food web **contains** / several food chains.

All food webs / begin with producers. They are plants / that use the sun's energy / to make their own food. These plants are eaten by animals, / called consumers. Consumers are organisms / that eat other organisms. Consumers can be classified / into three groups / **according to** the type of food / they eat.

Herbivores are plant eaters. They only eat plants. Cows and horses / are herbivores. So are / rabbits. Huge animals can be herbivores, / too. Both elephants and rhinoceroses / only eat plants. **Carnivores** are meat eaters. They are often hunters. They are **predators** / and must find prey / to catch and eat. The members of the cat family, / dogs, wolves, foxes, / and other **sharp-toothed** animals / are all carnivores. Sharks are also / meat eaters. Some animals eat / both plants and animals. They are called / **omnivores**. Humans are omnivores. So are / pigs, bears, and even chickens.

Every food chain and food web / ends with **decomposers** / such as bacteria. They **break down** dead organisms / **into** substances / that can be used by producers.

食物鏈 **food chain** 顯示了生態系統內的供養關係 **feeding relationship**。但是，大部分的供養關係並不單純，因為大部分的生物會吃許多不一樣的生物，也會被許多不一樣的生物吃掉。所以我們通常可以透過「食物網」**food web** 來顯現一個生態系統中所有物種之間的關係。食物網是個部分重疊食物鏈 **overlapping food chain** 的圖表。每個食物網涵蓋了許多條食物鏈。

全部的食物網都起源於生產者 **begin with producers**，就是利用太陽的熱能來生產自己的食物 **make their own food** 的植物。這些植物會被動物當成食物，在這裡的動物稱為消費者 **consumers**。消費者指的是那些以有機體為食 **eat organisms** 的生物。我們可以依照這些消費者所吃的食物類型把它們分為三類。

草食性動物 **herbivore** 是指吃植物的動物 **plant eater**。牠們只吃植物 **only eat plants**。母牛和馬是草食性動物。兔子也是。大型動物也可能是草食性動物。大象和犀牛也只吃植物。肉食性動物 **carnivore** 是指吃肉的動物 **meat eater**。牠們通常都是狩獵者 **hunter**，也是必須要找獵物 **find prey** 來吃的掠食者 **predator**。貓科動物、狗、狼、狐狸和其他尖齒動物都是肉食性動物。鯊魚也吃肉。有些動物則是動植物都吃，叫做雜食性動物 **omnivore**。人類就是雜食性動物。像是豬、熊、甚至是雞，也都是雜食性動物。

每個食物鏈與食物網都終結於如細菌等的分解者 **end with decomposers**。牠們將死掉的生物分解成 **break down dead organisms** 可以被生產者利用的物質。

Words to Know

- **food web** 食物網
- **organism** 有機體
- **overlapping** 部分重疊的
- **contain** 涵蓋
- **according to** 依據
- **herbivore** 草食性動物
- **carnivore** 肉食性動物
- **predator** 掠食者
- **sharp-toothed** 尖齒的
- **omnivore** 雜食性動物
- **decomposer** 分解者
- **break down into** 分解成

41 How Ecosystems Change 生態系統如何改變

Many ecosystems / are **thriving communities** / that are full of life. However, / many of them / were once empty / and were **barren lands**. But they changed / to become places / with many kinds of organisms.

The first step is called / primary **succession**. This happens / in a place / that has never had life on it. Soil must be made / first. Then **pioneer species** / come to the land. These are / low-level organisms / like **lichens** and **mosses**. Over time, / the soil starts / to be able to support / more **complicated** organisms. These are / various grasses. Once there is some **minor vegetation**, / animals / like insects and birds / move in. Eventually, / bushes and trees / start to grow. Finally, / even larger animals / move into the land.

Eventually, / the ecosystem will grow enough / that a **climax community** / will be formed. This means / that the ecosystem / is fairly **stable**. The ecosystem will not change anymore / unless something from outside / affects it. It could be / an invasive species. Or it could be / a natural disaster. But unless something / affects the ecosystem, / it will never change.

許多生態系統 **many ecosystems** 是充滿生命的繁榮群落 **thriving communities**，不過它們過去也一度 **once** 是空無一物的貧瘠土地 **barren lands**，最後卻變成了充滿許多有機體的地方。

第一個階段為初級演替 **primary succession**，發生在一地尚未出現任何生命時。先要有土壤 **soil**，接著先驅物種 **pioneer species** 進入這片土地。先驅物種是像地衣和苔蘚 **lichens and mosses** 這樣的低階有機體。隨著時間的過去，這裡的土壤開始可以維持更複雜的有機體，也就是各種的禾本科植物 **various grasses**。一旦有了一些低階植被，昆蟲和鳥類 **insects and birds** 等動物就會移入，灌木與喬木 **bushes and trees** 最終也會開始生長。最後，甚至連更大型的動物 **even larger animals** 都會進駐此地。

這個生態系統最後會發展完整，形成一個終極群落 **climax community**，表示它已經相當安定 **fairly stable**。除非有外來的影響，這個生態系統才會改變。有可能是出現了入侵物種 **invasive species**，或是發生天災 **natural disaster**。不過若是沒有外來影響，這個生態系統永遠不會改變 **never change**。

Words to Know

- **thriving** 旺盛的
- **community** 群落
- **barren lands** 貧瘠的土地
- **succession** 演替
- **pioneer species** 先驅物種
- **lichen** 地衣
- **moss** 苔蘚
- **complicated** 複雜的
- **minor** 少量的
- **vegetation** 植被
- **climax community** 終極群落
- **stable** 穩定

42 The Carbon and Nitrogen Cycles 碳循環與氮循環

Carbon is / one of the most important **elements**. All living things / are made from carbon. But it is **constantly** changing forms. This is called / the carbon cycle. In the atmosphere, / carbon is often **present** / in the form of carbon dioxide. This is / a compound / that has one carbon **atom** / and two oxygen atoms. Plants breathe in / the carbon dioxide / and use it / to produce nutrients. The carbon then becomes / part of the plants. These plants die / and then / often get buried. Over time, / these plants may turn into / **fossil fuels** / like coal or **petroleum**. People later burn / these fossil fuels, / which releases carbon dioxide / into the atmosphere.

Another important element / is nitrogen. There is also / a nitrogen cycle. Nitrogen is actually / the most common element / in the atmosphere. Around 80% of the air / we breathe / is nitrogen. We don't need nitrogen / like we need oxygen. But nitrogen is still important. There is often nitrogen / in the soil. Plants **absorb** the nitrogen / from the soil. When people and animals eat the plants, / they release the nitrogen / into their bodies. Bacteria / in people's and animals' bodies / can fix the nitrogen / so that the bodies can use it. Later, / when the people and animals / die and decompose, / the nitrogen returns / to the soil or the atmosphere. Then it can be reused / again.

碳 **carbon** 是最重要的元素 **elements** 之一，所有生物都是由碳所構成的。但它不停地改變型態，這稱為碳循環 **carbon cycle**。碳在大氣中最常以二氧化碳 **carbon dioxide** 的型態出現，這是由一個碳原子加上兩個氧原子而成的化合物 **compound**。植物吸入二氧化碳 **breathe in the carbon dioxide** 並利用它來製造養分，碳也因此成了植物的部分。植物枯萎死亡後常被掩埋 **get buried**，經過時間可能會轉變成了像煤炭或石油的化石燃料 **turn into fossil fuels**。後來人們燃燒這些化石燃料 **burn these fossil fuels**，釋放二氧化碳 **release carbon dioxide** 回到空氣中。

另一個重要的元素是氮 **nitrogen**，也有氮循環 **nitrogen cycle** 的存在。它是空氣中最常見的元素 **the most common element**，我們呼吸的空氣大約有百分之八十是氮。我們對氮的需求不如對氧氣，但它依然相當重要。土壤中 **in the soil** 常有氮，而植物從土壤中獲得氮 **absorb the nitrogen**。當人類與動物食用植物 **eat the plants** 時，植物便釋放氮到體內 **release the nitrogen into their bodies**。人類與動物體內的細菌會將氮轉化成身體可用的。等人類與動物死亡並分解 **die and decompose** 後，氮又回到了土壤或是空氣中 **return to the soil or the atmosphere**，便能再次受到利用。

Words to Know

- **nitrogen** 氮 • **element** 元素 • **constantly** 不斷地 • **present** 存在 • **atom** 原子
- **fossil fuel** 化石燃料 • **petroleum** 石油 • **absorb** 吸收

43 The Circulatory System 循環系統

The circulatory system / is the part of the body / that controls the **flow** of blood. It has many parts. The most important is the heart. However, / there are also / **arteries** and **veins** / that send blood throughout the body.

The heart has / four **chambers**. They are / the left and right **atria** / and the left and right **ventricles**. First, / blood flows / into the right atrium. Then it goes to the right ventricle / and into the lungs. In the lungs, / oxygen is added to the blood. Then the blood returns / to the heart. It goes into the left atrium / and then / into the left ventricle. From there, / it leaves the heart / by going to the **aorta**.

The aorta is / the body's main artery. It **feeds** blood / to the rest of the body. The body has / both arteries and veins. Together, / they are called / **blood vessels**. These blood vessels / take **oxygen-rich** blood / and transport it everywhere / in the body. The body then uses the blood, / which loses its oxygen. Then, / other veins and arteries / take the **oxygen-depleted** blood / back to the heart, / and the **cycle** begins again.

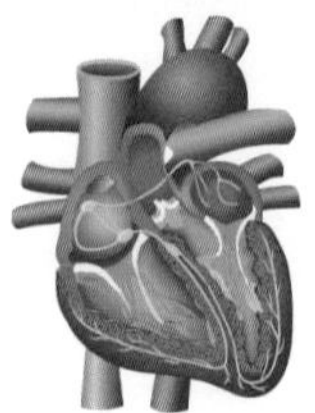

循環系統 **circulatory system** 能控制體內血液流動 **control the flow of blood**。它擁有許多部分，其中最重要的是心臟 **heart**。然而，動脈和靜脈 **arteries and veins** 也會將血液流送至全身。

心臟可分為四個腔室 **four chambers**。它們是左右心房 **left and right atria** 和左右心室 **left and right ventricles**。首先，血液流入右心房，然後進入右心室和肺部。在肺部 **in the lungs**，氧氣會進入血液中 **oxygen is added to the blood**。接著血液會回到心臟。血液通過左心房後，會由左心室流出心臟並進入主動脈。

主動脈 **aorta** 是身體的主要動脈 **main artery**，它供給全身各處的血液 **feed blood**。我們的身體有動脈和靜脈，它們被統稱為血管 **blood vessel**。這些血管帶著富氧血 **take oxygen-rich blood** 輸送 **transport** 至身體的每個地方。在被身體利用完後，血液會喪失氧氣。這時候其他的靜脈和動脈會將貧氧血 **oxygen-depleted blood** 帶回心臟 **back to the heart**，循環系統就會再次循環。

Words to Know

- **flow** 流動 • **artery** 動脈 • **vein** 靜脈 • **chamber** 室 • **atrium** 心房 • **ventricle** 心室
- **aorta** 主動脈 • **feed** 提供 • **blood vessel** 血管 • **oxygen-rich** 富含氧氣的
- **oxygen-depleted** 氧氣耗盡的 • **cycle** 循環

The Immune System 免疫系統

Every day, / the body **is attacked** / by bacteria, viruses, and other invaders. It is / the body's immune system / that fights these invaders. It helps / keep the person healthy. The immune system / is made up of / various cells, **tissues**, and organs.

White **blood cells** / are very important. They are also called / **leukocytes**. They move / through the body / in **lymphatic vessels**. There are / two types of leukocytes. The first / try to **destroy** / invading organisms. These are **phagocytes**. The second / are **lymphocytes**. They help the body / remember various invaders. This way, / it can destroy them / in the future.

Antigens often / invade the body. The body then / produces **antibodies**. They fight the antigens. If the antibodies succeed, / they will always remain / in the body. This lets the body / fight the disease again / in the future. This is very effective / against viruses.

People are often born / **immune to** certain diseases. This is called / **innate immunity**. But there is **adaptive** immunity, / too. This happens / when the body **recognizes threats** / to it. It then learns / how to defeat them. Also, / thanks to **vaccinations**, / people can become / immune to many diseases. Vaccinations help improve / the strength of the immune system.

人體每日都受到細菌、病毒與其他入侵者的侵襲。身體的免疫系統 **immune system** 負責對抗這些不速之客，以維持人體的健康 **keep the person healthy**。免疫系統是由不同的細胞、組織和器官所組成的。

白血球細胞 **white blood cell** 非常重要，它也稱做白血球，活動於淋巴管中。白血球有兩種類型，第一種是噬菌細胞，用來消滅侵略生物 **destroy invading organisms**。第二種是淋巴細胞，能幫助人體記憶各種侵略生物 **remember various invaders**。如此便能在以後消滅它們。

抗原 **antigen** 時常侵襲人體 **invade the body**，人體因而產生抗體 **antibody**。抗體對抗抗原 **fight the antigen**，若抗體獲勝，它們便會永遠存於體內。這使得未來人體能再次對抗疾病，對於對抗病毒相當有用。

人體生來就對某些疾病免疫，這稱為先天性免疫 **innate immunity**。但也有後天性免疫 **adaptive immunity**，發生於當人體辨認出威脅時，自行學會如何對抗病毒。還有多虧了疫苗 **thanks to vaccinations**，民眾能對許多疾病免疫 **immune to many diseases**。接種疫苗 **vaccination** 有助於提升免疫系統的效力。

Words to Know

- **immune system** 免疫系統
- **be attacked** 被攻擊
- **tissue** 組織
- **blood cell** 血細胞
- **leukocyte** 白血球
- **lymphatic** 淋巴腺的
- **vessel** 血管
- **destroy** 摧毀
- **phagocyte** 噬菌細胞
- **lymphocyte** 淋巴細胞
- **antigen** 抗原
- **antibody** 抗體
- **immune to** 對……免疫
- **innate** 與生俱來的
- **immunity** 免疫力
- **adaptive** 適應的
- **recognize** 察覺
- **threat** 威脅
- **vaccination** 疫苗接種

45 The Development of a Baby 嬰兒的發育

When a woman becomes **pregnant**, / a baby starts to grow / in her body. For the next nine months, / she will have another life / inside her. Until the baby is born, / the baby is called a **fetus**. The fetus **goes through** / several **stages** of development / over nine months.

At first, / the new life / is just an **embryo**. It starts / growing cells / and becoming larger. After three weeks, / the body's organs begin to develop, / and it takes a human shape. After two months, / most of the organs / are **completely** developed. Only the **brain** and **spinal cord** / are not.

In the ninth week, / the embryo is now said to / be a fetus. The fetus starts / to develop more quickly / now. By week fourteen, / doctors can **determine** / **if** it is a **male** or a **female**. And after about four or five months / of **pregnancy**, / the mother can feel her baby / moving around inside her. By the sixth month, / the fetus is able to survive / outside the **womb**. The fetus still needs / about three more months / to develop inside the mother. Finally, / during the ninth month, / most babies are born.

當一個女人懷孕 **become pregnant**，嬰兒就在她的體內開始成長。接下來的九個月裡，她的體內會孕育著另一個生命 **have another life**。小孩誕生前稱為胎兒 **fetus**，他在九個月裡 **over nine months** 會經歷數個階段的發展。

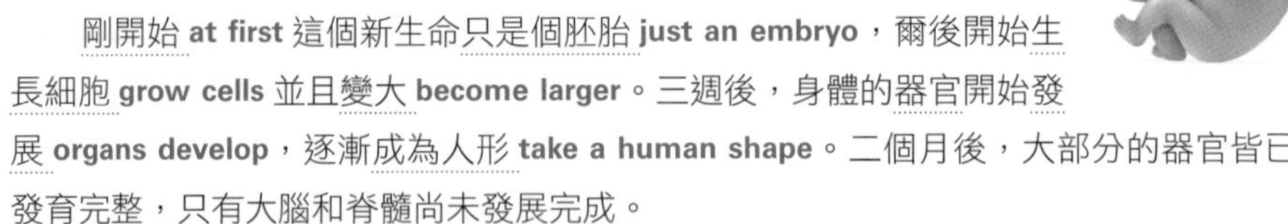

剛開始 **at first** 這個新生命只是個胚胎 **just an embryo**，爾後開始生長細胞 **grow cells** 並且變大 **become larger**。三週後，身體的器官開始發展 **organs develop**，逐漸成為人形 **take a human shape**。二個月後，大部分的器官皆已發育完整，只有大腦和脊髓尚未發展完成。

到了第九週時 **in the ninth week**，胚胎就會被稱為胎兒 **fetus**，生長的速度也更加快速 **develop more quickly**。到了第 14 週，醫生會檢查胎兒是男是女。懷孕的四到五個月後，母親可以感受到胎動 **move around**。第六個月時，胎兒已經可以在子宮外存活 **able to survive outside the womb**，不過仍須在母體內生長三個月，最後在第九個月時，大部分的嬰兒就會出生 **be born**。

Words to Know

- **development** 發展
- **pregnant** 懷孕的
- **fetus** 胎兒
- **go through** 經歷
- **stage** 階段
- **embryo** 胚胎
- **completely** 完全地
- **brain** 大腦
- **spinal cord** 脊髓
- **determine if** 確定是否
- **male** 男性
- **female** 女性
- **pregnancy** 懷孕；孕期
- **womb** 子宮

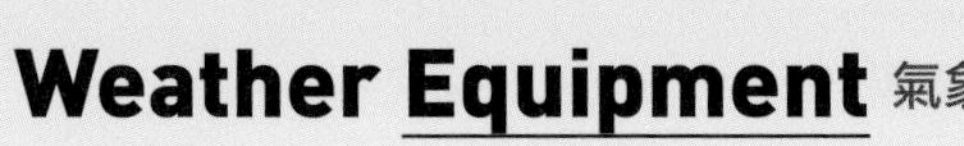

46 Weather Equipment 氣象設備

Meteorologists are people / who study the weather. They tell us / if it will be / hot or cold. They tell us / if it will be / sunny or rainy. They have / lots of equipment / to help them.

The most **common** piece / of equipment / is the thermometer. A thermometer **measures** / the temperature of the air. By looking at it, / people can tell exactly / how hot or cold / it is. Another common instrument / is the **barometer**. This measures / the air pressure. So people can know / if it is going to / rain or not. Usually, / when the air pressure drops, / bad weather is coming. And when it goes up, / good weather is coming. There is other equipment, / too. A **rain gauge** measures / the amount of rain / that has fallen / in a place. And an **anemometer** / is used to measure / how fast / the wind is blowing. It's really useful / on windy days! And some people even have / **weather vanes** / on their homes. They show / which **direction** / the wind is blowing.

氣象學家 **meteorologist** 是指研究天氣 **study the weather** 的人，他們告訴我們天氣的冷熱和晴雨。氣象學家有很多的輔助設備 **lots of equipment**。

其中最常見的就是溫度計 **thermometer**。溫度計用來測量空氣的溫度 **measure the temperature of the air**，經由觀測溫度計，人們可以得知確切的冷熱。另一個常見的儀器是氣壓計 **barometer**，用來測量氣壓 **measure the air pressure**，人們藉此可以得知未來下雨的可能性 **rain or not**。通常氣壓下降代表即將變天，氣壓上升則會有好天氣。還有另一種設備稱作雨量計 **rain gauge**，用來測量一地的降雨量 **measure the amount of rain**。風速計 **anemometer** 則用來測量風速 **how fast the wind is blowing**，遇到颱風天特別實用！有些人甚至在家中裝設自己的風向計 **weather vane**，可以觀測風向 **which direction the wind is blowing**。

Words to Know

- **equipment** 設備
- **meteorologist** 氣象學家
- **common** 常見的
- **measure** 測量
- **barometer** 氣壓計
- **rain gauge** 雨量計
- **anemometer** 風速計
- **weather vane** 風向計
- **direction** 方向；方位

47 The Water Cycle 水循環

There is / a **limited** amount of water / on the earth. In fact, / for billions of years, / the amount of water / has not changed. However, / water can often **appear** / in many different **forms**. These all / make up / the water cycle.

The first stage / is **evaporation**. This happens / when the sun's heat / on rivers, lakes, seas, and oceans / causes water to turn into water vapor. The water vapor / then / **rises** into the air.

The second stage / is **condensation**. As water vapor rises, / the air gets colder. This causes the water vapor / to turn into tiny water **droplets**. These droplets come together / to form clouds.

The third stage / is **precipitation**. The water droplets / fall to the ground / in some form. The most common kind of precipitation / is rain. But, in cold weather, / snow, **sleet**, or ice / may fall / instead.

The final stage / is collection. When water falls to the ground, / it may flow into rivers, lakes, seas, or oceans. Or it may / go down into the ground. There, / it becomes **groundwater**. But the water cycle / goes **on and on**.

地球上的水量是有限的。事實上，在這數十億年以來，水量一直沒有改變。不過，水通常以不同的形式出現，這些造就了水循環 **water cycle**。

第一個環節為蒸發 **evaporation**。這是指太陽溫度造成河水、湖水以及海水變為水蒸氣 **turn into water vapor** 的過程，水蒸氣會上升到空氣中 **rise into the air**。

第二個環節是凝結 **condensation**。隨著水蒸氣的上升，空氣會跟著變冷。這導致水蒸氣變成微細的水滴 **turn into tiny water droplets**。接下來，這些小水滴會聚在一起而形成雲 **form clouds**。

第三個環節是降水 **precipitation**。水滴會以某些形式在地表落下 **fall to the ground**。最常見的降水是下雨 **rain**。但是，天氣寒冷時，水滴可能以雪、凍雨或是冰 **snow, sleet, or ice** 的形式降下。

最後一個環節是匯流 **collection**。當水降至地表，可能會流入河流、湖泊、海或是大洋 **flow into rivers, lakes, seas, or oceans**。水也有可能進入土壤中 **go down into the ground**，這些水會變成地下水 **groundwater**。不過，水循環是生生不息的 **go on and on**。

Words to Know

- **limited** 有限的 • **appear** 出現 • **form** 形式 • **evaporation** 蒸發 • **rise** 上升
- **condensation** 凝結 • **droplet** 小滴 • **precipitation** 降水；降水量 • **sleet** 凍雨
- **groundwater** 地下水 • **on and on** 持續地

48 Ocean Resources and Conservation 海洋資源與保護

Oceans cover / around 71% / of the earth's surface. And they are full of / many different resources / that can **benefit humanity**.

For one, / the oceans are a great source / of fish and seafood. Fishermen / from **numerous** countries / sail the oceans / to catch fish / for people to eat. However, / humans are catching / too many fish. **Fish stocks** / are starting to become smaller. So humans need to be careful. They should not **overfish** areas. Instead, / they should catch / smaller numbers of fish. Then, / more fish can grow / and **repopulate** the oceans.

The oceans also have / many valuable resources / beneath their floors. For instance, / oil and natural gas / are pumped / from beneath the **seafloor** / in many places. But, again, / humans need to be careful. Sometimes, / **oil spills** release / large amounts of oil / into the water. This can kill / many fish, birds, and other sea creatures.

There are / even large amounts of certain **ores** / beneath the ocean. Gold, silver, and other valuable **metals** / could be mined / in the future. And people can even / use the oceans / for energy. **Tidal energy** could provide / cheap and **abundant** energy / in the future. But we need to / take good care of our oceans. They have / many resources, / but we need to / conserve them, / too.

海洋 **ocean** 覆蓋了約 71% 的地表，裡頭有許多資源能使人類獲益 **benefit humanity**。

首先，海洋是魚產和海鮮 **fish and seafood** 的重要來源，各國漁夫前往海上捕魚供人食用。然而人們過度捕撈 **catch too many fish**，使得魚貨量 **fish stocks** 減少 **become smaller**。因此，人們要多加注意，勿在區域內過度捕魚 **should not overfish**。反而應少量捕魚，讓更多魚生長並重新居於海洋中。

海底還有許多珍貴的資源，像是從海底 **beneath the seafloor** 多處地方抽出石油與天然氣 **oil and natural gas**。但再次呼籲，人類要注意 **be careful**。有時漏油 **oil spill** 使得大量石油流入水中 **release oil into the water**，造成魚類、鳥類與其他海洋生物的死亡。

海底甚至有大量的特定礦產 **certain ores**，金、銀與其他貴金屬 **other valuable metals** 未來皆可能受到開採。人們還可以利用海洋獲得能量，潮汐發電 **tidal energy** 在未來能提供便宜且充裕的 **cheap and abundant** 能量。不過我們要好好照顧海洋 **take good care of oceans**，它們雖擁有多樣的資源，但也需要我們的保護。

Words to Know

- **resources** 資源
- **benefit** 對……有利益；好處
- **humanity** 人
- **numerous** 許多的
- **fish stock** 魚類資源
- **overfish** 過度捕撈
- **repopulate** 重新移居
- **seafloor** 海底
- **oil spill** 漏油
- **ore** 礦石
- **metal** 金屬
- **tidal energy** 潮汐能源
- **abundant** 大量的；充足的

49 The Formation of the Earth 地球的形成

Billions of years ago, / the sun formed. There was a huge **disk** / of rocks and gases / in the **solar system**. Eventually, / these rocks and gases / began to form **planets**. This was about 4.5 billion years ago. The earth was / the third planet / from the sun. At first, / the earth was **extremely** hot. But, over millions of years, / it began to cool down. As the earth cooled, / **water vapor** started forming / in the **atmosphere**. This caused / the **creation** of clouds / all over the planet. Soon, / the clouds began dropping / huge amounts of water / all over the planet. This caused the creation / of the earth's oceans, seas, rivers, and lakes.

But the earth / 4.5 billion years ago / looked different / from the earth of today. Today, / there are / seven continents. In the past, / this was not true. There have been / different numbers of continents. Once, / there was / just one continent / on the whole planet. Why? One **clue** / is the **theory** of **plate tectonics**. There are many **plates** / that **make up** the earth's **crust**. These plates / are huge pieces of land. And they are **constantly** moving. As the earth ages, / the plates slowly **move around**. Today, / there are seven continents. In the future, / perhaps there will be / more or less.

太陽於數十億年前形成，岩石和氣體形成一巨大的圓盤 **a huge disk of rocks and gases** 環繞著太陽系 **in the solar system**。最後約 45 億年前，這些物質開始形成行星 **form planets**，地球 **Earth** 位於距離太陽的第三顆星球 **the third planet**。地球形成之初 **at first** 非常炙熱 **extremely hot**，數百萬年後 **over millions of years** 開始冷卻 **cool down**。隨著地球的冷卻，水蒸氣開始在大氣中形成 **water vapor forms**，造就了地球表面雲層的產生 **creation of clouds**。不久後，這些雲層開始落下大量的水 **drop huge amounts of water** 於整個地球，這使地球的大洋、海、河流以及湖泊 **oceans, seas, rivers, and lakes** 因此誕生。

但是 45 億年前的地球，和現今的 **today** 地球長得不一樣。今日的地球有七塊大陸 **seven continents**，以前卻不然，大陸的數量持續變動，曾經 **once**，整個地球僅有一塊大陸 **just one continent**。這是為什麼呢 **why** ？板塊構造理論 **the theory of plate tectonics** 是一個線索。地殼由許多板塊 **many plates** 組成，這些板塊是一片片巨大的陸塊 **huge pieces of land**，而且它們持續在移動 **constantly move**。隨著地球年齡的增加，它們也緩慢地移動 **slowly move around**。今天，地球上有七塊大陸。在未來，陸塊也許會變多或是變少。

Words to Know

- **formation** 形成；組成
- **disk** 圓盤物
- **solar system** 太陽系
- **planet** 行星；星球
- **extremely** 極度地；非常地
- **water vapor** 水蒸氣
- **atmosphere** 大氣
- **creation** 創造
- **clue** 線索
- **theory** 理論
- **plate tectonics** 地表板塊構造論
- **plate** 板塊
- **make up** 組成；造成
- **crust** 地殼
- **constantly** 不斷地；持續地
- **move around** 四處移動

50 Earthquakes 地震

Sometimes, / the ground suddenly / begins to shake. Buildings and bridges / move **back and forth**. They might even fall down. Places in the ground / begin to **crack**. This is an earthquake. Earthquakes happen / all the time / all around the earth. Most of the time, / they are so small / that we cannot even feel them. But sometimes / there are / very large earthquakes. These can cause great **damage**, / kill many people, / and even change the way / the earth looks.

The earth's crust / is its top part. The crust is formed / of many plates. These are called / **tectonic plates**. There are / seven large plates / and around twelve smaller ones. These plates are **enormous**. But they also move / really slowly. Sometimes / they move back and forth / against each other. This causes earthquakes.

The Richter scale / **measures** / the power of earthquakes. A level 2 **quake** / is ten times as powerful / as a level 1 quake. For each whole number increase, / the power of the earthquake / increases by ten. Levels 1 to 4 / are weak earthquakes. Level 5 earthquakes / can cause some damage. Levels 6 and 7 / can be dangerous. Levels 8 and 9 / can cause huge amounts of / death and **destruction**.

有時候地面會突然開始震動 **the ground suddenly shakes**，建築物與橋樑也隨之前後晃動 **move back and forth**，甚至倒塌 **fall down**，地面各處開始裂開 **crack**，這就是地震 **earthquake**。世界各地時時刻刻都在發生地震，通常很輕微，我們感覺不到。然而有的時候，也會發生非常大的地震 **large earthquake**，可能造成嚴重的損害 **cause great damage**，奪走無數性命 **kill many people**，甚至改變地貌。

地殼 **the earth's crust** 是地球的最上層，由許多板塊組成 **formed of many plates**，稱為構造板塊 **tectonic plates**。地球一共有七大板塊與大約十二塊較小的板塊。這些板塊很龐大，不過移動速度很緩慢。有時候它們會彼此碰撞，於是產生地震 **cause earthquakes**。

芮氏地震規模 **the Richter scale** 用來測量地震的威力 **the power of earthquakes**，規模二級是一級的十倍，每增加一個整數，威力也隨之增加十倍。規模一級到四級屬於輕微 **weak** 地震，五級會造成一些損害 **cause some damage**，六到七級非常危險 **dangerous**，八到九級會造成嚴重的死亡和破壞 **cause death and destruction**。

Words to Know

- **back and forth** 來回地
- **crack** 爆裂；破裂
- **damage** 損害
- **tectonic plate** 地殼構造板塊
- **enormous** 巨大的；龐大的
- **the Richter scale** 芮氏地震規模
- **measure** 測量
- **quake** 震動；搖晃
- **destruction** 破壞；毀滅

51 **Volcanic Eruptions** 火山爆發

Sometimes, / **volcanoes** suddenly erupt. They **spew** / tons of ash, gas, and **lava**. They might even kill / large numbers of people. What is it / that makes a volcano erupt?

Deep in the earth, / there is usually / a lot of **pressure**. Also, / the temperature / deep underground / can be very high. In fact, / it is often high enough / to **melt** rocks. Melted rock / that is beneath the ground / is called **magma**. The magma is constantly trying to **move up** / toward the surface. Under the earth, / there are / large pools of magma / that have **gathered together**. These are called / **magma chambers**. These magma chambers / often exist / beneath volcanoes. Eventually, / the pressure beneath the earth / becomes too great. The magma **forces its way** / to the surface. This causes / a volcano to erupt. When a volcano erupts, / it often **expels** / ash and gas. It can also expel magma. Magma / that is on the surface / is called lava. The lava often **creeps down** / the sides of the volcano / until it eventually cools and **hardens**.

The size of the eruption / depends on / the amount of pressure / that is **released**. Some volcanoes release / a steady amount of lava. These have / a low amount of pressure. Other volcanoes / erupt **explosively**. They can shoot ash / miles into the air. They can expel / lava and gas / very far in the area. These are / the most dangerous eruptions. Mt. Vesuvius, Krakatoa, and Mt. St. Helens / all had **explosive** eruptions / that killed many people.

有時火山會突然爆發 **erupt**，噴射出大量的灰燼 **ash**、氣體 **gas** 與熔岩 **lava**，可能會造成許多人死亡。是什麼造成火山爆發的呢？

在地球深處有很大的壓力，地底的溫度也相當高；事實上，溫度高到能將石頭熔化。地底下所熔化的石頭 **melted rock** 稱為岩漿 **magma**，岩漿不斷地想往地表上移動。地底下有叫做岩漿庫 **magma chamber**，是岩漿聚集之處。這些岩漿庫通常在火山下方，最後地下的壓力 **pressure beneath the earth** 實在太大 **become too great**，岩漿爆出地表，造成了火山爆發 **volcano erupts**。當火山爆發，常噴出灰燼與氣體 **expel ash and gas**。也可能會噴出岩漿 **expel magma**，地表上 **on the surface** 的岩漿稱為熔岩 **lava**，它通常由沿著火山邊緩慢流下 **creep down**，最後冷卻硬化 **cool and harden**。

爆發的規模取決於壓力釋放的多寡。有些火山 **some volcanoes** 壓力較小，釋放定量的熔岩 **release a steady amount of lava**。有些則猛烈爆發 **erupts explosively**，它能噴射數哩，將灰燼噴入空氣中。將熔岩與氣體噴得很遠，為最危險的火山爆發類型。維蘇威火山、喀拉喀托火山與聖海倫火山都曾經猛烈噴發，造成許多人死亡。

Words to Know

- **volcanic** 火山的 • **eruption** 爆發；噴發 • **volcano** 火山 • **spew** 噴出；湧出 • **lava** 熔岩
- **pressure** 壓力 • **melt** 融化；熔化 • **magma** 岩漿 • **move up** 往上移動
- **gather together** 聚集 • **magma chamber** 岩漿庫 • **force one's way** 用力推進
- **expel** 噴出；排出 • **creep down** 緩慢下移 • **harden** 變硬；硬化 • **release** 釋放
- **explosively** 爆發地 • **explosive** 爆炸性的；爆發性的

52 Mass Extinctions 大滅絕

Every once in a while, / a mass extinction occurs / on the earth. When this happens, / large numbers of species / all go extinct / at once. Scientists have **identified** / at least five mass extinctions / during the earth's history. During these mass extinctions, / up to 95% of all life / on the planet / was killed. The last mass extinction / happened / about 65 million years ago. Scientists **refer to** it / **as** the K-T Extinction.

65 million years ago, / the earth looked very different. There were no humans. Instead, / dinosaurs ruled / the land and the seas. This was a time / called the **Cretaceous Period**. Then, suddenly, / there was a mass extinction. Scientists are not exactly sure / what happened. But most of them believe / that an **asteroid** or **comet** / **struck** the earth. This caused a **tremendous** change / in the planet. Large amounts of dust / were thrown into the atmosphere. This **blocked** the sun. No sunlight / could reach the earth, / so many plants died. The animals / that ate the plants / then died. And the animals / that ate those animals / died, too.

The K-T Extinction killed / all of the dinosaurs. And about half of the other species / on the planet / died, too. Of course, / all life did not die. In fact, / some life **flourished**. After the K-T Extinction, / **mammals** began to increase / in number. Eventually, / humans **evolved**. So, without the K-T Extinction, / humans might not ever have existed.

每隔一段時間，地球上便會發生一次大滅絕 **mass extinction**。大滅絕發生時，極多物種同時絕種 **go extinct at once**。科學家發現在地球的歷史上，起碼發生過五次大滅絕。有高達 95% 的地球生物於大滅絕中死亡。最後一次的大滅絕約於六千五百萬年前發生，科學家將之稱為「白堊紀－第三紀滅絕事件」**K-T Extinction**。

六千五百萬年前的地球面貌相當不同，沒有人類，反而是由恐龍主宰陸地與海洋，此時期稱為白堊紀 **the Cretaceous Period**。接著突然發生大滅絕，連科學家們也無法確切了解發生何事。但大多數人相信，是行星或是彗星 **asteroid or comet** 撞上地球 **strike the earth** 造成地球的驟變。大量的塵土 **large amount of dust** 飄入空氣中 **thrown into the atmosphere**，遮住了太陽 **block the sun**。陽光完全透不進地球，造成許多植物枯萎 **plants die**，以植物為食的動物跟著死亡 **animals die**，食用動物為生的動物也死亡。

「白堊紀－第三紀滅絕事件」造成了全數恐龍絕種。半數的其他物種也跟著死亡。當然也不是所有生物都滅亡了，事實上有些生物還蓬勃地生長。「白堊紀－第三紀滅絕事件」後，哺乳動物 **mammals** 數量大增 **increase in number**，最終進化出人類 **human evolve**。若無「白堊紀－第三紀滅絕事件」，也許不會有人類的出現。

Words to Know

- **mass** 眾多；大眾
- **extinction** 滅絕；絕種
- **every once in a while** 時常；每隔一段時間
- **identify** 發現；確認
- **refer to . . . as** 指稱……為
- **Cretaceous Period** 白堊紀
- **asteroid** 小行星
- **comet** 彗星
- **strike** 打；擊
- **tremendous** 巨大的；極大的
- **block** 遮蔽；阻隔
- **flourish** 茂盛；繁榮
- **mammal** 哺乳類動物
- **evolve** 逐步形成；進化

The Inner and Outer Planets 內行星與外行星

The solar system has / eight planets / in it. These planets / **are divided into** two groups. We call them / the inner and outer planets. These two groups / have / their own **characteristics**.

The inner planets / are Mercury, Venus, Earth, and Mars. They are all / **fairly close to** the sun. Also, / these planets are all small / and made up of solid, **rocklike materials**. The earth is the largest / of the inner planets. And the inner planets all / have / zero, one, or two moons.

The outer planets / are very different / from the inner planets. The outer planets are much colder / than the inner planets. They are **farther** / from the sun. The outer planets / are Jupiter, Saturn, Uranus, and Neptune. They are all / very large. Jupiter is the largest planet / in the solar system. The outer planets are / **mostly** / made up of gas. Also, / the outer planets have / many moons. Jupiter has / at least 63 moons. The others also have / many moons.

太陽系共有八顆行星 **eight planets**。這些行星可分為內行星 **inner planets** 和外行星 **outer planets** 兩類，各自有其特色。

內行星包含水星、金星、地球以及火星 **Mercury, Venus, Earth, and Mars**，它們非常靠近太陽 **fairly close to the sun**。再者，這幾個行星的體積都很小，全都由堅硬如岩石般的物質組成 **made up of solid, rocklike materials**，地球是內行星中體積最大的，這幾個內行星各擁有零到兩顆的衛星 **have zero, one, or two moons**。

外行星與內行星差異甚大，外行星比內行星寒冷許多 **much colder**，因為它們離太陽較遠 **farther from the sun**。外行星包含木星、土星、天王星以及海王星 **Jupiter, Saturn, Uranus, and Neptune**，它們的體積都非常大 **very large**，木星是太陽系中最大的一顆行星。外行星大部分由氣體組成 **made up of gas**，並擁有許多衛星 **moon**，木星就有至少 63 顆衛星，其他的外行星也有很多顆衛星。

Words to Know

- **inner planet** 內行星
- **outer planet** 外行星
- **be divided into** 被分成
- **characteristic** 特徵；特色
- **fairly** 相當地
- **close to** 接近
- **rocklike** 像岩石的
- **material** 物質
- **farther** 更遠的
- **mostly** 大部分地；主要地

Are We Alone 宇宙只有我們嗎？

For thousands of years, / men have looked at the stars / and asked, / "Are we alone?" Men **are fascinated by** the stars / and the **possibility** of / there being life / on other planets. **Myths** in many cultures / tell stories / about **aliens** coming to the earth. But no one knows / if there really are aliens / or not.

Nowadays, / scientists are **searching for** life / on other planets. Some believe / there could be life / on Mars. Others think / the moons Europa or Io / could have life. And others are looking at / other **star systems**. They are trying to find / **Earth-like** planets.

What does life need / to survive / on other planets? Life on the earth / is all **carbon based**. That kind of life / needs a star / to provide heat and light. It needs / an atmosphere with oxygen. It needs water. Of course, / other forms of life / could be based on / different **elements**. We don't know / what they would need to survive. But we do know / one thing: / Men will continue / looking for **extraterrestrial** life / until we find it.

數千年以來，人們仰望星空問：「宇宙只有我們嗎？」**Are we alone** 人們陶醉 **be fascinated** 於漫天星斗，為其他星球可能存在生命所著迷。許多文化都有外星人 **aliens** 降臨地球的神話 **myths** 故事，卻沒有人知道外星人是否真的存在 **if there really are aliens or not**。

而今科學家 **scientists** 一直在尋找其他星球上的生命 **search for life on other planets**。有些人認為火星上 **on Mars** 可能存在生命，有些人則認為歐羅巴（木衛二）或埃歐（木衛一）可能存在生命，還有一些人試圖從其他星系 **star system** 尋找與地球類似的行星 **find Earth-like planets**。

其他星球生命生存的條件是什麼呢？地球上的生命 **life on Earth** 全是碳基 **carbon based** 生命，需要來自恆星提供的熱和光、充滿氧氣的大氣層，也需要水分。當然，其他的生命形式 **other forms of life** 可能以不同的元素為生命基礎 **based on different elements**，我們不知道他們需要的生存條件，但有一件事是確定的：在找到外星生物 **extraterrestrial life** 前，人們絕對會繼續探索下去。

Words to Know

- **be fascinated by** 被……所吸引
- **possibility** 可能性
- **myth** 神話；迷思
- **alien** 外星人
- **search for** 尋找
- **star system** 星系
- **Earth-like** 像地球的
- **carbon based** 以碳為基礎的
- **element** 元素
- **extraterrestrial** 地球外的；外星的

Conductors and Insulators 導體與絕緣體

Electricity can move / thanks to conductors. These are materials / that let electricity move freely. Gold and silver / are very good conductors. Some people make wires / out of them. But they are / both expensive. So, / people often use / other conductors / to make wires. Most electrical wires / are made from / a conducting metal, / such as **copper**.

What are some other conductors? Lots of metals / are conductors. So is / **graphite**. Water is / an excellent conductor. That's why it's a bad idea / to go swimming / in **thunderstorms**. Lightning can strike the water / and hurt or even kill a person. The human body / is also a conductor. That's why people need to be careful / around electricity.

Of course, / people may want to stop / the flow of electricity. To do this, / people use insulators. They prevent electricity / from moving / from place to place. What are some of them? Plastics are very good insulators. Paper and rubber / are also insulators. And glass and **porcelain** / are two more insulators. These materials are all useful / for stopping the flow of electricity.

由於有導體 **conductor** 的存在，電才能夠移動。有很多的材料都能使電自由移動 **let electricity move freely**。金和銀 **gold and silver** 是非常好的導體，所以有些人利用它們製造金屬線 **make wires**。然而金和銀都很昂貴，因此人們用其他導體來製造金屬線。大部分的電線是由像銅 **copper** 這樣的導電金屬 **conducting metal** 所構成。

還有哪些東西是導體 **some other conductors** 呢？許多金屬 **lots of metals** 都屬於導體，石墨 **graphite** 就是其中之一。水 **water** 也是最佳的導體。這也就是為什麼在大雷雨 **thunderstorm** 中游泳是個壞主意。閃電會擊中水並傷害、甚至奪走人的性命。人體 **human body** 也是導體之一。人要對周遭的電加以小心就是這個原因。

當然，人可能會想阻斷電流 **stop the flow of electricity**。為此，人們使用絕緣體 **insulator**，它們能阻斷電四處移動 **prevent electricity from moving**。那麼絕緣體有哪些呢？塑膠 **plastic** 是非常好的絕緣體，紙和橡膠 **paper and rubber** 也是絕緣體，還有，玻璃和瓷器 **glass and porcelain** 亦是絕緣體，這些材料都能有效阻斷電流。

Words to Know

- **copper** 銅
- **graphite** 石墨
- **thunderstorm** 大雷雨
- **porcelain** 瓷器

56 Sir Isaac Newton 艾薩克．牛頓爵士

Sir Isaac Newton lived / in the seventeenth and eighteenth centuries. He was / one of the greatest scientists / who ever lived. He worked with light. He invented **calculus**. And he also discovered gravity / and the three laws of motion.

Supposedly, / Newton was sitting / under an apple tree / one day. An apple fell / and hit him on the head. So he started thinking / about **gravity**. He realized / that it was gravity / that caused objects to fall to the ground.

Newton's three laws of motion / are incredibly important / to physics. The first law says / that the state of motion of an object / does not change / until a force is applied to it. It is often called / the *law of* ***inertia***. The second law of motion / is called / the *law of* ***acceleration***. It is often written / as / F = ma. That means / "force equals mass times acceleration." This is / the most important / of the three laws. The third law says / that for every action, / there is / an equal and opposite reaction. The third law means / that all forces are ***interactions***.

艾薩克．牛頓爵士 **Sir Isaac Newton** 生活在十七到十八世紀，他是史上最偉大的科學家之一。他研究光學 **work with light**、發明微積分 **invent calculus**，還發現重力 **gravity** 和三大運動定律 **three laws of motion**。

據說有一天牛頓坐在一棵蘋果樹下，被一顆落下的蘋果打中頭。因此他開始思考重力，他發現就是重力致使物體掉落到地面 **cause objects to fall to the ground**。

牛頓的三大運動定律 **three laws of motion** 對物理學非常重要。第一定律 **the first law** 說明，未受到外力前，物體的運動狀態保持不變。這通常稱之為「慣性定律」**the law of inertia**。第二運動定律 **the second law of motion** 稱為「加速度定律」**the law of acceleration**。它通常被寫為「F ＝ ma」，這表示「作用力等於質量乘以加速度」。第二運動定律是三大運動定律中最重要的一個。第三運動定律 **the third law** 說明，在每一個作用力都存在著一個相等且相反的力。第三定律意味著所有的力量都會相互作用 **all forces are interactions**。

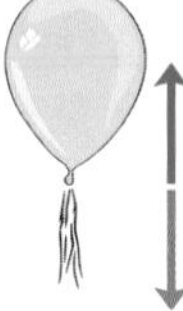

Words to Know

- **calculus** 微積分
- **gravity** 萬有引力
- **inertia** 慣性
- **acceleration** 加速
- **interaction** 互相作用

57 Elements 元素

The entire **universe** / is made of matter. And matter / is made of / elements or **compounds**. Compounds are **chemical combinations** / of two or more elements. What is an element? It is a substance / that **is made up of** / only one kind of **atom**, / such as **helium** or gold. Atom is the smallest **unit** / of an element.

There are / more than 110 elements. Most are natural. So they appear / in nature. But scientists have made / a few elements. They only appear / in labs.

All elements have / a similar **structure**. They have / a **nucleus**. This is / the element's core, / the center of an atom. Inside the nucleus / are **protons** and **neutrons**. Elements have / different numbers of them. For example, / **hydrogen** has / 1 proton and 0 neutrons. Helium has / 2 protons and 2 neutrons. **Oxygen** has / 8 protons and 8 neutrons. Gold has / 79 protons and 118 neutrons. Outside the nucleus / are **electrons**. They orbit the nucleus.

Electrons have / **negative charges**. But protons have / **positive** charges. Also, / an element usually has / the same number of protons and electrons. But they can / sometimes / be different.

整個宇宙是由物質組成的，而物質則由個別的元素或是化合物構成。化合物是指兩種或兩種以上元素 **element** 的結合。那麼什麼是元素呢？元素是只含一種原子 **made up of only one kind of atom** 的物質，例如氦和金。原子 **atom** 是元素的最小單位 **the smallest unit of an element**。

元素的種類超過 110 種 **more than 110 elements**，大部分是自然元素，存在於大自然中。但是科學家也會製造一些元素，就只在實驗室裡出現。

所有的元素都有一個類似結構，就是原子核 **nucleus**，這是元素的核心，也就是原子的中心 **the center of an atom**。原子核內部 **inside the nucleus** 有質子和中子 **proton and neutron**，每種元素的質子數與中子數並不相同。例如，氫有一個質子和零個中子，氦有兩個質子和兩個中子，氧有八個質子和八個中子，金則有 79 個質子和 118 個中子。原子核的外圍 **outside the nucleus** 有電子 **electron**，繞行 **orbit** 原子核運動。

電子帶負電 **negative charge**，質子卻帶正電 **positive charge**。此外，一個元素的質子與電子數量通常相同，偶爾也會相異。

Words to Know

- **universe** 宇宙 • **compound** 混合物 • **chemical** 化學的 • **combination** 結合
- **be made up of** 由……組成 • **atom** 原子 • **helium** 氦 • **unit** 單位 • **structure** 結構
- **nucleus** 原子核 • **proton** 質子 • **neutron** 中子 • **hydrogen** 氫 • **oxygen** 氧
- **electron** 電子 • **negative** 負極的 • **charge** 電荷 • **positive** 正極的

58 Atoms and Their Atomic Numbers 原子和原子序

All atoms have / different numbers / of protons, neutrons, and electrons. The protons / are **positively charged** / and are in the nucleus. Neutrons are also / in the nucleus. But they have no charge. And electrons orbit the nucleus. They have / negative charges. The number of protons and neutrons / in an atom / is often—but not always—the same.

Every element has / a different number / of protons. This helps / make it different / from other elements. An element's atomic number / is the same / as its number of protons. For example, / hydrogen has / only 1 proton. So this means / that it has an atomic number of 1. It is / the first element / on the **periodic table** of elements. Helium is / the second element. It has / an atomic number of 2. This means / that it has 2 protons in its nucleus.

There are / more than 110 different elements. Scientists often **recognize** them / **according to** their atomic numbers. **Carbon** is the **basis** / for all life on Earth. Its atomic number / is 6. Oxygen is / an important element. Its atomic number / is 8. **Iron** is / another important element. 26 is / its atomic number. Gold has / an atomic number of 79. And uranium's atomic number / is 92.

所有原子皆有不同數目的質子 **proton**、中子與電子。帶正電的 **positively charged** 質子與不帶電的中子 **neutron** 皆位於原子核中 **in the nucleus**，而帶負電的 **have negative charges** 電子則環繞著原子核 **orbit the nucleus**。質子與中子的數目通常是一樣的，但不是絕對。

每一個元素皆有不同數目的質子，使元素能互異於彼此。一個元素的原子序 **atomic number** 與質子數目 **number of protons** 會是相同的。舉例來說，氫 **hydrogen** 僅有一個質子 **has only one proton**，也就表示原子序為 1 **atomic number of 1**，是元素週期表 **on the periodic table** 的首個元素 **the first element**。氦為第二個元素，原子序為 2，代表原子核中有兩個質子。

元素有超過 110 種，科學家多以原子序來辨識它們。碳 **carbon** 為地球上所有生物的根本 **the basis for all life**，原子序為 6。氧 **oxygen** 是個重要的元素，原子序為 8。鐵 **iron** 是另一個重要元素，原子序是 26。金 **gold** 的原子序是 79，鈾 **uranium** 則是 92。

Words to Know

- **atomic number** 原子序
- **positively charged** 帶正電
- **periodic table** 元素週期表
- **recognize** 辨別
- **according to** 根據
- **carbon** 碳
- **basis** 基本成分
- **iron** 鐵

59 Energy and Environmental Risks 能源與環境風險

In the modern age, / human society / runs on energy. Most machines / need electricity / to **operate**. Humans have / many different ways / to create electricity. But some ways are **harmful** / to the **environment**.

For example, / **fossil fuels** are / the most common kind of energy. They include / coal, oil, and natural gas. First, / people have to mine them / from the ground. This can sometimes / harm the environment. However, / scientists are creating / cleaner and more **efficient** ways / to do that / these days. So the environment / is not damaged / as much. But when people burn / these fossil fuels, / they can **release** gases / that might harm the environment.

Tidal energy is another way / to make electricity. This uses / the ocean tides / to make electricity. But some kinds of tidal energy / can kill / many fish and other sea creatures. Also, / dams can create / lots of clean **hydroelectric** energy. But dams create lakes / and change the courses of rivers. So they can change the environment / very much.

Nuclear energy / is a very powerful form / of energy. It is cheap. It is also very clean. But many people are afraid of it / because it uses **radioactive** materials. Also, there have been / some accidents / at nuclear power plants / in the past. But the **technology** is much better / these days. So many countries are starting to build / more nuclear power plants / now.

現代生活中，人類仰賴能源生活，多數機器均需要電力才能運作。人類有許多不同製造電力 **create electricity** 的方法，然而有些方法卻對環境有害。

舉例來說，化石燃料 **fossil fuels** 為最普遍的能源，包含了煤、石油與天然氣 **coal, oil, and natural gas**。首先，人們需要從地底開挖它們 **mine them**，此舉有時會破壞到環境 **harm the environment**。不過近來科學家們為此想出更乾淨、更有效的方法，環境便不會受到如此大的傷害。但當人們燃燒化石燃料時，會釋出可能危害到環境的氣體。

另一個發電方式是潮汐發電 **tidal energy**，利用海洋潮汐 **use the ocean tides** 產生電力。不過有些潮汐能源會使許多魚類和海洋生物死亡。水壩 **dam** 也能產生許多乾淨的水力發電的能源 **hydroelectric energy**，但它需要造湖，改變河道，大幅地改變了環境。

核能發電 **nuclear energy** 是個強力的能源形式，價格低廉又非常乾淨。不過由於它使用放射性原料 **use radioactive materials** 而使許多人感到憂心，而且幾間核能發電廠在過去也曾發生意外。不過近來科技進步，所以許多國家正開始建造更多的核能發電廠。

Words to Know

- **risk** 風險 • **operate** 操作 • **harmful** 有害的 • **environment** 環境 • **fossil fuel** 化石燃料
- **efficient** 效率高的 • **release** 釋放 • **hydroelectric** 水力發電的 • **radioactive** 放射性的
- **technology** 科技

60 The Scientific Method of Inquiry 科學探究方法

Scientists have / a method / they use / when they are trying to learn / something new. It is called / the scientific method of inquiry.

The first step / is to ask a question. It could be / "Why do birds fly south / for the winter?" Or it could be / "How much heat does it take / for gold to melt?" It could be / about anything.

Then, / the scientist must do **research**. He or she should learn / as much / about the **topic** / as possible. Next, / the scientist makes a **hypothesis**. This is / an **educated** guess. It could be / "Birds fly south / for the winter / because they are cold." Or it could be / "Gold melts / at 200 degrees **Fahrenheit**." Now, / the scientist has a hypothesis, / so it must be tested. Scientists do this / by **conducting experiments**. Some do experiments / in **labs**, / and others do them / outdoors.

After the experiments are complete, / the scientist must **analyze** the **data**. Then he should **compare** it / with the hypothesis. Was the hypothesis / right or wrong? Even with a wrong hypothesis, / scientists can still / learn a lot. Finally, / they should write / about their **results**. That way, / other people can learn, / too.

科學家有一個用來試圖獲知新事物的方法，稱做科學探究方法 **scientific method of inquiry**。

第一步是要提出問題 **ask a question**。問題可以是「為什麼鳥會在冬天向南飛？」或者是「黃金需要多熱才會熔化？」。提出的問題可以是任何事情 **about anything**。

接下來，科學家會進行研究 **do research**。他們必須盡可能地瞭解研究主題。之後，科學家會形成一個假說 **make a hypothesis**。這會是一個有根據的猜測 **educated guess**。例如「鳥在冬天向南飛是因為牠們會冷」或是「黃金在華氏 200 度會熔化」。現在科學家有了假說，就要對它進行檢測 **must be tested**。他們通常會進行實驗 **conducting experiment** 來檢測假說。有些人在實驗室裡 **in labs** 進行實驗；有些人則在戶外 **outdoors** 進行。

實驗完成後，科學家會分析數據 **analyze the data**，並與假說加以比較 **compare it with the hypothesis**。假說是正確還是錯誤的呢？就算是錯誤的假說，科學家也能從中學到許多。最後，他們會把結果寫下來 **write about results**。如此一來，其他人也可以從中獲益不少。

Words to Know

- **research** 研究 • **topic** 主題 • **hypothesis** 假說；前提 • **educated** 根據知識或是經驗的
- **Fahrenheit** 華氏 • **conduct** 操作 • **experiment** 實驗 • **lab** 實驗室 • **analyze** 分析
- **data** 資料 • **compare** 比較 • **result** 結果

Mathematics

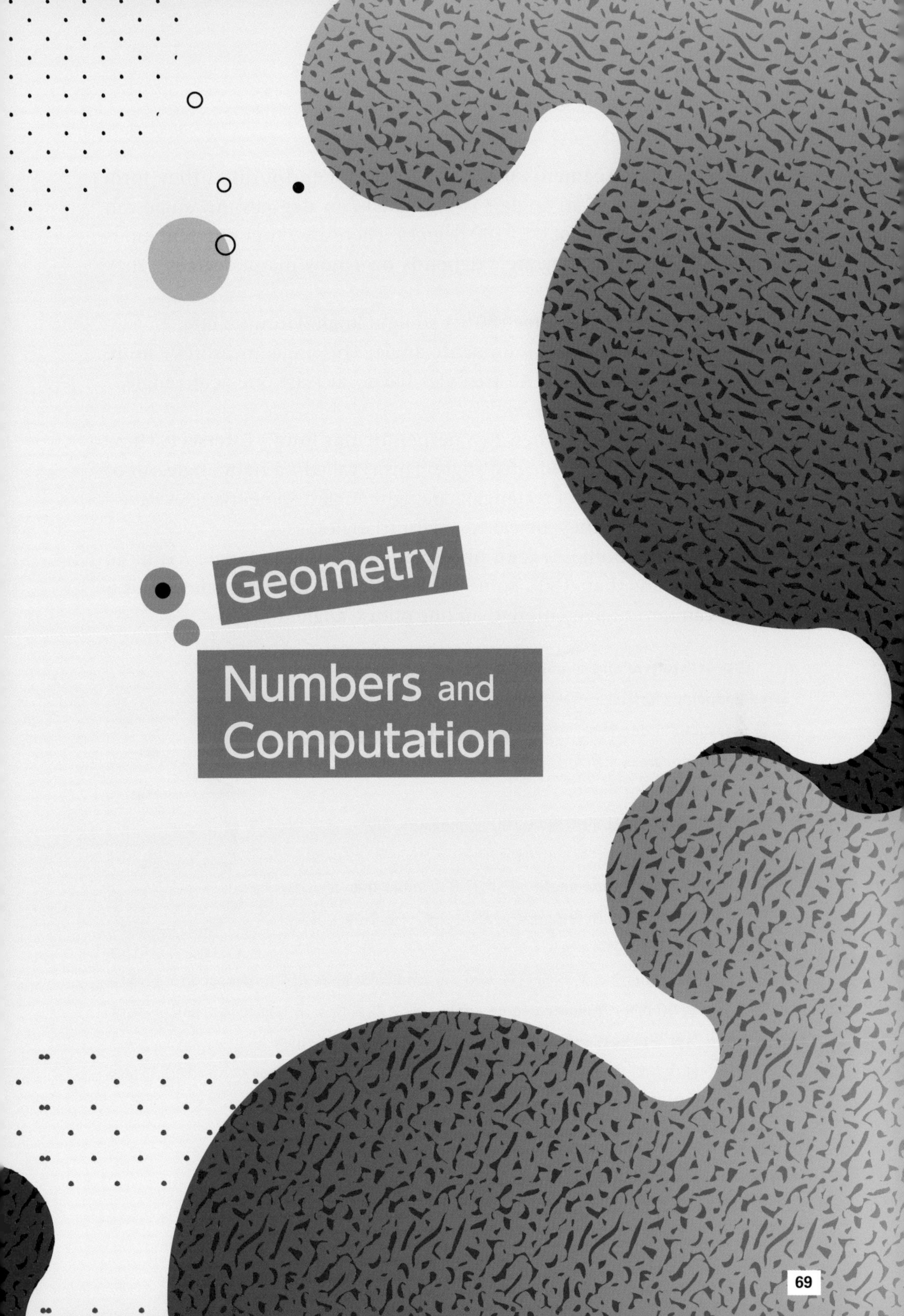
Geometry
Numbers and Computation

61 Angles 角

When two line segments meet / at the same **endpoint**, / they form an angle. The size of an angle / is measured / in **degrees**. An angle can measure / anywhere from 0 to 180 degrees. There are / four different kinds of angles. What type they are / **depends on** / how many degrees / they have.

A **straight** angle / measures 180°. A straight angle / forms a line.

The next kind of angle / is an **acute** angle. This angle measures / **more than** 0° but **less than** 90°. All triangles have / at least one acute angle, / and many have / three of them.

A right angle occurs / when two **perpendicular** lines / **intersect**. These two lines / form a ninety-degree angle. This is called / a right angle. All of the angles / in a square or rectangle / are right angles. Some triangles have / one right angle, / so they are called / right triangles.

The last kind of angle / is an **obtuse** angle. An obtuse angle / is more than 90° but less than 180°. Some triangles have / obtuse angles, / but a triangle can never have / more than one obtuse angle.

當兩個線段 **two line segments** 交會在同一端點 **meet at the same endpoint**，會形成一個角 **form an angle**。角的大小以度來測量 **measured in degrees**。角測量出來介於 0 度到 180 度之間 **from 0 to 180 degrees**。角可分為四種，它們的種類取決於度數的大小。

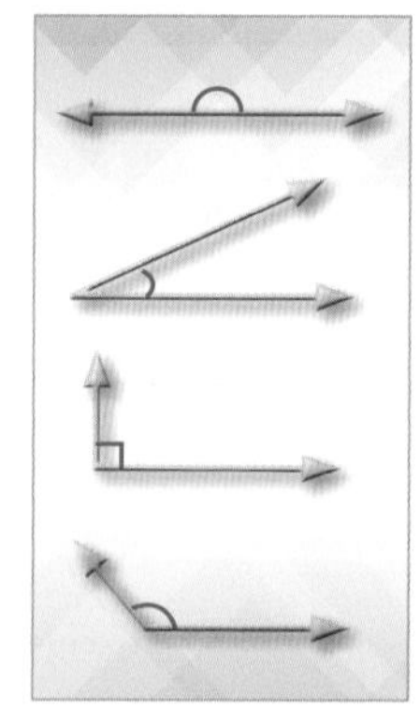

平角 **straight angle** 的角度為 180 度 **measure 180°**，它可以形成一條線 **form a line**。

另一種角為銳角 **acute angle**。它大於 0 度 **more than 0°**，小於 90 度 **less than 90°**。所有的三角形都至少有一個銳角，其中有許多三角形有三個銳角。

直角 **right angle** 形成於兩垂直線 **two perpendicular lines** 相交 **intersect** 時。這兩條線形成了一個 90 度的角 **ninety-degree angle**，稱之為直角。正方形和長方形中的角度都為直角。有些三角形有一個直角，因此它們被稱為直角三角形。

最後一種角為鈍角 **obtuse angle**。鈍角大於 90 度 **more than 90°**，小於 180 度 **less than 180°**。有些三角形有鈍角，但一個三角形不會有一個以上的鈍角。

Words to Know

- **endpoint** 端點
- **degree** 角度
- **depend on** 視……而定
- **straight** 直的
- **acute** 銳角的
- **more than** 超過
- **less than** 少於
- **perpendicular** 垂直的
- **intersect** 相交
- **obtuse** 鈍角的

62 Triangles 三角形

Triangles are **geometrical** figures / that have three sides. There are / several kinds of triangles. They depend on / the **type** of angles / in the triangles / and the **lengths** of the sides / of the triangles.

The first three types of triangles / are acute, right, and obtuse triangles. An acute triangle / is one / where all three angles / in the triangle / are acute. So each angle / is less than 90°. A right triangle has / one angle / that is 90°. And the other two angles / are acute. Finally, / an obtuse triangle has / one angle / that is more than 90° / but less than 180°. The other two angles / in it / are acute.

Next, / there are / three types of triangles / that **are characterized** / **by** the length of the triangles' sides. They are / **equilateral**, **isosceles**, and **scalene** triangles. Equilateral triangles have / three sides / that are the same length. All three angles are always 60°, / so they are also / acute triangles. Isosceles triangles have / two sides / with **equal** length. And all three sides / in a scalene triangle / are of different lengths.

三角形為三個邊的幾何圖形 **geometrical figure**，它可分為許多種類 **several kinds of triangles**。三角形的種類決定於三角形的角度和邊長。

前三種三角形為銳角三角形、直角三角形和鈍角三角形。銳角三角形 **acute triangle** 是指三角形的三個內角皆為銳角，所以每個角度都小於 90 度。直角三角形 **right triangle** 有一個為 90 度的內角，其他兩個內角都為銳角。最後，鈍角三角形 **obtuse triangle** 有一個大於 90 度且小於 180 度的內角。它的其他兩個內角為銳角。

接下來，有三種三角形可以根據邊長來分類。它們是等邊三角形、等腰三角形以及不等邊三角形。等邊三角形 **equilateral triangle** 的三個邊長皆相等，三個內角皆永遠為 60 度，所以它們也是銳角三角形。等腰三角形 **isosceles triangle** 有兩個相等的邊長。不等邊三角形 **scalene triangle** 的三個邊長都不相等。

Words to Know

- **geometrical** 幾何圖形的
- **type** 種類
- **length** 長度
- **be characterized by** 以……為特徵
- **equilateral** 等邊的
- **isosceles** 等腰的
- **scalene** 不等邊的
- **equal** 相等的

63 Solid Figures in Real Life 真實生活中的立體圖形

Solid figures **include** / cubes, **prisms, pyramids, cylinders**, cones, and spheres. Everywhere you look, / you can see / solid figures.

Many buildings / are **rectangular prisms**. A door is one, / too. So are / the **bulletin board** / in your classroom / and this book / you are reading right now.

Pyramids are not / very common. But some of them / are really famous. Think about Egypt / for a minute. What **comes to mind**? The pyramids, right? There are / huge pyramids / all over Egypt.

Cones are / among people's favorite solid figures. Why is that? The reason is / that ice cream cones are solid figures. There are often / many cones / in areas / where there is road **construction**, too. Construction workers / put **traffic cones** / on the street / to show people / where they can and cannot drive.

Of course, / spheres are everywhere. People would not be able to / play most sports / without them. They need / soccer balls, baseballs, basketballs, tennis balls, / and many other spheres. Oranges, grapefruit, peaches, plums, and cherries / are fruits / that are shaped like spheres, too.

立體圖形 solid figure 包含立方體 cube、角柱 prism、角錐 pyramid、圓柱 cylinder、圓錐 cone 以及球體 sphere，放眼所見幾乎都有立體圖形。

許多建築物 many buildings 是長方柱 rectangular prism，門 door、教室的布告欄 bulletin board 和你現在正在讀的書 book 也都是。

角錐 pyramid 並不常見，不過有些卻赫赫有名。想一下埃及，什麼出現在你腦海中呢？金字塔 the pyramids，對吧？埃及四處可見高大的金字塔。

圓錐 cone 是人們最愛的立體圖形之一。為什麼呢？因為冰淇淋 ice cream cone 就是立體圖形。道路施工處也常有很多圓錐出現，施工工人會在道路上設置交通錐 traffic cone，告知駕駛此處是否可通行。

當然，球體 sphere 也遍布各地。如果沒有球體，大部分的運動都無法進行了。人們需要足球 soccer ball、棒球 baseball、籃球 basketball、網球 tennis ball 以及其他球體。橘子、葡萄柚、桃子、梅子和櫻桃，也都屬於球狀的水果 fruits。

Words to Know

- **include** 包括
- **prism** 稜柱
- **pyramid** 錐體
- **cylinder** 圓柱；圓柱體
- **rectangular prism** 長方柱
- **bulletin board** 布告欄
- **come to mind** 突然記起或想到
- **construction** 建造
- **traffic cone** 錐形警告路標

64 Dimensions 維度

The physical world / we live in / has three dimensions. These three dimensions / can all be measured and charted / on a **graph**. They are / length, width, and **depth**.

Length / is the first dimension. It is represented / by a simple line. On a **three-dimensional** graph, / it is represented / by the x-**axis**, / which runs horizontally.

The second dimension / is width. When an object exists / in two dimensions, / it can **take the shape of** a plane figure, / such as a square, rectangle, triangle, or circle. **In other words**, / it can be represented / in both length and width. On a three-dimensional graph, / width is represented / by the y-axis, / which also runs horizontally.

The third dimension / is depth. It is also called / height. When an object exists / in three dimensions, / it can take the shape / of a solid figure, / such as a cube, pyramid, sphere, or prism. On a three-dimensional graph, / depth is represented / by the z-axis, / which runs **vertically**.

The fourth dimension / is time. Scientists have a name / for a cube / that exists in four dimensions. They call it / a **tesseract**.

So how many dimensions / are there? Scientists are not sure. Some believe / that there may be / eleven dimensions. Others claim / that there are even more. Right now, / scientists are searching for / extra dimensions. They have not found any yet, / but they believe / they exist.

我們所居住的物質世界 **the physical world** 有三維空間 **three dimensions**，此三維可在圖表上測量與繪製。它們也就是長度、寬度與深度。

長度為第一維度 **the first dimension**，可以以一條簡單的直線 **a simple line** 表示。但在立體圖中則以水平的 **run horizontally** X 軸 **x-axis** 呈現。

第二維度 **the second dimension** 則是寬度 **width**。當一物體存於二維空間中，便擁有平面圖形 **plane figure** 的型體，如正方形、長方形、三角形與圓形。也就是說它能以長寬來表現。寬度在立體圖中則以同樣水平的 Y 軸 **y-axis** 來呈現。

第三維度 **the third dimension** 則為深度 **depth**，又稱為高 **height**。當某物體存於三維空間時，會有像是立方體、三角錐、球體與角柱體般的立體形狀 **solid figure**。在立體圖中，深度則以垂直的 **run vertically** Z 軸 **z-axis** 呈現。

第四維度 **the fourth dimension** 則是時間 **time**。科學家替存於第四維度中的立方體命名為「超立方體」**tesseract**。

那到底有多少維度呢？科學家們尚未確定。有些人認為可能有 11 維，有些則聲稱要來的更多。科學家目前正在尋找更多維度，雖然尚未發現，但他們深信這是存在的。

Words to Know

- **graph** 圖表
- **depth** 深度
- **three-dimensional** 三度空間的
- **axis** 軸
- **take the shape of** 呈……的形狀
- **in other words** 換句話說
- **vertically** 垂直地
- **tesseract** 超立方體

65 Solve the Problems 解題

1. Two oranges / are the same size. Amy gets / $\frac{1}{2}$ of one orange. Tom gets / $\frac{1}{5}$ of the other. Who gets / more of the orange?
   → $\frac{1}{2}$ is / **greater than** $\frac{1}{5}$. So, Amy gets / the **larger** piece.
2. Eric has / one **candy bar**. He eats / $\frac{1}{3}$ of the candy bar / in the morning. **Later in the day**, / he eats / another $\frac{1}{3}$ of the candy bar. How much of the candy bar / is left over?
   → He ate / $\frac{2}{3}$ of the candy bar. So there is / $\frac{1}{3}$ left over.
3. Mary makes a pie. She cuts it / into 8 pieces. Steve takes / $\frac{1}{4}$ of the pie. Then Chris takes / $\frac{1}{2}$ of the pie. How much pie / **remains**?
   → $\frac{1}{4}=\frac{2}{8}$. And $\frac{1}{2}=\frac{4}{8}$. $\frac{2}{8}+\frac{4}{8}=\frac{6}{8}$. So $\frac{6}{8}$ of the pie / is gone. Now there are / $\frac{2}{8}$ (or $\frac{1}{4}$) of the pie remaining.
4. Daniel **goes shopping**. He has / $5\frac{1}{2}$ dollars. His brother goes shopping / with him. His brother / has $5\frac{2}{3}$ dollars. Who has / more money?
   → $\frac{2}{3}$ is / greater than $\frac{1}{2}$. So Daniel's brother has / more money.

1. 兩顆同樣大小 **the same size** 的橘子。艾美拿到其中一顆的 $\frac{1}{2}$ ，湯姆拿到另一顆的 $\frac{1}{5}$。請問誰拿到比較多的橘子？
   → $\frac{1}{2}$ 大於 **greater than** $\frac{1}{5}$，所以艾美拿到比較大塊 **large piece**。
2. 艾瑞克有一塊巧克力棒。他早上吃了 $\frac{1}{3}$ 的巧克力棒。當天不久後他又吃了另外的 $\frac{1}{3}$。請問巧克力棒還剩下 **left over** 多少？
   → 他吃了 $\frac{2}{3}$ 的巧克力棒，所以最後還剩下 $\frac{1}{3}$ 的巧克力棒。
3. 瑪麗做了一個派 **make a pie**，她把派切成八份 **cut it into 8 pieces**。史帝夫拿走派的 $\frac{1}{4}$，然後克里斯又拿走派的 $\frac{1}{2}$ 。請問派最後還剩下多少？
   → $\frac{1}{4}=\frac{2}{8}$，而 $\frac{1}{2}=\frac{4}{8}$。$\frac{2}{8}+\frac{4}{8}=\frac{6}{8}$ 。所以 $\frac{6}{8}$ 的派被拿走 **gone** 了，最後還剩下 **remaining** $\frac{2}{8}$（$\frac{1}{4}$）個派。
4. 丹尼爾去購物 **go shopping**，他有 $5\frac{1}{2}$ 塊錢，他的弟弟和他一起去購物，他有 $5\frac{2}{3}$ 塊錢。請問誰的錢比較多？
   → $\frac{2}{3}$ 大於 $\frac{1}{2}$ ，所以丹尼爾弟弟的錢比較多 **more money**。

Words to Know

- **greater than** 比……大
- **larger** 較大的
- **candy bar** 糖果棒；巧克力棒
- **later in the day** 當天晚一點
- **remain** 剩下
- **go shopping** 購物

66 Collecting and Organizing Data 蒐集和整理數據

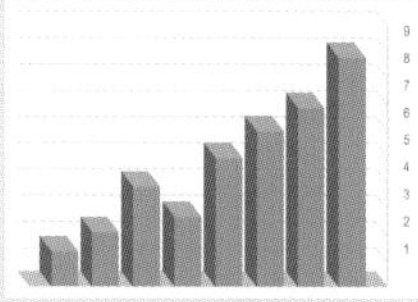

People often / conduct research. They may / research a topic / and find as much **information** / as they can / about it. Perhaps / they want to know / the daily temperature / in a region / for an entire year. Or maybe / they want to know / how many books / students read / during a **semester**. First, / they decide / what information / they want. Then / they collect the data.

But the **raw** data / they collect / could be **useless** / by itself. So they need to / organize it. One common way / to organize data / is to use **charts** and **diagrams**. This lets people / see the **visual** results / of their data. For example, / perhaps the researchers / have some data / on how many books / each student reads. They can put that data / onto a **bar graph**. This will let them / analyze it more easily. Or, maybe they know / the **average** temperature / for each day of the year. They can organize it / into a circle graph. This will show them / the **percentage** / of hot, warm, cool, and cold days / the area gets. By using these **visual aids**, / they can **interpret** their data / much more easily.

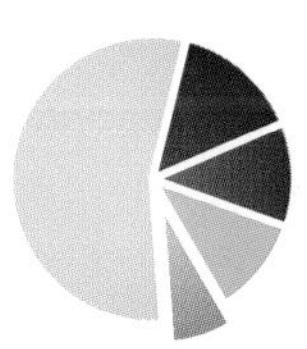

人們時常會進行研究 **conduct research**。他們研究一個主題 **research a topic** 並儘量蒐集相關資料 **find information**。也許他們會想知道一個地區一整年的每日氣溫。或是學生一學期要閱讀的書量。首先，他們必需先決定他們想要何種資訊 **decide what information they want**，接著才能蒐集數據 **collect data**。

然而，人們所蒐集的原始數據 **raw data** 本身可能一無所用。所以必須要整理數據 **organize data**。常見的方法之一就是利用圖表來檢視數據所呈現的視覺化資料 **visual result**。舉例來說，研究員擁有每個學生閱讀書量的數據。他們可以把數據放到直條圖 **bar graph** 上，以便於分析。或者，也許他們知道一年每日的日平均溫度。他們可以把數據整理成圓形圖 **circle graph**。此圖會顯示該區寒暖天數的百分比。藉由這些視覺輔助 **by using visual aids**，他們能更易於解釋數據 **interpret data much more easily**。

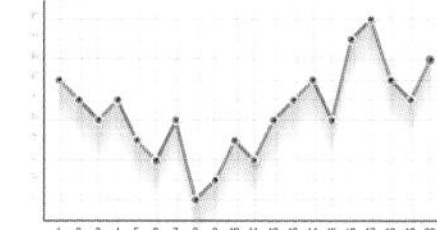

Words to Know

- **information** 資訊
- **semester** 學期
- **raw** 原始的
- **useless** 沒用的
- **chart** 圖表
- **diagram** 圖表；曲線圖
- **visual** 視覺的
- **bar graph** 長條圖
- **average** 平均的
- **percentage** 比例；百分比
- **visual aid** 視覺性的輔助
- **interpret** 解釋；詮釋

67 Roman Numerals 羅馬數字

We count with numbers / today. The **decimal system** / we use / is very easy. But not every **culture** / has counted / the same way. Many systems / are different. In **ancient** Rome, / the Romans used / Roman numerals. But these were not actually numerals. Instead, / they were **letters**.

The Romans used / the letters I, V, X, L, C, D, and M / to **stand for** certain **quantities**. For example, / I was 1, / V was 5, / X was 10, / L was 50, / C was 100, / D was 500, / and M was 1,000. To make larger numbers, / they just added / more letters. So 2 was II, / and 3 was III. 6 was VI, / and 7 was VII. However, / the number 4 / was not IIII. Instead, / it was IV. Why did they do that? When a letter was going to / change to one / with a greater value, / the Romans put the smaller letter / in front of the bigger letter. That meant / they should subtract that **amount**, / not add to it. So 9 was IX. 40 was XL. 90 was XC. And 900 was CM.

Doing that / was not difficult. But Romans could not / count very high / since it was hard / to write large numbers. For example, / what was 3,867? In Roman numerals, / it was MMMDCCCLXVII. How about doing / addition, subtraction, multiplication, or division? Can you imagine / dividing MMCCXII by CCLXIV?

今日我們都用數字來計數 **count with numbers**，我們所用的十進位制 **decimal system** 很簡單，不過並非每個文化都使用相同的計數法，方法各異。古羅馬人使用羅馬數字 **Roman numerals**，它們並非真正的數字，而是字母 **letters**。

羅馬人使用字母 I、V、X、L、C、D、M 來代表某些數 **stand for certain quantities**，例如 I 是 1，V 是 5，X 是 10，L 是 50，C 是 100，D 是 500，M 是 1,000。為了數出更大的數字 **to make larger numbers**，羅馬人會再增加字母 **add more letters**，因此 2 是 II，3 是 III，6 是 VI，7 是 VII。不過 4 並不是 IIII 而是 IV。羅馬人為什麼要這麼做？當一個數字要變成較大的數值時（如 III 變成 IV），羅馬人有時候是在大數字（V）前面放上小數字（I），表示要減去那個量，而不是加上（IV = V– I）。所以說，9 是 IX，40 是 XL，90 是 XC，900 是 CM。

這樣的作法雖不困難，但是羅馬人遇到特大的數字就算不下去了 **cannot count very high**，因為太難寫了。例如 3,867 要怎麼表示？用羅馬數字會變成 MMMDCCCLXVII。那麼又要怎麼作加減乘除？你可以想像用 MMCCXII 除以 CCLXIV 嗎？

Words to Know

- **decimal system** 十進位
- **culture** 文化
- **ancient** 古老的
- **letter** 字母
- **stand for** 代表
- **quantity** 數量
- **amount** 總數

68 The Order of Operations 運算順序

In math, / some problems / are easy to solve. For example, / this problem: / 2+3=5. That is / a simple problem. But sometimes / there are / more complicated problems. For example, / how about / this problem: / 2+3×4? How do you / solve this? Do you do / the **addition** or the **multiplication** / first? Is the answer / 14 or 20?

In math, / there is something / called / the order of operations. These tell / the order / in which you should solve a math problem. There are / three simple rules: /

1) Do the calculations / inside **parentheses** / first.
2) Moving from left to right, / solve all multiplication and **division** problems / first.
3) Moving from left to right, / solve all addition and **subtraction** problems / next.

Let's look at the problem above / one more time: / 2+3×4. How do we / solve it? First, / we must multiply / 3×4. That's 12. Then we add / 2+12. That's 14. So the correct answer / is 14.

How about / a more complicated problem? Look at this problem: / 3×(3+4)–1. First, / we must solve / the problem / in parentheses. So 3+4 is 7. Next, / we do the multiplication problem. So 3×7 is 21. Last, / we do / the subtraction problem. So 21–1 is 20. The answer is 20.

在數學中，有些題目很好解，例如 2+3=5 就是個簡單的題目 **simple problem**。不過有時候會碰到較複雜的問題 **complicated problem**，例如 2+3 × 4 要怎麼計算？要先作加法還是先作乘法？答案是 14 還是 20 ？

數學裡有所謂的運算次序 **the order of operations**，用來說明解題的順序。有三個簡單的規則：第一，括號內 **inside the parentheses** 先算；第二，由左向右 **from left to right** 先作乘除 **multiplication and division problems**；第三，由左向右再作加減 **addition and subtraction problems**。

再看一次上面的題目：2+3 × 4，我們要怎麼解 **how do we solve it** 呢？先將 3 × 4 得 12，再將 2+12 得到 14，所以正確答案為 14。

更複雜的問題怎麼辦？看看這一題：3 × (3+4)-1。首先要先算括號內的問題：3+4 是 7，接著作乘法：3 × 7 得 21，最後作減法：21-1 為 20，所以答案是 20。

Words to Know

- **order** 順序
- **operation** 運算
- **addition** 加法
- **multiplication** 乘法
- **parenthesis** 括號
- **division** 除法
- **subtraction** 減法

Percentages, Ratios, and Probabilities
百分比、比與機率

The **weatherman** may say, / "There is a 70% chance / of rain." He is telling you / the probability / of rain. At 70%, / this means / that, in the **current** weather conditions, / it will rain / 70 times out of 100. Weather forecasts / often use percentages. So do / sports. An **announcer** may say, / "The basketball player / **shoots** 52%." This means / that for every 100 shots / he takes, / he makes 52.

Ratios are a way / to compare two things / to one another. For example, / a classroom has / 20 children. There are / 12 boys and 8 girls. You can say, / "The ratio of boys to girls / is 12 to 8." Or you can write the ratio / as 12:8. Perhaps there are / 5 cats and 8 dogs. You can say / the ratio of cats to dogs / is 5 to 8 or 5:8.

Probability expresses / the **odds**, or chances, / of something happening. If you **flip** a coin, / there is / a 1 in 2 chance / of a certain side showing / because a coin has / two sides. If you roll a die, / there is / a 1 in 6 chance / of the number 4 appearing. Perhaps there are / 10 cookies. Three are / oatmeal cookies. If you grab one cookie / **at random**, / there is / a 3 in 10 chance / you will get an oatmeal cookie.

氣象播報員可能會說：「降雨機率 **chance of rain** 為 70%」，這是在說明下雨的機率 **probability of rain**。70% 表示以目前的天氣狀況來說，100 次的機會有 70 次 **70 times out of 100** 會下雨。氣象預報經常使用百分比 **percentage**，運動比賽也是，播報員可能會說：「這名籃球選手的命中率為 52%」，表示每 100 次的投籃有 52 次會投中。

「比」**ratio** 是用來比較兩件事物 **compare two things to one another** 的方法。例如，教室的 20 個孩童中，有 12 個男生、8 個女生，你可以說：「男女生的比 **the ratio of boys to girls** 為 12 比 8 **12 to 8**」，也可以寫成 12：8 。假設有 5 隻貓和 8 隻狗，你可以說貓比狗是 5 比 8、5：8。

機率 **probability** 表示事情發生的機會 **odds, or chances**。如果你輕拋一個硬幣，顯示某一面的機會為二分之一 **1 in 2 chance**，因為一個硬幣有兩面。如果你擲一顆骰子，出現 4 的機會為六分之一 **1 in 6 chance**。又或者有十片餅乾，其中有三片為燕麥餅乾，你隨機取一塊，拿到燕麥餅乾的機會是十分之三 **3 in 10 chance**。

Words to Know

- **weatherman** 氣象預報員
- **current** 現在的
- **announcer** 播報員
- **shoot** 投籃
- **odds** 可能性
- **flip** 輕拋
- **at random** 隨機

70 Square Roots 平方根

You have probably multiplied a number / by itself / before. For example, / two times two / is four.(2×2=4) Four times four / is sixteen.(4×4=16) Five times five / is twenty-five.(5×5=25) And ten times ten / is one hundred. (10×10=100) When you multiply a number / by itself, / you are squaring it.

However, / what happens / when you do an **inverse** operation? An inverse operation of squaring / is finding / the square root of a number. When the **divisor** of a number / and the result / are the same, / then that is / the square root of the number.

For instance, / the square root of 4 / is two.(=2) Why is that? The reason is / that four divided by two / is two.(4÷2=2) The divisor and the result / are the same. Also, / the square root of 49 / is seven. Forty-nine divided by seven / is seven. And the square root of 100 / is ten. One hundred divided by ten / is ten.

However, / not all square roots / are **whole numbers**. In fact, / they are usually / **irrational numbers**. For example, / what is the square root / of three? It is not / a whole number. Instead, / it is 1.73205. It actually goes on to infinity / because it can never be solved. And how about / the square root of six? It is 2.44948. It too goes on to **infinity** / and cannot be solved. Actually, / **the majority of** numbers / have square roots / that are irrational numbers.

你或許曾將一個數目乘以它自己 **multiply a number by itself**，像是 2 乘 2 **two times two** 等於 4、4 乘 4 等於 16、5 乘 5 等於 25，還有 10 乘 10 等於 100。當你將一個數字自乘，也就是在將它平方。

然而，當你反過來做 **inverse operation of squaring** 時會如何呢？平方的逆向運算便是找出該數的平方根。當一個數字的除數與答案是相同的 **the divisor and the result are the same**，即為平方根。

舉例來說，4 的平方根 **the square root of 4** 為 2 **is two**。理由為何呢？理由即在於 4 除以 2 **four divided by two** 等於 2 **is two**，除數與答案是相同的。還有 49 除以 7 等於 7，所以 49 的平方根是 7。100 除以 10 等於 10，故平方根為 10。

但也不是所有平方根都為整數 **whole number**，事實上通常為無理數 **irrational number**。例如 3 的平方根 **the square root of three** 是多少呢？它不是整數，而是 1.73205，事實上，數字無法被整除，所以答案無解。那 6 的平方根呢？是 2.44948，它也是無限小數，無法被整除。實際上，大多數字的平方根皆為無理數。

Words to Know

- **inverse** 相反的
- **divisor** 除數
- **whole number** 整數
- **irrational number** 無理數
- **infinity** 無限大
- **the majority of** 大多數的

71 Probability and Statistics 機率與統計

The probability of something / is the chance / that it will happen. This is often expressed / as a percentage. For example, / if you flip a coin, / the probability / of it being heads / is fifty percent. If you roll a die, / the probability / of it being the number one / is 16.67%, or $\frac{1}{6}$. You can **determine** the probability / by taking the number of ways / something can happen / and dividing it / by the total number of **outcomes**.

Statistics, / on the other hand, / is the field of math / that collects, organizes, and interprets data. Once data has been collected, / one of the easiest ways / to analyze it / is with graphs. For data / that involves probability, / circle graphs—or pie charts— / are the best to use. These can be divided / into 100 percentage points. Perhaps there is / a fifty percent chance / of something happening, / a twenty-five percent chance / of something else happening, / and a twenty-five percent chance / of something different happening. This can easily be shown / on a circle graph.

On the other hand, / other statistics are best recorded / on a bar graph. These are / simple charts / with an x-axis and a y-axis. For example, / perhaps the person is recording / some students' best subjects. The classes are / English, math, science, and history. These classes / go on the x-axis, / which is **horizontal**. The number of students / that do well in each class / goes on the y-axis, / which is **vertical**. This makes the data / easy to see and to interpret.

某事的機率 **probability** 即是發生的可能性 **chance**，常以百分比 **percentage** 表示。舉例來說，若你擲銅板，正面的機率是 50%。若你擲骰子，擲出點數 1 的機率為 16.67% 或是六分之一。你可以找出事物可能的發生方式共有幾種 **taking the number of ways**，再以結果發生的總次數除之，便得機率。

統計 **statistics** 在另一方面說來，是蒐集、統整與分析數據 **collect, organize, and interpret data** 的數學領域。一旦蒐集了資訊，其中一個最簡易的分析方式便是利用圖表。與機率有關，最適合的圖表有——圓形圖或稱圓餅圖 **circle graph or pie graph**，皆能分成 100 個百分點 **divide into 100 percentage points**。可能某事發生機率有 50%，另一件事發生機率有 25%，再另外一件事的發生機率也是 25%，都可簡易地顯示在圓餅圖上。

另一方面，條狀圖 **bar graph** 最適用於其他統計資料，而它們為有 X 軸與 Y 軸 **x-axis and y-axis** 的簡易圖表。舉例來說，有人正在紀錄幾位學生表現最好的科目，科目有英文、數學、自然科學與歷史。這些科目位於水平狀的 X 軸上，而表現良好的學生數量則在垂直的 Y 軸上。而這能使數據清楚又易於分析。

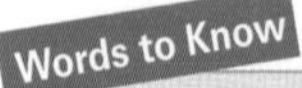

Words to Know

- **determine** 決定
- **outcome** 結果
- **horizontal** 水平的
- **vertical** 垂直的

72 The Metric System 公制

The metric system / is a system of **measurement** / that uses the base-10 system. It measures / length, **volume**, weight, pressure, energy, and temperature. There are / several units / in the metric system. But, / since it uses the base-10 system, / converting them / is quite easy.

The **meter** is the unit / used to measure length / in the metric system. But there are also / millimeters, centimeters, decimeters, decameters, hectometers, and kilometers. So, / in 1 meter, / there are / 10 decimeters, 100 centimeters, and 1,000 millimeters. Also, / in 1 kilometer, / there are / 10 hectometers, 100 decameters, and 1,000 meters. The most common units of length / are the millimeter, centimeter, meter, and kilometer.

The **liter** is the unit / used to measure volume / in the metric system. However, / there are also / milliliters, centiliters, deciliters, decaliters, hectoliters, and kiloliters. The method to convert them / is the same as / for meters.

The **gram** is the unit / used to measure weight / in the metric system. The most common units of weight / are the gram and the kilogram. There are other units, / but they are not commonly used.

Finally, / the metric system uses **Celsius** / to measure temperature. 0 degrees Celsius / is the temperature / at which water **freezes**. 100 degrees Celsius / is the temperature / at which water **boils**.

公制 **metric system** 是以十進位的測量系統 **use the base-10 system**，能測量長度、容積、重量、壓力、能量與溫度。公制中有許多單位 **several units**，不過由於它使用十進位制，便易於轉換。

公制中的公尺 **meter** 是用來測量長度 **measure length** 的單位，長度單位的還有公釐、公分、分米、十公尺（公丈）、一百公尺（公引）和公里。所以 1 公尺等於 10 分米，等於 100 公分，等於 1000 公釐。1 公里等於 10 公引，等於 100 公丈也等於 1000 公尺。最常見的長度單位為公釐、公分、公尺與公里。

公制中的公升 **liter** 是用來測量容積 **measure volume** 的單位。單位內還有毫升、釐升、分升、十升（公斗）、一百升（公石）與千升（公秉）。轉換單位的方式與公尺的方式相同。

公制中的公克 **gram** 是用來測量重量 **measure weight** 的單位。最常見的重量單位為公克與公斤，還有一些其他不常用到的單位。

最後公制中用攝氏 **Celsius** 是來作為測量溫度 **measure temperature** 的單位。水於攝氏零度時結冰，而於攝氏 100 度沸騰。

Words to Know

- **measurement** 測量 • **volume** 體積 • **meter** 公尺 • **liter** 公升 • **gram** 公克
- **Celsius** 攝氏 • **freeze** 結凍 • **boil** 沸騰

Language • Visual Arts • Music

Language and Literature
Visual Arts
Music

73 The Norse Gods 北歐眾神

Norse mythology / comes from Northern Europe. The Norse were Vikings. They lived in the area / that is Norway, Sweden, and Finland today. The Vikings loved to / fight and make war. So their stories / often / are very violent.

There were / many Norse gods. Odin was / their leader. He was very wise. Odin always had / two **ravens**. They were / **thought** and **memory**. They told him / everything / that happened in the land. Thor was / the god of thunder. He was / the most powerful / of all the gods. He carried / a great **hammer** / that he often used / to kill giants. Loki was / the god of **mischief** and fire / and was a half giant. He was also a **trickster**, / so he caused many problems / for the gods, / especially Thor. Frigg / was Odin's wife / and was also the goddess of marriage. And Freya was / the goddess of love. There were also / many other Norse gods and goddesses.

The gods lived at Asgard. They often had to / fight their enemies, / like frost giants and **trolls**. There are many stories / about their **deeds** / that people still enjoy reading.

北歐神話 **Norse mythology** 來自北歐 **comes from Northern Europe**。古北歐人曾是維京人，他們住在現今為挪威、瑞典以及芬蘭的區域。維京人喜愛打仗和製造戰爭，因此他們的故事都非常暴力。

北歐有許多的神 **Norse gods**，奧丁 **Odin** 為他們的領導者 **leader**。奧丁非常睿智 **very wise**。他身邊有兩隻渡鴉 **have two ravens**，分別代表思想與記憶 **thought and memory**。牠們告訴奧丁土地上發生的一切。索爾 **Thor** 是雷神 **the god of thunder**，是諸神中最強大的一個。他擁有一根常用來殺死巨人的巨鎚 **carry a great hammer**。洛基 **Loki** 是惡作劇之神與火神 **the god of mischief and fire**，同時是半個巨人 **half giant**。洛基也是個騙子 **trickster**，因此他替諸神帶來許多麻煩，特別是索爾。弗麗嘉 **Frigg** 是奧丁的妻子，同時也是婚姻女神 **the goddess of marriage**。芙蕾雅 **Freya** 是愛之女神 **the goddess of love**。北歐還有許多其他諸神。

眾神住在阿斯嘉 **live at Asgard**。他們常要和像寒霜巨人和山怪這樣的敵人戰鬥。至今人們仍喜愛閱讀關於諸神種種事蹟的故事。

Words to Know

- **raven** 渡鴉
- **thought** 想法
- **memory** 記憶
- **hammer** 鐵鎚
- **mischief** 惡作劇
- **trickster** 騙子
- **troll** 侏儒；巨人
- **deed** 行為

74 The *Iliad* and the *Odyssey* 《伊里亞德》與《奧德賽》

Two / of the greatest works of **literature** / are also very old. They are / the epic poems / the *Iliad* and the *Odyssey*. Both were told / by Homer / and tell stories / about the ancient Greeks.

The *Iliad* is about the Trojan War. Paris **abducted** Helen / and took her to Troy. Helen was the most beautiful woman / in the world. So all of the Greeks / joined together / to fight the Trojans. There were / many great Greek **warriors**. There were / Agamemnon, Menelaus, Odysseus, and Ajax. But Achilles was the greatest warrior / of all. The war lasted / for ten years. Many people died. Finally, / thanks to Odysseus, / the Greeks used the Trojan Horse / to win. The Greeks / **pretended to** leave. They left behind / a giant horse. The Trojans took the horse / into their city. But many Greek warriors / were hiding / inside it. At night, / the Greeks came out of the horse. Inside the city, / they managed to / capture and **defeat** Troy.

The *Odyssey* tells / the tale of Odysseus's return home / after the war. It took him / ten years / to get home. He had / many strange **adventures**. He had to / fight a **fearsome** Cyclops. He met / magical women / like Circe and Calypso. And all of his men / died. Finally, though, / with help from the gods, / Odysseus arrived home.

兩部最偉大的文學作品都非常古老，它們是史詩 **epic poem**《伊里亞德》**the *Iliad*** 與《奧德賽》**the *Odyssey***，兩者皆為荷馬所著 **told by Homer** 的古希臘故事 **about the ancient Greeks**。

《伊里亞德》是關於特洛伊戰爭 **the Trojan War** 的故事。帕里斯 **Paris** 誘拐 **abduct** 了世上最美麗的女人海倫 **Helen**，並把她帶到特洛伊，於是所有的希臘人 **all of the Greeks** 團結起來，對特洛伊人開戰 **fight the Trojans**。希臘有許多偉大的戰士，像是阿伽門農、墨涅拉俄斯、奧德修斯和阿賈克斯，不過其中最偉大的戰士是阿基里斯。戰爭持續了十年之久 **last for ten years**，許多人也因此戰亡。最終 **finally**，因為奧德修斯 **thanks to Odysseus**，希臘人利用特洛伊木馬 **use the Trojan Horse** 贏了戰爭。希臘人假裝撤退，只留下一座巨大的木馬。特洛伊人將木馬帶進城內，卻不知裡頭藏匿了許多希臘戰士。趁著黑夜時，希臘人走出木馬，從城內攻佔 **capture** 並擊敗特洛伊 **and defeat Troy**。

《奧德賽》是關於奧德修斯戰後返鄉 **Odysseus's return home** 的故事。奧德修斯花了十年的時間才回到家鄉，途中歷經許多奇特的冒險 **have many strange adventures**。他必須打敗可怕的獨眼巨人，也遭遇女巫瑟茜和卡呂普索。奧德修斯的士兵全都陣亡。他最後得到諸神相助，才得以返家。

Words to Know

- **literature** 文學
- **abduct** 誘拐
- **warrior** 戰士
- **pretend to** 假裝
- **defeat** 打敗
- **adventure** 冒險
- **fearsome** 可怕的

75 Types of Poems 詩的種類

Poets have / many different types of poems / to choose from / when they write. They can write / very long or very short poems. They can write / about many different subjects. And they can write / with different **rhyme schemes** / and in different meters.

One of the oldest types of poems / is the epic. This is / a very long poem. It can often be / thousands of lines long. An epic poem is / typically / about a hero and his adventures. There have been / many famous epic poems / in history. The *Iliad, Odyssey, Aeneid, Beowulf,* and *Gilgamesh* / are just a few / of the many epic poems.

On the other hand, / many poems are very short. **Sonnets** are / one type of short poem. They are poems / with fourteen lines. Usually, / the last two lines / in a sonnet / rhyme. Sonnets can be / about many different topics. William Shakespeare wrote / many famous sonnets. **Couplets** can be / long or short poems. Each **stanza** / in a couplet / has two lines. The last word / in each line / rhymes. **Quatrains** are / very short poems. They only have / four lines. And **cinquains** have / five lines. **Limericks** are also poems / with five lines. And **haikus** are poems / with only three lines. The first and third lines / have five **syllables**. And the second line / has seven syllables. They are / some of the shortest of poems.

詩人 **poet** 在作詩 **poem** 時，有許多文體可選擇。他們能寫下極長或極短的詩，或是許多不同的主題，還能以各種韻式 **rhyme scheme** 與格律 **meter** 來著作。

其中一種最古老形式的詩為史詩 **epic**，是一種極長篇的文體 **very long poem**，長度可達數千句之長 **thousands of lines long**。史詩通常是有關於一位英雄與他的冒險 **about a hero and his adventures**，歷史上就有許多著名的史詩—《伊利亞德》、《奧德賽》、《伊尼亞斯》、《貝武夫》與《鳩格米西史詩》，這些僅為史詩中的一些例子而已。

另一方面，也有許多短詩。十四行詩 **sonnet** 即是短詩的其中一種。此種有十四個句子 **with fourteen lines** 的文體，通常最後兩句 **the last two lines** 會押韻 **rhyme**。十四行詩能有各種主題，威廉·莎士比亞便寫了許多著名的十四行詩。對句 **couplet** 則可長可短。對句中的每個詩節 **each stanza** 有兩句 **have two lines**，每個句子最後的字 **the last word in each line** 必定互相押韻 **rhymes**。四行詩 **quatrain** 為極短詩，僅有四個句子 **only have four lines**。五行詩 **cinquain** 則有五個句子 **five lines**，五行打油詩 **limerick** 也是五個句子 **five lines** 的詩。僅有三個句子 **only three lines** 的為俳句詩 **haiku**，它的首句與第三句有五個音節，第二句則有七個音節；以上為最短詩的其中幾種。

Words to Know

- **poet** 詩人
- **rhyme scheme** 韻律
- **sonnet** 十四行詩
- **couplet** 雙行詩
- **stanza** 詩的一節
- **quatrain** 四行詩
- **cinquain** 五行詩
- **limerick** 五行打油詩
- **haiku** 三行俳句詩
- **syllable** 音節

76 Understanding Sentences 認識句子

All sentences must have / a subject and a verb. Some sentences can be / very short. For example, / "I ate," / is a complete sentence. Why? It has / a subject and a verb. Other sentences can be / very, very long.

People often **make mistakes** / when making English sentences. One common mistake / is the **run-on sentence**. Look at this sentence:

I went to the park I saw my friend.

It's a run-on sentence. A run-on sentence / is a **combination** of two sentences / that either needs punctuation or a **conjunction**. Here's / a complete sentence:

I went to the park, and I saw my friend.

All sentences need to have / subject-verb agreement. It means / that if the subject is **singular**, / the verb must be singular. And if the subject is **plural**, / the verb must be plural. Look at this sentence:

Jason like to play computer games.

It's a wrong sentence. Why? It doesn't have / subject-verb agreement. Here is / the correct complete sentence:

Jason likes to play computer games.

So watch out for run-on sentences, / and always make sure / your subjects and verbs / agree. Then you'll be making / lots of complete sentences.

所有的句子 **all sentences** 都有主詞和動詞 **have a subject and a verb**。有的句子非常短。例如，「我吃過了」是一個完整的句子 **complete sentence**。為什麼呢？因為它有主詞和動詞。有些句子則可以非常長。

人們在造英文句子時，常會犯錯 **make mistakes**。常見的錯誤就是連寫句 **run-on sentence**。看看這個句子「I went to the park I saw my friend.」。

它就是一個連寫句。連寫句是指兩個需要標點符號或是連接詞 **need punctuation or a conjunction** 來合併的句子。完整的句子應該是「I went to the park, and I saw my friend.」

所有的句子都需要主詞與動詞一致 **subject-verb agreement**。這意味著主詞為單數 **the subject is singular**，則動詞也要為單數形式 **the verb must be singular**；主詞為複數 **the subject is plural**，則動詞也要為複數形式 **the verb must be plural**。看看這句子「Jason like to play computer games.」。

這是一個錯誤的句子。為什麼呢？因為此句中的主詞與動詞不一致。正確且完整的句子應該是「Jason likes to play computer games.」。

所以要小心連寫句，並永遠確認主詞與動詞一致。你才能寫出許多完整的句子。

Words to Know

- **make a mistake** 犯錯
- **run-on sentence** 連寫句
- **combination** 結合
- **conjunction** 連接詞
- **singular** 單數的
- **plural** 複數的

77 Common Proverbs 常見的諺語

Proverbs are / short expressions / that people sometimes use. They typically pass on / some type of wisdom. The English language has / a very large number of proverbs.

One proverb is / "**Absence** makes the heart / grow fonder." It means / that people usually have / good memories / of events or people / from the past. Of course, / at the time, / they might not have thought / much of them. However, / over time, / the "absence" changed their memories, / so they remember / the events or people / **fondly**.

"All / that **glitters** / is not gold" / is another important proverb. Gold is very valuable, / and it glitters brightly. But many other things / glitter, too. However, / they may not be valuable. In fact, / they may even be harmful. So this proverb is a warning. People should be careful / because not every **shiny**, **good-looking** thing / is like gold.

"He / who **hesitates** / is lost" / is a popular expression. This proverb tells people / not to hesitate. They should / **make a decision** / and go with it. If they hesitate or wait / too long, / they might lose / an important **opportunity**.

Finally, / "**It's no use** / **crying** over **spilt** milk" / is another common proverb. Sometimes bad things / might happen to a person. But that person should not cry / about it. Instead, / the person should accept / what has happened / and move on. That is the meaning / of that proverb.

諺語 **proverb** 為人們有時會使用的短語 **short expression**，通常傳遞某類智慧 **pass on wisdom**。英語中有大量的諺語。

有一句話說：「距離產生美」**Absence makes the heart grow fonder.**，指的是人們通常對於過去的人、事、物懷抱美好記憶。當時他們當然並不會那麼想，然而要經過時間，「距離」改變了他們的記憶，他們便會深情地回想人事物。

「閃閃發亮的並非都是黃金」**All that glitters is not gold.** 是另一句重要的諺語。黃金非常珍貴並閃閃發亮，但也有許多不一定珍貴卻會發亮的東西，事實上還可能有害。所以這句諺語是在警告人們，不是所有好看、閃亮之物都如黃金般珍貴。

「猶豫者多失」**He who hesitates is lost.** 為一常見用語。這句話告訴人們切勿遲疑，應做出決定並順應它。若遲疑等待過久，可能會失去重要的機會。

最後，「覆水難收，悔恨無益」**It's no use crying over spilt milk.** 是另一句很重要的諺語。有時人會遭遇不好的事，不過無需悔恨。相反地，要接受事實並生活下去便是這句諺語的意義。

Words to Know

- **absence** 缺席；不在
- **fondly** 憐愛地；深情地
- **glitter** 閃閃發光
- **shiny** 發光的
- **good-looking** 漂亮的
- **hesitate** 猶豫
- **make a decision** 做決定
- **opportunity** 機會
- **it's no use V-ing** 做……沒有用
- **spilt** 灑出的；溢出的

78

Figures of Speech 修辭

Writers can be / creative. To do this, / they can use / figures of speech. There are / many of these. Four are / **similes**, **metaphors**, **hyperbole**, and **personification**.

Similes and metaphors / are both comparisons. But they are not the same. Similes use / "as" or "like" / to compare two things. For example, / "strong as an ox" / and "dark like night" / are similes. Metaphors are comparisons / between two unlike things / that seem to / **have** nothing **in common**. "The stars are diamonds in the sky" / and "There is a sea of sand" / are metaphors.

Hyperbole is also / a figure of speech. It is / a form of **exaggeration**. People often exaggerate / when they speak or write. For instance, / "There were a million people in the store" / is hyperbole. "I worked all day and all night" / is, too.

Finally, / people often give / objects and animals / human characteristics. This is personification. "The wind is **whispering**" / is one example. So is / "My dog is speaking to me." The wind and a dog / are not humans. But in both cases, / they have human characteristics. So they are / examples of personification.

作家也許要有想像力，因此他們會使用修辭法 **figure of speech**。修辭法有許多種，其中四種為明喻 **simile**、隱喻 **metaphor**、誇飾 **hyperbole** 和擬人 **personification**。

明喻和隱喻都是對比的手法，不過兩者並不相同。明喻使用 as 和 like **use "as" or "like"** 來對比兩件事 **compare two things**，例如，strong as an ox（壯得像頭牛）和 dark like night（漆黑如夜）都是明喻。隱喻是將兩件沒有相似處的事物作對比 **comparison between two unlike things**，「The stars are diamond in the sky（星星是高掛天空的鑽石）」和「There is a sea of sand（有一片沙海）」都是隱喻。

誇飾也是修辭的一種，是一種誇大的形式 **a form of exaggeration**。人們說話或寫作的時候經常會誇大其詞，舉例來說，「There were a million people in the store（店裡人山人海）」和「I worked all day and all night（我日以繼夜地工作）」都屬於誇飾法。

最後，人常會賦予物體或動物一些人的特質 **give human characteristics**，這就是擬人。「The wind is whispering（風在呢喃）」和「My dog is speaking to me（我的狗在對我說話）」都使用了擬人法。風和狗都不是人，但在兩個例子中，皆出現了人的特質，所以兩者都是擬人法。

Words to Know

- **simile** 明喻
- **metaphor** 隱喻
- **hyperbole** 誇飾法
- **personification** 擬人
- **have . . . in common** 有共通點
- **exaggeration** 誇張
- **whisper** 低聲說

79 Greek and Latin Roots 希臘與拉丁字根

English has more words / than any other language. Why is this? One reason is / that English borrows words / from many other languages. Then it turns these words / into new English words. Many of these words / come from Greek and Latin. These are called / roots. By studying roots, / a person can learn / the meanings of many different words / in English.

For instance, / the root *hydro* / comes from Greek. It means "water." From that root, / we get the words / **hydrate**, **dehydrate**, hydrant, hydrogen, and many others. The root *aster* / comes from Greek. It means "star." From *aster*, / we get the words / asteroid, asterisk, astronomy, **astronaut**, and many others. *Geo* also comes from Greek. It means "earth." The words / **geology**, **geometry**, and geography / all come from it.

Of course, / there are many roots / from Latin, too. For instance, / the root *vid* / means to "see." From that root, / we get / video, visual, visualize, and many others. The root *script* / means to "write." From it, / we get / **transcript**, **inscription**, and others. And *port* / means to "carry." From that root, / we get / transport, **portable**, **export**, and **import**, among others.

Without borrowing / from other languages, / English would have / very few words. But, / thanks to Latin and Greek / —and other languages, too— / English has many, many words.

英語的文字比其他語言要來的多，理由為何呢？其中一個理由為英文從其他語言中借用文字 **English borrows words**，再將之轉成新的英文字。這些字有很多都是從希臘文與拉丁文而來 **come from Greek and Latin**，稱為字根。人可藉由研讀字根來學習英文中多種字詞的意義。

舉例來說，字根「hydro」起源於希臘文，代表「水」**water** 的意思。由此我們可得「hydrate（使成水化合物）」、「dehydrate（脫水）」、「hydrant（消防栓）」、「hydrogen（氫氣）」等字。字根「aster」起源於希臘文，表示「星星」之意。由此我們可得「asteroid（小行星）」、「asterisk（星號）」、「astronomy（天文學）」、「astronaut（太空人）」等字。字根「Geo」也是起源於希臘文，代表「陸地」**earth** 的意思。「geology（地質學）」、「geometry（幾何學）」、「geography（地理學）」皆起源於此。

也有許多字根是起源於拉丁文。舉例來說，字根「vid」代表「看」的意思。由此我們可得「video（影片）」、「visual（視覺的）」、「visualize（使形象化）」與其他字。字根「script」代表「寫」**write** 的意思。由此我們可得「transcript（文字記錄）」、「inscription（題辭）」與其他字。還有「port」代表「運輸」**carry** 的意思。由此我們可得「transport（交通）」、「portable（便攜的）」、「export（出口）」、「import（進口）」與其他字。

英語若無借用其他語言，將會相當貧乏。多虧有拉丁語和希臘語以及其他語言，英語才有如此多的字詞。

Words to Know

- **hydrate** 使成水化合物
- **dehydrate** 脫水
- **astronaut** 太空人
- **geology** 地質學
- **geometry** 幾何學
- **transcript** 抄本
- **inscription** 碑文；題辭
- **portable** 可攜帶的
- **export** 出口
- **import** 進口

80 Gothic Cathedrals 哥德式大教堂

In **the Middle Ages**, / **religion** was / a very important part / of people's lives. Almost everyone / went to church / on Sunday. So building churches / was important. Some towns and cities / built huge churches. They were called / cathedrals. There were / many different styles. One important style / was Gothic. The Gothic Age lasted / from around the twelfth / to sixteenth centuries.

Gothic cathedrals / were **enormous**. Their builders / made them / to impress many people. So they look like / they are reaching up / into the sky. The reason / that they are so high / is that they have **buttresses**. These are / supports / that help the cathedrals stay up. The cathedrals also had / many **stained-glass** windows. These showed / scenes / from the *Bible*. Also, / they **allowed** a lot of light / **to** enter the cathedrals. Inside the cathedrals, / the ceilings were very high. This made them / look even more impressive. The outsides of cathedrals / often had many sculptures. These were called / **gargoyles**. The gargoyles looked like monsters. They were used to **ward off** / evil spirits.

中世紀時 **in the Middle Ages**，宗教在人們生活中佔有很重要的地位。幾乎每個人星期天都會上教堂。因此建造教堂相當重要。有些城鎮建造巨大的教堂 **huge church**，稱作大教堂 **cathedral**。大教堂有許多種不同的風格，哥德式 **Gothic** 是其中重要的一種。哥德時代大約從十二世紀持續到十六世紀。

哥德式教堂 **Gothic cathedral** 非常大 **enormous**。他們的建造者利用這樣的設計使許多人印象深刻 **impress many people**。所以這些教堂都看似高聳入雲 **reach up into the sky**。他們如此高大的原因來自拱壁 **have buttresses**。拱壁是用來幫助支撐教堂的輔助物。大教堂有許多彩繪玻璃窗 **have stained-glass windows**，它們展示了來自《聖經》中的場景。同時，這些玻璃窗也讓許多光線射入教堂。大教堂內的天花板非常高 **ceilings are very high**，這讓教堂看起來更加令人欽佩。大教堂外通常有許多雕像，它們被稱為滴水獸 **gargoyle**。滴水獸看起來像怪物，用來驅邪 **ward off evil spirits**。

Words to Know

- **the Middle Ages** 中世紀
- **religion** 宗教
- **enormous** 巨大的
- **buttress** 拱壁；扶壁
- **stained-glass** 彩色玻璃的
- **allow . . . to** 允許……做……
- **gargoyle** 滴水獸
- **ward off** 避開；擋住

81 Islamic Architecture 伊斯蘭建築

Islam began / in the seventh century. Since then, / there have been / many styles of buildings / designed by **Muslims**. They all **combine** / to make up Islamic architecture.

In Islam, / art is restricted. There should be / no images of Allah / – the god of Islam. Also, / there should be / no pictures of people / either. So / many of Islam's most creative people / became architects.

One of the main features / of Islamic architecture / is the **minaret**. These are / tall towers. They are found / in every **mosque**. There are usually / four minarets / at every mosque. There is one / at each corner of the building. They can be / very high towers. **Domes** are also / very popular features. Domes are rounded roofs / of buildings. Many mosques have / impressive domes.

As for famous buildings, / there are many. The Dome of the Rock / is in Jerusalem. It is / one of the earliest examples / of Islamic architecture. The Sultan Ahmed Mosque / is in Istanbul, Turkey. It is / another well-known building. And the Taj Mahal / is located / in India. Some say / it is the most beautiful building / in the entire world.

伊斯蘭教 **Islam** 於七世紀興起。自此，穆斯林 **Muslims** 便設計出許多風格的建築物，形成了伊斯蘭建築 **Islamic architecture**。

在伊斯蘭教中，藝術是受到限制的 **art is restricted**。不能有伊斯蘭教真主阿拉的圖像 **no images of Allah**，同時，人們的圖像也不能出現 **no pictures of people**。因此，許多伊斯蘭教最有創意的人都成為建築師。

伊斯蘭建築最主要的特色之一為尖塔 **minaret**。這些高大的塔樓 **tall tower** 出現在每一個清真寺中 **found in every mosque**。每個清真寺通常都有四個尖塔，座落於建築物的角落 **one at each corner**。它們可以是非常高聳的塔樓。穹頂 **dome** 也是非常著名的特色之一。穹頂是建築物上的圓形屋頂 **rounded roof**。許多清真寺都有令人讚歎的穹頂。

說到伊斯蘭教出名的建築物 **famous building**，可是多不勝數。位於耶路撒冷 **in Jerusalem** 的圓頂清真寺 **the Dome of the Rock**，就屬伊斯蘭建築早期的代表作之一。坐落於土耳其伊斯坦堡 **in Istanbul** 的藍色清真寺 **the Sultan Ahmed Mosque**，也是非常著名的伊斯蘭建築。印度的 **in India** 泰姬瑪哈陵 **the Taj Mahal** 也是，有些人說它是世界上最漂亮的建築物。

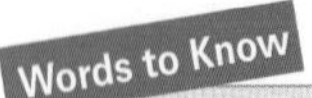

- **Muslim** 穆斯林
- **combine** 結合
- **minaret** 尖塔
- **mosque** 清真寺
- **dome** 圓蓋

82 Renaissance Artists 文藝復興時代的藝術家

During the Renaissance, / there were / many **brilliant** artists. These **included** / Raphael, Botticelli, Giotto, and Donatello. But two are considered / greater than the others. One is / Leonardo da Vinci. The other is / Michelangelo Buonarroti.

Leonardo da Vinci was / a true **Renaissance man**. He could do / many things / well. He was / an engineer and scientist. He was / an **inventor**, architect, and artist. He was / one of the greatest men / in history. As an artist, / he painted / one of the world's most famous pictures: / the *Mona Lisa*. Another famous painting / is / *The Last Supper*. It shows / Jesus and his **apostles** together. Leonardo made / many other famous works. But those two / are the most well known.

Michelangelo was / an **incredible** sculptor. He created / two of the most famous statues / of all time. The first was / *David*. The second was / *Pietà*. *Pietà* is / a sculpture of Mary / holding the body of Jesus / after he died. Michelangelo was also / a great painter. He painted the **frescoes** / on the ceiling / of the Sistine Chapel. The most famous of these frescoes / is the *Creation of Adam*. It shows / God and Adam / **reaching out to** one another.

文藝復興期間 **during the Renaissance** 有許多傑出的藝術家 **many brilliant artists**，包含拉斐爾、波提切利、喬托以及多那太羅，不過被視為最偉大的兩位是李奧納多．達文西 **Leonardo da Vinci** 與米開朗基羅．布奧納洛提 **Michelangelo Buonarroti**。

達文西是個真正的文藝復興人 **true Renaissance man**，他多才多藝 **do many things well**，不僅是工程師、科學家，也是發明家、建築師和藝術家，是史上最偉大的人物之一。身為一名藝術家 **as an artist**，達文西創作了世界上最著名的繪畫作品之一《蒙娜麗莎》**Mona Lisa**，另一幅《最後的晚餐》**The Last Supper** 也是名畫，畫中呈現耶穌與其門徒一起的畫面。李奧納多尚有其他無數知名的畫作，不過這兩幅最廣為人知 **the most well known**。

米開朗基羅是個天才雕刻家 **incredible sculptor**，他創造了兩座絕世的著名雕像 **two of the most famous statues**。第一是《大衛像》**David**，第二是《聖殤》**Pietà**。《聖殤》是刻畫耶穌死後，聖母瑪利亞懷抱著祂的雕刻作品。米開朗基羅也是個偉大的畫家 **great painter**，他在西斯汀教堂的天花板上繪製了濕壁畫 **paint the frescoes**，其中最著名的一幅當屬《創造亞當》**the Creation of Adam**，此畫表現出上帝與亞當伸手接觸的樣貌。

Words to Know

- **brilliant** 技藝高超的
- **include** 包括
- **Renaissance man** 文藝復興人；通才
- **inventor** 發明家；創造者
- **apostle** 使徒
- **incredible** 難以置信的
- **fresco** 濕壁畫
- **reach out to** 伸出手

83 Classical Art 古典藝術

The ancient Greeks loved art. They made / all kinds of works of art. This included / pottery, paintings, sculptures, and murals. The Greeks even considered / their buildings / to be works of art. So they made / beautifully designed buildings / as well.

Many examples of pottery / have survived / from ancient Greece. Pottery / in ancient Greece / had two **functions**. People used it / to eat or drink from. And they used it / for decorations. Many Greek **ceramics** have beautiful pictures / painted on them. These pictures often show / stories / from Greek mythology.

Sculpture **was highly prized** / in ancient Greece. The Greeks made sculptures / from either stone or **bronze**. Many stone sculptures / have survived / to today. But few bronze sculptures / have. The Greeks **depicted** the people / in sculptures / exactly as they looked in real life.

As for architecture, / many Greek buildings / still exist today. One important feature / of these buildings / is their **columns**. The Greeks made / three types of columns: / **Doric**, **Ionic**, and **Corinthian**. Doric columns / were the simplest. They had / very plain designs. Ionic columns had / flutes, or lines, / carved into them / from the top to the bottom. They were also / more **decorative** / than Doric columns. Corinthian columns / were the most decorative ones / of all. Their tops—called capitals— / often had flowers or other designs / on them. And they also had flutes.

古希臘人 **the ancient Greeks** 熱愛藝術 **love art**，他們製作各種的藝術品 **all kinds of works of art**，包含了陶器、繪畫、雕刻與壁畫。希臘人甚至視他們的建築物為藝術品，所以也建造了很多美輪美奐的建築。

古希臘留存下許多陶器 **pottery** 樣本。古希臘的陶器有兩個用處 **have two functions**，用於飲食 **to eat or drink from** 還有裝飾 **for decorations**。許多希臘的陶器上有美麗的圖畫，圖畫多為訴說希臘神話。

雕刻 **sculpture** 在古希臘更是受到讚賞。希臘人以石頭或青銅 **from either stone or bronze** 來雕刻，許多石雕存留至今，銅雕則不然。希臘人所雕出來的人就像是現實生活中的人一樣栩栩如生。

至於建築 **architecture**，許多希臘建築留存至今。這些建築的其中一個特點就是它們的圓柱，希臘人有三種類型的圓柱 **three types of columns**——多力克柱式 **Doric**、愛奧尼柱式 **Ionic** 與科林斯柱式 **Corinthian**。多力克柱式為最簡單的 **the simplest** 單純設計 **very plain designs**。愛奧尼柱式上有由上到下的雕刻凹槽，或說線條 **flutes, or lines**，比多力克柱式要來的多裝飾。科林斯柱式為這三種中最多裝飾 **the most decorative** 的柱式。又稱為柱頭的頂部常有雕花或是其他設計，也有凹槽的設計。

Words to Know

- **function** 功能
- **ceramics** 陶器
- **be highly prized** 受到高度重視
- **bronze** 青銅
- **depict** 描畫；雕出
- **column** 圓柱
- **Doric** 多力克柱式的
- **Ionic** 愛奧尼柱式的
- **Corinthian** 科林斯柱式的
- **decorative** 裝飾用的

84 From Baroque to Realism 從巴洛克到寫實主義

From around the late sixteenth century / to the early eighteenth century, / there was / a new type of art / in Europe. It was called / Baroque. There were / Baroque artists / in every European country. So they all had / slightly different styles. But there were / many **similarities** / that Baroque artists shared.

For one, / there were often contrasts / between light and dark / in Baroque paintings. The artists also / **focused on** movement. And they **stressed** / **facial expressions** / in the figures / they painted. This was / one way / they tried to show emotions / in their paintings. The works of Baroque artists / also had / symbolic or moralizing meanings. Many Baroque artists / painted religious topics, too.

One very important characteristic was / that Baroque artists were **realists**. So they painted their subjects / as realistically as possible. They knew about **perspective**. So they could show things / such as size and distance. They were also able to / use the space / in their paintings / very well. This ability made / many Baroque artists / quite famous. Today, / people still **admire** / the works of artists / such as El Greco, Rembrandt, and Caravaggio.

大約從 16 世紀後期 **the late sixteenth century** 到 18 世紀初期 **the early eighteenth century**，歐洲出現了一種稱作巴洛克 **Baroque** 的新型態藝術。每個歐洲國家都有巴洛克的藝術家。他們的風格皆有小小的差異 **slightly different styles**，但巴洛克藝術家間依然擁有許多共同點 **many similarities**。

舉例來說，巴洛克繪畫中總會有明暗的對比 **contrasts between light and dark**。藝術家們還著重於動作 **focus on movement**，他們強調畫中人物的臉部表情 **stress facial expression**，此為表現畫中情感的一個方法。巴洛克藝術家的作品通常有象徵或道德上的意義 **symbolic or moralizing meanings**，許多巴洛克藝術家也繪製以宗教為題 **religious topics** 的畫作。

非常重要的一點是巴洛克藝術家們是寫實主義者，因此他們都會盡可能寫實地描繪 **paint as realistically as possible** 主題。他們懂透視畫法 **know about perspective**，所以能展現出畫中物的大小與距離等等。他們還能在作品中善用空間 **use the space very well**，此能力讓許多巴洛克藝術家相當出名。直到今天，如葛雷柯 **El Greco**、林布蘭 **Rembrandt** 和卡拉瓦喬 **Caravaggio** 之流的藝術家作品依然受到讚賞。

Words to Know

- **similarity** 相似性
- **focus on** 著重於
- **stress** 強調
- **facial expression** 面部表情
- **realist** 寫實主義者
- **perspective** 透視法
- **admire** 讚賞

Nineteenth Century American Landscapes

十九世紀的美國風景畫

In the nineteenth century, / much of America / was not settled. So there were / few cities. Not many people lived / in the countryside. So there were / many beautiful places / for artists to paint landscapes.

One group of landscape artists / was called / the Hudson River School. The Hudson River / flows through New York. These artists / painted the land / in this area. Much of it / was forest. But there were also / farms, fields, and many mountains. Thomas Cole / was the first Hudson River School artist. Frederic Edwin Church and Asher Durand / were two others. The Hudson River School artists / were **Romantics**. So they **idealized** the landscapes / they painted. They painted the scenes / the way / they wanted the land to look, / not the way / that it actually looked.

Around the same time, / there was / another school of artists. They were called / **Naturalists**, or Realists. They painted nature / as it appeared. William Bliss Baker / was one of these artists. He also painted / in the Hudson River area. But his paintings look very different / from the Hudson River School artists' paintings. Baker's works are realistic. His painting / *Fallen **Monarchs*** / is one of the most beautiful / of the Naturalist paintings.

19 世紀時 **in the nineteenth century**，美洲大部分地區尚無人定居，也沒什麼城市。鄉村人口也不多，所以有許多美景可供畫家寫生 **paint landscapes**。

有一群風景畫家被稱為哈德遜河畫派 **the Hudson River School**。哈德遜河流經紐約，這些畫家就專畫這一帶的土地。這裡大部分是森林，也有農場、田野和許多山脈。湯瑪斯．科爾 **Thomas Cole** 是第一位哈德遜河畫派的畫家 **the first Hudson River School artist**，另外兩位是弗雷德里克．艾德溫．丘奇以及艾許．杜蘭。哈德遜河畫派的畫家是浪漫主義者 **Romantic**，他們會美化其所繪製的風景 **idealized landscapes**。他們所畫的風景是依照他們想呈現的樣貌，而非真實景色。

在同一時期，還有另一派的畫家 **another school of artists**，稱為自然主義者或寫實主義者 **Naturalist, or Realist**，他們將自然的真實樣貌呈現出來，威廉．布雷斯．貝克 **William Bliss Baker** 就是其中一位。他同樣描繪哈德遜河一帶，不過他的作品與哈德遜河畫派截然不同。貝克的作品走寫實 **realistic** 風格，《沒落君主》**Fallen Monarchs** 就是寫實畫派中最美麗的作品之一。

Words to Know

- **landscape** 山水畫；風景畫
- **Romantic** 浪漫派者
- **idealize** 理想化
- **Naturalist** 自然主義者
- **monarch** 大王；君主

86 Composers and Their Music 作曲家與他們的音樂

There have been / many great classical music composers. Three of the greatest / were Johann Sebastian Bach, / Wolfgang Amadeus Mozart, / and Ludwig van Beethoven.

Bach came first. He composed music / during the Baroque Period. Much of his music was / for the church. He wrote tunes / for orchestras, **choirs**, and **solo** instruments. The *Brandenburg Concertos* / are some of his most famous works.

Mozart was / one of the most brilliant musicians / of all time. He was / a child **genius**. He started / writing music / at a very young age. He wrote / all kinds of music. His opera / *The Marriage of Figaro* / is still famous. So is his *Great Mass in C Minor*.

Beethoven was / a great pianist and composer. His *Moonlight Sonata* / was very famous. He **went deaf** / later in his life. But he still **conducted** orchestras. His *9th Symphony* / is one of the greatest / of all **pieces** of classical music.

從古至今有許多偉大的古典音樂作曲家 **classical music composer**，其中有三位分別是巴哈 **Bach**、莫札特 **Mozart** 以及貝多芬 **Beethoven**。

巴哈為其先驅，他於巴洛克時期創作音樂 **compose music**。巴哈大部分的音樂是為教堂而作 **for the church**，曾為管弦樂團、唱詩班以及獨奏樂器譜曲，《布蘭登堡協奏曲》**The Brandenburg Concertos** 是他最著名的作品之一。

莫札特是史上最天才的音樂家之一，他自幼便是個音樂神童 **child genius**，很年輕就開始從事音樂創作。莫札特寫過的音樂涵蓋各種類型 **write all kinds of music**，其歌劇作品《費加洛婚禮》**The Marriage of Figaro** 至今仍為人所稱道，《C 小調大彌撒》**Great Mass in C Minor** 亦是。

貝多芬是傑出的鋼琴家兼作曲家 **pianist and composer**，他的《月光奏鳴曲》**Moonlight Sonata** 非常受到歡迎。儘管貝多芬晚年失聰，他仍繼續指揮管弦樂隊，他的《第九號交響曲》**9th Symphony** 是古典音樂史上最偉大的作品之一。

Words to Know

- **choir** 唱詩班
- **solo** 獨奏
- **genius** 天才
- **go deaf** 耳聾
- **conduct** 指揮
- **piece**（音樂作品等的）一首

87 Musical Dynamics 音樂的力度

When musicians play their instruments, / they must do more / than just **read the notes** / and then play them. They must know / the speed / that they should play the music. And they must also know / the dynamics. This means / they must know / if they should play / softly or loudly. How do they know that? They can look for / certain letters / on their **sheet music**.

On the sheet music, / they will see the letters / *p*, *pp*, *mp*, *f*, *ff*, or *mf*. These letters / **are** all **related to** / musical dynamics. They **indicate** / the **softness** or the **loudness** / that the musician should play.

p stands for piano. It means / the music should be played softly. There are also / *pp* and *mp*. *pp* means **pianissimo**, / which stands for "very soft." And *mp* means **mezzo piano**. This means / "**moderately** soft."

Of course, / some music should be played loudly. When a musician sees *f*, / it means **forte**. That stands for "loud." Just like with soft music, / there are / two more degrees of loudness. The first is / *ff*. That's **fortissimo**, / which means "very loud." And there is / *mf*. That's **mezzo forte**, / which means "moderately loud."

當音樂家演奏樂器時，他們不僅僅只是閱讀樂符 **read notes** 然後演奏。他們還要瞭解演奏樂器時的速度 **the speed** 以及力度 **the dynamics**。力度表示他們必須要知道何時要輕柔地演奏或是響亮地演奏。然而他們是如何得知呢？音樂家可以從他們樂譜上的特定字母 **letters on sheet music** 瞭解。

在活頁樂譜上 **on the sheet music**，他們可以看到 p, pp ,mp, f, ff 或是 mf 這樣的字母。這些字母與音樂力度 **musical dynamics** 息息相關。他們顯示了音樂家要演奏的力度大小 **softness or loudness**。

p 代表 piano，它表示音樂要輕柔地被演奏 **be played softly**。另外還有 pp 和 mp。pp 為 pianissimo，意味著「極弱的」**very soft**；mp 為 mezzo piano，表示「中弱的」**moderately soft**。

當然，有時候音樂也要響亮地被演奏。當音樂家看見 f，那代表 forte，也就是「強的」**loud**。與輕音樂相同，響亮的力度也有其他兩種。ff 為 fortissimo，代表「極強的」**very loud**；mf 為 mezzo forte，代表「中強的」**moderately loud**。

Words to Know

- **dynamics** 力度
- **read the notes** 讀譜
- **sheet music** 活頁樂譜
- **be related to** 和……有關
- **indicate** 顯示
- **softness** 柔和
- **loudness** 大聲
- **pianissimo** 極弱的
- **mezzo piano** 中弱的
- **moderately** 溫和地
- **forte** 強的
- **fortissimo** 極強的
- **mezzo forte** 中強的

88 Handel and Haydn 韓德爾和海頓

Two of the greatest / of all classical music composers / were George Friedrich Handel / and Joseph Haydn.

Handel lived / during the Baroque Period / in the eighteenth century. He was German. But he lived in England / for a long time. Some of his music / is very popular / and well-known / all around the world. He wrote / *Water Music* / and *Music for the Royal Fireworks*. These are / two easily **recognizable** pieces of music. But his most famous music / **by far** / is his *Messiah*. It is an **oratorio** / that tells the life of Jesus Christ. From the *Messiah*, / the most famous piece is / the *Hallelujah* **chorus**. Today, / when orchestras play / the *Hallelujah* chorus, / the **audience** always stands up. Why? When King George II of Great Britain / first heard it, / he stood up / during that part.

Joseph Haydn was / one of the best composers / of the Classical Period. He composed / hundreds of / **sonatas**, **symphonies**, and **string quartets**. He also **influenced** / many other composers. Beethoven was the greatest / of all his students. Two of his best works are / the *Surprise Symphony* / and *The Creation*, an oratorio.

古典音樂作曲家 **classical music composer** 中最有名的就屬格奧爾格·弗里德里希·韓德爾 **Handel** 與約瑟夫·海頓 **Haydn**。

韓德爾生活在十八世紀的巴洛克時期。他是德國人，但他有很長的一段時間住在英國。他的一些創作非常受到歡迎並廣為世人所知。他創作了〈水上音樂〉**Water Music** 與〈皇家煙火〉**Music for the Royal Fireworks**。這兩首是最為人所熟悉的樂曲。然而到目前為止，他最著名的樂曲就屬〈彌賽亞〉**Messiah**。這是訴說耶穌基督生命 **tell the life of Jesus Christ** 的神劇。〈彌賽亞〉中最出名的一首合唱曲為〈哈雷路亞〉**the Hallelujah chorus**。今日，當管弦樂隊演奏〈哈雷路亞〉合唱曲時，觀眾都會起立 **stand up**。為什麼呢？因為英國國王喬治二世第一次聽到此段音樂時，就站了起來。

約瑟夫·海頓是古典時期最棒的作曲家之一。他創作了奏鳴曲、交響曲以及弦樂四重奏 **compose sonatas, symphonies, and string quartets**。海頓同時也影響了許多其他作曲家 **influence many other composers**。貝多芬就是他最優秀的學生。他最出名的作品為〈驚愕交響曲〉**the Surprise Symphony** 與神劇〈創世紀〉**The Creation**。

Words to Know

- **recognizable** 可辨認的
- **by far** 到目前為止
- **oratorio** 清唱劇；神劇
- **chorus** 合唱團
- **audience** 觀眾
- **sonata** 奏鳴曲
- **symphony** 交響曲
- **string quartet** 弦樂四重奏
- **influence** 影響

89 Spirituals 靈歌

Music **is** often / **associated with** religion. In **Christianity**, / there are many kinds of songs / people sing. There are / **hymns**, **carols**, **chants**, and others. Another type of music / is the spiritual.

Spirituals were first written / in the eighteenth century / in the United States. They were written / because there was a **revival** / of interest in religion / in the U.S. / then. Spirituals were often / very **inspiring** songs. They were / about stories and **themes** / from the *Bible*. In style, / they were / a kind of folk music or folk hymn.

Spirituals were often sung / by black Americans. Yet / there were also / many white spirituals, / too. Many of the blacks / who made these spirituals / were slaves from Africa. So spirituals had / a strong African influence. They later combined / with European and American influences. The result was spirituals.

Nowadays, / spiritual music is called / **gospel music**. It is / a form of music / that is very religious. All kinds of people / sing and listen to gospel music. It inspires people / and gives them comfort / **as well**.

音樂經常與宗教息息相關 **be associated with religion**。在基督教中 **in Christianity**，人們唱著各式各樣的歌曲，有讚歌、聖誕頌歌、禱文及其他等等，還有一種叫作靈歌 **spiritual**。

靈歌誕生於 18 世紀的美國，當時一股宗教復興 **revival** 風潮，促成了靈歌的創作。靈歌常是激勵人心的歌曲 **very inspiring song**，內容取自《聖經》裡的故事和題材 **about stories and themes from the Bible**，風格屬於民間音樂或民間讚歌 **a kind of folk music or folk hymn**。

靈歌多由美國黑人演唱 **often sung by black Americans**，但也有許多白人靈歌。由於創作這些靈歌的黑人，許多是來自非洲的奴隸，因此歌曲受非洲的影響非常大 **have a strong African influence**。不久，這類型的音樂又受到歐洲與美洲的影響，造就了靈歌的出現。

現今靈歌音樂又被稱為福音音樂 **gospel music**，是一種非常虔誠的 **very religious** 音樂形式。各種民族都會演唱並聆聽福音音樂，它不僅鼓舞人們 **inspire people**，也撫慰 **give comfort** 了人心。

Words to Know

- **be associated with** 和……有關
- **Christianity** 基督教
- **hymn** 聖歌；讚美詩
- **carol** 聖誕頌歌
- **chant** 聖歌
- **revival** 復興
- **inspiring** 激勵人心的
- **theme** 主題
- **gospel music** 福音音樂
- **as well** 也

90 The Classical Period of Music 音樂的古典時期

The years / between 1750 and 1820 / saw / some of the greatest music / ever created. This time is now called / the Classical Period of music. Among the composers / who wrote during this period / were Mozart, Beethoven, Haydn, and Schubert.

By 1750, / people were **getting tired of** / the Baroque Period. So / they worked on / new forms of music. Thus / **arose** the Classical Period. It has / several important **characteristics**. For one, / the **mood** of the music / often changed. In a single piece of music, / there was not / just one mood / anymore. Instead, / the mood could suddenly change / anytime during a piece. The same was true of / the **rhythm** of the music. Music from this period / followed / several different rhythmic **patterns**. There were often / **sudden pauses**. Or the music would suddenly go / from being very slow / to very fast / or from very soft / to very loud.

Also, / music from the Classical Period / has beautiful **melodies**. The works / the composers created / are typically easy / to remember. Of course, / they are still / **sophisticated** works. But the ease / with which people can remember them / has helped increase / their **popularity**. Even today, / the works of composers / from this period / are among the most popular / of all classical music.

在西元 1750 年到 1820 年間，出現了一些最偉大的音樂創作。這段時期稱為音樂的古典時期 **the Classical Period of music**，此時期中的作曲家 **composers** 有莫札特、貝多芬、海頓與舒伯特。

1750 年時，人們對巴洛克時期感到厭倦 **getting tired of**，便開始創作新樂風，造就古典時期的崛起。此時期有許多特點 **important characteristics**，其中一點便是音樂的調子時常轉變 **mood often changes**。一首樂曲中不再只有單一曲調 **not just one mood**，調子反而能任意轉換。樂曲的節奏也是如此，此時期的音樂節拍有多種型式 **several different rhythmic patterns**，常有驟然中止或是音樂從極慢到極快，或是從柔和轉變成非常大聲。

古典時期的音樂擁有美妙的旋律 **beautiful melodies**，作曲家所創作的作品特別容易記得 **easy to remember**。當然這些作品為精心之作 **sophisticated works**，不過民眾能輕易記住這些曲子也使得這些曲子普及化。甚至到了今日，此時期作曲家的作品也是古典音樂中最為人所熟知的。

Words to Know

- **get tired of** 對……感到厭倦
- **arise** 產生
- **characteristic** 特點；特色
- **mood** 曲調
- **rhythm** 韻律
- **pattern** 型態
- **sudden** 突然的
- **pause** 暫停
- **melody** 旋律
- **sophisticated** 複雜的
- **popularity** 普及；流行

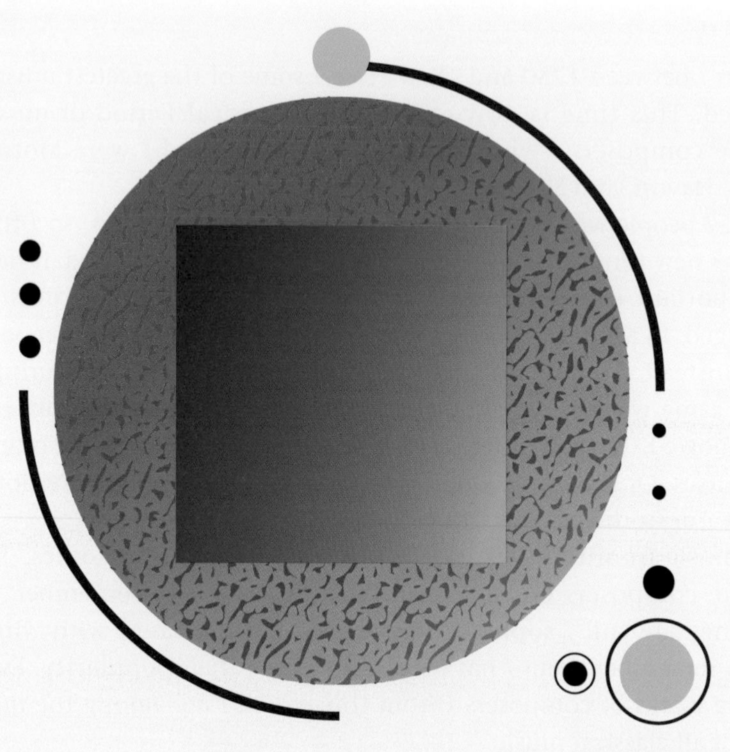

Answer Key

01 Kinds of Communities 社區的種類

1 (b)
2 a. millions b. Rural c. Suburban
3 a. population 人口 b. prefer 偏好 c. urban 城市的

02 Different Customs and Cultures 不同的風俗與文化

1 (c)
2 a. cultures b. shoes c. India
3 a. chopsticks 筷子 b. custom 風俗習慣
c. pass down 傳承

03 The Story of Israel 以色列的故事

1 (a)
2 (a)
3 a. covenant 契約 b. Israelite 古以色列人；希伯來人
c. descendant 子孫

04 Money Management 金錢管理

1 (c)
2 (a)
3 a. stock market 股票市場；股票交易 b. invest in 投資
c. budget 編列預算

05 Basic Economics 基礎經濟學

1 (c)
2 a. T b. T c. F
3 a. demand 需求 b. consume 消費；消耗
c. distribution 分配；分銷

06 The Three Branches of Government 政府的三大部門

1 (b)
2 a. laws b. legislative c. court
3 a. enforce 實施；執行 b. Congress（美國）國會
c. judicial branch 司法部門

07 The American Presidential Election System 美國總統選舉制度

1 (c)
2 a. Republican b. four c. primary
3 a. primary 初選 b. nominee 候選人 c. delegate 代表

08 A Nation of Immigration 移民之國

1 (a)
2 a. 1789 b. nineteenth c. little
3 a. Statue of Liberty 自由女神像 b. expand 擴張
c. immigrant 移民

09 Kinds of Resources 資源的種類

1 (c)
2 a. They are renewable, nonrenewable, human, and capital resources.
b. The energy from the sun, tides, water, and wind is renewable.
c. They are machines and tools used to produce goods.
3 a. human resources 人力資源 b. renewable 可更新的
c. capital resources 資本資源

10 Extreme Weather Conditions 極端的天氣狀況

1 (a)
2 a. It doesn't rain for a long time.
b. It is called a flood.
c. They drop several inches of rain in a few hours.
3 a. flood 洪水；水災 b. drought 旱災 c. thirsty 口渴的

11 Understanding Hemispheres 了解兩大半球

1 (b)
2 (b)
3 a. divide 劃分 b. prime meridian 本初子午線
c. hemisphere 半球

12 The Earth's Climate Zones 地球的氣候區

1 (b)
2 a. polar b. wet c. Antarctic Circle
3 a. temperate zone 溫帶地區
b. Tropic of Cancer 北回歸線 c. Antarctic Circle 南極圈

13 Climbing Mount Everest 攀登聖母峰

1 (a)
2 a. T b. F c. F
3 a. mountaineering 登山 b. expedition 探險
c. border 邊界

14 The Midwest Region of the United States 美國的中西部

1 (c)
2 a. There are twelve states in the Midwest.
b. They were all located beside the Atlantic Ocean.
c. They are five huge lakes located between the U.S. and Canada.
3 a. prairie 大草原 b. raise 飼養 c. agriculture 農業

15 Yellowstone National Park 黃石國家公園

1 (a)
2 a. F b. T c. T
3 a. bison（尤指北美）野牛 b. geyser 噴泉
c. regular 有規律的

16 The West Region of the United States 美國的西部

1 (b)
2 a. earthquake b. summer c. Forest fires
3 a. earthquake 地震 b. wildfire 野火 c. hit 襲擊

17 The Mayflower 五月花號

1 (c)
2 (b)
3 a. Pilgrim 朝聖先輩 b. festival 節日；慶祝活動
c. harvest 收成

18 The Colonies Become Free 殖民地獲得自由

1 (b)
2 a. T b. F c. T
3 a. independence 獨立 b. victory 勝利
c. command 命令

19 The French and Indian War Leads to Revolution 法印戰爭導致革命

1 (a)
2 a. It was the Seven Years' War.
b. The British won the French and Indian War.
c. They called them the Intolerable Acts.
3 a. Stamp Act 印花稅法 b. unfair 不公平的 c. revolt 起義

20 The Bill of Rights 權利法案

1 (a)
2 a. F b. F c. T
3 a. ratify 批准 b. speedy trial 迅速審判 c. assemble 集會

21 The American Civil War 美國南北戰爭

1 (c)
2 a. Civil War b. March c. Lincoln
3 a. bloody 血腥的；殘暴的 b. assassinate 暗殺
c. surrender 投降

22 The Roaring Twenties and the Great Depression 咆哮的二〇年代和經濟大蕭條

1 (b)
2 (c)
3 a. leisure time 空閒時間 b. go bankrupt 破產
c. recover 恢復

23 What Do Historians Do 歷史學家都在做些什麼

1 (b)
2 (c)
3 a. primary source 原始資料 b. journal 期刊
c. military 軍事的

24 Rome: From Republic to Empire 羅馬：從共和到帝制

1 (b)
2 a. F b. T c. T
3 a. overthrow 推翻 b. republic 共和的 c. corrupt 腐敗的

25 The Middle Ages 中世紀

1 (b)
2 (c)
3 a. invader 侵略者 b. starvation 飢餓 c. harsh 嚴厲的

26 Marco Polo and the Silk Road 馬可波羅與絲路

1 (b)
2 a. They went on the Silk Road.
b. The Chinese transported silk on the Silk Road.
c. He wrote a book called The Travels of Marco Polo.
3 a. adventurer 冒險家 b. advisor 顧問
c. trade route 貿易路線

27 The Age of Exploration 地理大發現

1 (c)
2 (a)
3 a. spice 香料 b. crew 全體船員 c. route 路線

28 The Spread of Islam 伊斯蘭教的傳播

1 (b)
2 a. Muhammad b. caliphs c. Ottoman
3 a. caliph 哈里發 b. dynasty 王朝；朝代
c. Muslim 穆斯林

29 The Cold War 冷戰

1 (b)
2 a. democracy b. Berlin c. Cold War
3 a. collapse 崩潰；瓦解 b. communism 共產主義
c. tyranny 專制

30 Globalization 全球化

1 (a)
2 a. World War II b. world c. easier
3 a. telecommunications 電信 b. affect 影響
c. advance 發展；進步

31 Organisms 有機體

1 (b)

2 a. T b. F c. T

3 a. asexual 無性的 b. reproduce 繁殖
c. protist 單細胞生物

32 Kingdoms 界

1 (a)

2 a. F b. F c. T

3 a. kingdom 界 b. pathogen 病原體
c. protozoan 原生動物

33 Heredity 遺傳

1 (c)

2 a. Because of heredity, children often look like their parents.
b. Genes have DNA.
c. There are dominant genes and recessive genes.

3 a. trait 特徵 b. heredity 遺傳 c. recessive gene 隱性基因

34 Sexual and Asexual Reproduction 有性生殖與無性生殖

1 (c)

2 (c)

3 a. bulb 球莖 b. stamen 雄蕊
c. sexual reproduction 有性生殖

35 Pollination and Fertilization 授粉與受精

1 (a)

2 a. The stamen is the male part of the plant.
b. The pistil is the female part of the plant.
c. The pollen must go in the pollen tube in the stigma to fertilize a plant.

3 a. nectar 花蜜 b. grain 顆粒 c. pollinate 給⋯⋯授粉

36 Tropisms 向性

1 (b)

2 (a)

3 a. tropism 向性；趨性 b. evolution 演化
c. gravity 重力；引力

37 The Five Kingdoms of Life 生命五界

1 (a)

2 a. F b. T c. F

3 a. prokaryote 原核生物 b. photosynthesis 光合作用
c. unicellular 單細胞的

38 Gregor Mendel 格萊高爾· 孟德爾

1 (a)

2 a. genetics b. pea c. dominant

3 a. crossbreed 雜配 b. hybrid 雜種 c. resistant 抗⋯⋯的

39 Pollination and Germination 授粉與發芽

1 (c)

2 (c)

3 a. dormant 休眠的 b. seedling 幼苗 c. anther 花藥

40 What Is a Food Web 何謂食物網

1 (a)

2 a. There are three groups of consumers.
b. They eat plants.
c. They eat both plants and animals.

3 a. carnivore 肉食性動物 b. ecosystem 生態系統
c. decomposer 分解者

41 How Ecosystems Change 生態系統如何改變

1 (c)

2 (c)

3 a. thriving 繁榮的 b. invasive species 入侵物種
c. barren 貧瘠的

42 The Carbon and Nitrogen Cycles 碳循環與氮循環

1 (b)

2 a. All life is made from carbon.
b. They turn into fossil fuels.
c. Around 80% of the atmosphere is nitrogen.

3 a. absorb 吸收 b. compound 化合物
c. fossil fuel 化石燃料

43 The Circulatory System 循環系統

1 (a)

2 (b)

3 a. aorta 主動脈 b. depleted 耗盡的 c. atrium 心房

44 The Immune System 免疫系統

1 (a)

2 a. F b. T c. T

3 a. phagocyte 吞噬細胞 b. antibody 抗體
c. antigen 抗原

45 The Development of a Baby 嬰兒的發育

1 (b)
2 a. fetus b. months c. womb
3 a. womb 子宮 b. fetus 胎兒 c. spinal cord 脊髓

46 Weather Equipment 氣象設備

1 (a)
2 a. A thermometer measures the temperature.
b. It measures air pressure.
c. An anemometer measures the wind speed.
3 a. meteorologist 氣象學家 b. weather vane 風向計
c. barometer 氣壓計

47 The Water Cycle 水循環

1 (a)
2 a. F b. T c. T
3 a. precipitation 降水 b. sleet 霙；雨夾雪
c. condensation 凝結

48 Ocean Resource and Conservation 海洋資源與保護

1 (c)
2 a. They cover around 71% of the earth's surface.
b. Fish, bird, and other sea creatures can die.
c. It could provide cheap and abundant energy in the future.
3 a. mine 採礦；開採 b. abundant 大量的；豐富的
c. repopulate 重新繁衍

49 The Formation of the Earth 地球的形成

1 (b)
2 a. 4.5 billion b. continents c. plate tectonics
3 a. continent 大陸 b. crust 地殼
c. plate tectonics 板塊構造論

50 Earthquakes 地震

1 (c)
2 a. There are seven large tectonic plates on the earth.
b. The Richter scale measures an earthquake's power.
c. They measure one to four on the Richter scale.
3 a. tectonic plate 地殼構造板塊 b. quake 地震
c. crack 裂開

51 Volcanic Eruptions 火山爆發

1 (b)
2 a. magma b. magma chambers c. ash
3 a. spew 噴出 b. explosive 爆炸性的 c. magma 岩漿

52 Mass Extinctions 大滅絕

1 (c)
2 (c)
3 a. asteroid 小行星 b. Cretaceous Period 白堊紀
c. flourish 茂盛；繁茂

53 The Inner and Outer Planets 內行星與外行星

1 (b)
2 a. F b. T c. T
3 a. moon 衛星 b. outer planets 外行星 c. solid 固體的

54 Are We Alone 宇宙只有我們嗎？

1 (c)
2 a. aliens b. life c. Mars
3 a. extraterrestrial 外星球的 b. star system 星系
c. element 要素

55 Conductors and Insulators 導體和絕緣體

1 (c)
2 a. It lets electricity move freely.
b. It stops the flow of electricity.
c. Plastics, paper, rubber, glass, and porcelain are insulators.
3 a. wire 金屬線 b. conductor 導體 c. porcelain 瓷

56 Sir Isaac Newton 艾薩克．牛頓爵士

1 (b)
2 a. F b. T c. T
3 a. inertia 慣性 b. calculus 微積分 c. acceleration 加速度

57 Elements 元素

1 (b)
2 a. T b. F c. T
3 a. proton 質子 b. atom 原子 c. matter 物質

58 Atoms and Their Atomic Numbers 原子和原子序

1 (a)
2 a. T b. F c. F
3 a. atomic number 原子序 b. orbit 繞軌道運行
c. hydrogen 氫

59 Energy and Environmental Risks 能源與環境風險

1 (c)
2 a. environment b. tides c. Nuclear
3 a. fossil fuel 化石燃料 b. hydroelectric 水力發電的
c. tidal energy 潮汐能

60 The Scientific Method of Inquiry
科學探究方法

1 (c)
2 a. method b. hypothesis c. labs
3 a. an educated guess 有根據的猜測
b. conduct 進行；處理 c. hypothesis 假說

61 Angles 角

1 (c)
2 (b)
3 a. obtuse angle 鈍角 b. straight angle 平角
c. acute angle 銳角

62 Triangles 三角形

1 (c)
2 a. acute b. right c. same
3 a. equilateral triangle 等邊三角形
b. isosceles triangle 等腰三角形
c. geometrical 幾何的；幾何圖形的

63 Solid Figures in Real Life
真實生活中的立體圖形

1 (a)
2 a. They are rectangular prisms.
b. They are pyramids.
c. They are cones.
3 a. cylinder 圓柱體 b. solid figure 立體圖形
c. rectangular prism 長方柱

64 Dimensions 維度

1 (c)
2 a. There are three dimensions.
b. They are length, width, and depth or height.
c. It is time.
3 a. horizontally 水平地 b. tesseract 四維超立方體
c. third dimension 三維空間

65 Solve the Problems 解題

1 (a)
2 (c)
3 a. left over 剩下 b. three sixths 六分之三
c. remains 剩下

66 Collecting and Organizing Data
蒐集與整理數據

1 (a)
2 (b)
3 a. raw data 原始資料 b. interpret 解釋 c. analyze 分析

67 Roman Numerals 羅馬數字

1 (c)
2 a. T b. F c. F
3 a. decimal system 十進位制
b. Roman numeral 羅馬數字 c. quantity 數量

68 The Order of Operations 運算順序

1 (a)
2 a. parentheses b. division c. left
3 a. multiply 乘；乘以 b. calculation 計算
c. operation 運算

69 Percentages, Ratios, and Probabilities
百分比、比與機率

1 (b)
2 (a)
3 a. odds 機會；可能性 b. ratio 比率
c. at random 隨機；任意

70 Square Roots 平方根

1 (b)
2 a. F b. F c. T
3 a. whole number 整數 b. square root 平方根
c. to infinity 無限

71 Probability and Statistics 機率和統計

1 (c)
2 a. probability b. data c. circle graph
3 a. pie chart 圓餅圖 b. statistics 統計 c. y-axis y 軸

72 The Metric System 公制

1 (a)
2 (c)
3 a. volume 容積 b. convert 換算；轉換
c. metric system 公制

73 The Norse Gods 北歐眾神

1 (a)
2 a. Northern Europe b. Odin c. Asgard
3 a. Viking 維京人 b. troll（北歐傳說中的）侏儒；巨人
c. mischief 惡作劇

74 The *Iliad* and the *Odyssey* 《伊里亞德》和《奧德賽》

1 (c)
2 a. F b. F c. F
3 a. adventure 冒險 b. epic poem 史詩 c. abduct 綁架

75 Types of Poems 詩的種類

1 (b)
2 a. F b. T c. F
3 a. sonnet 十四行詩 b. rhyme scheme 韻式
c. stanza 詩節

76 Understanding Sentences 認識句子

1 (b)
2 (b)
3 a. agree 一致 b. punctuation 標點符號
c. run-on sentence 連寫句

77 Common Proverbs 常見的諺語

1 (c)
2 (a)
3 a. fond 喜歡的 b. proverb 諺語 c. move on 繼續前進

78 Figures of Speech 修辭

1 (b)
2 a. figures b. Hyperbole c. Personification
3 a. metaphor 隱喻 b. simile 明喻 c. hyperbole 誇飾

79 Greek and Latin Roots 希臘與拉丁字根

1 (a)
2 a. roots b. Greek c. see
3 a. asterisk 星號 b. root 字根 c. geology 地質學

80 Gothic Cathedrals 哥德式大教堂

1 (c)
2 a. Buttresses helped support cathedrals.
b. They showed scenes from the Bible.
c. They are sculptures that look like monsters.
3 a. buttress 扶壁 b. gargoyle 滴水獸
c. stained-glass 彩繪玻璃的

81 Islamic Architecture 伊斯蘭建築

1 (b)
2 a. F b. T c. T
3 a. minaret 尖塔 b. dome 圓頂 c. mosque 清真寺

82 Renaissance Artists 文藝復興時代的藝術家

1 (a)
2 a. They painted during the Renaissance.
b. He was a true Renaissance man.
c. They were David and Pieta.
3 a. fresco 濕壁畫
b. Renaissance man 文藝復興人；博學家
c. apostle 使徒

83 Classical Art 古典藝術

1 (a)
2 a. They made pottery, paintings, sculptures, murals, and buildings.
b. They made sculptures from stone and bronze.
c. They were Doric, Ionic, and Corinthian.
3 a. ceramics 陶瓷器 b. mural 壁畫 c. flute 凹槽

84 From Baroque to Realism 從巴洛克到寫實主義

1 (c)
2 (a)
3 a. symbolic 象徵的 b. contrast 對比
c. perspective 透視法

85 Nineteenth Century American Landscapes 十九世紀美國的風景畫

1 (b)
2 a. F b. T c. T
3 a. idealize 理想化 b. Romantic 浪漫主義藝術家
c. school 學派；流派

86 Composers and Their Music 作曲家和他們的音樂

1 (c)
2 a. T b. F c. T
3 a. conduct 指揮 b. composer 作曲家 c. genius 天才

87 Musical Dynamics 音樂的力度

1 (c)

2 a. sheet b. pianissimo c. loud

3 a. moderately 適度地 b. dynamics 力度
c. sheet music 散頁樂譜

88 Handel and Haydn 韓德爾和海頓

1 (a)

2 (c)

3 a. string quartet 弦樂四重奏 b. oratorio 神劇
c. sonata 奏鳴曲

89 Spirituals 靈歌

1 (a)

2 a. religion b. eighteenth c. gospel

3 a. folk music 民俗音樂 b. carol 聖誕頌歌
c. spiritual 靈歌

90 The Classical Period of Music 音樂的古典時期

1 (b)

2 a. 1750 b. Baroque c. change

3 a. mood 基調；調子 b. sophisticated 複雜的
c. popularity 流行；受歡迎

Michael A. Putlack
專攻歷史與英文，擁有美國麻州 Tufts University 碩士學位

e-Creative Contents
一群專門為非母語英語課程及非母語英語教學學生開發英語學習產品的創意小組

國家圖書館出版品預行編目 (CIP) 資料

超級英語閱讀訓練 . 2 : FUN 學美國英語課本精選 / Michael A. Putlack, e-Creative Contents 著 ; Cosmos Language Workshop 譯 . -- 二版 . -- [臺北市] : 寂天文化 , 2020.02
面； 公分

ISBN 978-986-318-669-4 (第 1 冊 : 16K 平裝附光碟片)
ISBN 978-986-318-684-7 (第 2 冊 : 16K 平裝附光碟片)
ISBN 978-986-318-891-9 (第 1 冊 : 20K 平裝附光碟片)
ISBN 978-986-318-892-6 (第 2 冊 : 20K 平裝附光碟片)

1. 英語 2. 讀本

805.18 109000452

超級英語閱讀訓練 2

作者	Michael A. Putlack, e-Creative Contents
譯者	Cosmos Language Workshop
特約編輯	丁宥榆
校對	劉育如
主編	丁宥暄
內文排版	丁宥榆／林書玉
封面設計	林書玉
製程管理	洪巧玲
出版者	寂天文化事業股份有限公司
電話	+886-(0)2-2365-9739
傳真	+886-(0)2-2365-9835
網址	www.icosmos.com.tw
讀者服務	onlineservice@icosmos.com.tw
出版日期	2020 年 2 月 二版二刷 （200201）

郵撥帳號	1998620-0 寂天文化事業股份有限公司 訂購金額 600（含）元以上郵資免費 訂購金額 600 元以下者，請外加郵資 65 元 〔若有破損，請寄回更換，謝謝。〕